Enemies

A War Story

Kenneth Rosenberg

www.kennethrosenberg.com

Also by Kenneth Rosenberg

The American (Nathan Grant Thriller #1)
The Paris Conspiracy (Nathan Grant Thriller #2)
The Berlin Connection (Nathan Grant Thriller #3)
Russia Girl (Natalia Nicolaeva Thriller #1)
Vendetta Girl (Natalia Nicolaeva Thriller #2)
Spy Girl (Natalia Nicolaeva Thriller #3)
Mystery Girl (Natalia Nicolaeva Thriller #4)
Memoirs of a Starving Artist
The Extra: A Hollywood Romance
Bachelor Number Five
Bachelor Number Nine
The Art of Love
No Cure for the Broken Hearted

Forward

The following story is true. In depicting the people and events in this book, I strived to remain as close to the historical record as possible. In cases where sources contradicted one another, or where the information available was thin, ascertaining the truth invariably involves some speculation. Regarding the dialogue, some of it comes directly from interviews and court transcripts of those involved. As a fictionalized version of these events, however, some scenes and dialogue were created in order to advance the story. It is impossible to know exactly what some of these characters were actually thinking or saying at certain times, though this version is based on what is known of the people involved and their general motivations. This is a story, first and foremost, that deserves to be told. A number of non-fiction books and articles about this case exist, and you can find them listed at the end. This book, as far as I am aware, is the first fictionalized account, meant to bring together the story from the perspectives of those directly involved. Every reader will have his or her own interpretation of these events. One thing this story should remind us, however, is that history is rarely black and white. We might like it to be made up of good guys and bad guys, right and wrong, the virtuous and the evil. Reality, though, is more often colored in numerous shades of gray.

Part I – The Journey

Chapter One

Washington, DC., August 8, 1942

A thin sheen of moisture covered the walls, white paint peeling from the bricks. One narrow bunk, a small table and chair, rusted sink, and filthy porcelain toilet. And that smell… the nauseating odor of unwashed bodies and human waste, filling one's lungs with every breath. Twenty-one-year-old Herbie Haupt sat on his moldering mattress, trying to absorb what brought him to this place. Of course, he knew the story. He'd lived it, yet as he ran it over through his mind, time and again, he couldn't help but wonder what might have happened if he'd made one change here, or fate had intervened there. Regret was all that remained for him. Everything else was gone, cruelly stripped away by an indifferent world. Dank tendrils of hopelessness took root in his psyche, dragging him downwards. Outside his small window, a dark rain pounded the pavements.

Herbie heard the door at the end of the corridor rattle open and then clang shut, the stomping of boots, metal scraping against concrete. A guard appeared with a steel tray in hand. Leaning low, he slid it through a small slot along the floor. Without a word, the guard straightened up and moved on, delivering an identical breakfast to each of the seven other condemned souls.

Rising from his bed, Herbie moved to retrieve his tray, lifting it from the ground and placing it on the table before sitting down to examine his food. Under-cooked scrambled eggs, over-cooked bacon and two charred slices of toast, buttered. Haupt lifted a slice of bacon, breaking off the end as he took a bite and slowly chewed. He lifted a small spoon and stirred the eggs before scooping some onto the toast and lifting it to his mouth. Jailhouse food was consistently awful, Herbie thought. And they never gave him quite enough.

When he was finished with his meal, Herbie placed the spoon and tray back on the floor by the cell door and retook his place on the cot. He thought back once more over the events of the previous year, starting from the very beginning. He thought of Gerda Stuckmann. Was what she'd told him that day even true? Or had she simply made it up? All he knew was that those few words set everything in motion. Herbie closed his eyes and leaned his head against the wall, taking himself back to that day just over one year earlier when his whole life began to change.

Chapter Two

Chicago, May 3, 1941

Their bodies moved in rhythm, the squeaking mattress keeping time. Herbie tried to think of baseball. He pictured himself at work, grinding lenses for the Simpson Optical Company. Anything but what he was actually doing at this moment, though as Gerda Stuckmann's warm breasts heaved beneath him, Herbie inhaled her musky aroma and could hold out no longer. With one final spasm of convulsions, the chemicals of procreation flooded his brain.

"That's it!?" Gerda complained.

Herbie rolled onto his back. "Give me some time, I'll go again."

"I don't have that much." Gerda climbed out of bed and moved into the bathroom.

Herbie heard her turn the shower taps, the spray of water striking the tub. Slowly, he stood and retrieved his clothing, scattered around the bedroom. He slid on his blue cotton underwear, white undershirt, and then his pleated gray wool slacks. Herbie lifted his white collared shirt from the bed and gave it a quick inspection. A bit wrinkled, but not too bad. He donned the shirt and tucked it into his pants before buckling his black leather belt. Next, he moved to the bedroom mirror, examining his reflection. Herbie was a handsome man, five-feet, nine-inches tall with an athletic physique. He had dark eyebrows, a square jaw and thick, wavy black hair held firm by a hint of grease. Pulling a comb from his pocket, he carefully smoothed any wayward strands back into place. This was a man who cared about his appearance, who took pride in being a snappy dresser. Herbie took one last look and then slid the comb back into his pocket. It was Thursday evening. He wondered what his friends were up to. He might drag Hugo out for a beer or two. Maybe Wolf, too. Herbie thought about ducking out before Gerda finished her shower but then reconsidered. There'd be hell to pay if he left without a word.

Instead, he sat on the bed, kicking his legs up and leaning back against the headboard. Beside him on the bedside table was his watch, silver with a black leather band, along with a near-empty packet of cigarettes and a shiny silver lighter. He attached the watch to his left wrist before retrieving a remaining cigarette and striking a flame. Inhaling the smoke, his brain was hit with that sweet rush. After a few minutes of waiting, Herbie heard the taps shut off. Gerda emerged from the bathroom with one white towel tucked around her torso and another wrapped in a bun on the top of her head. "Let's have some coffee," she said. "We need to talk."

"I gotta get going," Herbie answered.

"You seemed to have plenty of time before!" Gerda raised her voice. "I'm asking for ten minutes!"

Herbie cringed. "Fine, I'll put the coffee on." He swung his legs over the edge of the bed and put on his socks and black leather wingtips before moving into the kitchen. A coffee pot sat disassembled in the sink. He fit the pieces together, filled the pot with water, and then opened the cabinet above, where Gerda stored ground coffee in a tin. He'd put the pot on to boil when Gerda came in wearing a light cotton dress, pink with white flowers. She took two mugs from another cabinet, put them on her kitchen table and then got out a bowl of sugar, container of cream, a cookie jar and two plates. Last, she pulled open a silverware drawer and pulled out two small spoons. It seemed like a big production to Herbie.

"Sit!" Gerda commanded.

Herbie did as he was told, gloomily dropping himself into a chair at the table. "What's this all about?"

Gerda didn't answer right away. Instead, she stood stock still, staring at the pot as the coffee percolated through a clear plastic handle. Something was gnawing at her. Probably the same thing as the last time they had a "talk" like this. When were they going to get married? It was all she seemed to think about. For Herbie, it was all he could do to put the whole thing off. Besides, Gerda was a widow, two years his senior. Marrying a girl like that just didn't look right. Maybe his parents hadn't come right out and said it, but their obvious disapproval enveloped him like a fog.

"I'm pregnant." Gerda spat it out without even turning to face him.

5

Herbie's mind struggled to process what his ears had just heard. What had she said? Wait… what? "No…" he shook his head, willing it to be untrue.

"I'm sorry, but yes."

"Not from me…"

"Yes, Herbie. From you. There's nobody else."

Only the sound of the boiling coffee pot broke the silence. Herbie was instantly alert, all of his senses heightened. Instinct told him to flee, to run for the door and never look back. Herbie didn't love Gerda. Not really. Not at this moment, anyway. He was in it for an afternoon fling once in a while. Never, ever, did he plan on this. Sure, he may have mentioned marriage in passing, but that was just to buy himself some time. Right?

"What have you got to say?" Her tone was filled with accusation. "You look like you're gonna pass out!"

"I...I..." Herbie stammered. "You're sure?"

"I'm sure, so you better prepare yourself to be a father because this baby is coming."

Herbie's peripheral vision narrowed, all focus straight ahead. "How long have we got?"

"I'm two months late. That means seven months, if you need some help with the math."

"Seven months..." he repeated.

"And I'd prefer not to have this kid out of wedlock."

"Of course." All Herbie could think was that in seven short months, life as he knew it would be finished. In fact, it was as good as finished already.

Gerda turned off the stove. She poured some coffee into Herbie's mug. "Have some of this, you look like you need it."

Staring at the steaming black liquid, Herbie ran through his options. "Isn't there somebody we could see about it?"

"Oh, no! Don't even think it! I'm not going that route! You can just forget about that!"

Herbie licked his lips. When he looked at Gerda now, he despised her. If only they'd never met… Yet he had to figure this out. There must be something he could do. For the time being, he would tell her what she wanted to hear. "We'll get married. But let's not rush it, huh?"

"How long do you plan to wait? I don't want to be showing on the altar!" Gerda countered.

"Sure..." What Herbie needed at this moment was some space. He needed air. He had to get out of there, to clear his head and think. "Look, I gotta go. I'll call you later."

Gerda poured some coffee into her own mug, a weariness overtaking her, evident in her slumped shoulders and tired expression. Gerda carried this burden all alone for over a month. Sharing the news with Herbie hadn't done a thing to lighten it. "I'm sorry. For what it's worth."

"Don't worry, we'll make it right." Even as he said the words, Herbie wasn't sure how much he believed them. He rose from his chair with an eye to the exit.

"Sure we will." Gerda's tone suggested she didn't quite trust him, either. "We better."

"I said don't worry." Herbie walked across the kitchen toward the front door. He turned to take another look at her, picturing Gerda's belly full to bursting, a passel of children running around her skirt.

"I said I was sorry," Gerda repeated.

"Yeah. Me, too." Herbie moved backward through the door, closing it behind him before he continued along the hall and then down the stairs, dizzy as he clung to the banister. What was he going to do? At this very moment, Herbie Haupt had no idea.

Chapter Three

Chicago, May 5, 1941

With his bulky frame wedged behind a drum set, Wolfgang Wergin lost himself to the rhythm as he played along to his favorite Glenn Miller record. Someday, maybe he'd be in a big band like that himself. For now, he could only dream, nodding his head to the beat as he riffed off the snare, tapped away at the symbols and kept time with the bass. When the song finished, he extricated himself from his stool and moved across to the player, lifting the arm and placing the needle back at the beginning. Wolf was six-feet tall with sandy brown hair and a youthful appearance. He wore blue dungarees and a white cotton undershirt, with no shoes on his large feet. At eighteen, Wolfgang was only one year out of high school, living at home with his parents on South Wood Street. Five days per week, Wolf worked at Simpson Optical Company, grinding lenses for the top secret Norden Bomb Site. Spare moments found him here in this room, pounding away at his drums. Wolf retook his seat. Before he began again, a shout echoed up from the street below.

"Hey Wolf, what are you doing?!" came the voice. Wolfgang set his drumsticks onto the snare and made his way to the open window. On the sidewalk below he saw Herbie Haupt and the tall and lanky Hugo Troesken. They wore casual clothing, with slicked back hair, not a strand out of place. "Are you ready?" Herbie called out.

"I guess I lost track of the time," Wolfgang was sheepish.

"We're coming up."

"Sure." Wolfgang moved away from the window, turned off his record player and then went to his closet. He laid a clean blue shirt and khaki trousers on the bed.

"Hey, Wolf!" said Hugo. "Amigo!" He patted Wolfgang on the shoulder and then moved across the room and took the seat behind the drum set. Hugo picked up the sticks and began to tap away at the snare. "You ready for a party?" he asked.

"Almost." Wolfgang unbuttoned his dungarees and dropped them to the floor. Herbie took a chair by the window, with a drab expression and slumped shoulders. "You all right?" Wolf asked.

"Sure. Fine. Why?"

Wolfgang slid on his clean pants and strung a belt through the loops. "No reason."

"He just can't wait to get to this fiesta." Hugo put down the drumsticks and flashed a grin. "Meet some little señoritas!"

"Sure," Herbie concurred. "Some señoritas."

"I guess that means Gerda won't be there?" said Wolf.

"I don't want to talk about Gerda!"

Wolfgang was caught off guard by the rebuke. He pulled on his dress shirt and tucked it in at the waist. Herbie would confide in them when he felt like it. Wolf slid into a blue sweater vest, then put on his socks and shoes before taking a quick look in the mirror. Lifting a comb from his dresser, he gave his hair a few quick swipes until he was satisfied. "Let's go." The others followed him out of the room and down the stairs.

Heading toward the front door, Wolf ducked his head into the kitchen where his mother, Kate, stood by the oven with a pair of mitts in hand. His father, Otto, sat at the kitchen table skimming through the evening paper. "I'm going out with the guys," said Wolf.

"Don't you want dinner?" said his disappointed mother. Through the doorway, Kate spotted Herbie and Hugo lurking behind her son. "I've got a meatloaf in the oven."

"We'll get something at the party."

"What kind of party is it?" said Otto.

"Cinco de Mayo, Mr. Wergin," said Hugo.

"Cinco de what? Is that some Puerto Rican thing?"

"Mexican," Herbie answered. "It's a fiesta."

"Well, you boys take care of my Wolfgang!" said Kate.

"Of course, Mrs. Wergin!" Hugo grabbed Wolf by the shoulders. "We'll look after him!"

"Why don't I believe that?" Kate rolled her eyes.

"You go have some fun," said Otto.

"Thanks, Mr. W!" said Hugo. The three young men ambled through the living room, out of the house and down the front steps.

Strands of colored lights hung overhead as a mariachi band played on a low stage. Revelers spun on a dance floor or gathered at rows of picnic tables. Wolfgang and his friends stood at the bar, taking in the scene.

"What'll you have?" a bartender asked.

"Three cervezas, por favor," Herbie answered.

"Since when do you speak Spanish?" said Hugo.

"Of course, I speak Spanish," Herbie answered. "The language of love."

"That's French, you idiot," said Hugo.

From a large ice bucket, the bartender pulled out three bottles of beer and popped off their caps before placing the bottles on the bar. "Anything else?"

"That's it," said Herbie.

"Ninety cents."

Herbie slid a dollar across the bar. "Keep the change."

"Thanks." The bartender took the dollar and deposited it in a cash register before moving on to the next customer.

The three men lifted their bottles and tapped the necks together. "Cheers," said Hugo.

"Cheers," Herbie replied. Each man took a drink. Two days since he'd heard the big news, Herbie still struggled to get his bearings. Here he was, out with friends on a Saturday night. Despite the cataclysmic development, the world hadn't ended. Not quite yet. He had some time, to figure out a plan. He took another drink and let the cool liquid run down his throat. They'd spoken of marriage, sure, but for Herbie that was mostly just talk. At least it used to be. Now there was a clock, tick-tock-ticking away. No more messing around. Herbie felt morose. He wasn't ready. Not yet. Of course, he understood that marrying Gerda was the right thing to do. He was responsible for her condition, after all. That knowledge didn't change the deep despair that he just couldn't shake. The three men wandered through the crowd, settling in at a table near the dance floor.

"What kind of food do they got here?" Wolf asked.

"Mexican, I guess," said Hugo. "What do you expect?"

"I'm gonna check," said Wolfgang. "Anybody else?"

"Get me something, will ya?" Hugo dug into his pocket for some coins.

"How 'bout you Herbie?"

"No thanks, I'm not real hungry."

"You better not eat any of mine, then!" said Hugo.

Wolfgang took Hugo's coins and headed off toward a food booth. Joining the end of a short line, he read over a menu board. Tacos; chicken, pork or beef, three for a dollar. What was a taco? He watched the customers ahead in line to see what they got. Each paper plate held three small pieces of some type of flatbread, folded over with fillings in the middle.

"What'll you have, bud?" A man in the booth stood ready to take Wolf's order.

Wolfgang gave another quick glance at the menu board. "Six tacos, I guess. Two of each."

"Two dollars."

Wolf counted out his coins and placed them on the counter. The man took Wolf's money and moments later, put his order up, divided onto two plates.

"Thanks." Wolf grabbed a small stack of paper napkins and then lifted the plates. Back at the table, he handed one plate to Hugo.

"Well looky here." Hugo lifted a taco and gave it a try, savoring the flavor. "Not bad."

"They're called tacos," said Wolf before trying a bite of his own. This Mexican food had some zing to it, he thought.

After finishing off his first, Hugo wiped his mouth with a napkin. "Go ahead, Herbie, take one, I was only kidding."

"Sure, I'll try one."

Hugo scanned the crowd. "Boy, I sure wish I had some work, I'll tell you what."

"Uncle Sam is hiring, so they say," Herbie replied.

"There's got to be a garage around that needs a good mechanic, you hear what I'm sayin'?"

"You'll find something." Wolfgang slid another bite of taco into his mouth and gulped it down, then licked his fingers and wiped them clean.

"I'm just damn tired of not having any money. I'm too old to be asking my folks all the time," said Hugo.

Herbie watched as a sultry blonde at the next table pulled a thin cigarette from a pack and held it in the air. A man in a dark suit moved close. Lighter in hand, he sparked the flint. The blonde leaned toward the flame, the tip of her cigarette glowing red before she gave the man a quick nod of appreciation.

"Looks like we're too late for that one," said Hugo.

Herbie produced his own pack of cigarettes and offered them to his friends. Hugo extracted one for himself.

"There's your friend Larry," said Wolf.

"Where?" asked Herbie.

"There." Wolf pointed.

Through the crowd, Herbie saw Larry Jordan striding in their direction. He was solidly built, in a tight-fitting brown sport coat. Jordan's face was long and narrow, his boxer's nose bending slightly to the left. "Hello, gentlemen!" He approached the group with a grin. "I guess they'll let just about anybody into this shindig, eh?"

"So it would appear," countered Hugo.

"Where ya been, Herbie? I haven't seen you around in a while."

"Busy, you know."

"Yeah, right. Busy. I heard about you, goose-stepping down Western Avenue with the Brown Shirts."

Herbie was equal parts annoyed and embarrassed. "Says who?!"

"Who cares? It's true, ain't it?"

"I don't see how it's any business of yours." Herbie stiffened.

"You trying to make some trouble, Larry?" said Hugo.

"I don't like it, that's all. We live in the United States of America, if you didn't notice."

"You don't know the first thing about it." Herbie leaned in close.

"I think I know plenty." Jordan faced Herbie down. "That Hitler character is a no-good son-of-a-bitch and so is anybody who supports him."

Herbie's frustrations rushed to the fore. There was nothing he wanted more at this moment than to punch somebody in the face, and Larry Jordan was the perfect target. He put both hands on Jordan's chest and shoved. Jordan stumbled backward before regaining his footing, then lunged, catching Herbie with a fist square on the chin. Haupt saw a flash of light, and then darkness as his body crumpled to the ground.

"Hey, hey, hey!" Wolfgang jumped between the two, putting his hands out. "Enough!"

Hugo knelt to check on Herbie, stunned but quickly regaining consciousness. "You all right, buddy?"

Jordan glowered from above, both hands clenched. Herbie wiped his mouth on the back of one hand and saw a thin red sheen. He felt the pain, pure and real. He yearned to land his own punch on that smirking jaw. Fury mixed with disappointment and fear… His whole life was changing and he just wanted somebody to pay. In this past week, he'd taken plenty. When was it his turn to dish some out?

"I think I made my point." Jordan walked off in the direction from which he'd come.

Hugo helped Herbie to his feet. To Haupt, the German Bund was just a patriotic organization. It gave his father somewhere to belong, to find a sense of camaraderie far from their ancestral home. They could be American and yet take pride in their heritage. Herbie could attend a rally with his father and still go out with his friends on a warm summer night.

"Forget about it." Hugo lifted a bottle from the table and held it out.

Herbie took hold of the beer and then searched the ground until he located his cigarette, crumpled in the dirt.

"Have one of mine." Hugo produced a pack, extracting a single cigarette and holding it out. Herbie used his own lighter, inhaling the smoke and holding it in his lungs. He watched the revelers, spinning on the dance floor to the music of a mariachi band. At this moment, all he wanted was to get away, to run as far from this place as possible. Maybe if he had one last taste of freedom, things would look different when he returned. Or maybe, just maybe, he'd never come back at all. "We should take a road trip," he announced.

Hugo inhaled a lungful of smoke himself and blew it out slowly as he considered the statement. "What kind of road trip?"

"I don't know… How about Mexico?"

"Mexico?!" Wolfgang was awe-struck by the mere idea. "That's kind of far, isn't it?"

"Three or four days to the border," said Hugo. "Give or take."

"I'd say I'm due for a vacation. Why not go down and have a look?" The more Herbie talked about the idea, the better it sounded. "I'll bet those señoritas would love to meet a few Americanos."

Hugo shook his head. "I gotta find a job. You know I ain't got no money."

"I'll bet you we could find some work down there. Maybe on a farm or something."

"It could be a laugh," said Hugo. "Whose car? The Pontiac?"

"My dad needs the Pontiac for work." Herbie turned to Wolf.

"Oh, no, don't look at me!"

"Your car is more reliable, anyway," said Herbie. "You don't want to break down in the middle of the desert, do you?"

"Who said I want to go at all? Besides, what about Simpson's?"

"We can ask for time off!"

Wolf watched the mariachi band, strumming their instruments to an upbeat tune. He admired and looked up to Herbie, though it did sometimes feel as though his friend was always pressuring him into one thing or another. Driving all the way to Mexico? That was an awfully big decision to make on such a whim. All the same, it would be an experience like none he'd ever had. "I guess we could see what they say," he conceded.

"That's the spirit!" Herbie broke into a grin. Escape was just within reach. "How about you, Hugo? You in?"

Tilting his head to one side, Hugo furrowed his brow. "Could be. Sounds like a good time."

"Sure it does. A real good time," Herbie held up the last of his beer for a toast. "To the open road!"

"I'm not making any promises," said Wolf.

"Come on, buddy. It's gonna be the trip of a lifetime."

"I'll think it over."

"I'm telling you, this'll be one adventure you won't want to miss." The friends tapped their bottles together and took a drink. Herbie's life wasn't finished, yet. He still had options. He would put three thousand miles between himself and his problems. For now, that was all he needed. The rest he could figure out later.

Chapter Four

Berlin, June 6, 1941

The crushing blow of a fist against his chin sent Ernst Peter Burger sprawling backward. Punched once, twice in quick succession, he slumped to the floor where he was set upon in earnest by a ravenous pack of guards, kicked by heavy boots in the stomach, the chest, the legs. Flashes of pain ricocheted through Burger's brain, yet he was oddly aware, hypersensitive to his surroundings, anticipating each strike. It was fifteen months since his Gestapo prison odyssey began. Fifteen months of beatings and misery and degradation. Small in stature, Burger was a brawler nonetheless; a street fighter with a party membership number far lower than any of the men administering this beating, and yet the blows kept coming.

"Enough!" A guard heaved Burger to his feet, spinning him around and pinning him against a brick wall. Blood streamed down the prisoner's face, flowing into his eyes and mouth. The guard leaned close, the fury of a wild beast in his eyes. Burger knew that look. He understood the ferocity behind it, the pure joy. He knew what it meant when a man's frustrations, his anger and his disappointments were vented through the swinging of his fists. Burger himself felt that exhilaration once upon a time, back in those early days. Finding himself on the other side of such beatings, there was nothing he could do but absorb the same pain he once dished out in the name of the Fuhrer. His life was in their hands. Or his death.

Yanking him by an arm each, two guards dragged him from the cellblock and up a flight of stairs to the commandant's office, where Burger was thrown into a wooden chair, a guard hovering close on either side. A wall clock ticked the seconds off one by one. Burger reached a hand up to wipe his left eye.

"Hands down!" shouted a guard.

Burger waited, eyes swelling shut. The door opened. The commandant hustled inside. He was a middle-aged man, gut bulging beneath his uniform. Probably an accountant before the war, Burger thought. Or a civil servant. Only a fortuitous change in circumstances gave him this unlikely position of power.

"On your feet!"

Burger struggled to stand, offering a halfhearted salute.

Eyeing Burger with contempt, the commandant took a seat behind his desk. He opened a file and flipped through the pages, weary of the entire process. "You've been granted a trial for the charge of falsifying state documents. What have you to say for yourself?"

Burger struggled to ascertain which document he might have falsified. Of course, the charges were preposterous. He'd written the report that was asked of him. His crime was honesty, though in the current environment that was a deadly miscalculation.

The commandant tilted his head back, peering down his nose at the prisoner. "Maybe we should send you back to the concentration camp, as an inmate this time. What would you think of that? Eh? Would you like that?" Turning his attention to the file, he made some quick notes. "Get him out of here," he said.

"Yes, commandant." The guards manhandled Burger through the office and then down the stairway toward the cellblock. Nothing decided. No change to the status quo. Just days on end stretching before him to slowly rot away in this Gestapo basement. He'd been through two trials already, yet it was just part of an elaborate game. For Peter Burger, there was no future. There was no past. Only the present. One step and then another.

Chapter Five

Chicago, June 13, 1941

Hospitals always made Herbie Haupt uneasy. It was the smells that got to him the most. Rubbing alcohol and antiseptic. The odors of illness and disease. Reminders of his mortality. As he walked down the corridor with his father by his side, Herbie sensed that Hans was anxious as well. A house painter by trade, Hans Haupt was a quiet man who kept mostly to himself, never quite comfortable outside the confines of his German-American community. The one person he relied upon was his wife, Erna. Hans clutched a bouquet of flowers in a clear glass vase. He wore his finest suit. His gray mustache was carefully trimmed. They found her alone in her room, sitting up in bed. Herbie wrapped lightly three times on the door. "Hello, mother."

"Look who we have here." Erna's voice wavered, though she managed a smile.

"How are you feeling?" Hans approached the bed tentatively.

"Wonderful now that you two handsome gentlemen are here," Erna replied.

"We thought some flowers might brighten up the room."

"How considerate!"

"I'll put them here on the windowsill where they can get some light."

"Thank you, dear."

Herbie kissed his mother on the cheek. "They say that if all goes well you'll be released next week."

"Yes, the doctor seems very encouraged by my progress."

Herbie saw his father's tension dissipate as he arranged the flowers. This was a man who truly loved his wife, more than anything in the world. Would Herbie ever feel that way about a woman of his own? The prospects weren't looking particularly good so far.

"Take a seat and stay awhile," said Erna.

Hans pulled up a chair while Herbie sat on the next bed over.

"Tell me, what's going on in the world?" Erna continued. "What have I missed?"

"Nothing out of the ordinary," said Hans. "We certainly miss you around the house."

"I hope you two are managing to feed yourselves."

"Yes, of course, we're getting by." Hans blushed at the insinuation that he and Herbie couldn't take proper care of themselves. Truth be told, it was an adjustment. The two men were fairly hopeless in the kitchen. "Your son has some news," said Hans.

"Oh? What news is that?!"

"Nothing very important." Herbie had dreaded this conversation. He would try to make it as brief as possible. "I've decided to go away for a while."

"Going away where?" Erna sounded worried.

"Just a little vacation. Me and some of the boys are going on a road trip."

"They're going to Mexico. Can you believe it?" said Hans.

"Mexico!" his mother gasped. "That's a long way, isn't it?"

"Just a few days on the road is all," said Herbie. "We're taking Wolf's car. Me, Wolf, and Hugo."

"How long will you be gone?"

"We don't know yet, for sure. Maybe just a few weeks."

"Maybe?"

"They might go all the way to Nicaragua." Hans envied his son's youthful independence. There was a time when he'd been just the same, traveling all the way to America on his own, in search of opportunity.

"I know a girl who has family there," Herbie explained. "She said maybe I could work on their plantation."

"What about your job here? You're not going to give that up?!"

"No, mother, they gave me permission to take leave."

Erna smoothed her bedspread with one hand. "What does Gerda think of this idea?"

Herbie's body tensed. He was hoping to get through this with no mention of his girlfriend at all. Erna made an effort to hide her disapproval whenever the subject arose, though her true feelings were always clear. Gerda wasn't good enough for Herbie. As far as Erna was concerned, the sooner this dalliance was over, the better. Not only was Gerda older than Herbie, and a widow, but she lived alone. Unmarried girls didn't live alone. Not respectable ones, in any case. Herbie couldn't tell his mother the truth about the current situation. Not yet, anyway. "She's not very happy about it," he said instead.

"I can imagine."

"She made me promise to send for her if I'm gone long."

"I don't blame her."

His mother's reaction left Herbie feeling confused. She was siding with Gerda on this? "I just…" he struggled for words.

"Don't you love her?" Erna came straight to the point.

"Do we have to talk about this now?!" Herbie snapped.

The color drained from Hans Haupt's face. "I don't believe you should speak to your mother that way!"

"I'm sorry…" A chastened Herbie dropped his head. For his entire life, he'd longed for his parents' approval. He wanted to make them proud. Deep in the recesses of his mind, he knew that he was letting them down. His parents were serious people, diligent in facing their responsibilities. As Germans living in America, they strived to prove that they belonged, as contributing members of society. Yet with their funny accents and foreign ways, his mother and father would always be outsiders. Among the three of them, only Herbie grew up here. Only the son fit in with the free-wheeling American culture. He didn't have to be so serious. He could afford to have a little bit of fun in life, though it was just this attitude that disappointed his parents. He did his best to make them happy. During summers he'd helped his father with his work. Lately, he'd gone along to Bund meetings. He treated his mother with the utmost respect. To Herbie, however, his parent's insular existence was suffocating. And now… now he'd let them down in the worst of all possible ways. The only solution was to go, as fast and far as he could. "I'm a little bit surprised by your question, to be honest. I never thought you cared for Gerda much."

"We like Gerda just fine," said Hans.

"She is a very nice girl," Erna conceded.

For Herbie, these words were an unexpected balm on his troubled soul, though he still needed this trip, more than anything. Less than six more months now, he realized. Soon she would start showing.

"I hope you'll send us postcards when you're gone," said Erna.

"Sure I will, mother. I'll send a truckload."

"Just promise you'll be careful down there."

"I promise. Everything will be fine."

"Don't let those other boys get you into trouble."

Herbie stood and moved across his mother's bed to kiss her on the forehead. "You don't push yourself too hard. Let father look after you."

Erna laughed. "You don't expect me to live on his cooking, do you? Maybe it's all right for you two…"

"Aunt Lucille ought to help on that score. She's an excellent cook."

"That she is."

"Look mother, I've got to run. I have some last-minute things to take care of."

"When do you leave?"

"The day after tomorrow."

"So soon?" Erna inhaled, a mother's concern in her eyes. "Well, I hope you boys have a lovely time."

"Thank you, mother." Herbie turned toward his father. "I'll see you back at the house."

"All right, son."

As Herbie moved out of the room, he took one last look through the door to see his mother wave farewell. Herbie waved back before moving on down the hall. He would miss her, that was true. He knew they loved him. That was never in doubt. He loved them, too, more than anybody else on earth. That was the reason it pained him so much to keep his dark secret. The truth would devastate them both. For the moment, all he wanted to do was hit that open road. The rest, Herbie would work out as he went.

Chapter Six

Chicago, June 15, 1941

The morning was bright and clear as Wolfgang walked down the front steps of his house with a duffel slung over one shoulder. Perfect driving weather. He was halfway across the yard when he spotted Herbie Haupt walking up the sidewalk with a bag of his own. "Hey, Herbie." Wolfgang felt alive with the thrill of anticipation. It hadn't taken him long to make up his mind. Herbie was right, this would be the trip of a lifetime. Wolf had hardly slept at all the night before, instead packing and repacking his bag until finally retiring to bed just to stare at the ceiling for half the night, imagining their imminent adventures. He was just five years old when the family emigrated to Chicago from Germany, but that trip he hardly remembered. In the past thirteen years, he'd never once traveled past the Illinois state border. Now he could hardly wait to get started.

"Is Hugo here?" Herbie met Wolf at the gate.

"We'll pick him up on the way." Wolfgang moved past and on to his black Chevrolet parked at the curb. After opening the trunk, the two men hoisted their bags inside.

"You all ready?" said Herbie.

"I need to say goodbye to my folks. Come on," Wolf nodded his head to one side. "They'll want to see you, too." The two men headed up the walk and through the front door. In the living room, they found Otto Wergin bent over his radio, twisting the tuner knob one way and then the other until hints of static faded away. A Mozart sonata drifted through. "Herbie!" Otto stood up straight. "Good morning!"

"Good morning, Mr. Wergin."

"You two all packed up?"

"We're all set, dad," said Wolf.

Otto rubbed his hands together, masking his apprehensions with a light smile. "Kate!" he called out. "The boys are leaving!"

Wolfgang's mother appeared at the top of the stairs. "Just like that?" she made her way down. "Can't I make you some breakfast before you go?"

"I already had something, Mrs. Wergin, but thanks all the same," said Herbie.

"You're sure?"

"We just want to hit the road, mom," said Wolf.

"OK…" Kate's disappointment showed. "At least let me give you something to take along. You just wait a minute. Mexico isn't going anywhere." She made her way into the kitchen. The men heard cupboards opening and then swinging shut. When Kate reappeared, she held a cardboard box in her arms. Inside they saw red apples, a loaf of bread in a paper bag, lunch meat, cheese and an assortment of tin cans. Kate handed the box to her son. "At least I know you won't starve for a day or two."

"Thank you, mother."

"How is Erna doing?" Kate asked Herbie. "Wolfgang tells me she's in the hospital!"

"That's right Mrs. Wergin, she had an operation, but she's in fine spirits. They say she'll be released next week."

"Well, that's good news. I should stop by the house with some schnitzel for her and your father."

"She sure would appreciate that. My dad, too."

"We better get going," said Wolf. "Hugo's waiting."

"Sure," said Otto. "We'll walk you out."

Herbie led the way, eager to put as many miles between himself and Chicago as possible, to carve out some distance from the problems he was leaving behind. All he wanted at this moment was to get in the car and drive.

"Do you boys have your route all mapped out?" Otto asked as they moved toward the Chevy.

"We sure do. Give me a sec and I'll show you!" said Wolf.

When they reached the car, Herbie raised the trunk once more and Wolfgang slid the box of food in next to the bags. After closing the trunk, Wolf walked to the front passenger door and reached inside for his map. Unfolding it, he spread the map across the hood of the car to show his parents. "First we're going to head to St. Louis, then south through Texas." Wolf pointed. "We thought we'd cross the border here, at Laredo."

"I sure envy you boys," said Otto.

Wolf refolded the map and placed it in the glove compartment.

"I'm counting on you to take care of my son, young man." Kate gave Herbie an earnest look.

"You bet, Mrs. Wergin. I'll look after him."

"Good luck, men." Otto offered a hand to Herbie and the two shook.

"Don't forget to write!" Kate grasped her son in both arms.

"I will, mom." Wolfgang embraced his mother in return before moving on to give his father a quick hug. Herbie climbed into the passenger seat as Wolf walked around to the driver's side and took his place behind the wheel.

"How far do you think you'll get today?" Kate said through the open window.

"We're hoping to make St. Louis." Wolfgang turned the key and the engine coughed to life.

"Safe journey, boys!" said Otto.

"Thanks, Mr. W!" Herbie called out.

Wolf pressed his foot on the gas pedal and the car eased forward. "So long!" He gave a last wave.

Kate and Otto stood on the curb arm in arm as the boys drove off down the street. Inside the car, Herbie took a deep breath. One quick stop to pick up Hugo and they'd be on their way, off toward new horizons. It was a valve being opened; all of the pressure he'd been under slowly starting to escape. Herbie needed this trip, far more than anybody knew.

Chapter Seven

Berlin, June 19, 1941

Day in and day out, the seconds ticked away on Peter Burger's life. Minutes, hours… it was all an endless, empty void. He thought often of his past, seldom of his future. What future was there for a man locked up and forgotten in a Gestapo prison? But the past… that was inescapable. Not that he would have done much differently if given the chance. Fate had conspired against him and there was nothing to be done about that. Burger was a man of conviction. It was not he who betrayed the movement, it was the movement that betrayed him. He remembered the day, nearly one and a half years earlier, when this darkness began. It was embedded in his mind forever; March 4, 1940, just after six o'clock in the evening. When he closed his eyes, those moments played out like a terrible dream…

Peter stood at his bedroom mirror, unfastening the collar on his uniform. A deep sense of melancholy was his constant companion. Depression stalked Burger his entire adult life, though this time there was a heavier sense of foreboding attached. This time he'd committed a grave offense, one with the power to destroy him, and there was no way to reverse it. If he could rewrite the report, he would. If he could adjust the wording a little bit… But it was too late for that. It was too late to keep those sentences from existing. He'd been given an assignment and he'd carried it out. Write a report on the administration of a concentration camp in Poland. On the face of things, it didn't sound so complicated. The difficulty, however, came from his innate desire to tell the truth. Under these circumstances, the truth was a dangerous commodity. What of the beatings and starvation, the executions and the degradation that he witnessed firsthand? Burger knew that he should keep his opinions on these matters to himself. These were Poles. Jews and Gypsies.

"Enemies of the state." Burger could have written the report the Gestapo bosses would approve of, but his bitterness at that organization made condemning their methods impossible to resist. Now it was Burger himself who was condemned. In his defense, he didn't know that his little report, written at the request of a university professor, would reach such lofty levels of the government. Only when he heard that the head of the Gestapo itself, Heinrich Muller, had read it, did Burger realize the extent of his recklessness. After learning that news, each morning that he put on his uniform, he wondered if it would be the last time. Surely, he'd lose his job at the Propaganda Ministry, but what then? Burger knew only too well what happened to men who disappointed their superiors. Even Ernst Röhm, his former boss, was not immune. Executed. Shot on Hitler's orders, along with three thousand of his men. It was a miracle that Peter Burger survived that purge, yet fate appeared to be catching up with him. Burger never should have left America. Things were hard there, but nothing like this. Yet Peter thought of his wife. If he hadn't returned to Germany they'd have never met. Bettina wouldn't be two-months pregnant in the next room, happily preparing his dinner. What could he say to her? How could he tell her that the future she dreamed of was hanging by a tenuous thread? The truth was that he couldn't. The best he could do was to go on, day by day. Maybe Muller wasn't so interested in this report. He must have better things to concern himself with. That was what Burger told himself, every single day for the past week. Just that afternoon he'd been summoned to the governor's office and made to answer questions. He knew it was only the beginning.

Peter unbuttoned the rest of his shirt and stripped it off, tossing it into a clothes hamper. When he'd hung the uniform pants and jacket in his closet, he put on a pair of dark slacks and a white shirt and belt. Next, he donned clean socks and a pair of leather shoes. Standing again at the mirror, Burger brushed his left shoulder with one hand and then ran his fingers through his hair, looking at his round, middle-aged face. He would have dinner with his wife and do his very best to pretend there was nothing wrong at all.

When Peter entered the kitchen, Bettina stood at the stove, frying a potato pancake. In a country with its fair share of tall, striking beauties, Bettina was a girl who spent much of her life overlooked.

Not by her husband, however. Peter's heartbeat sped up the moment he first laid eyes on her at the Propaganda Ministry. When she was assigned as his personal secretary, he worried that his growing infatuation would be impossible to conceal. Not that he didn't try, but slowly, day by day, he grew to understand that the feelings were mutual. They were in love. Bettina was always the sensible one, never expecting too much yet grateful for the good things that life brought her way. When Peter finally proposed, she didn't hesitate. And so, here they were.

"I hope you're hungry." Bettina turned off the flame and used a spatula to lift the pancake from the pan and place it on a stack on the dining table.

"That smells wonderful!" Burger came around the table and leaned close to give his wife a kiss. "You are too good to me."

"That's true, but only because you are so handsome."

"And you're a good liar, too."

Bettina offered a smile, her dark hair framing her round cheeks. "I thought we might have a picnic next weekend. We could take a basket with some lunch and find a nice spot in the Tiergarten?"

The pair took their seats at the table and Peter reached for a slice of bread, using a knife to spread a layer of butter across it. "That sounds like a fine idea." He tried to banish his distractions. The weekend. He would focus on that. Was he merely being paranoid? No, there was no such thing as paranoia these days in Germany. Röhm would be the first to agree, if he still could. Of course, Burger was no Ernst Röhm. He was small potatoes, but his report was a handy enough excuse for the Gestapo to do what they already wanted with him. Not that they needed excuses. Those they could manufacture out of thin air. It was what they did best.

Peter tried to calm himself. There was no use jumping to conclusions. If they'd wanted to arrest him, they'd had all week to do so. Just the fact that he was sitting here this evening, having dinner with his wife, was reason enough to be cautiously optimistic. Burger took another bite of his bread. "A picnic in the park would be lovely," he said. The sparkle in Bettina's eyes betrayed her innocence as she served them each a potato pancake. Peter didn't know if she was naïve or just pretending, though at this point, perhaps pretending was the best they could do.

He was washing the dishes at the sink when Peter heard a pounding at the door. They were here. He gave a quick glance to Bettina, whose wide eyes revealed her terror. "Who is that?" she asked.

"I'm sure it's nothing," Peter tried to calm her, though his own anxiety was impossible to hide. At this moment he could think only of his wife. He'd resigned himself as best he could to his fate, whatever it might be. If only they'd leave her and their unborn child out of it, to live their lives. A louder, more insistent knocking was followed by a voice.

"Ernst Peter Burger! Open the door!"

Burger wiped his hands on a dish towel, walked past his startled wife, and unlatched the lock. Before he could turn the handle, the door was thrust open to reveal two men in dark suits. "Ernst Peter Burger?" The first man was tall and solidly built with a rutted face and sunken eyes.

"Yes, I am Peter Burger."

The men pushed their way into the house, the first placing a document on the kitchen table. He pulled a pen from his front pocket and handed it forward. "Sign," he commanded.

"What is it?" Burger asked the question, though he already knew. His fate was sealed, just as he'd imagined.

"It is a request for protective custody," said the man. "Without it, there is no telling what might become of you."

Burger nodded. It was all a farce. A legal pretext. Everyone in the room knew it. Everyone except Bettina, who stood in one corner, pale as a ghost. Burger took the pen in hand. He had no choice. The men were plainclothes agents of the Gestapo. They would take him, with or without the document. He leaned down and signed before handing back the pen. The agent put it in one pocket and then folded the document and placed it in another. "You will come with us." His tone was clipped and efficient.

"What is this about?" Bettina asked.

"Official business, Frau Burger."

Peter saw the fear in his wife's eyes. He wanted to reach out and hold her in his arms. He longed to kiss her and tell her that everything would be all right, even if he knew it wasn't true. These men would allow him no such luxury.

"Let's go," said the second agent.

"Don't worry," Peter said to Bettina. "I'm sure we will have this all cleared up in no time."

Bettina tried to put on a stoic face but it was no use. She understood what happened when the Gestapo came to take a husband away. Rarely did that husband return. The three men walked through the door, down the stairs of the apartment building, through the courtyard and out. A car waited on the street. A driver opened the door and all three men slid into the back. The door swung shut and the driver quickly took his place in front before pulling the car into traffic. Outside the windows, Burger saw people going about their daily business, oblivious to his plight. This was how things were these days. Being oblivious was a means to survival. Don't notice anything, or say anything, or draw attention to yourself in any way. And by all means, never, ever, write an official report critical of the treatment of prisoners in a Polish concentration camp. Not if you know what's good for you. Burger broke that unwritten rule and there was nothing he could do about it but pay. The only question left was how much.

Chapter Eight

Southern Texas, June 21, 1941

The air was perfectly still as the three young men stood around a campfire, eating baked beans from metal cups, their blankets spread on the ground nearby. High above, the first evening stars flickered in a deep blue sky. Across a dusty plain, they saw the occasional headlights of a lonely car on state highway 35, a quarter of a mile away. This was as far south as any of them had traveled in their lifetimes and tonight would mark their last on U.S. soil before the real adventure began. Herbie Haupt's enthusiasm was infectious. Standing in this farmer's field with their future wide open, this was… freedom. They had gas in the tank and money in their pockets. Wolfgang, too, felt alive with expectation. "You think those Mexican girls like Americans?" he asked.

"They love Americans!" Herbie replied. "Why wouldn't they?"

"You think they hablo English?" said Hugo.

"Who cares?" Herbie grinned. "You're gonna wonder why we never came down here sooner."

Hugo chuckled to himself. "What about those local Mexicanos? Maybe they're a little possessive, you know… Don't want a bunch of Gringos coming after their women."

"Forget about the Mexicanos. We can take care of ourselves," said Herbie.

"Who's got that tequila?" Hugo finished his beans.

"It's in the trunk," said Wolf.

Herbie put down his cup and went to the car. He found the bottle and brought it back to the campfire. "We don't have any clean cups." He pulled out the cork.

"Forget the cups," said Hugo. "I ain't got no germs."

"That stuff will kill them anyway," Wolf agreed.

"To Mexico!" Herbie raised the bottle in the air and then took a good long swig before handing it over to Hugo.

"Viva Mexico!" Hugo drank and passed it on.

"To the pretty senoritas." Bringing the bottle to his lips, Wolf tilted his head back and felt a burn as the amber liquid rolled down his throat. One more day and their exploits would begin in earnest.

Warm, dry Texas air blew through the driver's window, caressing Wolf's face as they traveled south on highway 35. His pulse quickened as they drew ever closer to that magical line on their map.

"There it is!" From the front passenger seat, Herbie pointed to a highway sign. "Laredo. This is where we cross."

"Where do I go?" Wolfgang asked.

"Follow the signs for Nuevo Leon. That's the Mexican side."

"The Mexican side…" Wolfgang marveled at the prospect of driving his very own Chevy into a whole different country. Not long ago they'd sat at a Mexican fiesta in Chicago, and now this; just a few miles away from the real thing.

Herbie motioned toward another sign. "Nuevo Leon!"

"Almost there, my brothers!" Hugo leaned forward from his spot in back. "Hola Mexico!"

Wolfgang followed the signs, off the highway and through the town of Laredo. It seemed foreign already, with the dust and the heat, the dried-out grass and the few parched trees. Continuing into downtown, the storefronts were typical small-town America, with red brick buildings two stories high, clothing stores and a movie house. *Plaza Theater*. "Maybe we should get some beer?" said Hugo as they rolled past a liquor store.

"They got plenty of beer in Mexico," said Herbie. "That's one thing I know they have down there. I bet it's cheaper, too."

"Do we need to change our money?" said Wolfgang. "They got their own money, right?"

"Pesos," said Hugo. "Hey, right there! Money exchange! Cambio!"

A little shack stood in a corner lot with Mexican and American flags painted on the sides. *Best Rates in Town*. Wolfgang turned into the lot and parked the car. The three men climbed out, slamming the doors shut behind them and then stretching their arms and legs.

After three nights camping under the stars, their hair was dirty and uncombed, skin caked with a thin veneer of dust.

Inside the hut, a man stood behind a glass partition, like a bank but with only one teller. "Good morning, gentlemen," he said.

"Buenos dias." Hugo stepped up to the counter and shoved his American bills through a hole in the partition. "Pesos, if you don't mind."

The man on the other side took the money and laid it out. "Twenty-seven dollars." He did a quick calculation on a pad of paper and then placed the American bills in a cash drawer. After counting out Mexican pesos, he wrote up a receipt and slid both back through the slot. "There you go."

"Is that all you got? Twenty-seven dollars?!" Wolf hadn't expected his eighty dollars to go very far, but twenty-seven? This was starting to look like it might be a short trip after all.

"I told you boys I didn't have no money. You didn't seem to have a problem with it back in Chicago."

"Yeah, but twenty-seven bucks…" Herbie was a bit concerned as well. "Wolf is right, that's not gonna last very long."

Hugo was stung by the complaint, as his two travel companions ganged up against him. "You said we could find some work down here."

Herbie took out his wallet and counted the contents. "I've got eighty-two. How 'bout you, Wolf?"

"'Round about the same."

"That'll get us by for a while. We'll just have to find some work a little sooner than I thought," said Herbie.

Wolfgang wasn't convinced. "What if we can't find nothing down there?"

"You worry too much, Wolf. You've gotta learn to relax a little bit."

Hugo lifted his Mexican currency, examining his bills and coins. "This looks like play money to me."

Herbie went next, changing all but a few of his dollars. When it was Wolfgang's turn, his concerns were replaced by a heady sense of possibility as he pushed his bills through the slot. When the teller slid pesos back, Wolf counted them carefully before shoving the money into his pocket. "I guess that's it then. Next stop, Mexico."

Back at the car, Wolf spread their map across the hood once again. He spotted Laredo, right there on the border. With one finger, he traced the route south, slowing as he skimmed past exotic-sounding locales. *Barretillas, Los Cavazos, Salina Victoria…* He pictured dusty villages, old men in sombrero hats, burros tied to hitching posts. All that he knew of Mexico, he'd learned from the movies.

"I'll drive," said Herbie. After piling in the Chevy, the travelers headed on through the rising desert heat before joining a line of cars at the border. A sign stretched above the road ahead: MEXICO. Wolf peered into the cars that inched slowly forward around them; American families heading for vacation, Mexicans going home, or maybe to visit relatives south of the border. The lanes passed first through customs on the American side.

When it was their turn, Herbie eased the car up and stopped beside a booth. Inside, an American official in a blue uniform sat on a stool. He was roughly their age, with a blue cap resting atop his head. "Good morning, gentlemen. What's the purpose of your visit to Mexico today?"

"We're tourists," Herbie replied.

"And how much cash are you transporting?"

"'Round about a hundred and seventy bucks between us."

"How long are you planning to stay in Mexico?"

"A couple of weeks maybe. We haven't decided entirely."

"We thought we might find a little bit of work down there," Wolf added.

"Do you have work permits?"

"No, sir," Herbie admitted. "We figured we could sort that out once we got down there."

"I'm afraid you'd need to take care of that before you cross, not after," the officer informed them. "The Mexican consulate, that's who you'd apply to for a work permit."

Herbie turned to his accomplices, a hint of shame in his expression. He should have known that. He should have checked into it. Now it would be too late.

"I've got a job for y'all, though, if you want it," said the officer.

The comment caught Herbie by surprise. "What job is that?" His interest was mildly piqued.

"You see that old Ford over there, parked beside the office? The black one?" The officer used a pen to point just past the booth, where ten parking spaces fronted a small building with a red tile roof. In one of the spaces was a black Ford coupe.

"Yeah, I see it," Herbie answered.

"I need to get that car to California, pronto, but I don't have the time to drive it myself. I'll pay a hundred bucks to the man who's willing to take 'er there for me. Plus the cost of the gasoline, of course."

"A hundred bucks, that's good money," said Hugo. "How come you haven't found nobody else to take it for you?"

"Look, if you fellows want to discuss it, you best pull over, but only if you're serious. I don't want you wasting my time."

"Hell, it sounds good to me!" said Hugo.

"What about Mexico?!" Wolf blurted.

"Like I said, a hundred bucks..." Hugo shook his head. "You boys were the ones just telling me I ain't got enough. Anyway, I never been to California."

"You're just gonna leave us? Just like that?!" After all of their planning and anticipation, Herbie was astonished that his friend would give up on the whole thing in the blink of an eye.

"Pull over there and park by the Ford. I'll join you in a minute," said the officer.

Herbie did as instructed, easing the Chevy forward and pulling into an empty space.

"You boys could come, too," said Hugo. "Who says we have to go to Mexico, anyway?"

"You split it three ways, and a hundred bucks isn't all that much," said Herbie.

"True," Hugo conceded. "But if somebody wants to pay me a hundred dollars to go to California, I'll take it." Hugo hopped out of the car and the others followed.

"Are you sure about this?" Wolf was skeptical.

"What the hell," said Hugo. "Like Herbie said, we wouldn't last long in Mexico anyway on what we got."

They didn't have to wait long before the officer sauntered across from his booth. "Come on inside and we'll go over the details."

"You're really gonna do it?" Herbie pressed Hugo.

"At least let's see what the man has to say."

All three of them went inside. When they came back out ten minutes later, the customs officer handed Hugo the keys to the Ford. "You're doing me a big favor, I'll tell you what," said the officer.

"Sorry to ditch you fellas," Hugo said to his friends. "You can tell me all about Mexico when we get back to Chicago."

"Sure." Herbie was stiff. He didn't like being abandoned by someone he'd considered to be a loyal friend, though pride prevented him from complaining.

Hugo transferred his things from the Chevy to the Ford. "Just after I changed all my money to pesos, too!"

"How much is it?" said the officer. "Maybe I can take those off you."

"That would be swell. I got twenty-seven bucks worth."

"Sure, I'll change that for ya."

For Wolf, it was a surreal development. One moment the three of them were headed to Mexico, and just a few minutes later they were already down a man. "Take care of yourself," he said.

"You fellas, too."

Wolf and Herbie climbed back into the Chevy. They watched as Hugo handed his peso notes to the customs officer. "Can you imagine that?" Wolf said. "He has no idea what he's gonna be missing."

"We'll have plenty of fun without him." Herbie started the car, backed out of their parking space and then merged into the nearest lane before passing through another small booth, this time on the Mexican side. A customs officer in a green uniform met them with an air of boredom, as though he could hardly be bothered to sit in his small booth all day questioning American tourists.

"Identificacion."

The boys handed across their drivers' licenses. The officer took them in hand and examined them before lifting two brown cards from a stack on his small desk. He wrote the men's names, one on each card, and then stamped them. "Bienvenido a Mexico." He handed the cards and licenses back together.

"Gracias." Herbie tapped on the gas and they moved forward, leaving the U.S. of A. behind. The three musketeers were down to two.

Continuing into Nuevo Leon, Wolf gazed out the window at run-down buildings with shattered glass, unpaved side streets and feral dogs roaming broken sidewalks. "Kind of run-down, isn't it?" A sense of unease settled into Wolfgang's core. Maybe Hugo was the wise one after all.

"It's gonna be great, you'll see." Herbie tried to convince himself as much as his friend. This was not the romantic vision of Mexico evoked by their fiesta on the south side of Chicago. This was poverty, the likes of which neither had ever seen. All the same, it was too soon to be discouraged. There was a long way to go yet to Mexico City.

Chapter Nine

Polish-Soviet Border, June 24, 1941

The night was dark as ink, the swollen river lit only by the flickering points of a billion stars. No moon. Hermann Neubauer was but one in a sea of German soldiers, struggling to launch a collective flotilla of rubber boats. Water soaked Neubauer's trousers from the knees down, seeping into his boots as the deep mud sucked at them with each step. A pack and rifle were slung across his back, steel helmet on his head. Clutching a paddle, Neubauer heaved himself aboard his boat, sprawling across the legs of his comrades.

"Achtung!" Unseen hands pulled Hermann upright. He slid into place as the boat merged into a crowd of like craft, churning for the far bank.

"Paddle! Paddle!" the command rang out.

Ten men amongst ten thousand surged toward the opposite shore. To Russia. Water splashing, boats bumping, cries echoing in the night, Hermann did his best to concentrate on his one small task. Head down. Paddle, paddle, paddle. He strained from exertion, the taste of blood in his lungs. Attempting to spy the opposite shore, he saw only chaos all around him. Where was it? How far to go? Neubauer redoubled his efforts. When the boat finally lurched to a stop, Hermann launched himself into shallow water, trudging up the bank with the others to join the gathering troops. After months of preparation, his first taste of combat was coming. Soon. Already he heard the distant thump of artillery shells. But were they German or Russian? His heart raced with a mix of anticipation and fear. This could very well be his last day on earth.

"Fall in! Two lines!" his Sergeant called out. The men in his company scrambled into a semblance of order, coming to attention in the dark. The Sergeant gave a quick roll call. All accounted for. "Forward! March!" he hollered and the group moved off, following a long line of soldiers heading east, across Russian soil. Neubauer wondered how far his boots might take him, picturing photos he'd seen of Red Square. It was best not to think ahead. The life of a soldier was lived in the present. One foot in front of the other, marching toward his destiny, whatever it may be.

Neubauer's pack straps dug into his shoulders, the seams of his pants chafing his thighs, his damp socks bunched up around his heels. After five hours on the march, the promise of dawn glowed on the horizon before them. Hermann spotted a small village at the bottom of a valley, just a few kilometers away. With each step forward, the rumble of artillery seemed to grow until it was a roar, pounding the unseen positions just over the nearby hills. It was close. Too close, Neubauer thought.

The sun rose into the sky, warming Hermann's broad forehead as they reached the village, deserted but for a mass of German soldiers, lounging around smoking cigarettes or resting in the town square.

"Company, halt!" The sergeant checked his watch. "We rest here. Today we go over the top, so be prepared! You have six hours. Dismissed!"

Neubauer shifted his pack onto one shoulder before lowering it to the ground. Taking stock of his surroundings, he saw Cyrillic characters printed above the storefronts. He was a long way from home. One building appeared to house a small grocery, with perhaps a hardware store beside it, the windows blasted out of both. There'd been fighting here, though most of the action was taking place a few kilometers further east. Neubauer leaned down to open the top of his pack, rummaging through until he located his camera. "Klaus!" he called out to a tall, thin soldier nearby. "Can you take a photo of me?"

"Ja."

"Get me with some of those signs," Neubauer added. He handed the camera to Klaus and then unstrapped his rifle and carried it across the road to the front of the grocery.

"What does it say?" Klaus asked.

"Who cares? It says we're in Russia." Neubauer held the rifle in both hands. Despite his exhaustion, he was a dashing figure in his uniform. At least that's what Alma told him. Hermann was of average height, with a thin face, wavy dark hair and bushy eyebrows. He had a long, narrow nose above a small mouth. These were not movie-star features, though plenty of women found him attractive.

Klaus snapped a photo. "You can send it home to your wife."

Neubauer pictured Alma, back in Hamburg with his parents. His American wife, who barely spoke a word of German and would never forgive him for bringing her to Germany during wartime. Of course, he knew that she was right. They should have stayed in the U.S. as she'd said all along. His regret was like a deep, dark cloud that never left him. Alma hated it in Germany. Even worse was the very real possibility that she'd end up a widow. He'd made a mistake. All he could do at this point was survive as best he could each day. He carried Alma in his heart wherever he went, yet despite it all, deep down he still felt a thrilling sense of pride. To fight for his country was the reason he'd come back. After a journey that brought him halfway around the world, and months of training, that desire was about to be fulfilled. He was a soldier, no longer slaving away in a Chicago kitchen for a bunch of rich Americans. Neubauer was a German. He'd had little choice but to heed the call. It was as simple as that.

Klaus handed back the camera. "I'm going to lie down and rest."

"Yeah," Neubauer agreed. "Maybe behind that stone wall over there?"

Klaus nodded in agreement. Others were spread out on the square, leaning against their packs or digging out their rations to staunch an ever-present hunger. Some picked through the remains of the grocery store, trying to find anything left that was salvageable. Officers chose the largest building, most likely the city hall, as their temporary headquarters. Neubauer shouldered his pack once more and moved across to the loose stone wall just past the square. Klaus and a few others followed, dropping their packs and then doing their best to make themselves comfortable. Neubauer pulled out some rations of his own; black bread, a small piece of cheese and a canteen. His feet throbbed. His shoulders were chaffed and sore. The muscles in his back and his legs were grateful for any short reprieve.

"It sounds like those Russians are really taking it." Markus was small and wiry with dark-rimmed glasses. He sat munching on a piece of sausage.

"I hope so," said Klaus. "Kill them all, so we don't have to."

"There might still be a few left," said Neubauer.

"Maybe they'll run away, straight back to Moscow," said Markus.

"Don't bet on it," said Klaus.

Neubauer chewed his bread slowly. It wasn't enough. Not nearly, but until their supply convoy caught up, he'd have to make do. He nibbled on a piece of cheese. Should he eat it all, or save some for later? He broke off a bit more, popped it into his mouth, and wrapped the rest in paper before shoving it back into his pack. Maybe tomorrow he'd have a regular meal, he thought. If tomorrow came…

Reclining on the grass with eyes closed, scenes of battle ran through Neubauer's mind. Bullets whizzed past, shells exploding as he charged the Russian positions. How would he conduct himself? With courage? He pictured men falling and dying around him. It was a reality he would face soon enough. He wondered if he could take the life of another man, to snuff out the future of a fellow human being. He would follow orders. That was all. A soldier did as he was told. There was no time for compassion. In the end, it all came down to fate. Neubauer would either survive or not. He would go home when this war was over or he would not. There was no sense in obsessing over it. Instead, he shifted his thoughts to Alma, curled up in the spare bedroom at his parents' house. How he longed to be there, sleeping beside her. If he did survive, when the war was over he'd take her back to America like she wanted. Perhaps she should go already, to wait out the war. Transiting the Atlantic these days was a treacherous prospect, with few passenger vessels still making the journey. Neubauer thought back to the Lekala, the boat he'd bought in the states with his good friend Edward Kerling. Sailing back to the homeland on their own seemed like a good plan at the time, though the U.S. Coastguard had other ideas, intercepting them off Atlantic City and turning them back. And so, they'd sold their trusty sailboat and found a ship bound for Portugal, then traveled overland to Berlin. Even that route was now virtually cut off. Unfortunately, Alma would most likely have to wait it out, as long as the war lasted. With this incursion into Russia, that would likely be measured in years.

Slipping back into his present, Neubauer realized that he hadn't heard any shelling for some time. How long? Five minutes? Ten? He opened his eyes to check his watch. It was still two hours before their appointed time. Hermann shut his eyes once more. The first blast sent a shockwave ripping through his body, shaking his eyes in his skull, his eardrums nearly bursting. Hermann's lids sprang back open. Men rushed for cover through rolling smoke. Shouts of confusion blended with screams of agony. Neubauer crawled on his belly, inching toward the low wall. A volley of shells wailed overhead, exploding just beyond. Shrapnel pinged off the stones behind him as Hermann huddled close in confusion. What was happening? Where were they coming from? Officers streamed out of their makeshift headquarters as a shell hit the building, blasting out the windows and launching a stream of debris.

"We need to move!" shouted Klaus.

"Where?!" Neubauer's confusion quickly shifted to terror.

"Away!" Klaus scrambled along the base of the wall. Neubauer hopped to his feet and struggled to follow at a crouch. It was as though he were drunk, the ground swaying under his feet. Tripping over a prone soldier, Hermann fell onto his face in the grass.

"Stay down, you idiot!" the soldier shouted.

Next came the sensation of hot metal tearing into his flesh, burrowing into his arm, his back, his skull. When the stone wall collapsed on top of him, it was only the loss of consciousness that saved him from the pain. For Hermann Neubauer, the battle was over before it had begun.

Chapter Ten

Mexico City, June 26, 1941

The Lopez Restaurant had the kind of atmosphere that Wolfgang expected of Mexico, with piñatas and colored streamers hanging from the ceiling. It was a little grimy, sure, but festive. Perhaps that was why he and Herbie took to eating meals here each day. It was also near their hotel, and reasonably cheap. All of these were good reasons to frequent the establishment, though there was one additional incentive that kept them coming back. Lupita, the younger of two sisters, was Herbie's favorite, with porcelain-white skin and a deferential air. Wolfgang preferred Clara, the more self-assured sister, whose English also happened to be just a tad bit better. Today it was Lupita on duty as Herbie watched her move across the room with a tray of plates balanced precariously on one hand.

"We should ask them out."

"I thought we tried that already."

"We need to do it properly. We can't just tell girls like these to meet us for a drink somewhere. They're never gonna show."

"What else do you have in mind?"

Behind the bar, Señor Lopez washed beer glasses as he chatted with a regular customer, another gringo who was busy showing off a small Kodak camera. "We gotta take them someplace nice," Herbie said quietly. "You know, somewhere respectable."

Wolf stirred the beans on his plate. After the better part of a week, he craved a good old hamburger, or better yet, a serving of his mother's schnitzel and sauerkraut. They'd had the time of their lives so far, but their dwindling finances were never far from his thoughts. Herbie hardly seemed to notice, eager to spend their meager pesos at any opportunity.

"We could sell the car." Herbie suggested it as though the idea were a mere afterthought.

Wolfgang nearly choked on his beans. After carefully chewing and swallowing, he tried to maintain his composure. "MY car?! You can't mean that!"

"Why not? We could take the train back later, and then you buy a new car when we get home. I'll pay you back my half of whatever we get."

An incredulous expression crossed Wolf's face as he slowly shook his head. "You always have the answers."

"I'm just saying, it's an option."

Wolf recalled the pride he'd felt on purchasing the Chevy just one year earlier. It was his very first car. Holding those keys in his hand, it was as though that one moment signified his transformation into adulthood. His car meant freedom, to go where he wanted, when he wanted. To Wolf, it was more than simply the money. That car was a part of his identity. "Let's keep searching for other options, huh?"

"Sure, buddy, sure. We'll see how we go."

Wolf breathed a little easier as he looked back toward the bar, where he saw the gringo eyeing them. The man was in his 40s and wore a light tan suit. He often carried a newspaper, usually the *Herald Tribune*, but they'd overheard him speaking with a German accent. The boys speculated that he might have come by way of Chicago himself, based on his reading material. Was he listening in on their conversation? Wolf lowered his voice just in case. "Maybe we ought to start thinking about going home while we can still afford the gas."

"Don't tell me you're ready to go back already?! We only just got here!"

"I don't want to lose my job. I told them I'd be gone two weeks."

Just the mention of home filled Herbie with a sense of dread. Visions of a pregnant Gerda swirled through his mind; baby, diapers, the end of life as he knew it. When Lupita emerged from the kitchen, looking lovely in her white waitress' uniform, his spirits immediately lifted. "I'm not going back. Not yet."

From his back pocket, Wolf pulled out his wallet, opened it up and examined the contents, flipping through the bills with his fingers. "Ninety-six pesos. We'll be lucky to last out the week. How much you got left?"

"Wolf, you worry too much."

"Maybe you don't worry enough."

Herbie looked back toward Lupita, dark hair gleaming against her porcelain skin. When he caught her eye, he was sure that he detected the lightest of smiles. Thinking ahead was never Herbie's style. He was a man ruled by emotion, not logic, and that suited him just fine. "Relax, it'll all work out."

At times Wolfgang admired his friend's impulsiveness. Hanging around with Herbie was rarely dull. All the same, impulsive often bordered on reckless. Wolf yearned to be more like Herbie, to float through life without fretting about the consequences, yet he was beginning to feel that such a carefree attitude simply wasn't in his nature. He'd enjoyed the trip so far, more than he'd even expected he could. Herbie's influence was certainly good for him, though Wolfgang had his limits. He didn't want to end up flat broke and out on the streets. "At the very least, we ought to find a cheaper place to stay. That hotel we're in costs too much."

Herbie nodded. "We can ask around. Maybe Lopez knows something."

At the bar, the man in the tan suit placed his camera on top of his newspaper and drank from a glass of beer, though Señor Lopez was nowhere in sight. Herbie finished the last few bites of his lunch. "Let's get out of here." He waved a hand toward Lupita.

"All finished?" she called across.

"All finished!" said Herbie.

"OK, I bring the check."

Herbie and Wolf made their way across to a register on top of the bar.

"You boys are American." The man in the tan suit looked up. It was more of a statement than a question.

Herbie gave him the once-over. "That's right."

"Where from?"

"Chicago," said Wolfgang.

The man nodded. "Great town. I come from New York, myself."

"But you're German?" Wolfgang asked.

"Originally."

"You been down here long?" said Herbie.

"Quite some time, yes. You could say I've relocated, temporarily." He took another swig of his beer and then placed the glass on the bar before reaching out a hand. "Hans Sass."

"Herbie Haupt." The men shook hands.

"Wolf Wergin."

"And what brings you to this not-so-fair city?"

"We're just taking a look around," said Herbie.

"I see," said Sass.

On the other side of the bar, Lupita rang up their lunch. Mechanical numbers popped up on the register as she hit the keys. "Eight pesos and cincuenta centavos," she said.

"That's eight-fifty," said Sass.

"Yes, fifty," Lupita blushed.

"Sure, I know that much," said Herbie. He and Wolf counted out what they owed and placed it on the counter."

"Gracias!" said Lupita.

"I couldn't help but overhear a snippet of your conversation," said Sass. "I have to say, if you are in need of affordable accommodation I might be able to help."

Wolfgang shot Herbie a glance.

"What sort of accommodation?" Herbie asked.

"There's a boarding house just a few blocks from here. Clean, cheap… For fifty pesos per week, it's not a bad deal. I'm staying there myself. If you'd like I can take you by."

Wolf didn't have to think long about it. The place was less than half the cost of their hotel. At the very least it was worth a look. "Sure, we'll come by," he said.

"Excellent." Sass slid the camera into his pocket and folded his newspaper.

Señor Lopez emerged from the kitchen, wiping his hands on his apron. "Hola amigos! Que necessitan?"

"Nothing, Señor, we're all set!" said Herbie.

"Take your time, I'm in no hurry. Have another beer if you'd like," said Sass.

"I think we're ready," said Herbie. "We'd like to see this place of yours."

"Of course."

Wolfgang felt a glimmer of optimism. Perhaps this was a small change in their fortunes. At the very least, they might stretch their money past the end of the week. He had to give Herbie some credit. His friend was single-handedly shifting Wolf's perspective on what was truly important. For Wolf's entire life, he'd played it safe. Of course, he'd never quite realized that before they set out on this trip, but it was true. He'd lived in his parents' house, and followed their rules. After high school, he'd found a good job and showed up to work dutifully, on time each day. Wolf had never pushed any sort of boundaries in life. He'd known what was expected of him and strived to live up to those expectations. For the first time, he felt that he was living on his own terms. Despite his apprehensions, this whole experience filled him with an intoxicating sense of freedom. He was meeting people and seeing places that he'd never dreamed of beforehand. Wolf owed that all to Herbie, and just like his friend, he wasn't quite ready for it to end. Now that they were here, Wolf would breathe it all in, every last bit that he could. "How much do you think we could get for it?" he asked.

"What, the Chevy?" said Herbie.

"Yeah."

Herbie grinned. "Why don't we go by a dealership tomorrow and see what they say?"

Wolfgang wasn't quite ready to commit to the idea, but he wouldn't rule it out, either. He tried not to think about how hard he'd worked to buy that car. It was only money. He could always earn it back.

Chapter Eleven

Berlin, July 6, 1941

George Dasch was tall and ungainly; a garrulous man with a distinctive gray streak running through his dark hair. It was just before dawn as he sat at his desk with headphones on, listening to a speech by the American president. Facing him was his young assistant, Liselotte Piper, whose fingers rested on the keys of a stenograph machine. As Roosevelt spoke, Dasch translated the sentences into German while Miss Piper tapped the words onto her keypad. All day, every day, teams worked at the German Foreign Office in shifts to translate radio broadcasts from around the globe. When broadcasts were occasionally lost to static, Dasch enjoyed letting his creativity roam, using these occasions to invent reports out of thin air and bash the Nazi system that he'd grown to despise. "This evil regime must be stopped in its tracks before it infects the entire world with its warped and dangerous ideology! Adolph Hitler and his cronies are a dire threat to the principles of freedom and democracy!" Dasch would improvise as he went, always attributing these made-up quotes to somebody else.

On this particular morning, listening to Roosevelt made Dasch increasingly homesick for the country he'd lived in for the previous twenty years. He longed to return. He yearned to see his friends and even more so, his American wife Marie, who waited for him on the other side of the Atlantic; his little "Snooks," who'd tried to join him in Germany only to end up intercepted by a British naval blockade. It broke his heart to picture her, locked up in an internment camp in Bermuda. Dasch was powerless to help either one of them. His entire predicament really all came down to his mother. After two decades, she'd finally come to visit him in New York. She'd finally witnessed his life there firsthand. She'd learned what he actually did for a living. George hid that information from her for all those years.

He was an educated man. He'd always expected that his life would amount to something more substantial than waiting tables. It wasn't that he didn't feel some dignity in making his way in America, yet he couldn't entirely banish an underlying sense of shame. Working as a waiter was honorable work, sure. That's what he tried to tell himself and Dasch was able to put his pride aside, more or less, for two long decades. But then his mother arrived, and his insecurities overwhelmed him. "When are you going to come back to Germany?!" his mother implored him. "Things are better there now, you'll see! You'll be able to get a job! A good job! A job to be proud of!" His mother kept at him for the duration of her six-month stay. In the end, she simply wore him down. It was true, Dasch realized. If he stayed in America, he would probably never make much of himself. Maybe his mother was right. Maybe things really were better in Germany. Perhaps he could finally gain a position that he deserved, as an educated man. The family had connections. It was worth a shot, George finally conceded.

As soon as he'd boarded the ship for the first leg of his trip, from San Francisco to Japan, he realized what a terrible mistake he was making. The other Germans on board disturbed him, with their matching brown shirts, their Nazi emblems, and their constant *Heil Hitler* salutes. Tensions escalated. When Dasch refused to join them in expressing his fealty to the Nazi regime, he was punched in the face, his nose bloodied. By this time, it was too late to turn back. Dasch's fate was sealed.

Arriving in Germany, he'd been lucky to gain this government job. Lieutenant Walter Kappe, a fleshy, round-faced Nazi who'd previously lived in Chicago, was assigned to interview Dasch upon re-entry. Apparently, he spotted something in this former New York waiter that he admired. Perhaps they both recognized a little bit of themselves in each other, with their similar, outgoing personalities. Only, in Kappe's case, his optimism hid the darkness of the Nazi cause. The Lieutenant assumed that Dasch shared the same outlook. Why else would any good German return home but to support the war effort? Kappe offered him the position with the Foreign Office nearly straight away. George was grateful for the job, even if he was trapped in a Germany he barely recognized. A Germany that was being destroyed from within by the very government he now served.

All that Dasch could do, it seemed, was wait it out. In the early days, he told himself that the war would be over quickly. Surely it couldn't last too long. Then the Fuhrer invaded Russia. When George heard that news, he crumpled on his bed and cried. This war that he'd hoped would soon be finished was only just beginning. In public, Dasch did his best to maintain a stoic face, though that didn't stop him from taking his occasional liberties with the transcripts. It was a small way of maintaining his sanity in the face of overwhelming madness. On this morning, however, the broadcast came in loud and clear.

"We have sought no shooting war with Hitler," said Franklin Delano Roosevelt. "We do not seek it now. But neither do we want peace so much that we are willing to pay for it by permitting him to attack our naval and merchant ships while they are on legitimate business."

Dasch struggled to keep up. After two decades speaking English, his German was rusty. Words that would have once come easily to him now took some thought. Still, he managed. The job wasn't a difficult one. It kept him clothed and fed, and perhaps even more importantly, it kept him out of the Army. It allowed him to stay in Berlin, sleeping in the same bed every night instead of marching off to Poland or Russia to be shot at. Perhaps he was slower with the language than his colleagues, but his superiors seemed satisfied enough. Dasch stopped the recording and played it back, catching the last few sentences over again. When he was ready, he went on, relaying the German words to Miss Piper.

"I assume that the German leaders are not deeply concerned, tonight or any other time, by what we Americans or the American Government say or publish about them," Roosevelt continued. "We cannot bring about the downfall of Nazi-ism by the use of long-range invective, but when you see a rattlesnake poised to strike, you do not wait until he has struck before you crush him. The American people have faced other grave crises in their history -- with American courage, and with American resolution. They will do no less today."

When the speech was finished, Dasch reached up and pressed the button to turn off the tape recorder. "Did you get all of that?" He took his headphones off.

Miss Piper finished typing the last sentence into her stenograph machine. "Yes," she answered. "I got it." She pulled up the paper tape and read it over, checking for errors. Liselotte was a petite and gentle girl with big brown eyes. During the day she attended classes at Berlin University, working to finish her degree. She and Dasch worked well together, though he wouldn't go so far as to consider the pair of them friends. Socializing with anyone from the office generated unwelcome scrutiny from their Gestapo overseers. Lately, she'd seemed particularly distant, though George had no idea why. "Is everything all right?" he asked, hoping to garner a clue.

"Yes, fine!" Liselotte was startled by the question.

Dasch sat where he was, considering his response. He knew better than to press her. These days it was best to allow people their space. "I'm happy to hear it," he answered.

Miss Piper went about packing her things. Through their office window, a faint glow in the eastern sky signaled the break of day. It was nearly time to head home. Dasch rewound his tape recording and took it out of the machine. He placed the tape in its cardboard box and then rose from his chair. As he moved toward the door, Miss Piper peered up at him expectantly. "Perhaps you wouldn't mind escorting me home this morning?" she said.

Dasch stopped near the door. This was unexpected. He wasn't quite sure what to make of it. "Certainly," he replied. "I'd be honored."

"Of course, we shouldn't be seen leaving the building together," Liselotte stammered.

"No, of course not."

"I could wait for you, on the way to the subway station."

Dasch nodded slowly. Had the young woman taken an interest in him? Whatever her request regarded, he'd find out soon enough. "I'll just return the tape to the archive before I go. I won't be long."

"Fine. I'll see you shortly." Liselotte looked away, uneasy with the whole business.

Dasch walked out the office door. Whatever Miss Piper wanted to tell him was worth taking a risk. George passed a few of his colleagues from the American section on the way to the stairs. He saw Helen, a recent hire who was worse at the job than even Dasch. Compared to Helen, Dasch's German was excellent, but that didn't stop her from getting the job and keeping it. Dasch said hello and then continued down into the basement where a clerk sat at a desk. Behind him, rows of shelves were stacked with boxes of audio tapes from floor to ceiling. Dasch placed his box on the desk. The clerk read the serial number and then lifted a clipboard and used one finger to scroll down until he found the correct entry. He wrote down the time to signify that the tape was returned and then handed the clipboard to Dasch, who signed his name and handed it back. "Have a good morning," Dasch said.

"And you," the clerk replied.

By the time Dasch returned to his office, Miss Piper was gone. George gathered his jacket and hat before heading out himself. At the building's entrance, a dour Gestapo guard searched him for any forbidden materials. Nothing was to leave the building. Punishment for breaking this rule was severe, Dasch knew. He flashed a cheerful smile as the guard completed his search. "Good morning to you!" George said, though the guard was already moving on to the next man in line. Dasch walked outside into what was shaping up to be a glorious summer day. Was the continent really at war? How could it be, on a day such as this? Dasch folded his jacket in half and draped it across his arm before heading down the crowded sidewalk. Most of these people were on their way to work for the day, but all Dasch wanted was a precious bit of sleep.

As he moved toward the subway station, George passed men in gray suits and felt fedoras. He saw women in calf-length skirts and sensible shoes. And then there were the soldiers. Enlisted men on the way home from a night on the town. Officers on their way to jobs in the War Ministry. Civilians averted their eyes from those in uniform. Dasch, too, felt this compulsion to draw as little attention to himself as possible. But then, what were they likely to do? He was a government worker himself, at the Foreign Office no less. So why did he, too, feel this visceral sense of fear? Because he knew that if the Nazis suspected his true feelings, they might just shoot him dead on the street. Dasch kept his own eyes down and walked straight ahead. After a few blocks, he found Miss Piper, loitering in front of a shop window as she examined a display of leather shoes.

"Good morning, Miss Piper," said Dasch.

"Oh, hello," Liselotte replied.

"Heading to the subway?"

"Yes, as a matter of fact, I am." Miss Piper peered up and down the street, as though any one of these passersby might be watching them.

"Do you mind if I accompany you?" George added.

"Certainly not."

With that, the pair continued up the street, side-by-side. They made their way to the station and then down the stairs to the platform below where Dasch recognized a few other colleagues heading home for the day. In such a public place, he and Miss Piper refrained from speaking. Instead, they merely stood side-by-side amongst the waiting passengers. After a few moments, a train hurtled into view before screeching to a halt beside them. Dasch and the others moved aboard. He found a seat not far from Miss Piper before the train moved on. As they continued along beneath the streets of Berlin and out toward the suburbs, the carriage became less crowded with each stop. Before long, only a handful of passengers remained. Sitting across from Dasch, two men in their early sixties wore threadbare jackets and scuffed hats. One of them had deep creases in his face, the result of years of hard living. His companion had a waxy complexion and a large red nose.

"How about our boys, showing it to the Russians, eh?" said the first man.

"I hear we're licking them good," the second man agreed.

"It's about time. That Stalin had it coming."

"He'll sure be begging for mercy when our boys get to Moscow, eh?" The man let loose a grin that showed his missing teeth.

"It shouldn't be long at the rate they're going. Our Fuhrer is a military genius. Look what he did to the French."

"I bet we have the whole thing wrapped up by Christmas."

Both men seemed overjoyed by these developments. Dasch kept his eyes on his lap. When the train stopped again, Liselotte rose to her feet. George stood and followed her out of the carriage.

Up at street level, they continued down a sidewalk past multi-story apartment blocks. The day was warming as sunlight filtered through the tall green trees lining the street. There were no crowds this far out. Aside from the occasional passerby, it was just the two of them.

Whatever Miss Piper had wanted to say, she was free to do so, though she still seemed reluctant.

Dasch tried to make small talk. "This is a very nice neighborhood you live in, just the right distance from the center to be convenient, yet far enough to be quiet."

"I've lived in this apartment all of my life. It's my parents' home."

"I'm in a boarding room not far from the office, myself," said Dasch. "I'm from Speyer, originally. By way of Chicago, of course."

Liselotte didn't seem to care much for this biographical information. "Mr. Dasch," she said, "I have something to ask you."

"Yes?" This was the moment, George thought. Miss Piper was about to come clean.

"Sometimes I have the feeling you want Germany to lose this war, and as quickly as possible." This time she looked at him directly, as though daring him to deny it. "Before millions of people die and everything is destroyed."

"What makes you say that?!" Dasch was flustered by the accusation.

"Don't worry, I happen to agree, but you've got to be more careful. I don't think you fully understand how dangerous your views can be."

"I see…" It was a shock to be confronted this way by his assistant. "What makes you think that I'm not careful?"

Miss Piper's expression showed her incredulity. "I may not understand everything in these English broadcasts, but I've heard enough to know that you're making things up."

Dasch laughed out loud, a light blush reddening his cheeks. "Believe me, there is nothing to worry about! I only do that when the recordings are garbled. There's no way they can catch me!"

"You're a fool!" Miss Piper shot back. "That same broadcast will be made in a dozen other languages! Or maybe it will be broadcast another time, when the reception is better! They could easily check up on you and your goose would be cooked. Please be careful!" she pleaded. "Promise me you'll be more careful!"

Dasch was chastened. Of course, she was right. He *had* been reckless, as though it were all just fun and games. This was no game they were playing; it was serious business. The apprehension in Miss

Piper's eyes emphasized that fact. "I'm sorry," he said. "I will be more careful from now on. I promise."

"Good." Miss Piper was somewhat relieved. "You're not the only one who would be in danger. If they begin to suspect your loyalty, every person you associate with would be at risk."

"Yes, yes…" Dasch hadn't adequately considered that side of the equation.

Miss Piper's gaze shot straight ahead as they moved on up the sidewalk. "It's best to be careful. If I can see it, then somebody else can probably see it as well."

They came to an intersection and stopped to wait for a few cars to pass before hurrying across and continuing up the block. "Thank you for your concern."

"One more thing." Miss Piper stopped in front of the door to an apartment building. "Be careful of Helen. Watch what you say around her."

"Helen? Why should I worry about her?" Dasch was surprised. Helen, who he'd seen at the office just that morning, was thirty years of age and had spent most of her life in Detroit. She'd always been friendly. He had no reason to suspect her.

"Didn't you ever notice how poor she is at her job? She has no sense of history or politics or geography. Her reports are completely incoherent, yet they keep her on, even when others who are much better suited to the work are let go. Why do you think that is?"

Dasch shrugged. "You think she's reporting to the Gestapo?"

"Just be careful. You don't want to say the wrong thing to the wrong person."

The building behind Miss Piper was four-stories high, with a green plaster façade and empty flower boxes hanging from the apartment windows.

"What if *I'm* the wrong person? Did you ever think of that?"

Miss Piper laughed out loud for the first time that morning. "I'm sorry but you, I can read like a book." The gaiety didn't last, as a dark cloud of concern descended over her face once more. "Just be sure to keep this conversation to yourself, please."

"Of course," Dasch answered. "This is your place?"

Liselotte nodded. "Yes. I should go."

"Thank you for the warning. You took a risk in speaking to me like this."

"It was a bigger risk not to." Miss Piper removed a key from her jacket pocket and quickly opened the front door. "I'll see you tonight." With that, she moved inside and closed the door behind her. Dasch stayed where he was for a moment, looking up and down the street. It all looked so peaceful. A woman pushed a baby stroller up the sidewalk toward him. A few cars rolled past. Yet again, it was easy to forget they were at war. Here in Berlin, on a warm and sunny summer morning, the conflict seemed very far away. Of course, Dasch understood what was happening in Poland, and France, and now in the Soviet Union, too. He knew only too well. He heard the news reports every single day. Reports that most civilians had no access to. This war was serious business and Miss Piper was right. From now on, Dasch would be more careful.

Chapter Twelve

Mexico City, July 20, 1941

They sat all together at a table in the bar section of an upscale restaurant. Herbie and Wolf were side-by-side with Clara and Lupita Gomez directly opposite. The girls looked lovely in colorful cotton dresses with bare arms. They'd taken their time with their makeup and hair, striving to make the best possible impression on their American paramours. For their part, Herbie and Wolf donned the best suits they had available. All would have been wonderful except for one problem. It began with the seat beside the girls, occupied by their mother, and went on around the table to include an aunt, an uncle, an older brother, and lastly, Mr. Gomez himself seated directly beside Wolf. This was not at all what the boys bargained for when Lupita and Clara agreed on a date, but apparently, it was how things were done around here. It also appeared to be the custom for the two young gentlemen to pay the entire bill. Mr. Gomez, on his third beer, was content to sit quietly and absorb his good fortune. Other members of the family chatted with one another in Spanish, casting an occasional glance at the boys. That left Herbie and Wolf to make conversation with the girls, to the best of their ability.

"What do you call this?" Wolf pointed at his hand.

"Mano."

"Mano," Wolf repeated. "How about this?" He pointed to his head.

"Cabeza."

"I sure wish I knew a little bit more Spanish," said Herbie.

A waitress stopped by the table with the latest round on a tray, placing fresh drinks in front of each member of the group. Mr. Gomez pursed his lips, his cheeks flushing with delight. He quaffed the last of his previous beer and handed back the glass. "Gracias."

"De nada," the waitress replied before turning to the boys. "Veinte-cinco pesos, por favor."

"You got twenty-five pesos left?" Herbie asked Wolf as they each pulled out their wallets.

"Barely," Wolf replied. This was going horribly wrong. They'd already paid the equivalent of two-weeks rent at their boarding house on this family, and for what? With Mrs. Gomez staring him down from across the table, Wolf knew that a taste of Clara's sweet lips was entirely out of the question.

"Here's ten." Herbie handed over a bill. Wolf added fifteen pesos of his own and gave them to the waitress.

"Thank you," she said.

"De nada," replied Herbie.

"Hey Herbie, I gotta use the John," said Wolf.

"OK."

"I think you outta go, too."

"I don't gotta go, I just went."

"I think you outta go," Wolf repeated, tilting his head forward to accentuate the point. It took Herbie another moment to get it.

"Oh! OK. Yeah, I gotta go. Lo siento, girls! We need to use the bathroom. The, uh… el bano."

"Esta bien, no problema!" Lupita replied with a smile.

"Ladies, gentlemen…" Herbie stood and gave a nod to the others at the table. "Un momento."

Mr. Gomez raised his beer in the air, gave a nod, and took another drink. Wolf followed Herbie across the bar and into the men's room at the back. "What's up?" he said.

"What do you mean, what's up? We're out of money."

"Not that again! Come on Wolf, we've got some more back at the room."

"But how much? And what happens after the next round comes out? I only got ten pesos left!"

"So, we'll tell them they gotta pay for it! I mean, come on, they owe us that much!"

"I don't think it works that way."

An anxious expression came over Herbie's face. "We bought the guy four beers already!"

"They think we're just rich Americans! They think we can keep paying all night. Even if we do, what's it gonna get us?"

"I don't know," he conceded. "This whole thing isn't what I had in mind."

Wolf pushed the door open a crack and looked out toward the table. There was no escape without walking right past it. "We need to get out of here."

"Come on, how is that going to look?"

"I don't care how it looks. I'm not buying that fat bastard another beer. Or any of 'em."

"But think of Clara!"

"Forget about Clara. And Lupita. You want their old lady following you around all the time?"

"No." Herbie leaned against the wall and gave it some thought. "You're right, we outta go. Maybe we should say goodbye."

"Let's make it quick." Wolf exited the restroom with Herbie right behind. When they reached the table, Wolf cleared his throat. "Excuse me, but… buenas noches everybody."

"Hasta luego." Herbie raised a hand in the air.

"You go?!" Clara's panic-stricken expression melted Wolf's heart, but the decision was made.

"Yes. I'm sorry."

"No, no, you no go!" Mr. Gomez jumped to his feet and put an arm around Wolf, using his other hand to motion toward the chair. "Is early! You stay!"

A feeling of dread came over Wolf. They should have just walked on out without a second look. Now they were in danger of getting sucked right back in.

"I'm sorry, señor. We gotta go." Herbie physically pried Mr. Gomez's arm from his friend's shoulder. He gave one last apologetic look to the girls and then a quick nod to their mother. "Good night."

Wolf and Herbie headed for the door, but Mr. Gomez would not give up so easily. He followed behind, haranguing them as they went. "Is early! You no go! Uno mas!"

When they reached the street outside, Herbie gave a quick look to Wolf. "I think we'd better run!" Wolfgang needed no more persuasion. Instead, the pair of them took off up the sidewalk, weaving around pedestrians and moving as fast as their legs could take them. When they reached an intersection they turned left and continued up the block, their leather soles scuffing along the pavement. The exertion, the quick breaths in and out of their lungs, was invigorating. Long after they could have stopped, they kept on going, running and running and running until finally they entered a small plaza and doubled over from exhaustion. "Whew, I think we made it." Herbie straightened himself with a laugh and placed one hand on Wolf's back.

"I guess we'd better not go back to the Lopez Restaurant anymore," said Wolf.

"Yeah, maybe not." Standing in the dimly-lit square, they had no idea where they were, exactly in this enormous city. Music drifted out of a cantina on one corner of the plaza. "What do you say we grab a nightcap, just you and me?"

"No Mr. Gomez."

"Or any other Gomez."

"I wouldn't mind if it was just the girls."

The pair made their way across to the cantina and ducked inside. This was the kind of place they preferred. Dingy. Colorful. Cheap. They approached the bar and found two seats.

"Que quiere?" said a bartender.

"Dos tequilas, por favor," Herbie answered.

The bartender laid out two shot glasses, then lifted a bottle and filled them to the brim. "Cinco pesos."

"That's more like it." Wolf pulled out five pesos and placed them on the counter.

Herbie lifted a shot in the air. "What should we drink to?"

Wolfgang raised his glass. "I don't know. You're better at that stuff than I am."

"How about to Hugo? He sure missed some good times down here, didn't he? Even if we never got nowhere with the twins."

"You make it sound like the trip is all but over with."

Herbie's shoulders sagged as he faced the reality he had tried to avoid for so long. He placed his shot back on the bar. "I know what you think of me. That I never pay any attention to the money. You think I'm careless."

"I wouldn't say that exactly."

"Come on now, Wolf, I know it's true. You think all I want to do is have a good time."

"I'm having a good time, just being down here."

"I'm glad to hear it. I really am. I'm sorry we had to sell your car."

"It's all right. Come on, don't get all glum on me. Let's drink our shots."

Herbie perked up a bit. "Sure. To Hugo!"

"To Hugo." Wolf downed the fiery golden liquid, feeling the burn as it slid past his throat and hit his stomach.

When Herbie placed his empty glass back down, he took a moment to let his head clear. "Whew, that's rough."

"You get what you pay for, I guess."

"Yeah. One more on me?"

"Fine, I'll have another."

Herbie waved for the bartender. "Dos mas, por favor."

"Si, seguro." The bartender filled their glasses.

Herbie threw down the last five pesos in his wallet. "That car money sure didn't last too long, did it?"

"No." Wolf was tired of pointing out the obvious. Selling his car had allowed them one additional month. Now both were gone. "No, it didn't."

"It seems this is about the end of the line, huh buddy?"

Wolf nodded. It almost sounded as though Herbie was coming to his senses. For six weeks, Wolfgang traded his more pragmatic outlook for Herbie's boundless enthusiasm. It was liberating, to be sure, but their expedition was running on fumes. They still had enough to get back home if they left soon. They wouldn't be starving, flat broke and trapped down here. The only question was whether Herbie would finally admit it.

"It's been a good time, hasn't it?" Herbie's eyes took on a sentimental cast.

"Am I mistaken, or do those sound like the words of a man who's ready to go home?"

Herbie scanned the cantina. He spotted a middle-aged couple at a table against the far wall. Nearby a group of young local men gathered to drink beer. Further down the bar, an older gentleman swayed over a half-empty glass. "I'll tell you what, I'd rather stay a while if there was a way, but I see how it is. If it wasn't for you keeping an eye on things, we'd probably be out of cash already."

"Probably?"

Herbie gave a quiet chuckle. "OK, definitely."

"So, you're ready to call it a trip?"

"I guess so."

There was a sadness in the way Herbie said the words that caught Wolf off guard. "I'll tell you what, I can't wait for a home-cooked meal," said Wolf. "And my own bed. And my drum set. I miss my drum set."

"I wonder how my mother is doing…"

"I'm sure she can't wait to see you."

Herbie lifted his shot glass and heaved a deep sight. "To Mexico."

"To Chicago," Wolf countered.

"All right, Chicago." They tapped their glasses together and then downed their shots.

"We really did it, though, didn't we?" Herbie wiped his mouth with the back of one hand.

"We certainly did. I'll never forget it, for as long as I live," Wolfgang answered, though his mind was already drifting homeward. Back to the lives they'd left behind.

Chapter Thirteen

Northern Mexico, July 22, 1941

As their train churned through the arid landscape, Herbie's eyes remained fixed out the window. Whatever space he'd given himself by escaping to Mexico was rapidly shrinking. Aside from one postcard he'd sent from St. Louis, he'd had no contact with Gerda since leaving Chicago. Their unborn child was a responsibility that he couldn't ignore. People got married every day. They settled down and raised families. Herbie wanted the same for himself, eventually. He'd have preferred to wait a few more years, but it seemed that option was over. Perhaps it was time to make an honest woman of Gerda Stuckmann. Herbie thought back to the good times that they'd shared. He remembered the first time they met, at a picnic by the lake two years before. She'd radiated such confidence then, despite hardly knowing a soul. These were Herbie's friends, going back to childhood, yet she'd laughed and carried on like a certified member of the group. It was only after they got to know each other better that she revealed her vulnerabilities. Gerda married at eighteen. Her husband died at twenty, two years before she met Herbie. In those first few months, his presence was inescapable, hanging over them like a cloud. Slowly, she'd let Herbie into her heart. Gerda could love the man she'd married, keep a piece of him tucked away inside, and yet make room for someone else. Herbie remembered sitting high up in the stands at a Cubs game, Gerda's hand in his, their fingers intertwined. She'd looked so pretty that day, as the last rays of sun lit her rosy cheeks. If moments could be bottled and saved, that was one he'd like to keep. Yet if he married Gerda, there would surely be more. It might be a pretty nice life after all. Herbie wondered how his parents would take the news. It was an obstacle he dreaded, yet the truth was that he did love Gerda. Surely his parents could understand that.

"Are you OK?" said Wolf.

"Sure. Fine." The train moved through the outskirts of a small city, slowing as they neared the center.

"I can't wait for a big fat burger and a chocolate shake."

"How about a juicy steak with a baked potato?"

"Or a bratwurst with onions, cooked on the grill..."

The train crept through Nuevo Leon, past dusty, dilapidated buildings. Despite the challenges that faced him, Herbie was struck by an unexpected sense of anticipation. He missed his life in Chicago. He missed his family, and his friends, and even his job at Simpson Optical. The train pulled into the station, steam brakes hissing in relief. "This is it. End of the line."

The pair stood to retrieve their bags from a shelf above their heads. Here they would disembark, cross the border on foot, and catch another train on the American side. After exiting their compartment, they joined a line of passengers moving along the corridor. At the end of the car, they climbed down the steps to the platform. The heat was oppressive as they followed the crowd through the station and then out across the street.

"Do we know where we're going?" said Wolf.

"Wherever they're going."

Travelers moved like a slow river up the block, finally backing up at the U.S. border crossing. On their left, rows of cars and trucks stretched across several lanes, waiting their turn to go through customs and immigration. On the sidewalk, pedestrians lined up to pass, first through a Mexican checkpoint and then on to the American side. Wolfgang and Herbie dropped their bags to wait. Slowly the line crept forward under the broiling sun until they entered a small plaster building with a single fan overhead. Here the queue snaked back and forth behind ropes until it ended at a row of Mexican customs agents. When Herbie and Wolfgang made it to the front, they were called forward to a desk by an agent in a green uniform, his round, bald head covered by a thin strand of hair combed across the front of his scalp.

"Nacionalidad?" the officer asked.

"American," the boys replied in unison.

"Identificacion y tarjetas de entrada, por favor."

Herbie and Wolfgang took out their wallets. Their retrieved their driver's licenses and the cards they'd received upon entry to Mexico, six weeks before. When they'd slid them across the counter, the officer picked them up and read their names one at a time. As he looked over Wolfgang's entry card, his head tilted sideways. "Donde esta su carro?" he said.

"What?" Wolfgang answered.

"Su Carro! Su automovil!" The agent pointed to a stamp on Wolfgang's card. It showed the small symbol of an automobile.

"I think he wants to know why we're not in your car," said Herbie.

"It broke down! We had to leave it!" Wolfgang stretched the truth.

The officer shook his head. "You wait here." He walked to a door at the back of the room where he knocked twice and then passed through.

"They gotta let us cross, right?" Wolf laughed to hide his apprehension.

"Sure, we're Americans!" said Herbie. "They've got to."

"Just because we sold the car…"

"Don't worry, it'll be fine. He probably just doesn't speak English so good."

They stood waiting, nerves jangled. "What's taking him so long?" Wolfgang asked.

"These guys like to make you wait, just 'cause they can."

After a few more minutes, the agent reappeared, this time with a supervisor in tow. This man's uniform was cleaner and well-pressed. He was handsome, with only a slight paunch and flecks of gray in his well-trimmed hair. When the two agents approached the desk, Wolfgang saw that the supervisor held both travel cards.

"Good afternoon, gentlemen," the man said. "I see from your documents that you entered this country in an automobile."

"That's right," said Wolf. "We came in my car."

"And where is your car now?"

"It broke down."

"And did you pay the duty?"

"What duty?" Herbie was defensive.

"You must pay import duty when you sell a foreign vehicle in our country. Did you pay this tax?"

"No, the car broke down. We left it," Wolf tried again.

"You still must pay a duty of 20 percent of the estimated value of your vehicle. Do you have a bill of sale?"

"You expect us to pay right this minute?" Herbie was flabbergasted.

The supervisor raised both eyebrows. "I am sorry, señor, but if you expect to cross this border today, you will have to pay."

"And what if we don't?" Herbie persisted.

"Then you are welcome to stay here in Mexico until you do."

"Twenty percent of the value?" Wolfgang was aghast.

"That is the law, señor. I don't make the law. I only enforce it."

"But that car wasn't worth anything!" said Herbie.

"I can tell you, the tax is three hundred pesos, at least."

"Three hundred!" Wolfgang's face dropped. "We don't have three hundred pesos!"

"Then you will have to make arrangements to obtain it. I'm afraid I can't let you leave the country without fulfilling your obligations." The man slid the cards across the desk.

"We can give you fifty pesos." Herbie opened his wallet to count the remaining bills. "How much you got, Wolf?"

"I am sorry, sir, the duty is three hundred pesos."

"That's it then?" Herbie was dumbfounded. "We can't go home?"

"I am afraid not, señor. Not until you pay the fees you owe."

Wolfgang reached for the entry cards.

"Look, if you give us the form, we can send you the money from Chicago!" Herbie pleaded.

The supervisor, already walking back to his office, didn't even bother to turn around. The customs agent shrugged his shoulders. "I am sorry, señor." He waved the next traveler forward.

"Come on, Herbie." Wolfgang retreated, though Herbie stood where he was, unwilling to give up so easily. "Herbie!" Wolf repeated. "Let's go!"

Herbie's gaze shifted downward in dejection. Without a word, he followed his friend out of the building. Back into Mexico. As for American hamburgers and baked potatoes, the Chicago Cubs and Gerda Stuckmann… these would all have to wait.

Herbie and Wolfgang sat atop their duffel bags by the side of the road. They could see the other side of the border, just 100 yards away. The promised land of the United States of America was right there, so close that they could just about throw a rock and hit it, yet it might as well have been a million miles away. Unless they could come up with the cash, there was simply no way to get there. A surge of desperation flowed through him. "We could call our parents," he said. "Maybe they can send us the money."

"I can't ask my parents for money," said Herbie. "They've got their own problems. Besides, that would be admitting defeat."

"Maybe it's time we admitted it!"

"No," Herbie shook his head. "I'm not calling them."

"You said everything was going to be all right! You told me to sell my car!" Wolfgang's frustration crested. This whole mess was Herbie's fault. Now they were stuck here, on the wrong side of the border in the middle of nowhere, broke and with no good options. "What the hell are we going to do?!"

Herbie's face was pallid. "How much money we got left?"

Wolf pulled out his wallet and examined the contents. "I've got eighty-five pesos."

The pair sat where they were, considering their next move. Herbie looked at the dirt under his shoes. "I'll bet Hans would know what to do."

"But he's all the way back in Mexico City..."

"You got any better ideas?"

Wolfgang shook his head. "No."

Herbie rose to his feet. "We'll figure things out."

Wolfgang stood and lifted his bag. He took one last look across the border before the pair turned their backs and walked off toward the station.

Chapter Fourteen

Berlin, July 23, 1941

A malodorous stench lingered deep in Burger's nostrils, ever-present. Sixty men in one room, no windows, four toilets, two of them overflowing with human waste. When they'd first tossed him inside this hole, Burger thought he might pass out. After three weeks in this, the latest in a string of cells over sixteen months, Peter still struggled with each breath. The interrogations and the beatings provided his only respite from the stench. He almost wished they would just take him out and shoot him already, just to get it over with. Almost. Burger fought to keep up his strength, if not for himself than for his wife. He and Bettina were allowed one short visit per month, though he knew they might rescind that privilege at any time. As far as Burger could calculate, today was the day. Without a clock or any windows, it was hard to keep track. The best he could do was to count the meals, two per day, of mostly bread and gruel. The anticipation made his sorrow all the more severe.

When the guards arrived, Burger heard the metal bolt slide in the lock. He saw the door swing open. The rest of the men cowered in fear, but not Burger. Not on this day. Instead, he held onto the faint glimmer of hope that survived within him. Very quickly he saw that this time anyway, his optimism would not be rewarded. It was a new prisoner, shoved into the cell. He stumbled forward, dropping to the floor. A blanket was tossed in after and then the door slammed shut, the bolt turning in the lock once again.

"This is a mistake!" The new man scrambled to his feet. "I shouldn't be here!" He lunged toward the door, shouting after the guards as they retreated down the corridor. "If you'll only listen to me! Please! I beg of you!"

Peter Burger heard the cellblock door open and then close. The new man stayed where he was. "Please!" Slowly, his head dropped.

He turned to take in his surroundings, terror in his eyes. The man was middle-aged and rotund with a full, fleshy face. He wore gray wool pants with a black belt. A white cotton undershirt covered his bulging belly. "I shouldn't be here!"

Fellow prisoners eyed him with mild curiosity. "None of us should be here." A wiry older man with a long beard was stretched across a nearby bunk.

"You don't understand, I didn't do anything!"

"Then maybe you *should* be here." Another man, wearing a collared shirt and glasses, sat up on his bed. "Maybe if enough of us had…"

Burger understood that the new man might be a plant. It wasn't an uncommon Gestapo tactic, to put one of their own into the cell undercover. That prospect kept all of the prisoners on edge. But no, this man's fear did not seem manufactured. He was too confused, too out of sorts, to be faking it. A plant was more likely to be the quiet type, blending in to listen. At least one of the other men probably *was* working for the Gestapo, but who? One had to be careful. Sixty men together in a room and nobody said much. Utter the wrong words and it could quickly come back to haunt you.

"I didn't mean…" the new man tried to backtrack.

"Forget it."

With hesitation, the man slowly picked up his blanket. Probably a civil servant from the looks of him, Burger thought, or perhaps a lawyer. He was as wary of his forlorn cellmates as he was of his jailers. Half of the men rested in bunks along one wall while the others took up what space they could find on the floor. The new arrival shifted to his right and then sat beside Burger against the wall. "I shouldn't be here," he repeated to himself this time, his face flushed red. "I repeated some jokes… That was all. Only jokes!"

"The Fuhrer has no sense of humor," said Burger.

"On the contrary," said another man nearby. "Look what he's done so far! The greatest practical joke in the history of the world."

"Shhh…" said the old man in the beard.

"What does it matter? We're all doomed anyway."

"It was merely a joke," the new man muttered. If only he could explain himself properly these troubles might go away. This nightmare in which he found himself would end. He'd wake up back home with his family and his daily routine. Back before he was reported by a zealous neighbor. Just a little joke or two about the party. A crime against the state.

"You might as well get used to this place. You're going to be here awhile," said the man in the glasses.

The new arrival looked to his knees, tears escaping down his cheeks. Burger wished he could say something to cheer him up, but there was nothing. After sixteen months of shuttling from one prison to another, he knew better. Cheer didn't exist in a Gestapo basement. Only fear and terror, and if one were lucky, five minutes per month to speak with your wife. Burger tried not to get his hopes too high. Maybe he'd miscounted. Was it thirty days? Or maybe twenty-nine? "Can you tell me what day it is?" he asked.

The new man looked at him with some disbelief. "Saturday," he said. "The 29th of July."

"And do you know what time?"

"They took me straight from my bed. I barely had time to put my clothes on!"

Burger felt some small sense of relief. He'd counted correctly. Bettina would be here, if they still let her. Until then, Peter had nothing to do but sit and wait, breathing in the noxious fumes of sixty unwashed men and a sewer.

"Peter Burger!" a guard called. "Visitor!"

"Yes! Here!" Peter hurried to his feet, as though with hesitation the opportunity might be lost. He moved to the door where three guards ushered him into the corridor. When they'd locked the cell behind them, they escorted him down the block, through another door and finally into a long, narrow room with rows of tables separated by a steel mesh screen. Burger was seated at table number five. He waited, hands on the desk as two guards hovered behind him.

These visits from Bettina were a lifeline, though not without their trauma. For Peter, hearing about the harassment the Gestapo put her through was his worst torture of all; constantly imploring her to divorce him, telling her that her husband faced an eight-year sentence for stealing money from the party headquarters in Vienna. Bettina attempted unsuccessfully to point out that he'd never even been to

Vienna. The stress was debilitating, but it was the loss of the baby that pained them both the most. Ever since the miscarriage, Bettina's sorrow was embedded in her psyche, impossible to dislodge. All the same, when she entered the visitor's lounge, Peter's heart leapt at the sight of her. She looked so pretty, with her dark hair framing such a lovely face.

"Hello." There were many questions Peter wanted to ask. How were the neighbors treating her, the wife of an alleged traitor? Was she able to pay the bills? Did she have any word from his parents in Bavaria? "You look lovely," he said instead.

Bettina leaned close to the screen. "I have some news," she whispered. "Did they tell you?"

"No. Tell me what?"

His wife's eyes opened wide. Whatever she was about to share, her spirits seemed lifted. "They say the charges will be dropped! It was all mistake! You will be set free!"

"Who told you that?!" Burger snapped. False hope was just another form of cruelty. Peter knew a ploy when he heard one, to lift her spirits first only to crush them later.

"One of the guards told me!" Bettina's excitement rose. "He said that I wouldn't have to be coming here much longer!"

"They must be preparing to transfer me again." Peter thought of the commandant's threat, to put him in the same Polish concentration camp he'd once reported on. "I'm sorry, but if they were planning to let me out they would have told me." Rage built inside Burger. He wanted to smash the screen that separated them. He wanted to hold Bettina in his arms, to tell her that everything would be all right. They'd stolen his freedom, harassed his wife, murdered his child... Yet there was nothing that Peter Burger could do about it. He was on the wrong side. The party he'd once supported took everything from him. Peter put both hands against the steel mesh. "Bettina," he said. "I'm sorry."

Tears rolled down Bettina's face. "I want to believe it. I have to believe it. Why won't you let me?"

"Why should we believe them?"

"If you'd heard them…" she tried to explain.

Peter allowed himself to entertain the prospect for the briefest of moments. What if it was true? They could never just send him home, as though nothing had ever happened. Bettina lifted her hands and pressed them against his through the screen. "Don't give up," she said.

"Usually I'm the one to tell you that."

The couple gazed at each other in silence. Until the day came when he walked out a free man, Burger would keep his expectations in check.

"Number Five, time is up!" shouted a guard.

"I'll find out what I can," said Bettina.

"You must understand my skepticism."

"Someone in the party is looking out for you. I just know it."

Peter rose, refusing to fall into this trap even if his wife already had. "Goodbye."

"Goodbye. Don't give up."

Guards escorted Burger back out of the room, down the cellblock, and into his cell. As he faced the fetid stench once again, he considered what his wife had just told him. If he allowed himself the luxury of believing it, they might just break him after all. This was merely one more thing they could take away. Then again, hope was about all that he had left.

Chapter Fifteen

Mexico City, July 24, 1941

The streets were wet from an early rain as Wolfgang and Herbie walked toward the United States consulate. Wolfgang checked his watch. It was just after 8 a.m. His small sense of optimism was tempered by a hint of anxiety. He and Herbie were Americans. Somebody here had to help them. Right? As they rounded a corner one block away, they spotted the building; white brick, three stories high with a U.S. flag flying proudly out front. A small piece of American soil, right here in Mexico City. All they had to do was explain their situation. Perhaps they could get a loan, to pay for the import tariff. Somebody inside would know what to do.

As Wolf and Herbie made their way along the crowded sidewalk, a destitute man lurched forward to block their path; filthy clothing, grit smeared across his face, overgrown hair matted and dirty. "Hey, you're Americans!" He spoke the words with a rapid-fire southern accent.

"That's right," Wolf admitted, taking a step backward, his head tilted away from the man's heavy odor.

"You think you could help a fellow out?" the man continued. "I'm trying to get back to the U.S. and I'm flat broke."

"We got the same problem, Mister," said Herbie.

"Can you spare just five bucks? That's all I'm asking. Look, I've got my wife and kids." The man pointed to a woman sitting on a bench nearby, holding a newborn baby in her arms. A young girl in a ragged white dress clung to her mother's skirt. "We're trying to get back home to Texas. Can't you help us out?" Desperation showed in his eyes.

"Why don't you ask at the consulate?" said Herbie.

The man shook his head dismissively. "I already done tried. They ain't got no money to help a fellow. They already tol' me."

"I'm sorry, Mister. Really, I am."

"Sure you are." His voice was thick with disdain.

Herbie pulled five pesos from his pocket and shoved it into the man's hand. "Here's for some food. It's the best we can do."

The man took the money without a word and then swiveled around in search of another mark. Wolfgang and Herbie stood where they were. Just like that, the sliver of optimism Wolf carried was gone. "What do we do now?" he asked.

"I don't know…"

The two of them peered across at the consulate building. Two United States Marines guarded the entrance. A few well-dressed men and women filtered in and out. "You heard what the man said. They don't have any money to help guys like us," said Wolf.

"Maybe we should talk to them anyway."

As pedestrians filed past all around them, Wolfgang felt adrift, buffered by the currents in a tempestuous sea. He looked once more to the vagrant as he approached another passerby. "If they won't help a guy with a wife and kids, I don't see what chance we've got."

"What other choice do we have?"

"I don't know, you tell me." Wolf struggled not to place the blame on his friend, though it was a losing battle. He'd tried so hard to adopt Herbie's carefree attitude, yet look where it had gotten them! No car, no money, and no way to get home. "I'll be honest with you, Herbie, I'm getting a little bit tired of taking your advice."

"What do you mean?! I thought we were having a great time!"

"Maybe you are Herbie, but if you hadn't noticed, we got no money! Hell, we barely got enough to buy some food, and you're giving it away!"

Herbie's mouth dropped open. It was the first time he'd ever been so directly challenged by Wolfgang. The experience left him both stunned and saddened. "The man has a family, Wolf. I couldn't very well let his kids go hungry, now could I?"

A sense of shame came over Wolf. "No. I'm sorry." He hung his head low.

"I'm doing the best I can."

"That doesn't seem to be good enough. Look around!"

"What do you think we should do, then?!"

Wolf inhaled, trying to block out his frustrations. "Maybe Hans can lend us the money." This idea didn't sound very promising to Wolf either, but then again, he couldn't think of a better one.

"Sure, we'll talk to Hans. Maybe he can help us out." With that, the two of them turned on their heels and retreated the way they had come.

"Manzanillo is where you need to go." Hans Sass was quite sure of himself. "You can catch a ship to Los Angeles. Nobody is going to bother you about any import duty there. If you can't afford a bus, you can hitchhike back to Chicago."

"How do you know there's a ship?" said Herbie.

"My friend at the German consulate told me about it. They got jobs in Japan they're trying to fill. There's a ship leaving for Tokyo, but it'll stop in L.A. on the way. I'll tell you what, I'm considering going over there to Japan myself. I've had about enough of this country."

"What kind of jobs?" Herbie was intrigued. Maybe he didn't have to go back to Chicago quite yet after all.

"I don't know, it's on a farm, I guess. General labor, you know. Nothing glamorous."

"How would we pay for the fare?" said Wolf. "We don't have the money."

"We could ask at the consulate. They might loan it to you."

"It's worth a try," said Herbie.

"The German consulate?" Wolf was skeptical. "Why would they loan us the money if the U.S. consulate won't even do it?"

"I'll introduce you to Franz," said Sass. "Franz Von Wallenburg. He's a good man."

"Sure…" Herbie nodded. "We'll talk to him."

To Wolfgang, the prospect of taking a ship up the coast to California was a thrill in itself. Just when things seemed their darkest, here was a ray of hope. If everything worked out, soon they would be back in the good old U.S.A., hitching their way to Illinois. Wolfgang could hardly wait to get started. "When does this ship depart?" he asked.

"I don't know, a few days I think. Let's talk to Franz and see if we can't get things sorted out."

"That would be great," said Wolf. "Really great." Despite all of their exploits these past six weeks, he was ready. It was time to go home.

Chapter Sixteen

Manzanillo, July 26, 1941

The *Gynio Maru* was a rusted hulk, beaten and worn by decades plying the Pacific. Herbie and Wolfgang stood on the steel deck and watched as the last loads of scrap metal were loaded into the hold. Before them was the port of Manzanillo, with towering cranes reaching for the sky. Behind them was a stone breakwater, and beyond that, the open sea. Soon they would be on their way; first this short voyage and then a long trip hitching two-thirds of the way across North America.

"You think I should marry Gerda?" Herbie gazed across the misty harbor. "You know, make an honest woman out of her?"

"Ha!" Wolfgang couldn't help but laugh.

"What's so funny?" Herbie was stung by the response.

"What makes you think she'd even want to?"

Herbie paused to let this idea sink in. "She's having a baby, Wolf. My baby."

Wolfgang's eyes opened wide. It was as though a fog lifted as he connected the dots. "Is that what we're doing down here?"

"No, of course not."

"You dragged me all the way to Mexico just to get away from Gerda?!" Wolf laughed again, but this time in disbelief.

"I just... I needed some time to think."

"And now you want to marry her? First you want to run away and now you want to marry her?"

"It's the right thing to do."

"Do you love her?"

"Does it matter?!" Herbie snapped.

"You tell me. You're the one who's talking about spending the rest of your life with her."

Herbie couldn't answer. Part of him thought that settling down sounded like a decent idea. This was his child she was carrying, after all. Maybe the time had come for him to grow up and embrace his responsibilities. On the other hand, he was only 22 years old. The prospect of being a husband and a father left a pit in the bottom of his stomach. He yearned to take Von Wallenburg up on his offer, to work at a monastery in Japan. The ship was full of Germans headed across for that very purpose, including Hans Sass. Wolf dismissed it out of hand, yet for Herbie, it was still an open question. Only once they arrived in Los Angeles would he face the moment of truth. At that point, he would either get off the ship with Wolfgang or not. Deep inside, he was fairly sure what the answer would be. Herbie did have feelings for Gerda, that was true. All the same, he wasn't ready for this journey to be over. The freedom to go wherever he wanted, and do what he wanted, was like fresh air in Herbie's lungs. He had too much living left to do. Maybe he hadn't found work in Mexico, or even made it to Nicaragua, but this was a chance to experience someplace even more exotic. The Far East called out to Herbie. When he looked to Wolf, he knew that in another few days they would part ways. For the time being, Herbie would keep this information to himself.

"For what it's worth, I wouldn't have missed this for the world," said Wolf. "Are you kidding? Look at us! I'll never forget it. Not for as long as I live."

"Me neither, buddy. Come on, let's go check out the rest of the ship." Herbie gave Wolf a pat on the shoulder before the two of them crossed the deck and entered a passageway. Not since they were five years old had either of them been on an ocean-going vessel, and never on a cargo ship like this one. Herbie could hardly wait to get underway. Just the thought of crossing the Pacific made him feel… alive. No, he wasn't going back to Chicago. Not yet. He had the whole rest of his life to spend in America. For now, the world was Herbie's to explore.

On their second day at sea, Herbie and Wolf ate dinner with Hans Sass at a long table in the galley. Joining them was another German ex-pat, burly and with a full blond beard. Joseph Schmidt was larger-than-life and full of stories that fired Herbie's imagination. For the previous several years, Schmidt traveled through Canada, living off his wits as a fur trapper in the depths of the wilderness. After growing tired of the isolated lifestyle, he'd headed south to warmer climes, spending a few months in Mexico. Running short on funds himself, Schmidt was ready to give this monastery a try, though he didn't expect to stay for long.

"If all goes well, I'll be back in Germany before the winter sets in," Schmidt explained.

"That is my plan as well," Sass agreed. "I had planned to return by train, through Russia, but unfortunately that option is no longer available."

"No," said Schmidt. "The only mode is by sea."

"You're going back for the war?" Wolf asked.

Sass nodded in affirmation. "Every German ought to heed the call of their country. You boys as well. Don't you agree?"

This test of loyalty made Wolf uneasy. "Oh, I don't know. I'd rather stay out of it."

"But it is your duty!" Sass continued. "This is your Fatherland calling! How do you expect our nation to claim its rightful place in the world if able-bodied men like yourself prefer to *stay out of it?*" There was a mocking tone in his voice. "Am I right?" Sass turned to Schmidt.

The fur trapper took a sip of his soup and then shrugged. "A man must decide for himself."

"Certainly you must be joking!" Sass was flabbergasted. "How about you, Herbie? Tell me you're a true German! You support our Fuhrer, don't you?!"

"Sure…" Herbie, too, was uncomfortable with the question.

"I haven't been to Germany since I was five years old," Wolf tried to explain. "I hardly speak the language…"

"Then I would expect you to learn," Sass answered.

"You're planning to fight?" Herbie asked Schmidt.

"I will if I am called. I was hoping the war would be over by the time I arrived home. Now I'm not so sure."

"Don't tell me you think the Russians will put up a fight?" said Sass. "We'll be in Moscow by Christmas."

"I admire your optimism," said Schmidt.

"You don't agree?"

"I'm more of a realist myself. Of course, I hope you are correct."

"Herbie and I are getting off the ship in Los Angeles," Wolf explained. "With any luck, we'll be in Chicago this time next week."

"Los Angeles?" Schmidt was confused. "This ship is not stopping in Los Angeles. We're headed straight for Yokohama, my friends."

"No, no, we're stopping in California," Wolf assured him. "Von Wallenburg said so. We should be arriving any time now."

Schmidt shook his head. "Nobody said anything to me about California."

A sinking feeling crept back into Wolfgang's gut, though this time more pronounced than ever. He looked to Herbie. "That's what he said, isn't it? Isn't that what Von Wallenburg said? The ship stops in Los Angeles first and then Seattle. Right, Herbie? You said so yourself, didn't you Hans?!"

"If we were stopping in Los Angeles, I'd have thought we'd be there already," said Sass. "I may have passed along false information."

"But I need to get off!" Wolfgang wanted to run upstairs to the top deck, to scan the horizon for any sign of the California coast. Instead, he hurried across the galley. Behind a long metal counter was a Japanese cook, stirring noodles with a wooden spoon as a long ash from his cigarette hung over the pot. "Excuse me!" said Wolf. "Excuse me, sir, do you speak English?!"

A quizzical expression crossed the cook's face. "Eeengliish?" He shook his head. "No Eeengliish."

Nearby, a group of crew members ate their meal in silence. Wolf moved to their table. "Hello, does anybody speak English?" He was met with five blank stares, but then a sixth man nodded slowly.

"Leettle bit," the man said.

"Can you tell me when we will arrive in Los Angeles?"

The man's eyes narrowed. He appeared to not understand the question.

"Los Angeles," Wolfgang repeated. He pointed to his watch. "What time?"

The crewman shook his head.

Wolfgang pointed first to himself and then to the others at his table. He spoke slowly. "What time will we arrive in Los Angeles?"

"No Los Angeleees," said the man. "Yokohama."

"But first Los Angeles! Then Seattle?"

"No," the man repeated. "Yokohama. No Los Angelees."

Wolfgang stood where he was as the information settled in. The ship wouldn't stop in California after all. Nor in Seattle. He and Herbie were headed to Japan. His first reaction was pure panic. Whatever control he'd strived to regain was gone in a blink. He had no control whatsoever. Wolf walked back to the table and retook his seat.

"Don't take it too hard, kid," said Schmidt. "When else in your life would you ever get to see Japan? Chin up, you're in good company!"

"You got that right, Schmidty!" said Sass.

"Don't call me Schmidty."

"All right, relax. Don't get so worked up over it."

Wolf looked from one face to another. Schmidt was right, at least he and Herbie weren't alone. As his new reality settled in, a sense of calm slowly came over Wolfgang. There was nothing to do but accept his fate, whatever it may be. Japan. He laughed to himself. His friends back home would never believe it. "I hope they have jobs for us there, too." He saw a loopy smile on Herbie's face. "What?" Wolf asked.

"Nothing."

"I guess Gerda will have to wait." Wolf lifted his spoon. Despite the initial shock of it, he was beginning to feel an odd sense of satisfaction. For his entire life, he'd lived a sheltered existence, never straying outside the confines of his parents' constraining influence. Well, that was behind him now. Wolf was living his own life, adapting, learning to roll with the punches. So what if he lost his position at the Simpson Optical Company? He was young. There would always be another job, somewhere. These were experiences he would never forget and he was intent on making the most of them.

"I wonder what they'll have us do at that monastery, anyway," said Herbie.

"It's a farm," said Schmidt. "From what I understand, we'll be working in the fields."

"I guess that'll be all right for a while. I wonder if there are any girls out there?"

"At a monastery? You better forget about girls for a while," said Sass.

Minutes beforehand, Wolfgang thought he was headed home. Now he could hardly wait to get to Japan and whatever awaited them there. Maybe in a couple more weeks they could catch another boat back. Until then, he and Herbie would take in whatever came their way.

Chapter Seventeen

Stuttgart, Germany, August 4, 1941

Rows of hospital beds lined each side of a cavernous ward, all of them occupied by patients in varying states of distress. Some were missing arms. Some legs. Bloodied bandages covered their heads, or their torsos, hands or feet. Hermann Neubauer tried to shut out the incessant moaning of his fellow patients. His own face was wrapped tightly with bandages where doctors had tried, unsuccessfully, to remove all of the shrapnel from his cheek and just under his right eye. "It is too close to your brain," they explained. "We will have to leave some shards in place." The throbbing pain in his temples was incessant. At least the fragments in his leg were completely removed, and slowly those wounds were healing. Neubauer was learning to walk again, and talk again. For days after his evacuation, first by plane to Krakow and then onward by train, he'd been unable to speak at all. Only with time and patience did he learn to string a few words together. Even now, his language skills were like those of a child. And so, Hermann spent his days in bed listening to the agony of the men all around him as he struggled to contain his own unrelenting pain. For an hour each day, he worked with a nurse on his rehabilitation. Neubauer didn't know how long he would be here. He thought often of his regiment, advancing deeper into Russia without him. He thought of his wife. Poor Alma, at his parents' home in Hamburg with no friends and nothing to do. At least he had her letters to lift his spirits. With some luck, he would see her soon. Until then, each day blended into the next in seemingly endless repetition. Hermann closed his eyes and focused, willing the dull pain in his temples to vanish.

Chapter Eighteen

Tokyo Bay, Japan, August 5, 1941

Sailing through Tokyo Bay, Herbie and Wolfgang marveled at the sheer enormity of it. Ships of all sizes plied the waters around them; cargo ships, fishing vessels and oddly-configured sailing boats the likes of which they'd never seen. A massive naval destroyer passed a quarter mile off their bow. Herbie admired the enormous guns protruding from its decks, pondering the damage they could inflict if called upon.

Entering the harbor at Yokohama, the *Gynio Maru* eased past freighters being loaded and unloaded by armies of longshoremen. With the help of a tugboat, they were nudged into place and then tied up to the dock. "Welcome to Japan," Schmidt joined them along the rail.

"Thanks," Wolfgang replied. Japan. Wolfgang Wergin was in Japan. The whole chain of events still seemed entirely unlikely, yet here it was, right in front of him. Wolf's heart soared at the prospect. He could hardly wait to get off this old rust bucket and take a good look around.

Once cleared by a Japanese immigration agent in a smart gray suit, Wolf and Herbie shouldered their duffels and disembarked down the gangway, joining their small group of Germans on the dock. A representative from the German consulate took their names and passport details before escorting them to a nearby bus. It was all well organized, Wolf thought. He and Herbie were just along for the ride. Unlike in Mexico, they had no worries about finding jobs or a place to stay. Everything was taken care of. The group would be put up in a Yokohama hotel for the night, then taken by train into Tokyo where another consular official would provide them with one hundred yen apiece to pay their expenses, plus directions to the monastery, a further four hours away by train. It all sounded pretty good to Wolf. Maybe he hadn't expected this diversion to Japan, but he'd certainly make the most of it.

Two days later, the contingent of Germans boarded a train for Chingasaki. Wolfgang and Herbie found two seats and the train lurched forward before slowly picking up speed. Outside the windows passed the heart of Tokyo, slowly shifting to urban sprawl and then finally, the verdant green rice paddies of the Japanese countryside. "What kind of farm do you think it is where we're going?" Wolf asked. "You think they grow rice?"

"I guess they would," Herbie replied. "What else around here?"

"How do you grow rice, anyway?"

"You need a lot of water, that's all I know."

"I wonder what the accommodations are like…" Wolfgang pictured monasteries he'd seen in books. These were enormous complexes, made of stone and nestled into jagged mountain settings. He imagined monks in robes, wandering hallways with candelabras in hand, the smell of incense hanging in the air. "You think we'll have to make a vow of abstinence while we're there?"

"I don't think there's gonna be any women around there in the first place."

"Maybe there's somewhere we can go at night, like a town or something. Do they have bars in Japan?"

"Sure, they gotta…"

"I wonder how much they're going to pay us?"

"A bed to sleep in and three squares a day. That's all I expect out of this deal," Schmidt interjected from his seat across the aisle. "Not that I'll be here for long."

"Me neither," Hans Sass agreed. "I don't plan to sit this war out farming rice for a bunch of monks."

Wolf turned his gaze back out the window. He didn't care to discuss the war, or the Fuhrer. All of this talk about going back to fight for Germany left him feeling uneasy. Of course, the United States wasn't involved directly, but they might as well have been. Even in their German-American enclave back home, an "us against them" mentality pervaded the atmosphere. Wolfgang's father could be counted among the members of the Bund. The distrust directed toward them by everyday Americans was like a toxic cloud, though

Wolf and Herbie always had other things to concern themselves with. They were young and filled with the daily thrills of existence. Now that existence extended far past their small corner of Chicago, though this war had nothing to do with Wolfgang. Just because he was born in Germany didn't mean he had to rush back and fight for Adolph Hitler. These men could sacrifice themselves if they felt compelled to. He just hoped they'd leave him out of it.

Exiting the train after a four-hour journey, the men were loaded next into the back of an open flatbed truck. Wolf grasped his bag with one hand as they bounced down a rutted dirt road and then up a steep hillside. Rolling green pastureland gave way to sugar plantations. Men and women in triangular straw hats worked the fields, chopping at the stalks with long machetes. Soon that would be him, Wolf thought. What would his mother say if she could see him now? He'd send a postcard, the first chance he got. From the look of things, however, that might be a while.

When the road leveled off once more, the truck pulled into a clearing before skidding to a stop. Wolf took in their surroundings. It wasn't what he'd expected. No stone edifice loomed above them from atop a rugged mountainside. In fact, there were hardly any buildings at all; only a few flimsy wooden structures, several still under construction. In the center was a white church with a spire pointed toward the heavens. Beside that was a two-story home with a wrap-around porch. Two flagpoles stood in front, one flying the rising sun of Japan, the other a red square enclosing a white circle with a black Nazi swastika anchored in the center. A small German outpost in the depths of the Orient.

A monk exited the house and moved down the stairs toward them. He was a gaunt man with European features. The new arrivals climbed from the truck one at a time, their boots landing on rich dark earth. Past the church, Wolf saw two long, plain rectangular buildings and beside these a barn, where another brown-robed monk emerged briefly before ducking back inside. Past the barn, a rocky field was carved from dense jungle foliage. At the far edge, a group of men hacked at the undergrowth. Others hauled tree limbs through deep mud to a smoldering pile.

"This place sure doesn't look like much." Herbie didn't hide his disappointment.

"It's a farm," said Wolf. "We knew we'd be working on a farm."

"Welcome to Chingasaki, gentlemen. I am Brother Sebastian." The monk spoke in German. "You have come a long way. I hope that your journey was a pleasant one."

"This is a monastery?" said Schmidt. "It looks more like a work camp."

"We are proud to say that this is the very first monastery established in the country of Japan. Soon we will celebrate our tenth anniversary. With your help, we will build on what we've started here."

"They say you are Benedictine?" Sass queried.

"Yes, that is correct. We come originally from the Beuron Archabbey, in the upper Danube valley. Our settlement here is still a work in progress, though from humble beginnings great things are born. Please, let me show you to your quarters." He gestured with one hand.

The men hoisted their bags and followed Brother Sebastian across the dirt drive and into one of the rectangular buildings. Inside were rows of wooden bunks. The space was dimly lit, with a damp, musty odor. Dirty clothing, unwashed bodies…disease. Wolfgang recoiled, holding one hand over his nose. Most of the occupants were out, no doubt hard at work in the fields, though several men lay in their beds, sprawled under thin blankets.

"Please, take any free space," said the monk.

"What's wrong with those men?" said Schmidt.

Brother Sebastian struggled with discomfiture. "They are not feeling so well."

"What does that mean?" said Sass. "They're sick, or what? Is it contagious?"

"No, I think it's not contagious…" The monk's words lacked sincerity.

"Damn…" Schmidt chose a bunk as far from the sick men as he could. "I better not come down with whatever they got."

"What are they saying?" Wolf asked. "I can't understand."

"He says these men are sick." Herbie dropped his bag at a bunk near Schmidt. "Boy, it sure stinks in here."

"That's how they get us to work," Sass half-joked. "It's safer in the fields than in the bunkhouse."

"Hell, the fertilizer is probably what got these men sick in the first place," said Schmidt. "A bunch of cow shit."

"*Cow* shit if we're lucky…" said Sass.

"I'm starting to wonder if maybe we should have stayed in Mexico." Wolf took the bunk above Herbie.

"If you men follow me, we will serve lunch," said the monk.

"A little dysentery soup, perhaps?" Sass tried to make another joke but the monk didn't respond.

The men were led back outside and then into the other long building, this one holding rows of tables with benches. A small group of monks sat at one table, eating rice and what looked like cubes of white cheese covered in brown sauce.

"What the hell is that?" Herbie asked.

"Beats the hell out of me," said Schmidt.

"You will find all you need along the far wall," their guide motioned to another table that held cups, plates, utensils and several large pots and pitchers.

As the group approached, another man emerged from a kitchen in the back. Also of European descent with deep-set, hollow eyes, he wore dirty white pants and a stained shirt. In his hands, he held a large pot. When he saw the newcomers, he placed the pot on the table and retreated without a word. Herbie lifted the lid to look inside. "Rice," he said.

"You better get used to it," said Schmidt.

Each man took a plate and began helping themselves to the food. Besides rice, and the unidentifiable white cubes, there was a pot of limp mixed vegetables, another with sauerkraut and lastly, boiled potatoes. Herbie and Wolf avoided the cubes but helped themselves to the sauerkraut and potatoes, along with cups of water, and then found seats with the rest of their group. Further along the table were a few weathered men who looked as though they'd been in this place for far too long.

"Work will begin after lunch," said Brother Sebastian. "I will return to collect you." With that, he ducked out the door.

"We can't stay here." Herbie's tone betrayed his panic. "There's gotta be something else. Some other option."

"I'm with you," Wolf answered. "But what can we do? We hardly have any money."

"Enough to get back to Tokyo. Maybe the American consulate over here will help us?"

"I don't think they're going to be too sympathetic," said Sass. "Not when you came over with a ticket paid for by the German government, on German passports issued by the German consulate in Mexico."

"Maybe there's a ship going back that needs a couple of deckhands. Don't you think?" Wolf added. "There must be a way."

"I wouldn't try it." One of the men at the end of the table cleared his throat. He wore filthy brown pants and a cotton shirt that was perhaps white at some point in the distant past. His hair was combed back with grease. His features were creased.

"Why not?" Herbie took the bait.

The man answered the question without looking up. "Another man here tried that. German, but he came from America. He got a ship all the way back to San Francisco. American officials wouldn't let him disembark." The speaker turned to stare at them directly. "When the ship returned to Japan, German agents were waiting on the dock. That was the last anybody heard of him."

Herbie and Wolf let this information sink in. "So, we're trapped here?" said Wolfgang.

The speaker went back to his lunch.

"Maybe there's some other job they can find for us…" Wolf went on. "I mean, there must be something we can do."

Herbie nodded in agreement. "I don't even want to spend one night here."

"Why don't you give it a chance?! The place might grow on you!" said Sass.

Wolfgang looked to Herbie, hoping for some of his friend's boundless optimism. In this case, it seemed in short supply.

"It'll work out," Herbie did his best. "You'll see. We'll find something else."

Wolf used a knife and fork to eat some of the potatoes. They were bland and tasteless, but at least it was food; the first they'd had all day. After they finished, they would grab their bags and find a way back to Tokyo. This was a setback, Wolfgang thought, but it did little to diminish the thrill he felt at having come so far. They were in Japan! A trip like this was a once-in-a-lifetime experience. As long as they didn't starve to death, or contract a deadly disease, he and Herbie would have quite a story to tell.

Chapter Nineteen

Tokyo, August 10, 1941

The diplomat was a corpulent man. He leaned on his elbows, clasping thick fingers together as he faced Herbie and Wolfgang across his desk. He was not pleased. "You realize, of course, that we had an agreement. The German government paid for your fare to this country in exchange for your labor." He spoke English with a thick German accent.

"But Von Wallenburg said it was a loan," Wolfgang protested. "He said we could pay it back when the war was over. It's not that we don't want to work. It's just that, the conditions at that place…" He looked to Herbie for confirmation.

"Half of the men were sick with some intestinal disease," Herbie confirmed. "We didn't want to get sick."

"We heard that there was a ship we could work on. That's what they said at the German House. They said it was going to Europe."

The diplomat leaned back in his chair. He opened a drawer, pulled out a folder and placed it on his desk before flipping through a sheaf of documents, examining them one at a time. His eyebrows rose slightly. "I don't suppose you have any maritime experience to speak of?"

Herbie and Wolfgang looked to each other, as though trying to silently confer. "Not exactly," Herbie admitted.

This was not the response the diplomat was hoping for, though he continued. "The ship you speak of departs in approximately two weeks. We may be able to place you on board as ordinary seamen if you are willing to undergo a training period beforehand."

The boys' expressions lifted. "You bet!" said Herbie.

"Where in Europe will it go, exactly?" Wolfgang asked the obvious question, though the answer was largely immaterial. Just the thought of circumnavigating the globe was almost too good to be true.

"Portugal, I believe, though I can't be sure," the diplomat answered. "Around Cape Horn. It is a three-month voyage. Once you begin, there will be no backing out!"

"We'll take it." Herbie turned to his friend. "Right, buddy?"

"Sure!" Wolf agreed. "When does the training start?"

The diplomat appeared satisfied with the arrangement. "Immediately." He pulled another folder and took out two more documents, sliding them across the table, one to each man. "Fill these out." He gave them each a pen.

Herbie added his name in a box at the top.

"It's in German," said Wolfgang.

"I'll help you out," said Herbie. "Just let me finish mine first."

"OK." Wolf began filling out what he could. Once again, fate seemed to have smiled in their favor. Just when things looked their bleakest, providence came to their aid. Life with Herbie always seemed to work out that way, as though his optimism in the face of hardship was what saved them. For Wolfgang, a sense of relief mingled with anticipation. Ordinary seamen on a ship to Portugal… The adventure continued.

Chapter Twenty

Berlin, State Theater, August 24, 1941

Edward Kerling stood in the wings as the final act of a matinee performance drew to a crescendo. Behind him, a group of twenty young men lined up in ranks. They wore combat fatigues, with Nazi swastikas pinned to their chests. Some were bandaged on their heads, or their limbs. Each man carried a rifle slung over his shoulder. On stage was the carnage of battle, with Russian casualties splayed out and covered in blood. In the center, a German officer held a battered Nazi flag. He faced a full audience of Hitler Youth, brought into the city for an afternoon of culture and entertainment courtesy of the Propaganda Ministry.

"Atten-tion!" called out the officer.

"Atten-tion!" the soldiers in the wings chanted back.

"Forward, march!"

"Forward, march!" With a rumble of boots, the men moved forward to the drumbeat of a martial cadence. They passed the Russian corpses and lined up behind the officer.

"Close ranks!" came the next order.

"Close ranks!"

"You shall be all Germany! Where one sows the young seed, where one mows the ripe grain, where one drives the wheel and rod. The lofty brow, the mighty fist. Stand up, my brothers, when the oath clearly peels: We are eternally united! All Germany marches with us!"

The drums grew louder as Kerling brought the stage lights down and then lowered the curtain. The audience broke out in rousing applause. With the curtain down, the "Russian" soldiers rose to their feet and moved off, taking guns, helmets and fallen flags with them. The "German" soldiers resumed their positions, lined up at attention, with their commanding officer proudly center-stage, chin held high.

Kerling raised the curtain once again and the Hitler Youth were caught up in a fervor of hysteria, jumping to their feet to cheer. The officer's arm flew into the air. "Heil Hitler!"

Three hundred young arms shoot back. "Heil Hitler!!!" their eager voices reverberated through the theater.

"Deutschland uber alles…!" the officer led them all in a rousing rendition of their national anthem. When the song was finished, the curtain closed for the last time and Kerling brought the house lights up. The giddy youth filed up the aisles and out of the theater, brimming with enthusiasm for the Third Reich. These boys were ready to fight and die for their country. For Edward Kerling, it was just one more show. The faster he reset the stage, the faster he could get out of there for the day. When he'd first come back to Germany in support of the war effort, this was not what he'd expected his contribution to look like. He'd envisioned being a soldier himself, advancing on the enemy as part of Hitler's unstoppable war machine. Just like his audience members, the sight of the Nazi flag filled Kerling's heart with pride. Germany was finally standing on its own two feet and Eddie was playing his small part. Working for the Propaganda Ministry wasn't all bad. There was a certain thrill that came with life in the theater, especially in Berlin, where a stream of dignitaries came to watch the shows. Just a few nights earlier, Joseph Goebbels himself stopped by to see the play. No, Edward couldn't complain. He earned a decent salary, the respect of his countrymen, and unlike the troops on the front, he was able to sleep in the same bed each and every night. As the Reich marched further into Russia, however, he knew that it was a matter of time before his number was called. Eddie looked forward to that day with a mixture of anticipation and fear. He felt a tinge of guilt whenever he thought of his friend Hermann Neubauer, wounded in action on just the third day of the Russian assault. Well, Kerling's time would come. He merely had to be patient. Until then, his contribution meant getting this stage ready for the next performance. Germany was rising, and after a decade away in America, Edward Kerling was here to rise with it.

One hour later, Kerling sat in a bar full of rowdy servicemen, sipping a beer with Gerhard Schnell, his theater director. At forty-five years of age, Schnell was too old to serve in this war, but his memories of the last one were fresh in his mind. In these vigorous young men all around them, he saw himself at their age. He remembered the enthusiasm for battle; the blood lust. He knew all too well that it wouldn't last. Stick these men in a trench for eighteen months, pounded by artillery shells and bombs, decimated by snipers, gas attacks, cold and fatigue. Then see how eager they were to make war, if they survived at all. No, Schnell knew better. This time around he would keep his head down and stay out of it as best he could. What worried him was the fate of his sixteen-year-old son. How long would it take before the Fuhrer came calling for *him*? Already, Rudolph was a proud member of the Hitler Youth, just like the afternoon's audience at the theater. As Schnell looked to the soldiers at a table nearby, full of laughter and horseplay, he knew that before long Rudolph would be among them. In fact, there was nothing his son wanted more, despite Gerhard's best efforts. Rudolph's indoctrination into the cause was complete, so much so that Gerhard took great care with his own comments, lest the young man report him. It had happened before, to people Gerhard knew. Parents dragged off to prison for uttering the truth; that Adolph Hitler was a maniac and the whole world was doomed. Of course, Schnell knew better than to say such things in public as well. He could never admit his feelings, for instance, to the stage manager sitting across from him. Kerling had it easy, with his strong features, square jaw and full head of blond hair, he was a man who had no trouble attracting pretty women. Eddie had a wife and a girlfriend and a decent living over in the United States, yet he'd given it all up to return to Berlin, and for what? Schnell wondered how Kerling felt about it now that he saw his country again firsthand. "Tell me again about your girlfriend," Schnell said, avoiding a more direct line of questioning. "Where is she now?"

"Hedy?" Kerling looked wistful. "She's in Miami, working as a waitress. That's the last I heard anyway."

"And you have a wife as well?"

"Marie and I are separated. She knows about Hedy. They've met. In fact, they're quite close."

"So perhaps that is why you returned to Germany?" Schnell chuckled. "To avoid the complications?"

Kerling shook his head. "My country was calling. I had to come."

"To work in the theater?" Gerhard tried not to scoff. It was obvious that Kerling was haunted by the shame. One could see it in his eyes, in the way he peered at these soldiers all around them, wishing he was one of them. That was what he'd come for. Well, if Schnell knew anything, he knew that Edward Kerling would get his chance to fight. It was inevitable.

"It's not what I expected, that is true."

"I heard you tried to sail across from America all by yourself?"

"No, not by myself. There were others on board. Some friends of mine. We put our money together and bought a yawl. She was a beauty. The *Lekala*. You should have seen her."

"What happened? You had a change of heart?"

"Oh, no. We were on our way! Provisioned and prepared." Kerling's pride showed as he thought back to his grand plan. "It was our second day out, off the coast of Atlantic City. That's in New Jersey. A Coast Guard cutter caught up to us. They found it suspicious, a boatload full of Germans. We were escorted ashore and held for weeks. Finally, they let us go, but only if we changed our destination to Florida. We had to check in at every Coast Guard station on the way. When we got to Miami, I sold the *Lekala* at a loss and caught a liner to Lisbon, then made my way overland to Berlin."

"There was no stopping you."

"No."

"But you miss your Hedy?"

"Sure." Kerling drank from his beer and then took another look around the room, caught in the grip of a patriotic fervor from which there was no escape.

"To the Fuhrer." Schnell struggled not to choke as he spoke the words.

"Prost!" Kerling's face lit up.

The two men drank, Gerhard Schnell doing his best to bury his deep-seated sense of dismay while Edward Kerling savored his loyalty to the thousand-year Reich.

Chapter Twenty-One

South China Sea, August 27, 1941.

They were two weeks aboard a training vessel, the German liner *Schoenhorst*, where Herbie and Wolf learned the ways of the sea. It was day three when Sass and Schmidt showed up, tired of the misery that was life at the monastery. Together, the men were instructed by German naval officers in tasks that included standing watch, scraping rust, painting the ship and wiping oil from the enormous diesel engines. Whatever German Wolf couldn't understand, his friends were there to translate. When training was complete, the group shipped out aboard a cargo ship, the *Elsa Esburger.* Two days later, Herbie spotted what would be their permanent home for the next three months. It appeared first as a speck on the horizon but took shape as they drew closer. The ship was a freighter of similar size, though as they closed within 500 meters, it became clear that the vessel's best days were behind her. Herbie saw that all of her markings were obliterated. Where a name once graced the stern there were now only chisel marks covered with gray paint. Markings on the bow were similarly painted over. She flew no flag of origin.

"A blockade runner." Schmidt stood beside Herbie at the rail, cigarette hanging from his lips.

"As long as it makes it to Portugal, right?"

"Who said anything about Portugal?"

"At the consulate… That's what they told us."

Schmidt took a last drag on his cigarette and then flicked the butt into the churning sea below. "I wouldn't count on it."

The sudden prospect of running a military blockade struck Herbie with an unanticipated sense of terror. It represented the very real danger that they would be targeted at some point. He pictured artillery shells raining down on the ship, blasting it from the water.

Explosions, destruction, death… "You think painting over the name like that is gonna make any difference?"

"Maybe it will buy us some time. You better just hope we aren't spotted." Schmidt offered a sly grin. "Relax. We've got at least three months on board this beauty before we go to our watery graves."

"Thanks. I feel much better."

"You know the difference between a ship and a prison?"

"Is there one?"

"Sure there is. A prison can't sink."

"Right..."

Schmidt put a hand on Herbie's back. "Cheer up my young friend! We're off to Europe!"

With the two ships side by side, the more experienced deckhands shot lines across and carefully set up a system of pulleys. Wolfgang and Herbie helped ferry cargo and supplies from one ship to another. With the sway and motion of the seas, it was treacherous business. One could easily end up knocked overboard, or even flattened outright by a one-ton load of rubber.

"Achtung, Achtung!" an officer called out to Wolfgang, who quickly backed away from a swaying bundle.

The transfer took much of the day, but by late afternoon they were nearly finished. All that remained was the crew. Herbie was first up. Strapped into a harness and then swung over the rail, his stomach rose and fell as the lines grew slack and then taut, plunging him toward the sea before hurtling him skyward. He knew better than to look below, but still couldn't help himself. The turbulent waters swirled beneath him. Jerking his head back up, he focused on two sailors, arms outstretched and waving him in. At last, they pulled him aboard, his feet landing firmly on deck. The crewmen unhooked the harness and sent it back for the next man. One by one they crossed until Wolfgang came last. A broad smile radiated across his face as they whisked him over the tempestuous void. "Holy cow, what a ride!" he said upon landing. "Can we do it again?!"

"Hell no! Once was enough," said Herbie.

From the starboard flybridge of the *Elsa Esburger,* they saw that ship's captain overseeing the operation as his crew hauled in the lines. When the procedure was complete, he held a hand to his mouth and shouted to his opposite captain. Very faintly, Herbie heard the words "Viel glück!" drifting through the winds. *Good luck.* Then a last salute. The ships began to slowly part.

"Willkommen zu *Deutschland*," said a member of the crew.

"Dankashoen," Herbie replied.

"You are American?"

"Is it so obvious?"

"I no mind. You work, is good. Come." The newcomers lifted their duffels and followed the crewman across the swaying deck, through a door and down a passageway.

"Home sweet home," said Herbie.

"I guess we better get used to it," Wolf answered. The truth was, despite the hardships, it beat his life in Chicago hands down.

Chapter Twenty-Two

Berlin, September 26, 1941.

Buttoning his uniform before a barracks mirror, Peter Burger considered the irony of his situation. Just two months earlier he was a prisoner. Now he was a guard. They could have shot him if they'd wanted to. He'd half expected it. Instead, he was being "rehabilitated" as a private in the German Army, assigned to guard British POWs at a camp just outside the city. After seventeen months of incarceration, life on the opposite side of the fence was surreal. Burger's trauma still haunted him. He would never forgive the Gestapo. Especially not for the harassment they'd submitted his wife to, or the miscarriage that resulted. Yet here he was, back in a Nazi uniform, following orders. If his superiors knew how he felt about it all, they really *would* take him out and shoot him. Burger knew better than to give them any added excuse. Rehabilitation meant learning to keep your mouth shut. That didn't mean he would ever fully recover from the nightmares, or the depression, or the tremors that overtook his body at the most random of times. Heaven forbid he should ever have to fire his weapon. Just holding it, his hands shook. Burger fastened the last of his buttons and inhaled. He looked the part. He was a soldier. For eight hours every day, he would stand in a guard tower or march along the perimeter. At least it was easy duty. It could have been straight to the Russian front. Burger didn't want to think too much about that option. It would probably come soon enough. He'd heard rumors about the true state of affairs in the east. Operation Barbarossa was not going according to plan. Or at least so went the whispers. The Fuhrer was fallible. And there it was, another thought that could get Burger shot.

Peter slung his rifle over his shoulder and followed another guard out the barracks door. Making his way to guard tower six, he and a young private named Nordlinger climbed a ladder to relieve the two men on duty.

"Any excitement last night?" said Nordlinger as they entered the tower.

"Is there ever?" Another guard and his colleague gathered their weapons.

"Maybe we'll be lucky today and get to shoot someone," Nordlinger joked.

"I say we shoot them all and get it over with," said the other guard. "That's what the Ruskies would do."

"What do you think, Burger?" Nordlinger settled onto a stool. "Should we shoot them?"

Burger couldn't bring himself to answer. Instead, he took to another stool and sat silently.

"I don't think Burger wants to shoot them," said the other guard.

"I just want some sleep," the fourth man said as he and his colleague scrambled out and down the ladder, done for the day.

Looking out the window, Burger saw parallel barbed wire fences surrounding row upon row of prisoner barracks. On a parade ground inside the compound, prisoners gathered for morning assembly. He watched as they lined up at attention, as if they were still in active units, the war not yet over for them. After roll call, the camp commandant stepped atop a small podium to address the prisoners. Even over loudspeakers, it was too far away for Burger to understand his words. From their position in the tower, it all sounded like so much gibberish.

"What do you think he's telling them?" Nordlinger was tall, with a thin sheen of facial hair above his upper lip. Burger recognized the youthful enthusiasm in the boy, one long since vanquished in himself.

"I have no idea."

"Probably not to escape, or Burger and Nordlinger will take care of them!" he laughed again before pointing his rifle toward the camp and peering down the sight. "I wonder what it feels like to shoot one?"

Even here, high up in the guard shack, Burger couldn't help but picture himself on the other side of the fence. That was his reality for so long, shuttled from one detention facility to another. It seemed as though the whole world was made up of prisoners and guards. Even the soldiers on the front lines were prisoners in a sense, on both sides. It was up to Burger to survive as best he could. For now, that meant sitting in a tower with a juvenile soldier, guns at the ready. Burger just hoped that they'd never be called upon to fire them.

Chapter Twenty-Three

Berlin, November 9-24, 1941

Lieutenant Kappe was a gregarious sort, always eager to be the center of attention. It was the reason he hosted these weekly meetings. As the master of ceremonies, he enjoyed a position of respect. Kappe was a stout man, with a wide forehead and drooping eyes. His fleshy cheeks surrounded either side of a small, pouting mouth. Standing at the front of the room, full of pride in his German army uniform, he addressed the group with enthusiasm.

"We may not be at war with the United States," said Kappe, "but make no mistake, our two countries are at odds. For those of us who have lived in both places, it is imperative that we do all we can to support our fatherland. I understand that most of you returned to Germany for just this reason, with a sense of loyalty in your hearts. Each and every one of you is particularly predisposed to provide our government with assistance. Our leaders must better understand this nation across the sea; the land that you and I temporarily called home. Have no fear, your government will come calling and when it does, you should all be ready to heed that call. Thank you for coming, ladies and gentlemen."

George Dasch clapped along with the twenty or so others in the room. As he looked around the restaurant at these men and women, though, George couldn't help but wonder how many secretly despised the current German government, as he did. How many would return to America in a heartbeat if they could? Probably quite a few, Dasch surmised. He himself spent many hours contemplating how he might accomplish just this goal. He longed to escape this distorted reality that he currently found himself trapped in, where neighbors were afraid to speak above a whisper lest the Gestapo be listening. This country where being Jewish had somehow become a crime, punishable by death. Where fear seemed to stalk every man, woman and child, even those who did support the Fuhrer. As long as the war raged, all options for returning to America, and his wife, seemed to be cut off. Dasch was trapped, five thousand miles away from his Snookie. Sometimes, in his most desperate hours, he pictured himself being *sent* to the United States by the German government. He fantasized about being recruited as a German spy and spirited south into North Africa. He would catch a neutral ship, perhaps to Brazil and onward from there on an American vessel, sailing into New York past the Statue of Liberty itself. In these daydreams, George would turn upon arrival and help the Americans in their quest to free the Germany he loved from the clutches of this dictator, the so-called "Fuhrer." The grateful Americans would deliver Snookie from the British camp in Bermuda. On some level, Dasch knew this dream was far-fetched, yet the realization hadn't stopped him from making inquiries with certain party members. As this meeting of former ex-pats drew to a close, Dasch stood and made his way toward the door with the others.

"Ah, there he is!" Lieutenant Kappe approached him. "My protégé from the foreign office! How are things going for you over there Mr. Dasch?"

"Fine, thank you, Lieutenant."

Kappe bridled with energy. "I am happy to hear that."

"I did want to tell you…" Dasch considered how best to put it. "Not to sound ungrateful, but I feel that I should be doing something bigger and better for my country than transcribing news reports."

Kappe leaned in close, his hot breath on Dasch's ear. "Don't worry, Mr. Dasch, you just bide your time. I have a project that I would like to share with you, but I'm not authorized to discuss it just yet. I will call on you in due time, of that I promise." The lieutenant quickly moved on to mingle amongst the others, leaving George to consider his words. Leaving the restaurant, Dasch placed his hat on his head before moving up the sidewalk.

"A project…" Dasch said to himself. What kind of a project might that be? He knew better than to get his hopes too high. George had other contacts after all. At least one, anyway. It couldn't hurt to make other inquiries.

George Dasch didn't have to bide his time for long before Kappe called on him. *Report to the office of Lieutenant Walter Kappe, General Headquarters* came the message just two weeks later. As he sat across from Kappe that very afternoon, the lieutenant seemed annoyed. He tapped a pencil on his desk. "I understand you've been talking to Reinholt Barth. Poking around about a new job?"

"I know Reinholt quite well," Dasch tried to defend himself. "I merely asked if he might know of any opportunities…"

"I thought I made it quite clear that I had you in mind for a particular project. Did I not tell you that I would contact you in due time?"

"Yes, Lieutenant, you did say so. I apologize."

Kappe leaned back in his chair, allowing Dasch's contrition to sink in. "Ever since we first met, I knew that you could be quite useful. I was previously unable to share any details with you, but I am happy to report that certain obstacles have been overcome. The German High Command has seen fit to approve our plan." Kappe slid a single piece of paper and a pen across his desk. "George, I am authorized to disclose to you a few details but before I do that, I need you to sign this statement."

Dasch's curiosity was fully engaged. He quickly read through the document, slowing as he came to the most relevant section. *All information regarding this project is top secret, not to be revealed to any unauthorized persons on pain of death…* Dasch took a quick look at Kappe. This was serious business indeed. George signed.

The lieutenant retrieved the form and filed it away in a desk drawer before leaning back in his seat. His expression was that of the devil, having scored another soul. Pride of ownership. He licked his lips before continuing. "This plan, my plan, has been in the works for quite some time. Recent events have resulted in the Fuhrer taking a particular interest." Kappe paused for effect. "George, how would you like to return to America?"

Dasch struggled to contain his elation. "I thought that they were a neutral country?"

"Yes, officially they are neutral. Nonetheless, they are indirectly our enemy. The Americans are helping to supply the British with weapons, fuel, raw materials… Therefore, it is time for us to attack them. What do you know about industrial sabotage?"

Pressing the tips of his fingers together, George paused to think. Sabotage was not his area of expertise. He knew nothing about it, yet if he were to have any hope of taking part in this mission it was imperative that he prove his worth. "Of course, industries in the United States have certain bottlenecks which could easily be destroyed, thus slowing production to a crawl. Train networks, for instance, or various key factories."

"Tell me, George, would you mind writing up a report with all of your ideas?"

"Certainly!" Dasch let his enthusiasm slip.

"I would like two copies by the end of this week. Could you do that?"

"Yes, yes, I can do that."

"Wonderful." Kappe rose. "I will look forward to reading what you come up with."

"Thank you, Lieutenant." Dasch stood and shook Kappe's hand. As he left the office, George felt a joy swelling deep within his chest. America! How would he like to go to America? He laughed to himself as he ran the question through his mind once more. Yes, he would like that very much. George Dasch was determined to make it happen.

Chapter Twenty-Four

Atlantic Ocean, December 10, 1941.

Perched in a crow's nest high above the bow, Herbie Haupt heard only the whistling of a frigid winter wind. He felt a rhythmic rise and fall as the *Deutschland* powered forward, up and down through rolling ocean swells, their crests topped with billowing white froth. Lifting a pair of binoculars to his eyes, he scanned the horizon for any signs of enemy vessels. The job took on added urgency as they approached the British naval blockade. Enemies. Herbie took a moment to consider that prospect. Were the British his enemy? He'd grown up speaking their language. Never had he harbored any grudge against them. And yet, he was German at the core. An enemy of Germany was, by definition, an enemy of his own. Mostly it was the thought of being blown to smithereens by a British warship that kept him vigilant as he eyed the distant gray line between sea and sky. Nothing. Just clouds above and whitecaps below for three hundred and sixty degrees.

Alone in his perch for hours on end, Herbie's mind was wont to wander. Mostly he enjoyed the time, spotting the occasional whales or sharks, watching the shifts in weather, thinking about home. Doing the math, he figured that Gerda must be due any day. He pictured her in the hospital, cradling their newborn baby in her arms. His guilt was heavy, though at this point it wasn't entirely his fault. He'd tried to go home, hadn't he? He'd put in a good-faith effort. At the moment, all he wanted was to get off this ship. For one hundred and six straight days he'd been surrounded by a boatful of odorous German sailors. In one more day this portion of their journey would end. Updated orders reached their captain just a few days before. New destination: France. Bordeaux. Just the thought of those pretty French girls made his blood pressure rise. In the meantime, one more day on this tub, scanning the horizon and hoping they didn't get blown to kingdom come.

At first, he wasn't quite sure that the small gray speck was anything other than his imagination. Perhaps a cloud, low on the horizon? No, it couldn't be that. Herbie knew what a cloud looked like. This sky was nearly clear. Focusing his binoculars, the outline became more distinctive. It was a ship, definitely. And there toward the bow, he saw the faint horizontal lines of what appeared to be a battery of guns. Herbie put down the binoculars and lifted the handset of a small gray phone. With his other hand, he turned a crank.

"This is the bridge," the first mate answered.

"This is Haupt in the crow's nest. I see something," he reported. "A vessel at ten o'clock."

When he'd hung up, Herbie quickly found the ship again in his binoculars. The shape was even clearer this time. This was no liner, he was sure. Herbie held on with one hand as his ship heeled over beneath him, making a sharp turn to starboard. Until this point, the war was just an abstraction. It was something far away, in another world from the one that he and Wolf inhabited. As of this moment, all of that changed. Herbie was a part of it. He was in it. Wolfgang, too. There was a thrill in that knowledge, on some level. On another, however, Herbie could only hope that he'd be able to get back out.

One day later they tied up in port, safe at last. Herbie's thoughts turned again to the exotic French girls they were sure to find ashore. He could hardly wait to lay his eyes on them. With three months' wages coming, he and Wolf could afford to hang around a while. Maybe take a train to Paris. He sat in the galley with Wolf and the rest of the crew, playing dominoes while they waited for immigration agents to arrive. A German radio broadcast droned over the intercom. To Wolfgang, it sounded like gibberish, but Herbie understood every word. At first, he paid little attention. An announcer extolled German victories on the Russian front. There were references to the Japanese and their close cooperation with the German nation, followed by disparaging remarks about the evils of America. None of it concerned Herbie much. Then came the announcement that the German leader himself was about to give an important speech. Adolph Hitler, live on the radio. That was something Herbie didn't hear every day. He began to pay attention.

"Your move." Schmidt sat across the table with an array of dominoes between them.

"Shhh, I want to hear this part." Herbie pushed back his chair.

Even Schmidt couldn't feign disinterest once the Fuhrer began to speak. There was something mesmerizing about his words; uncontained passion, rallying the German people to a cause. Herbie picked up what sounded to his ears like a hint of insanity in the leader's pleas, yet this wasn't just any speech. The Fuhrer was building to something momentous. Something to do with America, it seemed.

"Despite the years of intolerable provocations by President Roosevelt, Germany and Italy sincerely and very patiently tried to prevent the expansion of this war and to maintain relations with the United States. But as a result of his campaign, these efforts have failed," Hitler cried out.

"Faithful to the provisions of the Tripartite Pact of September 27, 1940, Germany and Italy accordingly now regard themselves as finally forced to join together on the side of Japan in the struggle for the defense and preservation of the freedom and independence of our nations and realms against the United States of America and Britain."

All around the galley men fell silent, giving the radio their full attention. Only Wolfgang couldn't understand. "What did he say?"

"I think he said we're at war…"

"I thought we knew that."

"Not just Germany. I mean Germany and America are at war."

Wolfgang let this news settle in as the Fuhrer continued, "Germany, Italy, and Japan will together conduct the war that has been forced upon them by the United States of America and Britain with all the means at their command to a victorious conclusion."

"Where does that leave us?" Wolfgang's concern showed.

Hans Sass looked across from a table nearby. "You got German papers didn't you?"

"Sure, but Herbie and I are Americans…"

"Then it's straight to the POW camp for you two." Schmidt gave a smirk, only half joking.

"Deputies! Men of the German Reichstag!" Hitler continued at a fever pitch. "Ever since my peace proposal of July 1940 was rejected, we have clearly realized that this struggle must be fought through to the end! We National Socialists are not at all surprised that the Anglo-American, Jewish and capitalist world is united together with Bolshevism. In our country, we have always found them in the same community!"

"I need some air," said Wolf.

"Right behind you," Herbie answered.

The pair made their way topside where they were joined by Schmidt. Standing along the rail, they saw the docklands of Bordeaux stretching before them. In the distance, church spires rose from the peaceful-looking city. Closer at hand, two German naval police officers in winter coats stood guard at the bottom of the gangway.

"You don't think they'd send us to a prison camp, do you?" Wolf shivered in his thin cotton coveralls.

"They might," said Herbie.

"But we were born in Germany. That has to count for something."

"And you spent your whole life in Chicago," said Schmidt. "Hell, you don't even speak the language!"

"Come on, Schmidt, knock it off," said Herbie.

"You think I'm pulling your leg?! Two Americans showing up on the day Hitler declares war? Just hope they don't take you for a couple of spies or they'll shoot you dead on the spot."

Wolfgang felt a rush of panic. Would they do that? Maybe Schmidt was just trying to frighten them. If so, he was succeeding.

Herbie pulled a packet of cigarettes from the pocket of his coveralls, trying to push such thoughts aside. "Anyone?"

"Thanks." Schmidt pulled two cigarettes from the pack and handed one to Wolf. Each man took turns with Herbie's lighter.

"Nobody is going to shoot anybody." Herbie took a long drag on his own and then exhaled. "Don't listen to him, Wolf. We'll be fine."

"So, what will they do with us?"

Herbie shook his head. "I don't know."

Part II – The Fatherland

Chapter Twenty-Five

Bordeaux, December 13, 1941

After three months at sea, the *Deutschland* never felt more like a prison than here, tied up to the dock with Bordeaux in full view. Most of the crew were cleared days earlier. Only Herbie and Wolf were trapped aboard, their status unresolved. They were eating their lunch when Hans Sass came back aboard after a morning excursion into town. He entered the galley holding a paper sack with a baguette sticking out the top.

"There they are, my two American friends!" Sass beamed as he took a seat and put his bag on the table.

"What did you get?" Herbie asked.

"What did I get indeed?!" Sass lifted the baguette and placed it on the table before pulling out additional goods and arranging them before the boys. "Let's see, a couple bottles of wine, cheese, oh, and here are two bars of the best Swiss chocolate I could find."

Seeing these items made Wolf disconsolate. He wanted to go ashore, too. He wanted to purchase some Swiss chocolate. To see the sights. To get off this damned rust bucket.

"What do the girls look like?" Herbie asked.

"What do you think?" Sass smirked.

"Pretty, huh?" said Wolf.

"Prettiest girls I've ever seen."

"You're just saying that 'cause you've been stuck on this ship for three months."

"I'd be saying it anyway."

"What's this?" Wolfgang picked up a small envelope amidst Sass' loot.

"Photographs. I got my film developed."

"Can I look?"

"Sure, take a look."

Wolfgang opened the envelope and pulled out a stack of photos. Flipping through them, he saw some shots of Mexico, with Señor Lopez behind the bar in his restaurant, and another of Van Wallenburg sitting at a table. Next were pictures of Tokyo and one of Schmidt at the monastery, with a hoe in hand. Wolf paused when he came to a shot taken on the *Deutschland.* It was on the top deck, with Wolfgang on the left, kneeling in his dark coveralls, a white cap on his head. To the right, Herbie and Schmidt sat side-by-side on a wooden pallet. All three men looked toward the camera, smiles on their faces. "Look at this," Wolf showed the shot to Herbie.

Haupt held the photo up for closer examination. "That's a nice memento."

"Can I keep it?" Wolf asked Sass.

"Go ahead, I don't care."

Wolf took the photo back from Herbie. "Thanks!" He carefully folded it in half and then slid it into his wallet.

"How about one of those chocolate bars?" Herbie asked.

"You got the money, I'll buy you as many chocolate bars as you want."

"Can we make out a list?" said Wolf.

"Don't expect me to hang around here much longer. I'm catching a train first thing tomorrow."

"Where to?"

"Paris first, then Berlin."

"What are you gonna do there?" Herbie asked.

"I've got some people to see. Family, you know, and some friends."

"You still plan to join the army?" said Wolf.

"Of course. It's the duty of every good German to heed the call of his nation."

Before Wolf could reply, two men in suits that he'd never seen before entered the galley, satchels in hand. Wolf knew who they were at once. He'd been expecting two Gestapo agents to arrive all morning. "Wolfgang Wergin und Herbie Haupt?" said one.

Herbie raised a hand. "Ja."

"I'll leave you boys to it." Sass gathered the items back into his bag. When he'd moved on, the two agents sat at the table. Wolf pushed their lunch dishes aside.

"Reisepass," said an agent. He had a long, thin face, with round spectacles dangling from the tip of his nose. Herbie and Wolf produced the documents created for them in Mexico. The agent showed no emotion as he carefully examined them. "Wo bist du geboren?" he said.

"Stettin," Herbie answered.

"What did he say?" Wolf asked.

"He wants to know where we were born."

"Koenigsberg," said Wolf. "In East Prussia."

"And why have you decided to return to German territory at this time?" the other agent said in English. This man had full red cheeks and a shiny, smooth pate. It wasn't the first time these questions were asked. Herbie and Wolf went through the same drill, first with the German naval police and then with two consular officials. Nobody seemed to know what to do with them. Were they Germans? Were they Americans? The arrival of these Gestapo agents promised some resolution, one way or another. All the same, Schmidt's words were never far from Wolfgang's mind. *…they'll shoot you dead on the spot.*

While the second agent took notes, Herbie and Wolfgang related their stories once again. Herbie didn't seem worried. It was a thrill to encounter a pair of actual Gestapo agents firsthand. He was full of enthusiasm as he explained his role in spotting the British warship. Had they heard, the ship's captain was going to put them up for medals?

When the interview was complete, Herbie and Wolf were sent to their cabin while the agents decided what exactly to do with them. Herbie reclined on his bunk casually while Wolf sat in the cabin's single chair, rocking nervously back and forth. Neither said a word as the seconds ticked past. Finally, they were called back to the galley.

"We have decided that you will be sent to live with your grandparents," the bespectacled agent told them. "Haupt will travel to Stettin and Wergin to Koenigsberg. You will be escorted by naval police. On arrival at your destinations, you will register with the local Gestapo office. You will remain in constant contact with Gestapo agents while further inquiries are made into your claims. You will not travel further without explicit written permission. Do you understand these terms?"

"Yes." Relief settled over Wolfgang. No bullets in the head. At least not yet. He realized, of course, that this meant he and Herbie would be separated. And that he was being sent to live with a grandmother he had no memory of, who spoke not a word of English, for an indeterminate amount of time. He thought back to the very beginning of their journey. Two weeks. That was how long this trip was supposed to last. Two short weeks. The realization settled in that as long as this war dragged on, he and Herbie were trapped, with no way to communicate with their parents back home. Wolf took solace in the fact that he and Herbie weren't being arrested as spies, though it was small consolation. That fate might still await them.

For Herbie, the prospect of spending time in Germany was less daunting. He spoke the language. He could communicate with his grandparents, and perhaps he might be allowed to get a job. The responsibilities he was running from back home were far away indeed. The guilt remained, but what could he do about it? His destiny was beyond his control. Besides, he felt a small sense of pride at being back in his country of origin. He would live in the home that his father was raised in. As for the war, that was an unfortunate complication. He would simply have to wait it out. At least he had somewhere to go. He would be all right. He and Wolf both.

"You will board a train for Paris this evening," the Gestapo agent switched back to German. "Gather your belongings. Your escort will be sent to collect you shortly." With that, the agents packed away their papers and departed.

"What is my grandma going to think?" Wolf asked. "How will I even talk to her?"

Herbie shook his head.

"I just want to go home."

"We can't go home, Wolf. We'd better get used to it." The pair sat silently, considering the ramifications of that statement. "Come on," Herbie added. "We'd better pack our things."

"You think they'd let me go to Stettin with you instead?"

"I doubt it. It sounds like they've already made up their minds."

"My grandma is going to be awfully surprised when I come knocking at her door…"

Disembarking in Paris, the station was all noise and commotion. Crowds of travelers jostled on the platform. With only light sweaters to protect them, Wolf and Herbie shivered against the winter cold. Their escort, Lieutenant Becker, stayed close as the men approached a checkpoint. Wolf noticed small SS badges pinned to the officers' uniforms. He saw the machine guns slung over their shoulders. Becker handed over their travel documents. "Becker, naval intelligence."

The SS officer flipped through the passports and travel cards with brisk efficiency, peering at the dates and stamps. Without a word, he handed them back and gave a nod. Wolf and Herbie followed Becker past. The lieutenant led them through the station and out to the street where the scene was no less chaotic. More people, but with trams and buses thrown into the mix. They boarded one of the trams and rode several stops before clambering off. After hauling their bags a few more blocks through a cold December wind, they moved through twin doors into a hotel lobby. Here they saw families, couples, and a few unaccompanied men, all crowded toward two overwhelmed receptionists who stood behind a front desk. On the far side of the room, flames from a large fireplace cast a flickering glow, bathing the room in both light and warmth. "Wait here," Becker commanded.

"Sure." Herbie and Wolf dropped their bags to the floor as Becker moved off toward the desk.

"I guess this is it for tonight," said Wolf.

"It doesn't look so bad."

"The first time we won't be rocked to sleep in three months."

"I still feel like I'm moving. Don't you feel it? I'd swear this whole room is swaying back and forth."

"Yeah, I feel it." Wolf watched a small girl nearby, hopping up and down from one foot to the other. Spotting him, she stopped, but only momentarily before continuing with her game.

After several minutes, Becker returned with a bellman in tow. "You need winter clothes," Becker said. "This man will assist us."

Wolf and Herbie followed the bellman through a set of double doors and into a large dining room. Stacked on the floors and tables were clothes of all kinds, some in boxes, some draped over the backs of chairs, others thrown into disorganized piles. Coats, shoes, dresses, boots, shirts and pants... The room overflowed with them. "Take what you need." Becker stood by with arms crossed

"Anything?!" Wolf was astonished.

"Only what you need. Winter clothes."

Herbie and Wolfgang moved into the room, examining the contents. Herbie lifted a leather boot from a tabletop and checked the size, holding it beside one of his own. Too small. He put it back and searched for a larger pair. Wolf found a passable fedora and then a scarf. When he saw a pristine wool overcoat, his eyes lit up. He tried it on, sliding his arms slowly into silk-lined sleeves. Wolfgang would never have made such an extravagant purchase on his own. The fit was perfect, just right in the shoulders. He looked around the room for a mirror but there were none. "Hey Herbie, how does it look?"

Herbie raised his head from a stack of wool trousers. Taking in Wolf's fancy new coat, he was impressed at first but then his expression dropped. "No, I don't think so." Herbie shook his head.

"Why not?! It's perfect!" Wolf checked the length of the sleeves. "You just want it for yourself."

"Pick another one!" Herbie snapped.

Wolf slid the coat off dejectedly. "I don't see why…" Scarcely had he spoken the words when he noticed it. Stitched across the chest on the right side were thread marks outlining the distinctive shape of a Jewish star. "Oh." Wolf's heart sank. "I'll find something else." The two of them continued to shuffle through the piles until they'd picked out some manageable alternatives.

"Come on, let's go," said Becker.

Moving back through the lobby, the bellman pushed a cart holding their bags along with their new acquisitions. Wolf's mind raced. What happened to all of those people, represented by all of those clothes? Where did they go? These were questions it was best not to dwell on. That much he already knew.

After a night of fitful sleep, their first ashore, the boys boarded a train bound for Saarbrucken. They shared a compartment with Becker and a group of women and children. Wolf sat by the window with Herbie pressed up against him. In the seat across was a German woman in a plain blue dress, her hair tied up in a white scarf. On her lap she held a precocious young boy, bouncing up and down as he struggled to escape his mother's grasp. "Ruhig, Oskar! Bitte!" she pleaded for him to behave.

As the minutes turned to hours, Wolf's legs and buttocks grew numb. He shifted in his seat, desperate for some relief. "You want to walk around a little?" he asked Herbie.

"Have you seen the corridor?"

Wolf leaned forward to get a better view, then rose, stepping gingerly between legs and feet as he approached the door. Herbie was right. Men, women, and children took up every bit of space as they sat or sprawled on the ground. Turning around, Wolf made his way back where he'd started. At least he could stand and stretch a little bit. Up and down, he managed some deep knee bends as Oskar began to wail. Out the window, he saw rows of barbed-wire fencing, trenches, and then earthen fortifications. Machine gun nests and watch towers were manned by German soldiers, while others patrolled with dogs. The brakes hissed as the train slowed to a halt. Seconds later, he heard the clanging noise of the door to their car opening, followed by shouting and some commotion.

"Papiere!" came a stern voice.

Wolf retook his seat.

"Deutschland!" The woman across the aisle had a hopeful expression as she nodded out the window.

Wolf looked once again. So, this was it. The land of their fathers, literally. He wondered what his parents would think. When the door to their compartment slid open, a tall man in an SS uniform faced them. "Papeire!" he repeated. The passengers shuffled to produce their papers. Herbie and Wolf pulled their documents from their pockets. The officer made his way down the opposite row, checking travel permits one at a time. Wolf was sure this man would smell the fear on him. It seemed impossible to hide. At least the lieutenant was here to vouch for them. When it was his turn, Wolfgang tried to maintain a blank expression as he handed over his documents.

"These two are with me," said Becker. "I am escorting them to Saarbrucken."

The SS officer examined Wolfgang's papers before handing them back and moving on. He made his way through the rest of the compartment and then continued out the door.

"Welcome to Germany," said Herbie.

"Thanks," Wolf answered. Under different circumstances, he might have been happy traveling back to the land where he was born, yet from the view out the window, it looked more like a prison.

Becker's responsibility ended in Saarbrucken, as soon as the two men were safely aboard their respective trains. For Wolfgang and Herbie, each step along the sidewalk brought them closer to their separation. After six months of constant companionship, this was the end. That reality was not lost on either of them as they passed through the entryway and lined up for yet another document inspection.

"I guess this is it, huh?" Wolfgang said it quietly, trying not to draw attention with his English.

"I guess, so."

"You think they'll let us visit each other, at least?"

"I don't know. I can't see why not."

"Maybe you could come out to Koenigsberg?"

Herbie didn't seem thrilled by this prospect. "Maybe you can come to Stettin."

"I'd like that," Wolf answered.

When they'd shown their documents, Becker gave the boys their tickets and walked with them to platform number two. Herbie's train was already waiting, shrouded in an early-morning mist. They located his carriage and the three men stood to wait. With only a few minutes before departure, Wolf was disconsolate. Throughout their journey, he'd had Herbie by his side. When times were tough, he relied on his friend's bright outlook to help get them through. The thought of facing the unknown without Herbie was daunting. It felt as though their adventure was officially over. This was the end. From here on it was all about survival.

"Take care of yourself." Herbie read the apprehension in Wolf's eyes.

"Yeah, thanks. You too."

"Don't worry, we'll be all right."

"I know."

"I'll write if I can."

"That would be great."

Neither man wanted to be the one to break the bond and walk away. It was Becker who expedited the parting. "You'd better climb aboard," he said. "I don't want the train to leave without you."

"Yeah, sure." Herbie took a step forward, embracing Wolf in a giant bear hug. "So long, buddy."

"You better watch out for those German girls." Wolf laughed as they let each other go. "You don't want to knock one up. You can't run off to Mexico, this time!"

"That was low, Wolf."

"Come on, you know I'm kidding."

"I'll tell you what, though, think of all these local boys away at the front. The girls around here are gonna be crazy for us! You'll see."

"You've always got an angle, haven't you Herbie?"

The train whistle blew. "Alle einsteigen!" called the conductor.

"Let's go, hurry along," said Becker.

Herbie moved up the steps and onto the train. He walked a short distance down the aisle and placed his bag in an overhead rack before waving through the window. With another shrill whistle, the train shuddered, lurching forward. Wolfgang watched until the last carriage moved past and out of the station. That was it, then. From this point forward, he was on his own.

Chapter Twenty-Six

Berlin, January 12, 1942

George Dasch heard the crunch of dry snow under his boots. Walking briskly up the sidewalk, he clutched a manila folder in one hand. Inside were the latest additions to his plan. Aluminum factories. That was the key. The American war effort relied on them. If the Germans could disable aluminum production… With these ideas, Dasch would do all he could to convince Kappe that he was indispensable. He didn't want to merely plan the mission. Dasch was intent on taking part and even leading it if he could. Not that he intended to carry out these sabotage plots, but it was imperative to play the part of a zealous Nazi, to convince Kappe that he was eager to strike a blow against the American menace. The lieutenant had already shown Dasch a list of potential recruits, all of them former U.S. residents. Very soon, the process of interviewing these men would begin. To Dasch, the makeup of the final group didn't matter so much, as long as he was among them.

Arriving at Kappe's address, Dasch rang the buzzer and was let in. It was a simple residential building, with offices on the top floor. Kappe posed as the editor of a small magazine, *Der Kaukakus*. Though the magazine published irregular issues, it was primarily a front for his intelligence operations. Kappe could interview recruits under the pretense that it was all just for a magazine article. Potential candidates who were rejected would be none the wiser.

After climbing the stairs to the fourth floor, Dasch let himself in through the office door to find Kappe's receptionist sitting behind a desk. "Ah, Mr. Dasch. He's expecting you. Go on in," she said.

"Thank you!" Dasch took off his overcoat and hung it on a rack, along with his hat. On the other side of a wooden door, he heard Kappe's booming voice. George leaned forward and knocked three times.

"Yes!" Kappe called out. "What is it?"

Dasch cautiously opened the door. The corpulent Kappe sat behind his desk, leaning back in his chair. Facing him was a tall, thin man who Dasch didn't recognize. The newcomer had a long face and sunken eyes. He wore a loose gray suit.

"Ah, George, come in!" Kappe motioned with one arm. "I'm sure you'll want to hear this."

Wary of anyone associated with Kappe, Dasch eyed the new man with suspicion. From his strained expression, it seemed the feeling was mutual.

"This is Lieutenant Hoffman, army intelligence," Kappe said. "George is helping me with that special project I told you about."

Hoffman's hard demeanor eased somewhat. "Ah, yes, your project."

"The lieutenant was just telling me about his experiences in Kyiv."

"Is that right?" Dasch took a small chair in the corner. "Go on, I don't want to interrupt."

"As I was saying, those Russians are sneaky bastards. Very clever, but bastards nonetheless."

"They blew up our divisional headquarters!" Kappe brought Dasch up to speed.

"Yes, but how they did it! That was the clever part. Those Russians, they burrowed underground to set the explosives beneath the building. Not just the headquarters, but many other buildings we occupied as well. They used radio signals to set off the charges, blowing up all of them at once. Can you imagine? By radio!"

"Astounding," said Kappe.

"Yes," Hoffman shook his head in amazement. "Well, we taught them a lesson after that. We rounded up all of the Jews in the city. Thirty-five thousand men, women, and children. We split them into groups of two to three hundred people, gave them shovels, and made them dig their own graves. Then we shot them in the back of the head and kicked them into the hole." A gleeful smirk appeared on Hoffman's lips.

Dasch struggled to mask his revulsion. "Did you shoot some of them yourself?"

"No, not me. I was merely an observer. Officers of the SS were in charge of the details." Hoffman gave a hearty laugh before continuing. "They shot so many people, the executing officers had to be periodically replaced because their trigger fingers got so tired!"

Kappe rocked in his chair with a look of merry contentment.

"That's not all!" Hoffman went on. "I saw one dirty old Jewess who sat on the road near the dead body of a young woman. The old Jew refused to leave. The only way they could get that woman away was by shooting her right there in the place!"

Kappe and Hoffman broke into raucous laughter. Dasch did his best to force a smile. He knew what was happening to Jews. He'd seen the brutality firsthand; the confiscation of property, public beatings and humiliation, and finally, expulsion to distant camps from which they never returned. He'd heard rumors of mass killings, but never had the horror struck him as it did when he saw the glee on these men's faces. Until this moment, he'd tried to pretend to himself that those rumors weren't entirely true. Faced with the joy in the telling of this story, Dasch could pretend no longer. A deep sense of helpless melancholy overtook him. How had the world come to this?

"I'll leave you two to your planning." Lieutenant Hoffman rose from his chair. Dasch and Kappe stood as well and each man shot an arm in the air. "Heil Hitler!"

"Come back and tell us more stories any time!" said Kappe.

"I will, Lieutenant. I wish you luck with your project."

When Hoffman was gone, Dasch retook his chair, still flushed. "For Christ's sake, that's an awful way to kill people."

Kappe's face glowed red. "What kind of a German are you?!" he snapped. "We Germans have one thing to do above all others, and that is to kill all of the Jews! Don't you be so chicken-hearted!"

"Yes, I'm sorry…" Dasch stammered. "My mistake. They were Jews, I must remind myself."

Kappe examined his protégé. "Don't let it happen again."

"No, Lieutenant. Certainly not."

After some reflection, Kappe seemed satisfied. More important was the issue at hand. His pet project. The lieutenant reached into a drawer and pulled out a folder of his own before opening it on his desk. "Let's take a look at our prospects, shall we? I'm interested in your opinion. I think we have some good men here."

"Yes, let's see." Dasch leaned closer, reading over the names on a list. He tried to moderate his breathing, to calm his pounding heart.

For the time being, he was a Nazi, devoted to the Fuhrer above all else. For Kappe to believe it, Dasch had to believe it himself. If only he might take part in this mission, his true feelings would emerge eventually, far, far away across the sea. "What can you tell me about them?" he asked.

Chapter Twenty-Seven

Stettin, March 3, 1942

Herbie Haupt shifted uncomfortably in his seat. No matter how many times he was called in for questioning, it never got any easier. This room, this chair, the desk at which he sat facing two Gestapo agents, were better-known to him by this time than any other place in Stettin. Three, sometimes four days per week he was made to appear. Usually, they were the same questions asked over and over again as the agents tried to catch him in an inconsistency. All he could do was come in each time, sit in this chair, and give the same old answers.

"How many dental fillings do you have?" one of the agents asked.

"Five."

The agent jotted down the number in a notepad. "And where did you get them?"

"At my dentist, in Chicago."

"Chicago, in the U.S.A.?"

"Yes."

"Your parents," the other agent cut in. "Are they German, or American?"

"German-American."

"Yes, but their citizenship? Of which country are they citizens?"

"My parents were born German citizens, in Germany. They became American citizens in 1929."

The first man jotted down this fact. The same fact he'd jotted down countless times before. "American citizens."

"Yes."

"And what does that make you?"

"I became an American citizen at the same time they did. I was born a German, here in Stettin."

"And what do you consider yourself?" the first agent asked. "Are you German, or American?"

"I don't know," Herbie shrugged. "Both, I guess."

The agents looked at each other for a moment and then back to Herbie. "That will be all for today," the second agent said.

"Do you think I might be able to get a work permit sometime?" Herbie pressed them. "I'm trained as an optician. It's awfully hard just sitting at my grandparents' house all day. I could use a job…"

"You must understand," the first agent had a hint of condescension in his voice. "We can't be sure whose side you are on. We are at war, you realize."

"I'm just trying to survive."

"Good day, Mr. Haupt."

Herbie stood from his chair and slipped from the room. His life had become an exercise in futility. Exiting the building, he turned up the sidewalk, though there was nowhere in particular to go. Nothing to do. Just walk the city, shadowed by one of these same Gestapo agents. Or he could go home and sit in the house with his grandparents. Neither option was appealing. It was what every day looked like, one after another. Herbie took a deep breath and headed home. He thought of Wolfgang. They hadn't seen each other since Saarbrucken. Nobody in Chicago had any idea that Herbie and Wolf were trapped in Germany. Thinking of Gerda filled him with a deep sense of melancholy. He'd never imagined that he could miss her so much. At this moment, he wished for nothing more than to be curled up with her in bed, their baby sleeping soundly in a nearby crib. If he ever managed to find a way out of here, if he got back to Chicago, Herbie would marry Gerda. He was ready, if she'd still have him.

Trudging through Stettin, Herbie peeked backward from time to time to see the agent trailing from a few blocks behind. Herbie couldn't help but feel guilty, though of what, he wasn't sure. Continuing on his way, his thoughts turned to the more immediate future. If only he could find a job, he might carve out some sort of a life while he was here. Enough money to ask out the girl at the grocery store he'd had his eye on. Maybe even buy a car to take her on a Sunday drive? Not one of these bulbous Volkswagens he saw all over, but something with style. He remembered the BMW coupe he'd seen the week before, parked in front of City Hall. Now that was a car! Sleek and lean, it looked like a silvery rocket ship, with sloping lines that concealed what could only be a massive V-12 engine. All of the cars here were different than any he saw back home. When he came across a shiny blue Opel parked by the side of the road, he stopped to take a look. This would do, he told himself. The car had four doors, sculpted fenders, and a round, bullet-shaped nose. Maybe someday.

On a corner across the street, he saw the loitering Gestapo agent. Herbie kept walking, past two young soldiers on leave, looking smart in their matching gray uniforms. What must it be like to wear the uniform of their country? The girls must go crazy for it, he thought… Herbie pictured himself flying a fighter plane for the Luftwaffe, buzzing over the countryside at three hundred miles per hour. He imagined drinking beers in a small village pub, the pilots of his squadron raising their glasses in celebration of a successful mission. Forget about a car, if he was going to dream, why not make it an airplane? Anything but the mind-numbing boredom of his current existence, where each day ticked by more slowly than the last.

When he arrived at the house, Herbie looked back one more time for the Gestapo agent, but there was no sign of the man. Checking his grandparent's mailbox on the way inside, he half expected to see another postcard calling him back in for questioning. Instead, he found a few letters addressed to his grandfather, but then one more. This last letter was addressed to Herbie, but it wasn't from the Gestapo. The return address was Berlin. *Der Kaukasus*, it read. Editor-in-Chief, Lieutenant Walter Kappe.

Moving inside, Herbie placed his grandfather's mail on the front table before continuing into the kitchen. Curiosity overtook him as he tore open his envelope and pulled out a letter typed in English.

Herbert Haupt,

Allow me to introduce myself. My name is Walter Kappe, editor of Der Kaukasus, a general interest magazine distributed to our proud soldiers on the Russian front. I have recently been made aware of your extraordinary journey halfway around the world, and the medals you received for running the British naval blockade. I would very much like to interview you for a story in our magazine. Would you be willing to meet with me in Berlin? A story such as yours would help very much in keeping up the morale of our troops. Please let me know when you might be able to see me.

Kind regards,

Lieutenant Walter Kappe

For a brief moment, Herbie was enthused by the idea of appearing in a German magazine. Just as quickly, he considered the logistics. How could he travel to Berlin? Even if the Gestapo gave him permission, Herbie had no money for train fare. He folded the letter and put it back into the envelope. No, he thought, *Der Kaukasus* would have to find another story to entertain the troops. Herbie wasn't going anywhere.

Chapter Twenty-Eight

Berlin, March 17, 1942

Emerging from an underground station, Herbie was disoriented. Cars rushed past on a busy boulevard. Pedestrians crowded the sidewalks. After pushing his way to the nearest corner, he checked the street names on the side of a building and then pulled out a small map that he'd drawn by hand. Herbie spun the map until the streets lined up with those before him. With his bearings restored, he traced the route with one finger. Three blocks up and then two over. Herbie started off down a narrow side street. He checked his watch. Right on time.

Of course, he hadn't expected to be here in Berlin at all. When a second letter from this mysterious magazine arrived, however, Herbie began to reconsider the idea. Any opportunity to get out of Stettin was too good to pass up. How could the Gestapo deny him travel papers when he had a written invitation from a lieutenant in the German army? Herbie set about raising the money, borrowing some from his grandparents and the rest from an uncle. He would pay them back as soon as he could, he promised. Setting off on the train felt like a temporary prison furlough; two whole days to explore the capital he'd heard so much about.

And so, after a night in a seedy hotel near the railway station, here he was, navigating these unfamiliar city streets. When he found a building marked with the correct address, he was confused. This was an apartment building, not an office. Herbie had pictured an imposing government building, with army personnel streaming in and out past security checkpoints. Peering through the front window, he saw a small, unoccupied lobby. Along the right-hand wall, stacks of mail were piled atop a wooden bureau. Herbie stepped back and found the name *Der Kaukasus* on a door plate and then pushed a corresponding button.

"Der Kaukasus!" came a young woman's voice.

"This is Herbert Haupt. I am here to see Lieutenant Kappe."

The door buzzed and Herbie made his way inside. After climbing carpeted stairs to the top floor, he found a door with the name of the publication etched on a bronze plaque. Herbie turned the handle and let himself in. The young woman sat behind a desk. To the left was a large potted plant. To the right, two chairs were pushed up against the wall on either side of a small table. A hallway past the woman's desk led to several more doors, all closed. "Good morning," she said. "Have a seat. The lieutenant will see you in a moment."

"Thank you." While he waited, Herbie lifted an issue of the magazine from the table. It wasn't much. Just a few pages, black ink printed on white paper with some grainy photos. The front page featured updates on German army victories. Inside were human interest stories; one about a group of soldiers' wives collecting supplies for their husbands' unit. Another article reviewed the latest theater offerings from the Ministry of Propaganda. Herbie set the magazine down just as one of the doors opened to reveal a pudgy man in an officer's uniform. On seeing Herbie, the man broke into a smile. "You must be Herbert! Come in, come in! I'm Lieutenant Kappe." The man spoke fluent English, albeit with an accent.

"Nice to meet you, sir." Herbie rose.

"The pleasure is all mine, I assure you." Kappe shook Herbie's hand and then ushered him inside his office. "Please, have a seat!"

Herbie settled into a chair while Kappe moved around to sit behind his desk.

"Thank you for coming. I trust you had a pleasant journey?"

"Yes, sir. It was fine."

"I understand you have quite a story regarding your return to Germany!" The lieutenant was filled with enthusiasm.

"It was an unusual set of circumstances."

"And you were awarded some medals, correct?"

"Yes, sir." Herbie's chest swelled with pride. "One for running the blockade, and then I got an Iron Cross for spotting a British warship. I was on watch, up in the crow's nest…"

"Excellent. Did you bring those medals along with you?"

"No, sir, I left them in Stettin."

Kappe was disappointed. "That's all right." He took out a notepad and a pencil. "Why don't you tell me your story? Go ahead and start from the beginning."

"I'm surprised that you heard about me. Was it because of the medals?"

"No, not exactly. I happen to know a friend of yours. Hans Sass?"

"Oh! You know Hans! How is he? I haven't heard from him since we arrived."

"Hans is well. He's joined the SS mountain troops. I believe he is undergoing training as we speak."

"The mountain troops!" Herbie was in awe. "I guess he got what he wanted."

"Hans is a good man. But about you, Herbert. How did you end up back in Germany? You grew up in Chicago, is that right?"

"Yes. That's right." Herbie thought back to that day, nine months earlier, when he and two friends first set out. "A few of us decided to take a road trip. To Mexico…"

After Herbie finished his tale, Kappe's expression seemed to shift. The carefree enthusiasm was replaced by a more serious demeanor. He opened a file and scanned a few pages while Herbie shifted in his seat.

"So you lived in Chicago from the time you were five years old, is that right?" Kappe asked.

"Yes, sir."

"And you are a United States citizen?"

"That's correct. I became a citizen in 1929, when my father was naturalized."

"I see. And you have four uncles still living in Germany?"

"Yes." Herbie wondered if he'd said something wrong. This was beginning to feel uncomfortably similar to one of his Gestapo interviews.

"According to my information, your mother's oldest brother is currently being held in a concentration camp."

Herbie sat up straight. What was this all about?

"And your father's brother was previously in such a camp?" Kappe went on.

"You have quite a lot of information about me," Herbie answered. "More than I expected."

Kappe looked up from his papers. "You've had a hard time finding work in Stettin. Isn't that right?"

Herbie examined his hands, folded in his lap. The pride he'd felt in telling his story was replaced with a dark cloud of anxiety. What was this all about?

"I understand that the Gestapo and the local police have made your life somewhat difficult."

"I don't know what this has to do with your article..." Herbie wondered if this lieutenant might be a Gestapo agent himself. Perhaps this was just some cruel ploy to glean more information from him. But why have him come all the way to Berlin for that? It made little sense.

"You'd like to see your uncle released from the camp, wouldn't you, Herbie?"

"Of course." Herbie recognized the underlying threat. "But I'm in no position to help him."

"Life certainly seems to be difficult for you here in Germany. I'll bet that if you could, you'd like to return to the United States. Isn't that right? It seems to be the only thing left for you."

Herbie was afraid to answer, but in the end he couldn't resist. The lure was too strong. "Sure, I'd like to go home. If there was a way."

A smile returned to Kappe's face; the fisherman reeling in a prize catch. "I might be able to help you in this regard. Of course, there would be certain duties required of you."

"What sorts of duties?" Herbie's skepticism ran deep.

"We can discuss that in due time..."

"There is no magazine article, then?"

"I apologize for that little ruse. This magazine of ours, well, it serves a purpose."

Herbie took it all in. The prospect of returning to Chicago was nearly overwhelming. To see his mother and father, to sleep in his own bed... To get his job back and return to his old life... And, yes, to see Gerda and meet his newborn child. Herbie would hear the lieutenant out. There was also his uncle to think of. That message was clear. "What's the next step?"

"I like your enthusiasm!" Kappe beamed. "If all goes well, we will arrange for your transportation back to the United States. Does this sound like something you'd like to consider?"

Herbie nodded.

"Wonderful!" Kappe slid a single sheet of paper and a pen across the desk. "Before I can discuss our project in any greater detail, I ask that you please sign this document."

Herbie scanned the paper. *All information regarding this project is top secret, not to be revealed to any unauthorized persons on pain of death…* It sounded dramatic, but he lifted the pen and signed his name across the bottom of the page before adding the date.

Kappe lifted the page and examined the signature. "Welcome to Operation Pastorius. You understand, our meetings must not be discussed with anyone. This is strictly top secret."

"I have a friend," Herbie spat out. "Wolf Wergin. He's the one who came with me from Chicago. He might be interested, too."

Kappe nodded. "I will take it under consideration."

"Wolf is very reliable. And smart! Perhaps you could meet with him?"

Kappe folded his arms. "I will meet him. My receptionist can arrange for train fare. You will be reimbursed for your travel expenses as well."

"Thank you, sir!"

"Regarding Wolf, I can't make any promises."

"He's a stand-up guy. You'll see."

"I am sure that he is."

"What sorts of tasks would we be responsible for, if we agreed to take part?"

"Enough to keep our enemies guessing. We want to sew discontent, to diminish the American people's support for this terrible war."

To Herbie, that one word still struck a nerve. *Enemies.* There it was again, but this time in reference not to the Brits, but to the only country he'd ever called home. Even so, Herbie was overtaken by the first hint of optimism he'd felt in months. Chicago. Just the thought of it made him deeply, inconsolably homesick. With a bit of luck, he and Wolf might be back there very, very soon.

Chapter Twenty-Nine

Koenigsberg, March 24, 1942

It was late afternoon as Wolfgang loaded four heavy steamer trunks onto a wobbly luggage cart and then pushed it slowly up the railway platform. Though the days were growing longer, the seasons seemed locked in perpetual battle, sunny and warm on one day yet spitting down the last winter snowflakes the next. On this particular evening, a cool wind blew scraps of discarded newspapers along the tracks below him. High above, patches of deep blue appeared and then vanished amid dancing gray clouds. Wolf shivered before putting his back into it, easing his load into the dimly lit baggage office where his boss sat at a desk behind a worn wooden counter. The wiry old man had spent a lifetime in this station, overseeing luggage stored on rows of shelves that stretched out behind him. Though Wolf's language skills were improving day by day, the older man communicated with Wolf in short bursts of German mixed with hand signals. "Das ist alles?" he said.

"Ja."

Across the counter, a valet approached with a tag in one hand. "Lichtman?"

"Ja," said Wolf. "Lichtman."

The valet placed his tag on the desk. Wolf pushed the cart back out of the office, following the valet to the street before helping load the trunks into the back of an enormous convertible black Mercedes. Wolfgang had never before seen a car like this one, long and square, with flowing fenders along each side of a gigantic engine compartment. At the front were mounted two small flags, one on each side. Red, with a white circle and the ubiquitous Nazi swastika in the center. When the trunks were safely stored, Wolf stood beside his empty cart and admired the vehicle.

"Danke." The valet climbed into the passenger seat. A driver with black leather gloves and a tan scarf fired up the rumbling engine.

Wolfgang watched wistfully as they headed off down the road. "You're welcome," he responded to nobody in particular before guiding the cart inside. Even with the wartime labor shortage, his job prospects had been extremely limited. It was only upon approval of the Gestapo that he managed to secure this position. Wolf didn't mind it. He didn't have to speak to anyone, much. More than anything, he was just relieved to have somewhere to go each day, and a small paycheck at the end of the week.

When he clocked out a few minutes later, Wolf left the station and began the long walk home, back to another dinner staring across the table at his grandmother. At least he could contribute now, instead of merely being a drag on her. Finances were tight, that much he understood. Milk, eggs, meat, and other staples were expensive, and sometimes difficult to come by.

Strolling up the sidewalk in the fading evening light, he spotted hardy green buds on some of the tree limbs. Spring was coming, and none too soon. Nature didn't care about the war. Seasons changed and the world went on, despite whatever else was happening. One day it would all be over and Wolf would go home. Until then, he would master the language and get by the best he could. He already had a schoolbook to practice with, handed down from a niece who lived on a farm outside the city. The book was meant to teach English to German students, but that didn't stop Wolf from pouring over the conjugation tables in the back, memorizing as many verbs as he could each day, along with tenses, prefixes, suffixes… Early on, he began to separate in his mind where one word ended and another began. Later, he was recognizing individual words and beginning to pick up on pieces of conversation. Lately, he was able to converse in basic German himself. Wolf looked forward to surprising his parents when he got back to Chicago. For the foreseeable future, however, Koenigsberg was his home.

Letting himself in his grandmother's front door, Wolf retreated to his room where he collapsed on his bed. His body ached from a long day on his feet. This was his mother's room once, long ago. Wolf wondered what her life had been like then. He peered at a framed photo perched on the desk. A teenage version of his mother gazed back, frozen in time. She and two girlfriends wore traditional dresses, along with bright smiles on their faces. His mother seemed on the verge of laughter. What was being said, at that moment, to bring her such joy? Whatever the words, they were now lost to the ages. A loud knock jolted Wolf back into the present. His grandmother stood at the threshold holding an envelope in one hand. "Für sie," she said. This was a surprise. He could tell right away that it wasn't the typical Gestapo postcard.

Wolf rose to meet his grandmother in the doorway. She was a slight woman, yet sinewy and strong. Upon his arrival, she'd met Wolf with a suspicion that never quite went away. She seemed unable to figure out what to make of him, this young American suddenly living under her roof. For Wolf's part, he found his grandmother to be equally puzzling. She led a lonely life, with her only daughter five thousand miles away in America, and her son and his family living outside the city and visiting only on occasion. All the same, Wolf could tell it was an adjustment for his grandma to have someone else living in the house after so many years alone. Surely she missed her husband, Wolf's deceased grandfather, though Wolf was no replacement. In the early days, he could hardly speak to her. After three months, they were now able to converse, though his grandmother was not the talkative type. Mostly, Wolfgang was left feeling that his presence was an imposition. Both of them were keenly aware that they had no other choice in the matter. "Danke." He took the envelope and examined the return address as his grandmother retreated. The letter was from Herbie. Wolf wasted no time in tearing it open and pulling out the hand-written pages. Any news from his only friend in Germany was more than welcomed. He read quickly through the text.

Greetings Wolf! I hope you're surviving there in Koenigsberg. Have you found some work? Is the Gestapo on your case? I better be careful, they'll probably read this. That's OK, though, I think I found a way for us to get back home. If you come to Stettin, I will tell you all about it. Come see me as soon as you can. Don't worry about the fare. If you can borrow the money, I will pay you back when you get here. The enclosed document is from the department of military intelligence. If anyone asks for your travel papers, just show this to them and it will be all right.

Your friend,

Herbie

A second page was printed on official government stationery. Wolfgang couldn't make out quite what it said, but he saw that it was signed by a man named Lieutenant Walter Kappe. Who was Walter Kappe? All of this intrigue filled Wolfgang with a deep curiosity, mixed equally with apprehension. Whatever this was about, though, any chance to see Herbie was one that Wolf couldn't pass up. Of course he would go, as soon as he was able.

Chapter Thirty

Berlin, April 2, 1942

"I don't get it. Is this a magazine or isn't it?" Wolf asked Herbie as they walked along a residential sidewalk in the heart of the city. Five-story apartment blocks lined each side of the narrow street.

"It is. Sort of."

"What do you mean, sort of?"

"I mean, yeah, it's a magazine, but they do more than that, too."

"Why all the hush-hush? This whole thing seems awfully shady if you ask me. How come you can't just tell me what the hell it's all about? What does this have to do with Chicago?"

"The lieutenant will explain it. I can't say any more than that. I signed a vow."

"What kind of vow?" Wolf's tone betrayed his disbelief.

"You'll see."

The pair crossed an intersection and continued up the block. "How did this guy find out about us, anyway?"

"Hans Sass."

"What about Hans Sass?"

"I don't know. The lieutenant met him somewhere. Look, you're just gonna have to trust me. You'll find out all about it from the lieutenant."

Ever since Wolf arrived in Stettin the day before, this was about all he'd been able to pry out of Herbie. He knew that this lieutenant contacted his friend three weeks beforehand, requesting an interview for some army publication. *Der Kaukasus* it was called. Herbie wanted to tell Wolf more about it, but he simply couldn't. Only Kappe could do that. Hence the quick trip back to Berlin. Very soon, the mystery would be revealed.

"This is the one." Herbie stepped up to the front of an unassuming apartment building and pressed the last button on a column of doorbells.

"Der Kaukasus!" came a young woman's voice.

"This is Herbert Haupt. I am here to see Lieutenant Kappe."

With a buzzing sound, the lock clicked open and the boys moved inside. "This is a magazine office?" Wolfgang mused as they began to climb the stairs, the smell of grilled sausages wafting through the halls.

It was only forty minutes later that the pair made their way back down the stairs and exited to the street. For Wolf, any semblance of hope was extinguished. Instead, he felt deflated, as though the untenable nature of their circumstances was just shoved in his face. The whole setup was preposterous, starting with this rosy-cheeked lieutenant's affable demeanor. His smile hid an insincerity that put Wolf on his guard from the very start. Wolfgang didn't trust this man. Blow up factories? In his own country? The FBI would be all over them. Wolf had seen the movies. He knew what those G-men were capable of. Hell, they'd gunned down Dillinger right there in Chicago! No, this wasn't for Wolf. He wanted no part of it. From the tension in the room, it was clear that this lieutenant wasn't keen on him either. When Kappe blithely mentioned the draft, Wolf felt particularly uneasy. Was that a threat? "Have you received any notification from the Army?" the lieutenant had asked. No, Wolf replied. He had not. Why would he? Wolf was an American citizen. What business would the German Army want with an American in their ranks? Kappe didn't answer this question, instead merely offering a sly smile.

"What did you think?" said Herbie as they moved up the sidewalk.

Wolfgang didn't know what to say. Frankly, Herbie's enthusiasm shocked him. How best to convey this sentiment without insulting his friend? "I don't think the lieutenant liked me very much," he said.

"What do you mean? He liked you just fine!"

"I'm not so sure. Besides, I don't know if this idea is for me."

"But come on! It's a surefire way to get back home! Don't you want to go home? You can't want to stay here?!"

"Of course I want to go home. Just not like this."

As the pair continued up the street, Herbie was disappointed. "Come on, we'll catch the train back to Stettin. You can stay with us tonight."

"Thanks."

"I thought you'd be more excited about this whole idea."

"I don't know… It all sounds a little crazy if you ask me."

Wrinkles formed on Herbie's forehead. "Who knows when another opportunity like this might come along? I'll tell you what, I just don't want to wait. I've had as much of this place as I can take."

"I can't argue with you there." When they got to the underground station, the boys headed down the stairs.

"Maybe we can look around Berlin a little. Before we catch the train." Wolf didn't want to talk about this stuff anymore. The whole idea disturbed him.

"Yeah, sure. We can look around." The boys each slid a token into a turnstile and then pushed their way through. "What should we see first?"

"How about the Brandenburg Gate? And maybe the Tiergarten, too."

They stopped to consult a transit map mounted on a wall. For the rest of the afternoon, all Wolf wanted was to have some fun with his old friend. He'd put the rest of this dismal business as far out of his mind as he could.

It was late at night as the two friends sat up in the kitchen back in Stettin, sharing a bottle of wine with bread and cheese. Once again, they talked about the plan, with Herbie describing how he would put one over on them all. "First, three weeks in this training program, and then it's right back to the United States. Home sweet home! I'll tell you, Wolf, I can't wait to get back. I've had enough of it over here. I just wish you'd come with me."

"But Herbie, you're not going to make it!" Wolfgang protested. "You go back like that and the G-men are going to get you and put your ass in jail!"

"No, no, no…" Herbie shook his head with a laugh. "I'm just going to disappear. You'll see. Nobody has to know how I got there." After refilling his glass, Herbie swallowed a gulp of wine. His eyes took on a distant cast, as though he'd drifted off to somewhere else entirely. Wolfgang watched in puzzlement as his friend processed the entirety of his predicament. All Herbie wanted, desperately and without condition, was to return to his family, his friends, and the mother of his child. The emotions swelled inside Herbie's chest, overwhelming him. Without warning, he placed his glass on the table and burst into tears, sobbing uncontrollably as Wolfgang shrank backward in shame. This was Herbie, the friend Wolf looked up to; older and mature. Here in this small kitchen, their roles reversed in an instant. Herbie leaned his head into his hands, tears streaming through his fingers, misery flowing from him in cascading waves. Slowly the sobs subsided with a last few spasms of grief, yet Herbie was still unable to raise his head. At this dark moment, neither friend could face the other.

"It's late," Wolf offered. "Maybe we should go to bed."

Eyes damp and bloodshot, cheeks flushing red, Herbie sat upright and corked the wine bottle without a word. Wolfgang wrapped the bread and cheese in paper before moving into the living room where a pair of blankets and an extra pillow were laid out on the couch. "Goodnight, Herbie." Wolf watched as his friend headed up the stairs, head hung low in defeat. When he was gone, Wolf dropped his pants and switched off the light before climbing under the blankets. Here in the dark, on this couch in Stettin, the future was entirely blank. They both knew the risks. Each was given a choice. In the morning, Wolfgang would catch a train back to Koenigsberg and their paths would diverge, perhaps for good this time. The lieutenant's mention of the draft still haunted Wolf, leaving him unable to banish this deeply disturbing prospect from his mind. With a little bit of luck, perhaps he could wait out the war as a baggage handler. Wolf would take his chances. He and Herbie had each made their decision. The outcome from this point on was not up to them. Their futures were held firmly in the hands of fate.

Chapter Thirty-One

Brandenburg an der Havel, April 12, 1942

Joseph Schmidt slung his duffel over one shoulder and boarded a streetcar. Taking a seat near the rear, he dropped the bag to the floor as the car eased forward toward Quenz Lake. Schmidt was skeptical of the whole project. He didn't much trust this flabby lieutenant, Walter Kappe. The man seemed incompetent, overcome by an inflated sense of self and an ideological fervor. Schmidt was a far more practical type of man, but any chance to get back out of Germany was worth investigating. He'd keep an open mind. For the time being, this "school for sabotage" might not be so bad. Three weeks with a roof over his head and three square meals per day sounded all right. Plus, it was hard to turn down the chance to spend some time playing with explosives. That part sounded like a whole lot of fun.

The streetcar moved through the outskirts of town, with Schmidt's fellow passengers disembarking a few at a time until he was the only one left on board. At the very last stop, he lifted his bag and climbed down the steps before ducking his head back inside and calling out to the driver. "Quenzsee?" he asked, unsure where exactly to find the lake.

The driver pointed down a small road. "Dieser weg."

"Danke." Schmidt adjusted his shoulder strap and began walking down a country lane hemmed in by forest on either side. When the road eased to the left, he saw the lake to his right, spread before him like an inland sea. Further on he came to a compound, hidden behind a tall fence topped with barbed wire. "This must be the place," he said to himself. When he found the front gate, two armed guards demanded to see his papers. Schmidt pulled the documents from his bag and handed them over. After a close examination, the guards waved him through.

Moving past the sentries, Schmidt couldn't help but scowl. He'd never cared much for authority. It was a way of life in Germany these days, a country that seemed addicted to the power of the uniform. Schmidt preferred the wilds of Canada and living by his wits. Well, you had to make do with the reality you faced, he thought. As he continued through the property, forestland gave way to tilled fields until eventually he came to a large, two-story farmhouse facing the lake, with a few outbuildings on one side and a large barn nearby. From a distance, he saw two men standing on the front porch of the house. As he drew nearer, Schmidt laughed. If it wasn't his old shipmate, Herbie Haupt himself. Kappe hadn't mentioned this detail. When Schmidt turned up the front path, young Herbie's face lit up in recognition.

"Schmidt!" Herbie exclaimed. "How'd they ever let a rogue like you in here?"

"Look who's talking, the skirt-chasing boy wonder from Chicago!" Schmidt climbed the steps, sizing up the third man with a critical eye. This fellow was tall and thin, with a slight stoop and a pronounced gray streak running through his hair.

"This is Dasch," Herbie introduced him. "George Dasch."

"How are you, George?" Schmidt reached out a hand.

"Very well, thank you!" Dasch flashed a smile as he pumped Schmidt's arm with a frenetic energy. "It's good to meet you. Why don't you come inside and we'll get you settled?"

"Lead the way."

The three men moved on into the farmhouse. While Schmidt was happy to see his young friend, he couldn't help but question the wisdom of including the kid on such a mission. This was serious business. Could the kid be trusted to keep his mouth shut? Or would he give the whole thing away, bragging about it to a couple of girls in a Chicago bar? This Dasch character didn't inspire much confidence either, from the looks of him. He wasn't the hardened type. You could see it in his eyes. Dasch was the sort who thought that book smarts were the measure of a man. He was soft, that much was clear. A man who belonged behind a desk, not on a secret mission in the field. His quick smile was a sure sign of insincerity. Schmidt was not enthused, but at least the farm was nice. Spending some time in this place wouldn't be bad. Whether he'd ultimately take part in this mission was another question entirely.

The full contingent gathered in the morning to begin their training. The classroom was located in one of the outbuildings, with a desk for each man, a podium in the front and a chalkboard hanging on the wall. Sitting in the back of the class, Schmidt sized up his fellow saboteurs. There was Herbie, who he already knew quite well. Then there was Dasch, whose ingratiating demeanor could only spell trouble. Burger was the quiet one, eyeing the others with suspicion. Neubauer, injured in the war, seemed eager to make a good impression. Kerling, the handsome one, was a die-hard supporter of the cause whose enthusiastic "Heil Hitler" salutes let everyone know it. As for the rest, Quirin, Heinck, and Thiel, there was nothing much to distinguish them. Working-class one and all, they would do as they were told. Recently returned from the Russian front, Ernst Zuber seemed in a constant fog, an enduring case of shell shock haunting his every thought. The last man, "Scottie," was small and wiry, with eyes that darted nervously to and fro. He was an incessant talker with a thick Scottish accent, constantly punching at the air as he discussed boxing and all of the fights he'd promoted in his day. All-in-all, Schmidt was none too impressed, yet a trip back to North America was at stake. How hard would it be for him to slip unnoticed back across the border into Canada and merely vanish? For the moment, he would keep an open mind.

When the door opened, Kappe strode into the room wearing his lieutenant's uniform, followed by a thin, weathered man in civilian clothes. The trainees fell silent, sitting up a bit straighter at their desks. "Good morning, gentlemen!" Kappe addressed them. The other man passed out notepads and pencils before taking his place beside the lieutenant at the lectern. "Welcome!" Kappe continued. "The mission we will prepare you to undertake is a dangerous one, but I cannot stress enough how important it is to the war effort. The Fuhrer himself is counting on each and every one of you." Kappe paused to eye each man for effect. "During your training, we will speak in English at all times. I want each of you to become re-accustomed to speaking in this language. That means no German from this moment on. Once the mission begins, you will be operating in two groups. Each group will be transported aboard a submarine to the United States where your primary task will be to cripple aluminum production. No aluminum means no airplanes. No American airplanes means we win the war. It is as simple as that. According to our experts, if the electrical power to an aluminum factory is cut off for as little as eight hours, the molten aluminum will harden inside the baths, completely destroying them. One bomb carefully set at the base of an electrical tower can render an entire plant useless for three months or more." Kappe peered around the room to let this information sink in. "Now, let me introduce one of your instructors, Doktor Konig!"

The man beside Kappe raised a hand in acknowledgment. "Good morning."

"Please open your notebooks," Kappe went on. "Doktor Konig will begin your first lesson on how to build a bomb."

Konig lifted a piece of chalk and began to draw a diagram on the board. "Our first incendiary device can be made from materials purchased at any neighborhood drug store."

Schmidt lifted his pencil to copy the diagram into his notepad. One never knew when the ability to make a bomb from household products might come in handy…

In the evening, the men's time was their own. A thirty-minute walk through the woods led to the nearest village pub. Once they'd settled in at a table near the back, the group ordered one round and then another, with Scottie chasing each beer with an additional glass of whiskey. Speaking to each other in English, the men drew quizzical looks from regular patrons. Most pretended not to notice. They'd learned not to ask questions. Just as they hadn't said anything when the village's Jewish residents were rounded up and loaded onto a train a few days before. No, the locals didn't question what was going on at the farm on the lake, formerly home to a longstanding Jewish family and from whence they now heard gunfire and explosions emanating at all hours of the day and night. These things were none of their business. Just as these newcomers gathered in their local pub, speaking the language of their enemies, was none of their business. In Germany, keeping one's head down was a means of survival. The trainees and the locals did their best to pretend each other did not exist. All except for Herbie. When two unaccompanied women entered the bar, his attention was drawn. The girls were a bit older, yet still attractive. One was tall and strong, with blue eyes and long blond hair weaved into a braid. The other was petite, with dark hair hanging loose over a white blouse. The pair ordered two small beers and shared a single cigarette, handing it back and forth as they lost themselves in conversation.

"Hey, Schmidt," Herbie said. "Look at those two."

"Settle down, Romeo."

"Aw, come on!" Herbie persisted. "Take your pick, I don't care. You can have the blondie if you want."

"Don't forget what we're on about here. Our training is strictly secret."

"So? We don't have to tell them nothing."

"Keep your seat," Schmidt growled. "This isn't the time."

Herbie's dejection showed "So when *is* the time?"

"Don't worry, my young friend, we'll get you a woman. But not tonight."

Herbie lifted his beer and drank half the glass. The one thing he wanted more than anything else was to be home. Chicago called out to him. His old life, his family and friends, Gerda. Just a few more weeks and he would be off to America. All he had to do was get through this training, land on a beach somewhere and then steal away from his group. He could do this. Yet for the present, loneliness filled his heart. It was the loneliness that a woman might cure, if only temporarily. Instead of pursuing it, however, he nodded to Schmidt. "Fine then, not tonight."

Chapter Thirty-Two

Koenigsberg, April 13, 1942

Standing beside an accommodating clerk inside the railway station, Wolfgang waited while she read a letter he'd received in the mail. Unable to entirely decipher it himself, he'd asked her to translate it for him. Wolf already suspected the worst, yet when the clerk read the text word for word, his heart still sank. "Wolfgang Wergin, you are hereby notified that you are called to duty in defense of the Deutsches Reich. Report to the main railway station, Koenigsberg, at 08:00, 23 of April, for transport to training camp, Sixteenth Army of the Wehrmacht. You are allowed one bag with civilian clothing for three (3) days. Heil Hitler!" And just like that, the trajectory of his life shifted once more. Wolf would not spend the war lugging bags for passengers in this out-of-the-way Baltic station. He would be right in the thick of it, fighting for a country he'd hardly known firsthand, in an army whose language he was still learning to speak. Maybe Wolf was born here in Germany, but he was an American through and through. Baseball, apple pie, and the sounds of Glenn Miller. That's what he'd grown up with. If this war dragged on long enough, he might even face his old schoolmates across the front lines. For the time being that wasn't a concern, Wolfgang realized. He was headed straight for the Russian front, to bleed and perhaps even die for a cause he felt little connection to.

Less than two weeks later, Wolf stood on the platform, this time with his grandmother by his side. He glanced around with curiosity at his fellow inductees. Most were about his age, just out of high school, or perhaps even a bit younger. A few were athletic, though others small and thin. Some had yet to work off a layer of baby fat. Adolescents are what they were, not really men at all. Most had parents along to see them off, and younger siblings bounding with energy along the platform. Some would never return. Which among them were saying farewell for the very last time? Wolfgang himself? He turned to his grandmother. Despite the gravity of the situation, he imagined that she must be relieved on some level. Taking care of him these past months wasn't easy on her. Perhaps this was for the best. He tried to convince himself as the recruits began boarding the train. "Goodbye." He gave his grandmother a warm embrace. Wolf was surprised when his grandmother used her sleeve to dab at tears running down her cheek.

"Du bist ein gutter junge, Wolfgang," she said. *You are a good boy.*

"Dankeshoen. For everything."

"Auf wiedersehen, mein enkel."

The two stood staring at one another. Wolf hesitated before lifting his bag. He wasn't sure what else to say, or even how to say it. His grandmother was distressed by his departure. Perhaps Wolf hadn't understood the situation as well as he'd thought. Only now did he realize how much he'd eased her loneliness. His grandmother had a sharp personality, there was no denying it, yet that didn't mean she wasn't grateful for his company. Or was she just afraid that he might never return? The time for coming to any sort of better understanding was behind them. Instead, Wolf leaned close and kissed her damp cheek. He hoisted the strap to his duffel over one shoulder and moved across the platform, up the steps and into the nearest carriage. When he'd found a seat, he stuffed his bag in an overhead rack. The car overflowed with nervous energy as recruits waved to families out the window or sat chattering to each other in German. Never before had Wolf felt so out of place. What would they think when they found out he was American? A sworn enemy?

"Ich habe lange auf diesen tag gewartet!" the boy beside him said with glee. He was one of the skinny ones, barely old enough to be considered a soldier.

Wolfgang nodded, translating the words as best he could in his mind. *I've been waiting a long time for this day.*

"Endlich können wir uns auf den Kampf einlassen!"

"Ja," said Wolf. "Endlich können wir kämpfen."

The boy's face dropped. His glee was replaced with incredulity as he processed the accent. "You are English?!"

"No." Wolfgang looked around uneasily as the train lurched forward. "German. But I grew up in America."

The boy laughed in disbelief. "America! But you fight for Germany?!"

"Yes."

The boy thought this over and then offered a hand. "Otto. Otto Schreiber."

"Wolf Wergin."

"Welcome to the sixteenth army."

Out the window, Wolf caught a last glimpse of his grandmother standing alone at the back of the platform, one hand in the air. He raised his own in return as the train eased out of the station. He'd come an awfully long way from the quiet house on South Wood Street, Chicago, Illinois. He wondered if he'd ever see that place again. Wolf didn't have the luxury of saying farewell to his parents as he headed off to war. They had no idea what had even become of him. As far as his mom and dad knew, their son went to Mexico for a two-week vacation and simply never came home. There was a postcard he'd sent from Japan, but after that, complete silence. His heart yearned to contact them, to let them know that he was still all right. He *had* been able to get a letter off to Herbie in Stettin, just a few days beforehand, but there was no knowing if his friend would even receive it. Maybe if Herbie did get back to America, he could convey this news to Wolf's parents. Herbie, who was bound to end up in a federal prison if he made it that far. In hindsight, however, perhaps Herbie's *was* the better way. Just go home and disappear. Maybe the FBI would never catch on after all. As for Wolf, he'd do his best to survive, both the war and the deep homesickness that descended upon him like a fog. One day at a time, for as long as those days lasted. That was all he could do.

Chapter Thirty-Three

Quenz Lake, April 24, 1942

With less than one week to go in their training, Edward Kerling was not happy. He'd learned valuable lessons about building bombs and setting fuses. He knew how to blow up a rail line and take down a bridge. Kerling was eager to set about these tasks as soon as possible. The problem, as he saw it, lay with his collaborators. First there was his old friend Hermann, who still had metal shards lodged in his head. What if they led to medical complications? If Hermann went to an American hospital, he could never explain where this embedded Russian shrapnel came from. Then there was the Haupt kid, who cared about nothing but girls and money. And Burger, who'd previously been locked up in a concentration camp. How could *his* loyalty be trusted? Zuber and Scottie were another story entirely. The pair didn't have more than half a brain between them. Scottie was drunk whenever he could manage it. Zuber left his cognitive abilities behind somewhere on the front, if he'd ever had any to begin with. Not only could he barely speak English, he didn't even communicate in German very well. Perhaps worst of all was Dasch, who never shut up. Besides that, he paid almost no attention in their training courses. When tested, Dasch failed time and again, unable to remember how to assemble an explosive device, or set a fuse, or even follow through on a simple task, like sending a message with invisible ink. Worse yet, he was excruciatingly smug. When the group snapped to attention with a Heil Hitler salute, Dasch shoved his hands into his pockets, a sly smile on his lips. Could Kappe see none of this? Kerling worried that Dasch might actively betray the entire mission. Maybe it wasn't too late to have some of these men removed. It was the reason Eddie sat facing the lieutenant in this empty classroom, doing the best he could to make his case about each of them. As Kappe listened to these concerns, the veins on his forehead throbbed.

"I see your point about Scottie and Ernst," Kappe admitted. "I've had my doubts about those two. I am willing to send them packing, but as for the rest, I believe you've misjudged them."

"But Dasch?!" Kerling complained. "He hasn't learned a thing the entire time he's been here! It's as though he couldn't be bothered!"

"Yes, I did notice. George and I have discussed this. He assures me that he is enthusiastic, but he's not a nuts and bolts type of man. He's leaving that to the others. Dasch's role is as a leader. Don't underestimate his knowledge of America. He was there for twenty years. That is a long time."

"We all lived in America, Lieutenant."

"And while you were there, how many baseball games did you attend? What do you know about baseball at all? Anything?"

Kerling's shoulders dropped. "I'm not interested in baseball."

"No, but Dasch is. He knows everything there is to know about it. Other than Haupt, none of the men can pass themselves off as American better than George."

"Who's to say he doesn't consider himself one?"

This prospect gave Kappe pause, yet he pushed any doubts aside, preferring to believe in the loyalty of his man. "Leave these decisions to me. I trust George. He came back to his fatherland in time of need to support the war effort. He's going to get that chance. George is a good man, you'll see."

Kerling was not convinced, yet his worries were falling on deaf ears. The only remaining option was to take matters into his own hands, literally if necessary. He licked his lips slowly before broaching the possibility. "Fine," he conceded. "Dasch stays, but if I find evidence that he is not with us, do I have the authority to rectify the situation, by force if necessary?"

The question came as a surprise to Kappe. One group leader asking if he could eliminate the other? It was unexpected, but if circumstances required it, then Kappe would offer no objection. "Certainly," he assured Kerling. "You must do everything you can to assure the success of the mission."

The answer was enough to satisfy Kerling, to some degree. He'd successfully lobbied for the removal of Scottie and Zuber. He had permission to remove Dasch on his own if he had to. Kerling's heart beat faster as he imagined using lethal force. He must do whatever it took to bring glory to the Reich, and to save his own hide at the same time.

Chapter Thirty-Four

Quenz Lake, April 29, 1942

For their final exam, the men were divided into pairs. Herbie was partnered with Eddie Kerling. Neither was thrilled with the matchup. Something about the way Kerling looked at him made Herbie always feel that he was being judged. Nothing Herbie did seemed good enough for Eddie, who complained about both his attitude and his aptitude. Herbie sometimes tried to lighten the mood with a joke, yet to Kerling there was no room in their training for humor. Sure, Herbie knew this was serious business, but he wished that Kerling would ease up a little.

For their assignment, the two men were tasked with entering a guarded stone cottage on the far side of the farm and setting off a small incendiary device. Others had similar orders. Dasch and Quirin were to set a similar device in another building, designated as a "factory." Schmidt and Burger had to sneak into a cellar to take out a make-believe oil refinery. Others were set to destroy rail lines. Each pair had twenty-four hours to complete their assignment without being caught.

Assembling their device in the laboratory, Kerling was intent as he dampened sawdust and mixed it with saltpeter in a jar. For a fuse he combined three-parts potassium chloride and one-part powdered sugar, layering it on top.

"How do we ignite it?" Herbie asked.

"Didn't you learn a thing?" Kerling sneered.

"Sure," Herbie recoiled. "I just can't remember, exactly."

"Sulfuric acid." Kerling held up a small bottle. "One drop of this stuff and 'poof!'"

"Oh, right."

Whatever annoyance Kerling may have felt was replaced by his pride in the small incendiary device he'd created. Now they just had to find a way to sneak inside the building, past instructors posing as security. "The guards have to stay up all night. I say we get some sleep and make a run at it later on. Right about the time they're nodding off themselves."

"Sounds good to me."

"I will wake you at 04:30."

"I still don't see how we're supposed to get in there…"

"Maybe we can create a distraction."

"Or catch them sleeping."

"If we're lucky."

"I'll see you in the morning." Herbie left the laboratory and made his way to his bunk room. A few of the other men were already in bed, apparently with the same plan as Kerling for an early-hours raid. Others were off scoping out their assignments, or perhaps trying to complete their tasks before bed. As he pulled down his bed covers, Herbie heard a small blast, followed by what sounded like firecrackers and then shouting. Apparently, things had gone wrong for some of his colleagues. Not that it mattered. After all that they had been through so far, Herbie couldn't imagine being cut loose. The groups were set. Nine men divided into two subs, heading back to America. Herbie was ready to get going already. He'd had enough of this place and all of the rules and the endless Heil Hitler salutes. Everybody here seemed to have something to prove, each man constantly showing his loyalty to the cause. It was the same all across Germany. Display your fealty to the regime, or… Or what? Or the Gestapo might follow you around all day. They might cart you off to a concentration camp as they had with Herbie's uncle. Or Burger. They might have done so with Herbie, too, if he'd refused to take part in this mission. Well, if things went according to Herbie's plan, the last laugh would be his. They were giving him exactly what he wanted most. A one-way ticket home.

Herbie climbed into bed and pictured that journey home. He imagined himself aboard an actual submarine, plying the ocean depths. He'd only ever seen a sub in the movies, firing torpedoes at an enemy ship, or being blasted from above by depth charges. It felt to Herbie like he was living in a movie himself. What a story he would have to tell when it was all over. As he pictured himself rowing ashore on an American beach, sleep slowly overtook him.

When Eddie shook his shoulder in the predawn hours, Herbie's eyes sprang open. "What?!"

"Come on, let's go."

Herbie sat up, still fully clothed. "OK, I'm ready." He slipped on his shoes and the two of them crept out of the bunkhouse before snaking through the compound by the light of the moon. Approaching their target, they ducked behind a row of bushes to observe.

"Do you see anyone?" Herbie whispered.

"No."

"We should check the other side."

"Right."

Walking in a wide perimeter, they circled the entire building. No guards were in sight.

"They could be sleeping." Herbie had a hopeful tone.

"I wouldn't count on it." Together, the two men slunk silently toward the cottage, the incendiary device and small bottle of acid in Kerling's hands. There were two options for entry; a front door or a window. Both were closed.

"How do we get in?" Herbie whispered.

"Shhh…" Kerling tried the door handle. It was unlocked. He pushed slowly. "Keep an eye out!" he hissed.

Herbie turned to look behind. The next moments were a frenzied blur of noise and motion. A blinding flash of light accompanied the concussion of a small explosion. Disoriented, Herbie didn't know where the "guards" came from, except that the shadowy figures were there, tossing a handful of firecrackers that snapped and popped at his feet as he hopped and skipped in the air.

"Nice job. You're dead," said a guard.

"Scheisse!" Kerling's frustration boiled over.

"English, my man!" said the other guard. "Speak English!"

"Why should I?" said Kerling. "I'm already dead."

"Go back to your barracks. Your final exam is complete."

Retracing their steps, the tension between Herbie and Kerling was palpable. "That didn't go so well," said Herbie.

"Shut up, Haupt." Eddie clutched his unused device.

"I'm just saying… Maybe we should have tried the window."

"They saw us the whole time." Eddie glared at Herbie in the dim glow of the moon.

"Hey, it wasn't my fault!"

When they'd returned to the bunkhouse, the two separated without another word. Herbie entered the room he shared with three others. One man was still out slinking around the property. Two other shapes reclined in their beds. "How did it go?" Schmidt asked as Herbie stripped off his clothing.

"Not so good."

Schmidt laughed. "They caught you, huh?"

"How about you?"

"At least we set off our device first. They got us on the way out."

"We didn't even get a foot in the door. It was over before it started."

"Relax," Schmidt tried to ease Herbie's anxiety. "They wanted to put us under some pressure, that's all. To see how we'd react. I don't think they expected any of us to get away with it. Not with the guards watching the whole time. It will be easier once we get to the states. How many guards will be watching an electrical tower, or a rail line? Compared to this, it'll be a piece of cake."

"Yeah." Herbie slid into his bed. "A piece of cake." The prospect of actually blowing up an electrical tower filled him with dread. He had no intention of doing so, but what if the others followed through? Wolf's warnings about the FBI echoed through his mind. In just a few short weeks Herbie and the others would depart. He remembered Kappe's veiled threat, to keep his uncle locked up in the concentration camp indefinitely if Herbie didn't go along with the plan. Yet, once he got home, how would Kappe even know what he was up to? "Good night, Schmidt," Herbie said. His friend answered with a muffled snore. Schmidt, who always seemed to have everything figured out. It did offer Herbie some comfort to have the big guy along. Schmidt was smart. If the FBI was on to them, he would know what to do. Herbie rolled over and closed his eyes, trying to rest before they roused him again in another hour.

Chapter Thirty-Five

Berlin, May 2, 1942

The gray light of a new dawn crept around the edges of the bedroom curtains, casting a pale glow on a sleeping Bettina Burger. Peter watched her chest slowly rise and fall beneath the covers beside him. It was almost as though he were dreaming. Over the past two years, he had longed for just one moment alone together, nearly giving up hope that this wish would ever be fulfilled. Yet here they were. With one finger, Peter eased a lock of her dark hair from in front of her eyes. Bettina murmured softly and rolled to one side. Draping an arm across his wife's warm body, Peter snuggled close, inhaling her sweet scent. If only this moment could last forever, he thought. Instead, he would store the memory away, to sustain him in times of loneliness. After this two-week furlough, Bettina assumed he was heading to Russia like so many other German soldiers. He was forbidden from divulging the truth. Yet still, she deserved that much. After everything they'd been through, their only real loyalty was to each other.

When Bettina stirred, Peter propped himself up on one arm. His sleepy wife opened her eyes. "Guten morgen." A dreamy smile crossed her face.

"Guten morgen mein lieber." Peter slid his body on top of hers under the sheets and gently kissed her lips.

"Not wasting any of our precious time?"

"No. Not a moment." Gazing at each other, what Peter saw on her face was… contentment. A small upturn on the corners of her mouth. A light in her eyes. A calmness in demeanor so absent these past few years. Peter felt it as well. He didn't want to think about the future. He didn't want to think about the past. All that mattered was right here, at this very moment in time. For these precious few days, they were free. Nobody could take that away. Peter and Bettina had their whole lives to live over the next week and a half. After that, there were no guarantees.

Bettina ran both hands down Peter's back before grasping firmly at his buttocks. "Hallo liebes..."

Peter laughed. "Hallo an euch."

Preparing his breakfast, Bettina was filled with a joy that had proven so elusive for so long. Happiness swelled within her heart as she gathered together what ingredients she could manage. These days, they were harder and harder to come by. No eggs, nor sausage. They'd make do with toasted black bread, sliced tomato, cucumber, and a bit of cheese, plus some coffee she'd managed to save. It was enough. This would be their last breakfast together in the apartment. They didn't regret giving it up. Bettina would be better off with his parents, in Bavaria. The war was more distant there. Food was easier to come by in Wurzburg and at least she'd be looked after. When the war ended, Peter would join her there. That was the dream they both clung to. Not a brief furlough with the end of the world hanging over them, but an actual future. Peter lifted his coffee cup and blew across the top. For the next twelve days, the present was all that mattered.

"It's a little bit weak, I'm sorry," said Bettina. "It was the best I could do."

"I'm sure it's perfect." Peter took a sip. "Thank you."

Bettina blushed lightly. "You're welcome."

"Are you sorry to leave Berlin?"

"No. Not one bit."

"My parents are thrilled to have you."

"I appreciate your saying so."

"But it's true. It was my mother who suggested it."

"That was very kind of her. It is kind of them both."

"I never want you to feel as though you are a burden to them. That is the furthest thing from the truth."

Bettina swallowed hard, trying to keep her tears from flowing. She was grateful to have a place to go. If she couldn't be with Peter, at least living with his parents would provide some connection to him.

"There's something else I want to tell you." Peter sat up straight in his chair.

"Yes?"

"I'm not going to Russia. I'm going to America."

Silence hung over the table as Bettina let this information settle in. "What will you do there?"

Peter looked down at his hands. "I can't tell you that. I'm not supposed to tell you anything at all but I thought you should know. Please don't repeat it. Not to anybody, not even my parents."

"You won't be fighting, then?" Bettina sounded hopeful.

"Not exactly."

"What does that mean? You will be a spy? Is that it?"

"I can't say any more."

"You can't, or you don't want to?"

"Both."

Bettina saw that this line of questioning was leading her nowhere. "Will I be able to write to you?"

"You can send letters through a Lieutenant Kappe in Berlin. I'll give you his address. I can't promise that I will receive them, but I hope that you will try. Just know that every word will be read by others, possibly on both sides. You must be discreet."

"Of course."

"I will try to write to you if I can." Peter considered his options. Could they communicate indirectly somehow, through an intermediary? But how to trust such a person? "I'll give you a password," he offered. "If anybody should come to you with this word, know that you can trust them and do whatever they ask."

"This all sounds very mysterious. What's the word?"

"How about… spaetzle?" If a stranger approaches and tells you *spaetzle*, then you will know the message comes from me." Peter stood from the table and went into the bathroom. He opened a medicine cabinet above the sink and rummaged through until he found a box of laxatives and a bottle of aspirin. He brought these to the table and then found a box of toothpicks in the kitchen, along with a small glass of water. Lastly, he opened a drawer in his desk and retrieved a blank piece of paper. Clearing the breakfast dishes aside, he retook his seat. "I'm going to show you a simple method for writing with invisible ink."

"Is this what they've been teaching you these past three weeks?"

"In part."

"I see. Go ahead, then." Maybe Peter hadn't told her everything, but Bettina could put it together. This was a mission that put his life in grave danger, should he be found out.

Peter opened the box of laxatives. "First you take a tablet," he explained, "and break it up into a powder."

Bettina watched with rapt attention, ready to commit the process to memory and beginning to feel a bit like a secret agent herself.

Chapter Thirty-Six

Baltic Coast, May 14, 1942

Hermann Neubauer sat outside with his wife Alma on a warm spring afternoon, sipping lemonade from blue glasses. Behind the pair was his aunt's small farmhouse. Stretching before them, the wide expanse of the Baltic Sea. It was almost pleasant. If only the circumstances were different. If this had been her family's holiday home near the shores of Lake Michigan, for instance… Instead, a near-constant tension existed between them, derived in equal measure from Hermann's impending departure and from the shrapnel-induced headaches that still plagued him. "We will travel to Berlin in the morning," he said. "I must meet some members of my company before I report for duty, to make arrangements for our journey."

"Are you sure that you want me to come?"

"Of course!" Hermann looked at her accusingly. "Why wouldn't I?"

"I don't know, Hermann. I just don't know."

As far as Alma knew, Hermann was headed back to the Russian front, leaving her alone with the fear and uncertainty that he might never return. The last time he'd only been injured. This time, who knew? He yearned to tell her the truth. Instead, Hermann lowered his head into his hands, wishing that the throbbing pain would somehow go away.

Arriving in Berlin the following evening, Hermann and Alma checked into a hotel. "We'll meet my friends at a tavern not far away," he explained as Alma laid a dress across their bed, doing her best to smooth out the wrinkles. She remembered buying this dress, linen with a pink flower print, at a shop in Chicago one summer day a few years past. It was one of her favorites, more appropriate for a balmy evening outdoors than a smoky Berlin pub. Alma did not want to go to this meeting. She wished they could do something else… anything but spend time with the men who would be taking him from her.

"Eddie will be there," Hermann took on a hopeful air.

"Kerling?" Alma was surprised. "Isn't he working for the Propaganda Ministry?"

"Not anymore."

"Will you be in the same unit?"

"Yes." Hermann cleared his throat and looked away.

"Does Marie know?"

"No. How would she?"

"Maybe it's better that she doesn't. She'd be so worried."

The comment hung in the air. Hermann could have told his wife not to worry, but what was the point? Maybe he wasn't going to Russia, but his mission was likely just as dangerous. Hermann was a soldier, following the orders he was given. Eddie, too. "Come on, let's get dressed, we're going to be late," he said.

Alma stripped down to her undergarments and then lifted the dress over her head. Hermann stepped close and fastened the back. One more night together. Perhaps their last, they both seemed to realize. Alma would try to make a good impression on the other soldiers, smiling at the right times, not saying too much. At least she could talk to Eddie, she thought, reminiscing about their times together in America. The prospect gave her little comfort.

Sitting at a table with his fellow saboteurs, Herbie Haupt peered around the dingy pub. He was unimpressed. The place was nearly deserted. No women at all, unless you counted the middle-aged waitress or the flashy redhead accompanying Lieutenant Kappe. Haupt had never seen the lieutenant so happy. This mission, his little pet project, was finally coming to fruition. The very next day they would take the train to Paris. From there it was on to Lorient, where the two groups would board submarines bound for the U.S.A. Everything was coming together. Last to arrive at the pub was Neubauer, who appeared in the doorway wearing a loose gray suit with his hat pulled low. He looked like a gangster, Herbie thought. Just the type to raise suspicions… At his side was a dark-haired girl in a flower-print dress. When they'd approached the table, Neubauer removed his hat before putting one arm around the girl.

"Ah, here he is!" Kappe stood and clicked his heels together, throwing an arm in the air. The rest of the men followed suit with Herbie scrambling to catch up, never quite used to these formalities.

"Heil Hitler!" the men said in unison.

"Heil Hitler," Neubauer responded. "This is my wife, Alma," he added as the men retook their seats.

Eddie Kerling made room for them at the end of the table. "Hello, Alma, it's good to see you."

"You, too." Alma took a seat on the bench.

"Hi, Eddie." Neubauer slid in alongside his wife.

"Somebody bring them a beer!" Kappe flagged down the serving woman.

Looking from one member of the group to another, Herbie saw that only the lieutenant and his lady friend had smiles on their faces. Unless one counted the usual smirk from George Dasch. As for the rest, it was as though a deep depression had settled over them. How could the lieutenant not see it? Was he so distracted by his mistress' sweet perfume? These men didn't like each other, Herbie understood. Just the day before, Schmidt confided his deep animosity toward Dasch. "I'll strangle that son-of-a-bitch with my own two hands if I so much as suspect he isn't with us," Schmidt had promised. Now Herbie peered across the table at the obsequious Dasch, eyeing that same vulnerable neck in question. And what would Schmidt think of Herbie's uncertainties? Would he strangle Herbie, too?

The server placed two more beers on the table.

"I would like to propose a toast!" said Kappe. "To Operation Pastorius!"

"Operation Pastorius," the men lifted their glasses and then took a drink.

Alma turned to Hermann with a quizzical expression. Her husband merely shook his head, signaling her to remain silent.

"I have every confidence in your great success!" Kappe continued.

"As do we, lieutenant!" said Dasch. "As do we! Thanks in no small part to your extraordinary leadership!"

Kappe held one hand in the air and shook his head in a gesture of humility, though it was clear that the words had worked their magic. The sly grin remained plastered on Kappe's face as he canoodled with this mistress young enough to be his daughter. Just one more day, Herbie thought, and the final leg of his circumnavigation would commence. One more night in Berlin and he would be heading home at last.

When Hermann's second beer was nearly empty, he lifted the glass and quickly downed the rest. "I'm sorry but we should be going," he announced.

From his place at the end of the table, Kappe's face dropped. "But tonight we celebrate!"

"Yes, lieutenant, of course." Hermann turned a desperate eye toward Alma.

"You must understand," she said to Kappe. "A soldier's last night with his wife…"

"Ah, yes. I do understand." Kappe gave a conspiratorial wink. "Thank you, fraulein, for joining us tonight."

"It was our pleasure."

Hermann quickly stood and snapped a Heil Hitler salute. The others responded in kind and then sat back down. Neubauer offered a hand to Alma, who grasped his fingers and rose.

"I'll walk you out," Kerling offered. The threesome moved across the room. Reaching the doorway, Eddie seemed reluctant to let them go. "You know we'll be leaving for Russia soon," he said to Alma.

"Yes. Hermann told me. I'm just glad he'll have you along this time. Maybe you can look after him."

"I'll do my best." Kerling wrapped his arms around Alma for one last hug. "Take care of yourself." He paused for a moment, as though trying to convey some unspoken message.

"What is it, Eddie?"

"Nothing… It was swell to see you. Good night to you both." Kerling moved back to the table, head down, shoulders slumped.

Alma followed her husband out onto the sidewalk. Side-by-side, they walked back to their hotel through eerily quiet wartime streets, Alma's mind churning with regret. She remembered that day, five years before, when she'd stood at the altar with Hermann by her side,

Eddie and his wife Marie just a few steps away. Alma was so happy then. The future so bright. She and Hermann were in love. They would make a beautiful life for themselves. They never should have left the safe confines of America. What was Hermann thinking? Of course, he never would have come to Germany if not for Eddie's encouragement. First, there was the asinine plan to buy a boat, the *Lekala*, and sail back by themselves. When the Coast Guard turned them around off Long Island, Alma was naïve enough to think that might be the end of it. Then Hermann insisted they embark on a ship bound for Lisbon. She'd tried to talk him out of it. If only she'd been more persistent. Her frustration built inside with each step, anger rising as she focused the blame on her husband. *It was a new Germany*, he'd said. *I want to be a part of it*. Well, he was part of it all right, subsumed into the madness of war. Alma was a part of it too. She'd done as he asked and in return they were paying the price, the both of them.

As they entered the small lobby of their hotel, a sallow-faced woman sat listening to a radio behind the front desk. Seeing the young couple approach, she lifted their key from a series of boxes and slid it across the counter.

"Dankeshoen," said Hermann. The woman didn't answer, immersed as she was in the latest news reports. The Neubauers made their way up two flights of stairs in a musty, carpeted stairwell, inhaling the pungent odors of cigarettes and mold. Moving down the hallway, Alma's rage simmered until they entered their room and locked the door behind them. "We never should have come here!" Her pain and sorrow burst forth in a stream. "How many times have I had to tell you? We never should have left America! Why didn't you listen to me?!" Alma threw her purse onto the bed and then turned to face him, her cheeks flaring. "They treat me like a criminal here! The police always following me around... *Why don't you work? Why don't you have a baby???*" Alma seethed with resentment. "How could you have ever thought this was going to be a good idea, Hermann?! A new Germany? Ha! What has this new Germany done for you? For either one of us? I can't take it anymore! I just can't! Every single day I wake up wishing it was all just some terrible dream, but it's not. This nightmare is real and there's nothing I can do about it! I just want it to be over!" Alma's voice trailed off, a few lonely tears cascading down her cheeks.

"What do you expect of me?!" Hermann sputtered in his own defense. "I'm a German. I did what any good German must do! Surely you can understand that. Your own family, after all…"

"No, Hermann. I don't understand. We had a good life! Why give it up? Why drag us into this war? I'm an American, Hermann. So what if my parents were born here? Do you have any idea what it is like for me? All day long, I sit around just waiting to hear the news that you've been killed. The anxiety, Hermann… Do you have any idea?"

Hermann stood stock-straight, chin jutting forward. "I am a soldier, Alma. Can't you understand? This is my duty."

"Your duty…" Alma repeated the words in disbelief.

"Would you rather be married to a coward?"

"Yes, Hermann. Yes. I would prefer that."

Hermann's posture dropped, the fight draining from him. "I can't apologize. I won't." The couple stood a few feet apart, their last night together, perhaps forever. After everything that they'd been through, this reality heavily hung over them both. "Don't be angry with me. Please. I don't want to fight."

Slowly, husband and wife came together until Hermann held her in his arms. As the sobs began, Alma buried her face in his shoulder, losing herself to the deep well of emotions. He wasn't perfect, but she loved him.

Chapter Thirty-Seven

Paris, May 24, 1942

The river blazed in a riot of pink and white, spring blossoms bursting from the limbs of chestnut trees lining both banks. Delicate petals drifted downward like a soft rain, covering the pathway as Herbie Haupt strolled with a petit mademoiselle under his arm. For the first time in as long as he could remember, Herbie felt happy. This was the adventure he'd longed for. Paris, the Seine, love… or at least what might pass for it in a pinch. His companion clung to his waist as they went. In his left hand, Herbie held a half-empty bottle of red wine. He paused long enough to take a long drink, then offered some to the girl who finished it off before hurling the bottle into the river. "Finit!" she shouted.

"That's right," Herbie replied. *Finished.* He could nearly say the same of his travels. The following morning, he would board a train for the submarine base at Lorient and then, barring any last-minute complications, he and the other men would be on their way. Finally, Herbie would be able to put the whole big mess behind him. Until then, he had the girl's attentions to take his mind off any lingering unpleasantness.

Arriving at his hotel, Herbie spirited his companion up the stairs and into his room. These French girls were easy, he thought. It hadn't taken much to lure her away from the bar where they'd met, just that afternoon. Maybe it was the wine, or the fact that he was an American. As far as Herbie could tell, he must have been about the only Yank in Paris. Perhaps she was lonely. Whatever her reasons, he didn't much care. As soon as the door closed, the girl was on him, peeling off his cardigan and dropping it to the floor before unbuttoning his shirt. "You don't waste any time, huh?" Herbie leaned in to kiss her as she grasped at his belt buckle, fumbling to unlatch it. When she'd yanked down his pants, the girl pushed Herbie backward onto the bed. He kicked off his shoes and watched quietly as she disrobed. The girl was thin, with ribs showing through pale skin. Her hair was strawberry blond, hanging down just below her shoulders. She was no great beauty, though her face was pleasant enough. Long nose, slightly irregular. Bright red lipstick. Perhaps a bit severe overall, though not that it mattered much. How long it had been since Herbie felt the touch of a woman. His whole body tingled in anticipation, craving her flesh against his own. When she'd removed her bra and slid out of her panties, the girl gave Herbie a quick smile before falling onto the bed and sidling up beside him. Herbie felt her soft breasts against his chest. He rolled over on top of her, kissing her once more. Yes, it had been far too long.

"Vous fils de pute, tu me dois 800 francs! Donne moi mon argent!" the girl screamed at Herbie as they stood in the hallway outside his door. Any tenderness in her gaze was long gone, replaced by a seething hatred. She wore only underwear as she pounded him on the chest, punched him in the arm, and then slapped at his face. Herbie pushed her back.

"Get the hell away from me! I don't even understand you! Speak English!"

This time the girl kept her distance but the verbal assault continued. "Vous Allemands trou du cul que vous pouvez venir ici et tout simplement profiter de nous pauvres petites filles françaises! Est-ce correct? Nous sommes juste le butin de guerre?!"

Schmidt and Quirin emerged from the stairwell to find themselves witness to the escalating dispute. "What have we here?" A smirk crossed Schmidt's face. "A little disagreement?"

"She keeps talking about 800 francs," Herbie complained. "I don't have 800 francs!"

"Did you partake of her services?"

"It wasn't like that! We met in a bar."

Schmidt eyed the girl, red-faced, with fists clenched. "I'm afraid it was like that, my friend. Just give her what you have and get rid of her."

Herbie's shoulders slumped in defeat. "I spent all of my money already."

"For Christ sakes, it's forty Reichsmarks. You don't even have that?" Schmidt took out his wallet and extracted some bills before shoving them into the girl's hand. After examining them carefully, she stalked back into the room to retrieve her clothing, chin held high. When she was dressed, she shoved the money into a pocket, hurried past the men as quickly as she could, and then disappeared down the stairs.

"You thought she merely fell for your charms?" Schmidt laughed.

Herbie shrugged. "Why not? It's not like it hasn't happened before."

"Let me give you a piece of advice. Every girl in France is a whore these days. Nothing is free. Especially when it comes to Germans. To her, we are a means to survival, that's all."

"All right, all right. I heard you."

"I've got forty Reichsmarks," a hopeful Quirin peered down the stairs after her.

"I think you missed your chance," said Schmidt.

"You guys want to get another drink somewhere?" said Herbie.

"No thanks," answered Quirin. "I'm going to relax a while."

Schmidt looked to Herbie. "On my dough, of course."

Herbie shrugged. "I'll cover it next time."

"Come on. We'll get some wine and sit by the river."

"Sure." Herbie perked up. He could use the wine and the company both.

It wasn't hard to find an open shop. They were still plentiful, even if the merchandise inside of them was not. Walking in the door, Herbie saw rows of nearly bare shelves. A few bags of rice, dried noodles, bread… The French always had their baguettes, poking up out of round wicker baskets near the register. They also had wine. Schmidt browsed the musty bottles before lifting one, more or less at random, and placing it on the counter. "Combien?"

The proprietor was a man in his late sixties, with what seemed to be a perpetual scowl on his aged face. His pate was bald, with gray hair at the sides. His glare showed no soft spot for the country's German guests. He probably fought in the last war, Herbie thought. All of those lives lost on both sides, and yet in the end the Germans rolled right back in and took over. Herbie wished he could explain that he was an American citizen, but it wouldn't have mattered. As far as the French were concerned, he was all German.

"Dix," the old man growled.

Schmidt dropped two coins onto the counter and held the bottle forward. "Ouvre?"

The proprietor put the Reichmarks into his register before taking the bottle. With practiced hands, he used an opener to quickly remove the cork. After reinserting it partway back into the neck with his fingers, he handed the bottle back.

"Merci," Schmidt glared back at him, no love lost on either side of this transaction. Herbie followed his friend out of the shop and the pair walked in silence to the river. The Seine flowed through a deep brick channel, cutting the city in half like an open wound. They found a bench and sat. Schmidt pulled the cork and took a long drink before handing the bottle over.

"Maybe we should have got two." Herbie took a drink of his own.

"Don't push your luck."

"Where'd you learn French, anyway? They teach you that in school?"

"School? Nah, I didn't learn it in school. I picked up a bit in Canada. You gotta get by, you know?"

"That's right... Canada." Herbie drank some more and handed the bottle back. "Thanks for covering me back there at the hotel."

Schmidt laughed as he shook his head in wonder. "You are a piece of work, kid. One naïve son-of-a-bitch."

"How was I supposed to know?!"

"Don't even get me started."

Herbie crossed his arms and turned his head the other way. He wasn't sure which hurt more, Schmidt's condemnation, or the fact that it wasn't Herbie's charms that attracted the girl after all. He'd felt so good about himself, so proud, that with just a short conversation she'd wanted to accompany him. Herbie was a good-looking guy. An American. Why wouldn't she be interested? But then, picturing her there, screaming at him in the hallway… He wanted to forget the whole thing. "Hey, let me have another." Herbie took the bottle and drank. "You think the FBI is going to catch us? That's what Wolf said. He thought we were crazy to even try it."

"I'll be honest with you; I don't like it. Don't like it at all. You already know what I think of Dasch, that sorry excuse for a human being. How could the lieutenant put a guy like that in charge? It's incompetence, that's what it is. Kappe is an idiot."

Herbie let Schmidt's opinion sink in. Sitting here with the morose outdoorsman by his side, the reality of their situation seemed untenable. This unfolding drama had Herbie trapped with no discernible way out. "So, what are we supposed to do about it?"

Schmidt sat up straight, cheeks flushing. "I'm still working on that."

"On what?" Herbie was surprised.

"There are always options in life." Schmidt looked Herbie in the eye. "Always. I just need to figure out what mine are."

For Herbie, his options seemed extremely limited. If he made it to Chicago, the Germans couldn't touch him. As far as he was concerned, this whole thing would be just a distant memory. And what of Wolfgang? A twinge of guilt ran through Herbie when he thought of his friend, whose letter he'd received while on furlough. Wolf was most likely in the middle of basic training by this point. After that, straight to the front. A sense of responsibility weighed on Herbie. Wolf's future was in part up to him. The lieutenant made that clear. Play ball when he got back stateside or… To Kappe, Wolfgang was just an extra piece of insurance. But Wolf would make it, Herbie told himself. Someday this war would end and they'd laugh about it. Stories to tell their families, that's what this would all become.

The men drank in silence, passing the wine back and forth until it was empty. Schmidt dropped the bottle onto the gravel beside the bench before standing. "Come on, let's go." He nodded his head to one side.

The western sky glowed a soft yellow as they retraced their steps to the hotel. *Paris.* Herbie looked again toward that famous tower, looming above the rooftops. Yes, he certainly would have stories to tell.

Chapter Thirty-Eight

Paris, May 25, 1942

Under the watchful eyes of armed security officers, the men loaded four water-tight crates of explosives, fuses, weapons and ammunition on board the train. The wooden boxes were one-meter tall but narrow. Weighing roughly 25 kilos apiece, each crate could be carried by a lone individual. Overseeing the operation was Kapitan Lieutenant Willhelm Ahlrichs. Tall and thin himself, his uniform hung loosely from a narrow frame. This was a man whose taut expression demonstrated the gravity of his chosen profession. Unlike Kappe, the Kapitan Lieutenant was a career officer. Ahlrichs was a military man long before the Nazis came to power and if he survived, he would remain so after the war was over. Kappe was a Nazi first and an officer second. For Ahlrichs it was the other way around. He was here to accomplish whatever task was asked of him. For the next several days, that meant accompanying a group of intelligence operatives to the submarine base in Lorient. He stood by as Dasch and Schmidt stacked the last of their crates in the cargo compartment. "That's all of it, then?" he asked.

"Yes, Kapitan Lieutenant. That's the last of them," said Dasch.

"Good." Ahlrichs examined the boxes, making sure that they were stable. When he was satisfied, he nodded to Dasch. "We will take our seats."

"Yes, sir."

Dasch and Schmidt followed the officer into the next carriage, moving down the corridor until they found two compartments with large paper signs taped to the windows. *Reserviert.* Ahlrichs paused at the door. "What is it that you will do in America?" he asked.

"Just look inside our boxes!" George flashed a conspiratorial grin. "We're going to blow up some factories!"

Furrows formed on Ahlrich's brow. "I see."

"You ought to watch your mouth," Schmidt castigated Dasch.

"It's all right," George countered. "There's nothing we can't share with the Kapitan."

"We're on a public train!" Schmidt raised his voice.

"I did ask," Ahlrichs raised a hand in the air. "But your colleague is correct. These discussions are best held in private."

Ahlrichs moved to join Kappe in the next compartment. When the officer was gone, Schmidt leaned closer to Dasch. "I don't care what his rank is, you keep your big trap shut." Schmidt clenched his hands into fists. When the door slid open once more, they were joined by Burger, Thiel, Quirin and Haupt. The men took facing seats. The train carriage shook and then began to move forward.

"Off we go!" Dasch's spirits were still high. "Next stop, America!"

"No train went from Paris to America that I ever knew," Schmidt answered under his breath.

"Yes, well, one step closer," Dasch replied.

Sensing the tension, the rest of the men remained quiet as Schmidt crossed his arms, his face burning red. It was Dasch's sly pretension that was so hard to take, but Schmidt knew better than to attack a group leader in front of the others. He would bide his time, searching for a weakness to exploit. Schmidt glared from one man to the next, finally resting on Peter Burger. "What are you looking at?!" he barked.

"Me? Nothing!" Burger replied.

"Don't think we aren't on to you! We know your story. They had you locked up, just two months ago, in a concentration camp! Don't try to hide it."

Burger looked to the others. What was being said behind his back? "I've nothing to hide."

"They tell us you have been *rehabilitated*." Schmidt pronounced this word with derision. "How do we know you won't betray us all as soon as we arrive in America?! You tell me that!"

The blood drained from Burger's face. "I… I was always loyal, from the very beginning…"

"Loyal to who, the party or yourself?!"

"Relax, Schmidt," Herbie tried to interject. "Take it easy."

"Shut up, Herbie!" Fire glowed in the big man's eyes, as though at any moment he might plant a fist on the nearest jaw.

"The kid is right," Dasch interjected. "Our nerves are all a little frayed, it's only natural. We have a long way to go."

Schmidt grit his teeth and fell silent, though Herbie knew this wasn't the end of it. The bad blood simmered. This would be a long ride, stuck in a small compartment with men who wanted nothing more than to tear each other to pieces. He glanced out the window as they moved through the outskirts of Paris. Under different circumstances, he might have enjoyed this journey. As it was, he just wanted it to be over with.

It was late in the evening when they arrived at the base. They hadn't killed each other, yet, Herbie thought. There were still several weeks to go aboard a cramped submarine. Anything could happen. If Kappe picked up on the tension between his men, he did his best not to show it as he gathered them in a small meeting room to address the group one last time. "You will each be issued with a uniform of the German navy," he said. "These will be worn when boarding the submarines, so as not to create any suspicion amongst possible witnesses. They will also be worn upon landing on the American shore. If by the stroke of unfortunate circumstances you happen to be captured, these uniforms will ensure that you are treated as prisoners of war and not spies. I don't have to tell you, but your very lives are at stake. The best remedy, of course, is to simply avoid being caught. Once you are safely ashore, you will bury the uniforms along with your supplies." From under a desk, Kappe retrieved two leather satchels and placed them in front of him. Next, he pulled out nine canvas money belts and arranged them on the desk. He unfastened a strap on one belt and pulled out a bundle of green American bills, separating them into individual denominations. "I have here the funds that are to be issued to each of you in order to finance the mission."

At the sight of all of that money, Herbie perked up in his seat. Never had he seen so much cash in all of his life. What a man could do with that!

"Each of you will be given $4,450 to be used for personal expenses. Each leader will receive an extra $50,000 to go toward operational expenses plus an additional $5,000 per man from which monthly salaries will be drawn."

With his eyes glued to the money, Herbie pictured the high-end suits he could buy. A nice watch. A new car. And a diamond wedding ring? Returning to his old life, this money would give him a fresh start. Kappe ordered each man to approach the desk one at a time to sign a receipt before being handed their belt of cash.

Herbie's heart pounded as he took hold of his share. Returning to his chair, he opened the belt and began to flip through the crisp, clean bills. Many had never seen circulation. Herbie marveled at his newfound wealth, $50s and $100s, one after another, until he came to a bill that stood out. This wasn't green like the rest. Instead, it was printed on gold-colored paper. A fifty-dollar gold certificate. He looked around the room, checking to see if his colleagues had spotted any, but the other men sat impassively in their seats. Herbie quickly went through his entire stack, pulling out one gold certificate after another, four in total. "Hey!" he finally raised his voice. "What's the idea sending us over with these gold certificates?!"

"Excuse me, Herr Haupt, is there a problem?" Kappe was annoyed.

Herbie held up one of the offending notes. "These haven't been in circulation since 1934! Are you trying to get us arrested or something?!"

Kappe's face turned a shade lighter. The rest of the men sat up in their seats before opening their belts and pawing through their bills, each finding similar gold certificates mixed in.

"What's the big idea?" Kerling complained next. "This is a sure tip-off! You expect us to blend in over there, flashing these things around?!"

"It's no big dilemma," Kappe tried to calm their nerves. "Just go through your bills and remove any gold certificates."

"How could intelligence make such a dumb mistake?!" Schmidt raised his voice. "How can we trust anything they tell us?"

Quiet rumblings swept through the room as each man confronted his own level of distress. "Maybe we should call the whole thing off before it's too late," said Kerling. "This project is too dangerous. We need to rethink it."

"We are not going to call off the mission!" Kappe tried to retake control. "Remove the gold certificates and hand them back to me. The mission will go ahead as planned!"

The men slumped in their chairs. Dasch and Kerling emptied their entire satchels and filtered through tens of thousands of dollars apiece. When all of the gold notes were separated out, each man brought them to the front, where Kappe stuffed them into a satchel of his own. "Remember, this is the Fuhrer's money!" he said. "Use it wisely, in the name of the Fuhrer!"

Herbie was careful not to scoff. His money would be spent however he saw fit. If he wanted a new car, what was Adolph Hitler going to do about it?

"Gather your things and come with me," Kappe continued. "We will issue your uniforms."

The men stuffed the money into their pouches and then rose, following the lieutenant out the door.

Under cover of darkness, Kerling's group was the first to board their submarine. Rain poured down as they hurried across the gangplank with their heavy wooden crates. They would depart tonight, the other five men in a few days' time. Like the rest of them, Herbie had never laid eyes on an actual sub before. He thrilled at the thought of spending the next few weeks in one. Perhaps they would intercept a convoy along the way, or even sink an American ship… Or might they be the ones sent to a watery grave? Herbie thought again of the friend he was leaving behind. It was Herbie's plan after all, to run off to Mexico. Nobody could have foreseen the consequences. Wolf certainly didn't blame him, yet as Herbie stepped foot on the deck, he was weighed down by remorse. He was the one about to complete his journey back home to the family who awaited him. Wolf was on his own.

When they'd maneuvered their supplies down the ladders and into the sub, the men carried the boxes forward toward the torpedo room. Herbie inhaled the heavy aroma of diesel fuel. He heard the dull thrum of the engines. The passageways were tight, filled with food and supplies, as Herbie, Kerling, Neubauer and Thiel made their way through. Only when the men's boxes were stowed and lashed was the crew allowed to board. It was the second officer who gave the newcomers a brief tour. Here was the galley, here were their berths. They would have free access to all areas of the sub during the voyage except for the radio room. Just being aboard filled Herbie with an undeniable sense of excitement. It was just like all of the subs he'd seen in those movies. He could hardly wait to tell his friends back home.

Just one hour later, as the saboteurs played cards in the galley, Herbie heard the engine noise increase. Vibrations moved along the hull, through the table and into his cup, where small concentric rings formed on the top of his coffee. Shouts echoed down the hatch as crew members untied the lines. Moments later he felt a sway from side to side as the sub eased away from the dock. "Here we go," he said.

"Yeah. Here we go." Kerling paused only briefly before turning his attention back to the game.

Chapter Thirty-Nine

Lorient, May 27, 1942

Joseph Schmidt ducked out of the barracks and hurried across the base. He was running out of time. Their group was due to depart that evening and unless Schmidt acted quickly, he too would be on board. Schmidt had other ideas. When he spotted a small grocery, he went inside. Two sailors stood by a magazine rack, perusing the periodicals. Just past them, a woman sat smoking a cigarette behind a cash register. "Is there a pharmacy here?" Schmidt asked.

"Next door," said the woman.

Schmidt moved back outside. On the window of the next building, he saw the tell-tale green cross. Pushing his way through the door, he found a pharmacist in a white lab coat standing behind a wooden counter. Schmidt took a quick look around before approaching the pharmacist. "Hello, I want to know if you can help me with something," he asked.

"What do you need?" The pharmacist was impassive. This was a man used to sailors and their personal hygiene problems. It was all the same to him.

"Do you happen to have hydrogen peroxide solution?"

At this, the pharmacist eyed Schmidt with mild suspicion. Why the secretive nature over something as basic as H2O2? "Yes, of course. Wait here." He disappeared through a doorway in the back.

Schmidt bounced from one foot to the other as he ran the plan through his mind. Would it work? He couldn't say. He only knew that this was his one last hope. When the pharmacist returned, he held a small glass bottle in one hand. On a white label was written, *Wasserstoffperoxidlosung 3% (H2O2).*

"And one plain syringe," Schmidt added.

"What is this for?" the pharmacist asked.

"I'd rather not say. Do you have a syringe?"

The pharmacist considered a response but then relented. It was better not to know. He placed a wrapped syringe on the counter. Schmidt paid the man, took possession of the items, and then hurried back to the barracks.

After locking himself in a bathroom stall, Schmidt quickly pulled down his pants and then removed his underwear. Taking the cap off his bottle, he brought the open container to his nose. Clear. Odorless. It looked like water. He tore open the paper package and quickly inspected the syringe before injecting the tip into the bottle. He withdrew the stopper until it was full. Sitting on the toilet, he composed himself for a moment, holding one hand in a fist as he prepared for the pain he was likely to endure. There was no time to waste. Schmidt squirted a small amount of the liquid onto his penis, rubbing it into the shaft first and then his balls. Next came the real test. Inserting the tip of the needle into the end of his penis he squeezed the stopper further. Schmidt winced as the solution flooded his insides. Leaning forward with one hand on the stall door, he struggled not to cry out in agony as a thick brown foam bubbled forth. Rocking himself backward and forward, the stinging began to slowly subside. He recapped the bottle and placed it and the syringe on the floor behind the toilet, then pulled up his pants and fastened his belt. Quickly, lest the effects dissipate, he hurried from the bathroom in search of Kapitan Lieutenant Ahlrichs. Schmidt knew better than to attempt this stunt on Kappe. The lieutenant would never go for it, but Ahlrichs… He was a man who went by the book. That was Schmidt's only hope. He found the Kapitan Lieutenant in a break room, sitting at a table with several documents spread before him. After approaching the table, Schmidt stood silently for a moment. Gaining no response, he cleared his throat. "Excuse me, Kapitan."

"Yes?" Ahlrichs looked up.

"I have something that I would like to discuss."

"What is it?"

Schmidt shifted nervously. A few men whom he didn't recognize occupied a table on the far side of the room. No matter, he thought. This was it. Now or never. "I believe that I might have picked up a disease while we were in Paris."

"What kind of disease?" A dubious expression crossed Ahlrichs' face.

"I think you know," Schmidt answered.

"I am sorry, Mr. Schmidt, but you will have to be more specific."

"From a prostitute, Kapitan Lieutenant."

"I see..." Ahlrichs' concern showed. He gathered his papers and then rose to his feet. "Come, you will show me!"

"Yes, sir." Schmidt's spirits rose. So far so good.

The two men walked through the barracks until they entered Schmidt's room. Without a word, he closed the door behind them.

"Go ahead," said Ahlrichs.

Schmidt dropped his pants.

Ahlrichs tilted his head to one side and took a quick look. "On the bed, please."

Schmidt did as he was told, reclining onto his back with his pants bunched around his ankles. Foam still bubbled from his private parts, oozing from the tip.

"I see." Ahlrichs leaned forward. "From a prostitute, you say?"

"Yes, Kapitan Lieutenant. In Paris. I must have caught it there."

"I've seen enough." Ahlrichs took a step back.

Schmidt stood and pulled his pants up, then fastened his belt.

"Do you realize that naval regulations prohibit any man with a venereal disease from entering a submarine?"

"No, Kapitan Lieutenant! I did not know this!"

"I'm afraid it is true." Ahlrichs considered the implications. "I'm sorry to report that this disqualifies you from our mission."

"But I've trained so hard!"

"You will catch the next available train to Berlin where a proper medical evaluation will be conducted. You will remain there while undergoing any necessary treatment."

"But sir!..."

"Regulations must be obeyed," snapped Ahlrichs. "They were written for a reason. We cannot simply disregard them."

"I understand, Kapitan Lieutenant. If you think it is for the best." Schmidt lowered his eyes. "And will you be informing Lieutenant Kappe?"

"Don't worry about Kappe. I will take care of him. Return your money belt and uniform to me. I will write up your orders myself."

"Yes, sir, Kapitan Lieutenant, whatever you say, sir."

As soon as Ahlrichs left the room, Schmidt sat again on his bed, a giant wave of relief settling over him. This mission, so doomed to failure, would go on without him.

Part III – The Mission

Chapter Forty

On board U-254, Bay of Biscay, May 26, 1942

Girding himself against the pitch and sway of the vessel, Herbie Haupt clutched tightly to his mattress. Adding the noise and vibration from twin diesel engines, and sleep seemed nearly impossible. Peering forward toward the bow, he saw a small sliver of the control room. With the top hatch open, a few precious rays of morning light poked inside. Across the passageway, and less than two meters away from him, Eddie Kerling reclined in his own berth. Neubauer was below. Directly beneath Herbie, Thiel quietly moaned to himself as the effects of seasickness took their toll. Herbie felt it too, though for him it was merely a mild nausea. More significant was the pressure he'd felt building in his abdomen for the past 30 minutes. Herbie could put it off no longer. It was time to use the head. Very carefully, he climbed down from the bunk and set his feet on the deck. He moved forward, slowly becoming more accustomed to the rhythmic movement as he adjusted his stride. Once inside the small cabinet, he held onto a sink on one side and the door on the other, managing to relieve himself without missing his target, much. When he was finished, he struggled to remember the instructions for the toilet. Open the valve, pump the handle three times, close the valve, pump the bowl dry. Not so hard.

Back in the corridor, Herbie squeezed past two sailors coming in the opposite direction as he made his way back to his berth. Thiel lay huddled below with his back turned, still moaning. "You all right there, buddy?" Haupt asked.

Thiel rolled over. His face was the color of an avocado. In a rush of panic, he bolted from his bunk and flung himself down the passage, disappearing into the head. The sounds of retching followed. "Some ride, huh?" Herbie said to Kerling, who propped himself up on one arm.

"It's not bad when we're submerged."

"I don't see why we have to surface at all."

"We can't go all the way to Florida on electric motors. Even if we could, it would take forever. You want to spend two months in this tin can?"

"I don't want to spend two weeks in this tin can. I thought it was fun at first. At least I'm not Thiel…" Herbie looked up the corridor. The faint sound of a grown man vomiting filtered back.

"He'll get used to it," said Neubauer.

At least Herbie went to the head before Thiel and not after. Just the thought of that acrid odor made a hint of bile rise in his throat. After climbing into his bunk, Herbie rolled onto his back and closed his eyes. He was on a German submarine, crossing the Atlantic. After a year of shocking twists and turns in his life, this one neared the top of the list. With each passing moment, he was that much closer to resuming the life he'd left behind. He considered what he might say to his parents. Would he tell them the full truth? He couldn't imagine trying to hide it from them. Besides, his father was sure to be proud of him. As Herbie pondered this thought, a shout from the bridge echoed down the conning tower and through the passageway. It was a lookout's urgent voice. "Alarm!" the man yelled. "Enemy airplane!"

"Flood! Flood! Flood!" the captain shouted over the intercom. "All hands forward!"

A burst of alarm bells sounded and a stampede of crewmen rushed past the bunk, headed for the bow. Looking toward the control room, Herbie saw the lookouts drop from the bridge through the hatch. He heard a gurgling noise as the sub took on water and slipped below the surface. With the diesel engines off, all went quiet. Rocking waves gave way to a smooth glide as the nose pitched down and they entered the shadowy depths.

"Twenty meters!" a crewman called out.

"I wonder if they saw us," Herbie whispered.

"We'll know soon enough." Fear showed in Kerling's eyes.

"Forty meters!"

Onions from the galley rolled past on the deck.

"Sixty meters!"

"Sounding!"

The first explosion rocked Herbie to his core, nearly lifting him from his mattress. Seconds later came another, and then another.

"Three! Four!" a man called out after each blast. Could the sub withstand such abuse? Herbie expected to see water spraying through the hull, though so far they appeared to be intact.

"Eighty meters!"

Boom! Another blast, and then another. "Five! Six!"

Was this the end, after all that he'd been through? Herbie was going to die right here, on the bottom of the Atlantic. His parents would never know. Or Gerda. He pictured a son never understanding what had become of his father.

Boom! The sub quaked with violence.

"Seven!"

"One hundred meters!"

Herbie saw crewmen, huddled forward in the passageway. They looked as worried as he felt. Was this routine? It didn't seem to be. Kerling looked upwards, as though he might see the plane circling above them.

Boom! This one nearly shook loose his fillings.

"Eight!" A sense of relief passed through the crew as smiles broke out on some of their faces.

"Is that it?" Herbie tried not to sound too hopeful.

"I don't know," said Kerling.

"One hundred twenty meters!"

Thiel crept back from the head, his face still a deep shade of green. He climbed into his bunk without a word. Herbie braced himself for another round of explosions, though as the seconds ticked past he slowly began to accept that they had survived this attack. With the vessel level, he released his grip and rolled onto his back. He wouldn't end up at the bottom of the sea after all. At least not this time. There was still no telling what the next two weeks might bring. Whatever romanticism he'd previously harbored about life aboard a submarine was gone.

Chapter Forty-One

Novgorod Oblast, Soviet Union, June 7, 1942

Bouncing down a rutted country road in the back of an open troop transport, Wolfgang Wergin looked like any other soldier in the Wehrmacht. He wore the gray wool tunic with a bottle-green collar and shoulder straps, and a round steel helmet. In one hand he clutched a Mauser Karabiner 98K rifle. He used his other hand to hang onto his seat. While he may have looked like the rest of the newly minted soldiers packed in with him, he certainly didn't feel that way. It began at the very start with basic training, where Wolf was the only man who hadn't spent his entire youth in preparation for war. Wolf alone had no experience in the Junior Hitler Youth, or later the Hitler Youth itself. He'd never attended the camps, where the rest of the boys learned orienteering, weapons training, marching, and other essential soldiering skills. Luckily, Wolfgang was a quick learner. He also excelled at physical challenges. When it came to sprints, distance running, long jumps, or the obstacle course, Wolf could more than hold his own. As the only American in the group, he'd had to. All of the attention was on him. Wolf's drill sergeant never quite trusted him, at the shooting range especially, as though he expected this kid to turn against them at any moment.

Still, some of the other recruits were enthralled by Wolf's tales of growing up in Chicago. Those who spoke some English even helped him to improve his German. He didn't consider himself fluent yet, though he was close. With America in the war, Wolf sometimes pictured friends back home being called up and shipping off to basic training themselves. If he'd stayed at home he probably would have been among them, entering the same war on the other side.

Not that Wolf had much use for speculation. Reality was enough to occupy him. The convoy he traveled in pulled to a halt in the center of a sprawling camp. Under threatening gray clouds, Wolf saw tents lined up in grids across a damp field. A few of the larger tents had the familiar red cross on them. Armored personnel carriers rumbled through mud as soldiers on crutches hobbled past, trying not to be run over. They were filthy to a man, unshaven, with a far-off look in their eyes. These were the supermen of the Fuhrer. Wolf knew that many spent the better part of four months trapped in the Demarysk pocket. Completely encircled by Russian troops, they were supplied entirely by air. It was only a matter of a few weeks since they'd broken through the Russian lines, at great cost. Wolfgang and those with him were replacements. When the tailgate of his truck dropped, they shouldered their packs and climbed onto Russian soil. Looking around, Wolf felt embarrassed by the cleanliness of his uniform. It only proved how green he was, though that wouldn't last long, Wolfgang knew too well. A wounded soldier hobbled past on a makeshift crutch. In his mind, Wolf conjured the horrors that caused that vacant stare. Artillery pounded in the distance as the men dropped their packs in a pile on wet ground. The earth shook with each blast, vibrating up through Wolf's boots. Standing beside the truck, he was nearly run over himself by a barreling ambulance, the driver laying on his horn as he careened past the men and skidded to a stop. The back doors swung open and two medics emerged. Wolf watched as they unloaded a bloodied soldier, screaming in agony, his right leg torn off at the knee.

"Landmine," a replacement speculated.

"Artillery," said another. "A mine would have killed him."

"And an artillery shell wouldn't?"

An unteroffizier whose name tag read Dreyer approached the men with a clipboard in one hand. "Fall in!" he called out. Shorter than Wolf by a good four inches, the man was stocky and strong. Wolfgang imagined him as a plumber in civilian life. Or perhaps he'd worked in a mine, deep underground. As the medics rushed their charges into a nearby tent, the replacements lined up at attention.

"I will call the role." Dreyer went through his list, name by name, each man calling back in turn. They stood stiff and straight as scattered raindrops fell from above. An oberleutnant approached, black boots sloshing through the mud.

"All men present and accounted for!" said Dreyer.

The oberleutnant walked up and down the line, lifting his nose in the air as he examined each man, as though dismayed by some malodorous affront to his senses. "Welcome to our lovely camp. Don't expect to stay here for long. You will be joining your units this afternoon. The unteroffizier will show you to the mess tent. Enjoy it. This may be the last warm food you have in quite some time. You have one hour!" With that, the oberleutnant turned and stalked off. To Wolfgang it was clear. He was nothing more than cannon fodder in this man's estimation.

"You heard the oberleutnant. Grab your packs," said Dreyer.

"One hour," said a soldier. "They don't waste any time."

"German efficiency. It's why we will win the war," said another.

"Sure, that much sooner for you to bag your first Russian."

"I bet I'll bag mine before you do."

With packs slung on their shoulders, the men followed Dreyer. Wolf imagined being hauled back to camp in an ambulance himself, one leg blown off at the knee. Maybe Herbie was the smart one after all… Wolf followed the others into the mess tent for their last hot meal as the earth continued to tremble. Very soon he'd find out how it felt to be directly beneath that exploding artillery. At the moment, it would take all he had just to eat.

Chapter Forty-Two

On board U-202, June 12, 1942

"Ohhhh…" Seaman Hans Zimmerman wreathed in agony, his sheets damp with sweat. An excruciating pain emanated from his abdomen. At first, it was only mild, but in the previous twenty-four hours the pain increased exponentially until now it nearly overwhelmed him. Captain Linder stood beside the bunk with Weber, the sub's radioman and impromptu medic. The ship's doctor, normally present for such emergencies, was left behind due to lack of space. His bunk was needed to accommodate one of this voyage's four extra passengers. Without the doctor's advice and assistance, Linder was forced to consider alternative solutions. "What do you think?" he asked his medic.

"Acute appendicitis," the radioman answered.

"Are you sure?"

"We can't be sure unless we cut him open, but he is showing all of the symptoms, captain."

"What else might it be?"

"Food poisoning, perhaps. Though if that were the case, he wouldn't be the only man to have it."

"Yes. And what can be done?"

"He needs proper medical attention as soon as possible. If it is the appendix, it will need to come out or Zimmermann…" He didn't want to say the words in the man's presence.

"He will die," Linder completed the sentence for him.

"Yes, captain. If we could pass him to another of our submarines. One with a proper doctor…"

"I'm afraid that nothing can be done on that account. Not until after we've delivered our passengers."

Weber's expression turned grim as he looked to the patient.

"I will do it myself, if it comes to that," said the Captain. "Do you have any medical implements on board?"

"Not a scalpel, captain."

"A kitchen knife then."

Despite his pain, Zimmermann focused on these few words. A kitchen knife. He was to be sliced open by a man with no medical training, using a kitchen knife.

"How long can we wait?" the captain asked.

"I don't know. Perhaps twenty-four hours."

"Give him something for the pain."

"Aye, aye, captain."

As his medic went to fetch some opium and an ice compress, Linder headed back to the control room, eager to get these "passengers" off his boat already. If all went well, he would be dropping them onto an American beach that night. It couldn't happen soon enough.

In the galley, Burger sat with Dasch sharing a meal of spaetzle, the small German dumplings that reminded him of home. The cook had prepared them especially for Burger as a way to lift his spirits, though they weren't doing much good. Burger still felt doomed by the whole affair, missing his wife and convinced that the mission would go badly as soon as they arrived. That moment was coming near. On board the sub, the current time was a few minutes shy of midnight. Berlin time. Up above, off the coast of Long Island, it was six o'clock on a cloudy Friday evening. If they weren't intercepted by a roaming American patrol boat, the submarine would make landfall under cover of darkness in just a few more hours. Stirring his noodles with a fork, Burger didn't have the appetite to finish them.

"What's wrong, don't you like your spaetzle?" Dasch shoveled some of his own down with gusto.

"It's fine." Burger took another bite and forced himself to chew.

"Otto isn't going to appreciate it if you don't finish your meal. He went to such trouble to prepare it for you."

Burger saw Quirin and Heinck enter the galley. The men looked away before taking the farthest table they could. In such a small space, that wasn't far. Not far enough for any of them. The tension between the pairs had grown day by day until they hardly spoke to each other at all. Whenever Burger approached within earshot, Quirin and Heinck immediately fell silent. Burger knew. They were complaining, about Dasch and Burger both. About the mission. About the stench inside the sub, of unwashed men and dirty clothing. Somehow Burger was connected with Dasch in their eyes. An enemy, not to be trusted. Burger didn't trust them either. Not Quirin or Heinck, and not even Dasch. His entire life seemed to have depended on the whims of others; on Kappe and Dasch, on the Gestapo and the Abwehr. Burger was a tiny droplet in a monstrous storm, blown through life by forces far greater than himself. If he'd stayed in the U.S. when he had the chance, years of pain and misery would have been avoided. Yet, in that case, he'd never have met Bettina. It was not a trade off he would make. His wife was the one thing that saved him. Memories of waking up in bed beside her kept Burger plodding through from day to day. Perhaps he would survive, after all. Maybe when the war was over they could settle down somewhere in Bavaria, eating spaetzle and never having to worry about orders, or sabotage, or being locked in a Gestapo prison and beaten to the edge of consciousness. A future free from worry was the dream he clung to. Until that day arrived, he would blow whichever way the storm took him. In a few more hours that would be a beach on Long Island. Peter took another bite of his spaetzle and slowly chewed.

Peering through the periscope, the captain saw nothing but darkness and fog. There was no way to verify their position through visual landmarks. He couldn't even be sure how close they were to shore. Linder lifted the handles to retract the periscope and then moved to his chart table. "I believe we are here." He tapped a spot to show Dasch his best estimate of their location, just off the coast of Amagansett. "We will surface here and ease ourselves toward shore on electric power until we come to rest on the sand. Two of my men will help you row ashore. Once you are safely on the beach, you and your men will change into civilian clothing and pass your military uniforms to my crew."

"I was told to bury the dungarees on the beach, sir."

"No, you will return them. I want no unnecessary evidence of German involvement left on that beach. You bury your supplies, but that is all."

"Yes, Captain."

"Assuming there are no complications, my crewmen will then return to our vessel. The incoming tide will lift us from the bottom and we will be on our way."

"And if there are, as you say… complications?" Dasch asked.

"Any witnesses that you come upon are to be overpowered and sent back to me." Linder gave Dasch a stern look. "My men will be well armed."

"Yes, Captain. Does this apply to civilians?"

"*Any* witnesses! If you are unable to subdue them, then you must eliminate them. They shall be brought back to the sub by any means necessary."

Dasch let that single word settle in. Eliminate. An order to kill. He shuddered, but this was war. All he could do was hope that the coast was clear. And if not? He would figure that out as he went.

"Tell your men to empty their belongings of any matchbooks or cigarette packets. Anything that could compromise the secrecy of this mission."

"Yes, captain."

"It is time to make ready." Linder moved to the sub's intercom. "All hands prepare to surface!" he called out.

Dasch hurried to the galley where his men sat in gray dungarees, their boxes and bags spread across the tables. George unzipped his small personal bag and pulled out his pair of dungarees. "This is it, boys, we're going ashore." He quickly changed. On top of his Navy coveralls, he slid into his favorite red sweater, zipping it up the front. Over that, he put on a gray mechanic's coat. It was a lot of clothing, but better to wear it than to carry it. On his feet, he wore white tennis shoes. Lastly, he placed his brown fedora on his head. When he was ready, he shoved the rest of his things into an over-sized sea bag. "Let's go, fellas, put your stuff in here."

The others crammed their things into the one big bag. They carted this and their crates to the cramped control room, where a crew member opened the hatch above them. Dasch heard the sound of breaking waves. They were close indeed. Two crew members in navy coats and caps dragged in the collapsed rubber dinghy. George eyed the sub-machine guns slung over their shoulders. An unnecessary detail, he hoped. Another sailor brought a foot pump and an armful of collapsible paddles.

Linder was the first man through the hatch. When he reached the bridge, the captain quickly called down the ladder. "Let's go, landing party on deck!"

George went next. Emerging topside, he was met by fog so thick he couldn't see from one end of the sub to the other. "Perfect," he marveled to himself. If only they could determine which way it was to shore. Dasch swiveled his head, trying to zero in on the noise of the breakers. They would manage. He leaned back down the hatch. "Hand me the duffel!"

Over several trips up and down the swaying ladder, the group transferred their four cargo boxes, duffel bag, two shovels, paddles, and the rubber raft and pump onto the deck. In one hand, Burger held an extra case stuffed with money. It was his special charge. Picturing all of those bills washing out with the tide, he clutched the case tightly to his chest.

The landing party stood aside on the gently rolling deck as the crew members quickly inflated the raft. When all was ready, the sub eased forward silently. A paddle was passed to each man. One sailor tied a long rope to the sub, the other end to the rubber raft. "In case we get lost," he explained to Dasch. "So we find our way back."

Carefully, the submarine slid onto a sand bar, easing slowly to a halt. "All stop!" the captain called down from the bridge. The electric motors shut off. "This is it," said Linder. "As far as I take you. Launch the boat!"

With the four heavy boxes already in the raft, the men lowered it over the side. The first sailor climbed aboard, followed by Burger with his briefcase. Thiel handed across the duffel. When the shovels were stowed, the rest of the men took their places in the boat, oars at the ready. Pushing away from the sub, they began to paddle feverously, straining to discern the direction of the crashing surf. Burger sat in the bow. An image of George Washington crossing the Delaware River flashed through his mind. Another war, another century. Would these men catch the enemy sleeping as well?

"Good luck!" the captain called out as they disappeared into the fog.

"Thank you, captain!" Dasch replied. "Heil Hitler!"

"Heil Hitler!" Linder gave them his final salute.

Within moments, the entire submarine disappeared into the mist. The men saw nothing before them and nothing behind. Only a thick soup of clouds all around. "We're going the wrong way!" Heinck complained.

"How do you know?" said Burger.

"I hear the waves over there!" Heinck pointed with a paddle.

"Well I hear them over there!" countered Burger, pointing in a different direction.

"Quiet!" Dasch demanded. He swung his head from one side to another, pausing at 90-degree angles. Were they rowing in circles? He pointed to their two o'clock. "Come on boys, this way! Let's get to it!"

The men resumed their efforts until they were surrounded by breaking crests. A wave snuck up from behind and sent the raft spinning sideways, dousing the men as it nearly tipped them over. After skidding into a small trough, they were quickly struck again, and then again, seawater filling their small craft as Heinck's hat washed away, along with Quirin's paddle. Each successive wave washed them further shoreward until Dasch stuck his paddle straight down and struck sand. "This is it, boys, we've done it!" He leaped from the boat, landing in waist-deep water. George steadied himself with one hand on the raft and began trudging toward the beach, pulling the others along until the rest hopped out and waded toward dry sand. They had arrived. American soil. The United States. But they weren't quite home-free. They had to get off this beach, and as soon as possible. Dasch may have intended for this mission to fail, but not yet. Not upon landing. If they were caught in the act it would mean certain disaster, for him, too. No, to play the hero's role he'd have to be smart about it. All in good time. "Let's go, grab those boxes!"

The sailors helped hoist the crates out of the boat and into the arms of the saboteurs, who hauled them up the beach, feet churning through dry sand. Burger alone struggled with the additional sea bag slung over his back, and the briefcase perched on his crate. He caught up to the others at a low saddle, partially hidden from view.

"Drop them here!" Dasch hissed. "Let's change out of these dungarees, boys, quickly!"

Burger placed his cargo on the sand beside the other boxes. After opening the canvas duffel, he pulled out a rubber raincoat, spreading it on the beach before reaching back into the bag to retrieve clumps of wet clothing. These he laid out on the coat as the other men unfastened their dungarees and began to strip them off.

Impatient, Dasch peered through the fog toward the sailors whose dark forms could be seen scurrying around in the water near the rubber boat. What were they up to? Had they lost something? George just wanted them gone already. "Get changed," he said to his men. "I'll go check on the navy boys." He hurried back across the sand where the sailors were floundering at the tide line. "What are you men doing?"

"We lost two paddles!" a sailor explained.

"Forget the paddles! They don't matter."

"We should leave no sign that we were here!"

"I said forget it! They'll wash out to sea. Come, let's drain the water from your boat!"

The sailors acquiesced, heads bowed as they joined Dasch at the raft. Together, the three men tipped the boat into the air, dumping out most of the seawater before dropping it back down.

"Tell the captain the landing was perfect," said Dasch. "You men should return to the submarine."

"We must take the dungarees!" said one sailor.

"And the sea bag!" said the other.

"Yes, the dungarees…" As he spoke, George sensed some unexpected movement coming from just up the beach. Turning his head, he saw the bouncing beam of a flashlight illuminating the fog. The men were not alone. It was Dasch's worst fear.

"You there!" an unfamiliar voice called out. "What's up here? What are you doing?"

George hustled across the sand, intercepting the man before he could approach the German sailors, submachine guns at the ready. As Dasch moved closer, he made out a tall figure in a Coast Guard uniform. The man stopped abruptly. He was young. Barely out of high school, Dasch would guess. And nervous, doing his best to keep some small distance.

"You men aren't supposed to be on the beach at this hour. Only uniformed military personnel are allowed down here after sunset. What are you up to?" He shone his flashlight up and down Dasch's figure.

"What do you care what we're doing? We were fishing. We left East Hampton to go down to Montauk Point and we got lost."

"What do you mean East Hampton and Montauk Point? Do you know where you are?" The boy switched off his light.

"No, I already told you, we got lost! You should be able to tell us where we are. Where is your station?"

"It's right up there," the man gestured behind him. "My station is Amagansett."

The pair faced off in the darkness. Dasch needed to get rid of this kid, and quickly, but how?

"What are you planning to do now?" the coastguardsman asked.

"We'll stay here until sunrise. Don't worry about us, we'll be all right."

"It's four hours until sunrise. You'd better come back with me to the station. You can spend the rest of the night there."

Dasch hesitated. He needed time to think! If he let this coastguardsman get anywhere near the two sailors, it would mean the end of the kid. Murder in cold blood. Dasch couldn't let that happen. "All right," he agreed. They walked a few steps together back along the water before Dasch slowed again. He couldn't just show up at the Coast Guard station. Of course, that would never do. But what were his alternatives? "I'm not going with you." He halted.

"Why not?"

"Because, I don't have a fishing permit or any identification."

"That's fine, you come along!"

"No, I'm not coming!"

"I insist!" The coastguardsman reached out to take Dasch's arm.

"Now wait a minute!" Dasch pulled away. "You don't know what this is about!"

"No, I don't think I do."

Dasch peered toward the sailors, standing at the edge of view beside their rubber boat. They didn't have to kill the kid. With three against one, they could easily overpower him. They'd tie him up and send him out to the sub as a prisoner of war, just as the captain had ordered. But what would become of him then? Dasch took a few steps toward the raft. The coastguardsman hesitated to follow, his fear evident even in darkness. But George Dasch just couldn't do it. He couldn't doom this boy to captivity. What if Linder stuffed the boy into a torpedo tube and flushed him into the depths? No, this was Dasch's first test. He drew close to the coastguardsman once again. "How old are you, boy?"

"I'm twenty-one years old, sir..."

"You have a mother?"

A pause followed this question. "Yes..."

"And a father?"

"Sure, I have a father."

"Well, I wouldn't want to have to kill you." Dasch let this statement settle in. From the direction of the dunes, another dark figure approached. It was Burger, wearing only a bathing suit and dragging the wet duffel behind him. "Ich habe die latzhose hier!" he called out.

"Shhh!!!" Dasch hissed in return. "You damned fool! Shut up and go back to the other guys!" Dasch made out a shift in the coastguardsman's posture as he heard German being spoken; a physical recoil as the boy leaned away. Burger slunk back into the fog. George leaned in and took the coastguardsman's arm this time. "Come over here." He led the boy a short distance further down the beach. "Forget about this and I can give you some money and you can have a good time."

"I don't want any money."

"I'll give you three hundred dollars. How about that?" Dasch reached into his pocket and pulled out a tobacco pouch. Inside was a wad of $50 bills. "You have undoubtedly given your oath to do your duty, and I am telling you that by taking this money that I am offering, you are doing nothing else than your duty, so *please* take it." Dasch shoved some of the bills into the coastguardsman's hand. "Go ahead and count it."

"No, it's all right." The boy slid the bills into his pocket.

Dasch's head jerked up and down. "What will you do with it?"

"I don't know. I guess I'll give some to my parents. Some of it I'll put in the bank. Maybe I'll have a good time."

"Boy, you do just that, but wait a minute." Dasch reached up and pulled off his hat. "Look at my face. Take a good look at me. Do you know me?"

"No, sir, I never saw you before in my life."

"Look in my eyes. Take a good look." The coastguardsman switched his light back on and shone it into Dasch's face, making a mental note of his unusual streak of gray hair. Dasch leaned back and put his hat back on. "You might see me again in East Hampton sometime. My name is George John Davis. What is your name, boy?"

"Frank Collins, sir."

"You'll see me again, Frank."

"That's good, sir." The coastguardsman took several steps backward, keeping an eye on the three men in view. As "Davis" moved toward the dark figures at the water's edge, the seaman turned and walked briskly in the direction from which he had come.

"Who was that?" one of the sailors demanded of Dasch.

"Nobody. Just a boy out looking for clams. Forget about it."

"Why didn't you detain him?!"

"I said forget it. You two men need to go back to the submarine."

"But you haven't given us your dungarees!"

"Don't worry about the dungarees. We will bury them!" Dasch began walking back across the beach to the others before stopping to look back. The sailors stood indecisively beside their raft. "Go!" Dasch added. "You've done your job! You can tell your captain it was a success." With that, Dasch marched on up the sand. It was time to get off this beach.

The dense fog enveloped Seaman John Cullen like a cloak. Out of sight from the mysterious strangers, he ran full tilt, following the waterline for half a mile and then traversing up a small hill. Breathing hard, he passed a Navy radio beacon with a small station house attached. A few hundred yards further, he arrived at the two-story Coast Guard station. Exhausted, he rushed inside and began to holler. "There's Germans on the beach! There's Germans on the beach!" He gave a quick scan of the main floor. Finding it deserted, he scaled the stairs and then pounded on the door of his boss,

Boatswain's Mate Carl Jennett. "Hey Boat! There's Germans on the beach! Get up!"

When the door opened, Jennett stood in his pajamas with a bewildered expression on his face. "What is this? What Germans?"

"On the beach!" Cullen struggled to speak and breathe at the same time. "We need to wake up the guys!"

"Slow down!" Jennett was skeptical. "Give it to me straight. What's the story?"

"I was doing my patrol, just like usual," Cullen explained. "A half mile down, that's where I seen them. They were German all right!"

"How do you know that?"

"'Cause I heard them, talking German!"

"How do you know it was German?"

"Listen, Boat, I know what I saw. The one guy, he threatened my life. Then he told me that if I kept my mouth shut, he'd give me this!" Cullen pulled the soggy bills from his pocket.

Jennett's incredulity quickly faded. "How many men were there?"

"I don't know. Four that I saw, but maybe more!" Cullen handed over the money.

As Jennett examined the bills, his face lit up. "Oh, boy, this is big. This is the real McCoy! I've got to notify Map Hague! Wake up the men!" Jennett hurried to the nearest phone.

Cullen bolted into the sleeping quarters, flipping on the light to reveal four slumbering figures. "Get up! There's Germans on the beach! Everybody up!"

"What's the big idea, Cullen?" A sleepy coastguardsman rolled over and opened his eyes.

"Get your sorry asses out of bed! There's Germans on the beach!"

After their uninvited visitor departed, Dasch and his men retreated further into the dunes with their precious crates, coming to rest in a low spot near a wooden fence.

"How could you let him go?!" Heinck seethed.

"He'll report us!" Quirin seconded. "We were supposed to send him out to the sub! You heard the captain!"

"Relax, boys," Dasch tried to calm them, though he was anything but calm himself. "He won't tell anybody. I paid him off. We'll be fine."

"How can you be sure?!" said Heinck. "We should have killed him!"

"Calm down, this is not the time to lose our heads."

"They'll be looking for us!" Quirin hissed. "It's all your fault!"

"Dig!" Dasch commanded. "Let's get to it, boys! We'll get this evidence in the ground right here!"

Burger picked up one shovel and Quirin the other. Together they made a hole roughly one and a half meters square. When it was deep enough, they lowered in their boxes side by side. Burger threw in the sea bag, full of sodden uniforms.

"Where are my clothes?!" Dasch was hit with a rush of panic. Underneath his coat and sweater, he still wore his own dungarees. He remembered pulling his other personal items from the duffel, back near the water's edge. Shirts, slacks and shoes in a brown leather travel bag.

"You told us to change!" Quirin complained. "Why didn't *you* change?!"

"We left the raincoat, too…" Burger admitted.

"Somebody help me look…," said Dasch. "Peter, you come with me."

Heinck clutched his arms around himself in a vain attempt to generate warmth. The tension between the men was as thick as the heavy blanket of fog that enveloped them. Burger followed Dasch back over the dunes where the pair began to scour the sand. Every moment they spent searching was that much more time for the Coast Guard to arrive in force, yet it would do no good for Dasch to leave the beach in a German naval uniform. They had to find that clothing. "Keep looking!" he said to Burger.

When the coastguardsmen were dressed and assembled, Boatswain's Mate Jennett hurriedly sorted through a bulky key ring, trying one key and then another until he was able to unlock the station's gun cabinet. Opening the solid wooden door revealed a long rack of .30 caliber rifles. "How many of you men have fired a gun?"

Jennett was met by blank stares all around. "None of you? Not one man knows how to fire a Springfield rifle?!"

"Nobody ever showed us before."

"It's time for your first lesson." Jennett handed a rifle to each man and then passed out boxes of ammunition. "You see this?" he pointed to a small switch on his weapon. "It's the safety catch. You want to shoot something, you make sure this is set to *Fire.* That's forward. Never point this weapon, or any weapon, at anything you don't intend to shoot. I never want to see you pointing these guns in the direction of one another at any time, you got it?"

"Sure boss, we got it."

"If you think there's a German, you be ready to aim through these sites and pull the trigger. This is serious business, understand?"

"Yeah, boss, we know."

Jennett handed his rifle to Cullen and then opened a box of ammo, holding up one bullet. "Here's how you load it." He took his gun back and proceeded to demonstrate, sliding in one cartridge after another. "You got that?"

"Yeah, we got it."

"Good, load up and make it quick!" The men did the best they could while Jennett moved from man to man, speeding along the process. "Montgomery, you stay here and guard the station."

"By myself?"

"What's the matter, you scared?"

"No, Boat."

"Good. The rest of you guys grab a light and let's go."

Montgomery helped pass out the flashlights, downcast at the prospect of missing all the action. When all the lights were checked and operational, Jennett grabbed a flare gun. He slid it into one pocket, with extra flares in the other before leading the party out the front door and down the steps. Thick clouds of mist billowed past the station in spectral waves. "How the hell did you see these guys?" Jennett asked Cullen.

"I don't know, Boat. I got lucky, I guess. I came right on 'em."

Cutting through the fog, the men saw a lonely pair of headlights moving straight for them down the road. "This could be someone coming to pick up the Germans!" said Jennett. "Quick men, get in the bushes!" The party fanned out, half of the men hiding on each side of the road. "I'll stop them. You boys cover me!" As the car approached, Jennett bounded into the center of the road. The vehicle skidded to a stop, nearly running him over.

The driver rolled down his window. "What's the big idea?!" he hollered.

"What are you doing out here?" Jennett switched off his safety as he came around the car.

"I'm coming from the radio station! What the hell are you doing out here?!"

"You're Navy?"

"Damned right I'm Navy. What the hell is going on?!"

"You got some identification on you?"

"Not unless you start explaining things!"

Jennett leaned close to get a better look in the dark. "How come you're not in uniform?"

"'Cause my damned shift is over, that's why! What's it to you?"

"Uh-huh." Jennett began to let his guard down. This man certainly didn't seem like a foreign agent. "We have reason to believe there might be Germans on the beach."

"Germans?!"

"That's right, now let me see some ID." The driver fumbled for his wallet as the other men rose from their hiding places and surrounded the vehicle. When the man handed his ID through the window, Jennett gave it a look under his flashlight. Radioman George Blackwell, U.S. Navy. "He checks out." Jennett handed the ID back. "Be careful," he said to the driver. "I don't know what these Nazis are up to."

"How do you know they're Nazis? You sure you didn't just imagine all this?"

"I'm sure." Jennett looked to his men. "Let's go." The group of coastguardsmen moved on, down the hill and past the radio station. As they reached the sand, the unmistakable rumble of diesel engines met them from somewhere across the water. "Look sharp, men, we are definitely not alone down here."

After a quick search, Dasch and Burger found the sodden duffel. Nearby was Dasch's travel bag. Beside it, sodden clothing sat atop the sandy raincoat. The men scooped everything up and hurried back to the others. "We found it," George announced. He quickly tore off his shoes and clothing, shoving the dungarees and sneakers into the duffel before tossing it into the hole. Next, he pulled on his wet slacks and jacket before extracting a pair of brown leather loafers from his small bag and sliding them onto his sandy feet. "Let's go men, fill this in. It's time we got moving!"

"Bury the shovels!" said Heinck. He threw in one and Burger the other before the men used their hands and arms to push sand into the hole. After smoothing the sand out, Quirin and Burger gathered dry grass from nearby and spread it on top. "That's good, let's get out of here." Dasch didn't have to convince anybody. The group crept further inland, through the dunes, until they came to a row of small houses fronting the beach. Light shone through an open door. Dasch motioned with one hand and the men ducked low behind some grass. Through the dark night, they heard the ringing of a telephone. A screen door creaked open and then slammed shut. Muffled voices just inside. A door gently closed. When Dasch peeked over the grass once more, the light was out.

"Where do we go!?" Heinck was paralyzed with fear.

"Follow me…" Staying low to the ground, Dasch led the men along the row of homes, searching for an opening. To their left, a white beacon of light flashed on and then off at regular intervals. From somewhere in the distance came a popping sound, followed by the faint green glow of a naval flare.

"We're surrounded!" Heinck exclaimed. "They're going to catch us!"

"Quiet!" Dasch demanded. In the direction of the beacon, they saw a road. The headlights of a single car moved toward them. "Get down!" The men dropped to the sand as the vehicle rumbled past. "We'd better hide out, boys, until things settle down a little." Dasch motioned to a small cluster of bushes on their left. "In here. We'll lay low for a while." He pushed his way through the scrub until he was completely hidden from view. The others waited a moment, each one calculating their best course of action. What was the alternative? Separate and go it alone? None of them wanted that. Better to stick together, out of sight. They slid into the brush to wait. Sandy, wet and shivering, they heard the sound of engines just offshore, roaring then idle, roaring then idle, up and down.

"What is that noise?" asked Quirin.

"It must be U-202 headed straight out to sea," Dasch replied.

"Or a coast guard patrol boat, coming after us," countered Heinck.

"Relax, boys. No use losing our heads. We'll wait until things settle down and then move inland."

No matter what Dasch might have told them, relaxing was nigh impossible for these men, hunted like dogs by soldiers no doubt patrolling the beach already, just a few hundred feet away. If the group was still in these bushes by the time the sun came up, that would be the end of the line and every one of them knew it. Here they were, so close to success, huddled on American soil. "We should have killed that guy," Heinck repeated. "We never should have let him go."

"Forget about it!" Dasch ordered. "Just keep quiet, will you?"

Cold, wet, and terrified, the men fell silent but for the rattling of their teeth, each lost to his misery as they waited for the moment to make a quick break on a dismal Long Island morning.

Inside the radio station, Chief Radioman Harry McDonald heard the engines, too. Moving to the window, he peered outside, struggling in vain to see where the sound was coming from. The unmistakable odor of diesel fumes drifted up to his station. McDonald picked up his telephone and dialed the nearest Coast Guard headquarters. "Hello, this is Chief Radioman McDonald at the Naval Radio Station, Amagansett. I think I might have a German submarine down here! You guys have any information on that?"

"I'm sorry, I am not permitted to give out information pertaining to enemy activity," said a coastguardsman.

"Hey, I've got my wife and kids here! You've got to tell me something!"

"I'm sorry. I'm not authorized to discuss it."

McDonald hung up and quickly found another number. This time he dialed the army base five miles down the beach. The 113th Mobile Infantry Division. "I think there's an invasion going on!" he pleaded to a lieutenant on the other end of the line. "You've got to send some men!"

"I'm sorry, but we can't leave the base without orders from my captain."

"Then get the captain! I'm afraid they might try to blow up my station!"

"What are you doing, trying to start something?!" the lieutenant complained.

When McDonald hung up this time, he hurriedly woke his wife. "What's going on?" she asked in a panic.

"Get dressed, I'm sending you and the children to the Bradfords'. I don't think it's safe for you here."

"Not safe?" His wife was still sleepy. "Why wouldn't it be safe?"

"Just get dressed, dear. Please hurry."

On the darkened beach, Jennett and his men strained their senses as they followed the water's edge one half-mile from the station. "Are we close yet, Cullen?"

"I don't know, Boat. I think so, but it's hard to tell."

The men halted where they were as Cullen shone his light on the ground, searching for any signs. "The one man, he was dragging some kind of a sea bag."

"Let's take a look around here." Jennett directed the men in a loop, up toward the dunes and then back. No other men were in sight.

"Hey Cullen, you sure you weren't just putting us all on?" said Caldwell.

"You think I'd do that?!"

"Why not? It gets pretty dull around here."

"After tonight, I'll take dull any day."

"You smell that?" said Jennett.

"Yeah, I smell it. Diesel," Brooks replied. The men felt a vibration trembling through the sand. "You think that's a sub?"

"I don't know. Could be," said Jennett.

"Maybe they're stuck?" said Caldwell.

With the fog beginning to clear, Cullen spotted the outline of a low vessel just a few hundred yards offshore. "You see that?"

"Yeah, I see it," Jennett answered. A small light on the vessel blinked on and off, on and off, in time.

"Does that look like a sub to you?" said Caldwell.

"It sure doesn't look like any other kind of boat I've ever seen," Cullen replied.

"Dowling, you come back to the station with me," said Jennett. "I need to update HQ. The rest of you guys stay here and keep your eyes open. Be careful. I don't want any of us shooting at each other!"

"We got it," said seaman Brooks. As Jennett and Dowling retreated the way they had come, Brooks, Caldwe and Cullen stayed put, lights off as they strained to detect any signs of a German invasion.

"You think they might shoot at us from out there?" said Caldwell.

"They might," Cullen replied.

"Maybe we ought to back up a little bit," said Brooks.

"Good idea." The men scooted up the beach toward the dunes.

"Hey, Cullen, how many men did you say were on the beach before?" Caldwell asked.

"I don't know for sure. I think I saw three. No, wait, it was four."

"Did they have any weapons on them?" Caldwell was anxious.

"I didn't get a very good look at them. I only saw the one guy up close."

"Let's hope they don't have no guns."

"If they'd wanted to kill me, I think they'd have done it already."

"You never know."

"You guys think it's safe to turn our lights back on?"

"I'm not so sure that's a good idea."

"I want to look around." Cullen switched on his light and pointed it toward the sand. "I swear that guy was dragging a sea bag. It must have left a groove in the sand. You'll see…" It took less than a minute of searching before the coastguardsman spotted a small square object. Leaning down to pick it up, he brushed the sand off with his thumb before examining it more closely. In his hand was a half-empty cigarette pack. The brand he didn't recognize, but Cullen could make out one word at the bottom. "Hamburg," he read out loud. "That's in Germany, isn't it?"

"Damn right," said Brooks.

“We better get this to the skipper!” All three men peered further toward the dunes. Any lingering doubts about the presence of Germans on the beach were gone.

Chapter Forty-Three

On board U-202, June 13, 1942

"Full power! Give me full power, electric motors and diesel!" Captain Linder called over the intercom. The entire sub was tilted at an angle of 40 degrees, resting on a sandbar and pushed further ashore with each successive wave. Their situation was growing increasingly desperate.

"Aye, aye, captain, full power!" replied the chief engineer.

"Blow the tanks!" Linder commanded.

"Blow the tanks, aye, aye captain!"

"Forward torpedo room!" Linder called. "Remove all torpedoes from the tubes! We must lift our bow!"

"Yes, captain!" the torpedo officer called back.

Despite his best attempts, Linder's stranded submarine would not budge. He'd rocked the boat from side to side, one prop forward the other reverse, back and forth. He'd dumped diesel fuel to lighten their load. He'd blown the tanks, flooded, and blown again. And he'd revved the engines, full power, despite the threat of giving away their position. Anybody within half a mile would have heard them by this time.

"All stop!" the captain called back to the chief.

"All stop!"

The engines ground to a halt. Linder grasped the ladder and quickly climbed the rungs through the hatch. Bracing himself against the angled conning tower, he was able to clearly make out the shore. Headlights moved in both directions along a frontage road, not more than 300 meters from their position. Somewhere in the darkness a dog barked, long and loud. Linder saw a small building almost directly abreast, with a radio tower attached. Further along a low bluff, spotlights shone upward, scanning the clouds.

"Why are they searching the sky?" The first officer passed through the hatch to join the captain's side.

"Perhaps they think our engine noise comes from airplanes." Linder heard next what sounded like a gun firing, at some distance. If he was unable to dislodge the boat by daybreak, he would be forced to surrender, his entire crew consigned to prison for the remainder of the war. Perhaps an even worse fate, those spotlights might shift in direction and find their target. When that happened, the sub would certainly be fired upon, by artillery if it was available. Compounding his problems, low tide was not due for nearly an hour. Linder's thoughts shifted to the boat's Enigma machine and codebooks. Every captain in the German navy understood the magnitude of their importance. Above all else, he had to keep them from falling into enemy hands. "Prepare the boat for demolition," he ordered. "I want explosive charges set bow to stern, every five meters. Double in the radio room. I want one charge strapped directly to the Enigma machine. No, make it two."

"Yes, captain." The first officer hesitated.

"What is it?!"

"Zimmermann, captain. He's very ill."

"I am well aware of the situation." Linder peered through the glare toward the beach. "Perhaps the Americans can save him."

"Shall we row him ashore?"

"Not yet."

"Then when?"

"Not yet!"

"Yes, captain." The first officer gave a quick salute and headed below.

Linder followed his first officer back down the canted ladder. The captain picked up his microphone and switched on the intercom to address the crew. "This is the captain speaking! You are all aware of the predicament in which we find ourselves. We will continue our attempts to free the vessel. On the chance that those efforts are unsuccessful, I am asking every man to prepare for surrender. Pack a few items of clothing and be ready to abandon ship on my orders."

A murmur arose throughout the vessel as the men contemplated the previously unthinkable. While the first officer and second engineer went about setting explosive charges, Linder sat down to type what very well might prove to be the last coded message he sent as the captain of U-202.

After an hour in the bushes, Heinck's nerves were more frayed than ever. Spotlights lit the dunes, scanning back and forth on two sides. Shouts emanated from the shoreline. "I told you, we're surrounded!" he repeated yet again.

"Shut up, Heinck!" Burger complained.

When a troop transport rumbled past on the nearby road, Dasch decided that it was finally time to move. "Come on, boys, let's make a break for it!" There was no dissent. The men followed each other out from their hiding spot and then slinked inland.

"Someone's going to see us!" said Quirin.

"Be quiet, Richard!" Dasch stepped out onto the darkened highway. Which way to go? He turned to the right. The others followed. After a short distance, they came to a smaller dirt road on their left. "We'll take this one!"

"Do you even know where we are?!" Quirin complained.

"Sure! I think so."

"You *think* so?"

"I have an idea." Continuing up the dirt road, the men passed a campground, quiet and still in the early hours of the morning. A lone dog barked. When this road ended, the men continued straight ahead through a fallow field, walking over large clumps of dirt. The fog cleared in earnest as they moved away from the coast. On the far side of the field, they entered a line of trees, passing through a short stretch of forest before emerging into another clearing. Before them was a set of railroad tracks stretching left to right. "Ah, now I know!" Dasch was elated. "The Long Island Railroad! We're nearly there, boys. We're almost home free." Dasch turned to his left, toward New York City. All they had to do was find the nearest station.

Hurrying along the tracks in the dark, nobody said a word. One mile. Then two. Where was the station? No trains passed. No signs of life, yet every step took them away from that beach and the soldiers searching for them. Even so, each man expected to be caught at any moment. Would more soldiers be waiting at the train station? Were they already laying an elaborate trap? After three miles, the men approached the outskirts of a village. Farmhouses.

Barns. A few businesses lining an empty road. They arrived at a small, deserted station. "Amagansett," read a sign above the platform. The men climbed up off the tracks and onto the platform. Dasch alone approached the station house, trying his hand at the door. Closed up tight. He peered through a window, hoping in vain to spot a station master. What he saw was a small lobby, vacant but with a ticket window on one side.

"Maybe we ought to clean ourselves up," said Burger. Standing under a single bulb, the men eyed one another. They were covered in dirt and sand, their hair and faces a mess.

"Good idea," Dasch agreed. Moving along the platform, they came to a small restroom. George tried the door. It was open. When he flipped on a light, the men crowded inside around a single mirror, taking turns at the sink to wash their faces and smooth out their hair. Dasch examined his pants, torn to shreds while he'd crawled through the bushes. There was nothing to do about that.

Back outside, they stood close together. "Today is a Saturday," said Burger. "What if there aren't any trains on Saturday?"

"We'll wait and see," Dasch replied. "It's still early. We'll wait. There must be trains on Saturday." He took a seat on a bench nearby. After some hesitation, the others joined him, still shivering, cold and wet, each man lost to his own anxieties.

As the angled deck heaved and swayed beneath them with each passing swell, two crewmen struggled to lower a groaning Zimmermann into the waiting rubber dinghy. With the vessel's opium supply exhausted, the sailor's pain was unrelenting. Captain Linder oversaw the operation from the bridge above. He wasn't sure if this man would survive long enough to even reach the shore. And if so, what then? There was no telling if their enemy would transport him to a hospital in time. Wedged beside the captain on one side of the bridge was a lookout, binoculars raised to his eyes. On the other side was his English-speaking second mate. The officer would accompany the shore party, to explain the situation. After that, Zimmerman's fate would be left to the moral conscience of these Americans.

"You must be clear that we intend to surrender," Linder explained.

"Yes, captain."

"Tell them that our men will be coming ashore unarmed. We expect to be treated in accordance with the laws of war."

"I will convey your message, if they don't shoot us on sight."

Linder's typically expressionless face showed a hint of despair. "It has been my pleasure to serve with you."

"The pleasure is mine, captain."

With the sailors and their patient aboard the dinghy, the second mate scrambled down and across the deck to join them. Pushing off the hull of U-202, the men paddled toward the beach, bobbing further across the waves with each stroke. For Captain Linder, after three hours trapped on this sandbar, it was time to make the announcement. With the faint glow of light already showing in the east, soon the shelling would begin. He had to get his men off this submarine while they still had a chance. As the captain lowered himself back down the ladder, however, he was struck by an observation. The angle… It was less than it had been, even when he'd climbed up just a short time before. Standing in the control room, he took a moment to get his bearings. Indeed, where the boat had keeled over earlier at roughly 40 degrees, it was now perhaps 30. Maybe less. It swayed more, as well, back and forth with the waves. The tide was coming in. He checked his watch. They could try one last time. One more shot at salvation before scrambling into life rafts and then blasting their craft to pieces. Linder picked up his handset. "We will make a last attempt to free the boat!" he announced. "If it fails, we will go together to captivity. Remember the first commandment; silence is golden. I want all men aft, on the double!" The captain waited while the men scrambled toward the stern, giving their bow just a little more buoyancy. When all was ready, he made a last call to the engine room. "Give me full power straight ahead!" he commanded. "Diesel and electric!"

"Full power, aye, aye!" cried the chief.

The sub shuddered as the engines surged. With each passing swell, the boat rocked further, to and fro, to and fro. "I think she's moving, captain!" the first officer called out. "I can feel it!"

"Come on, come on!" the captain shouted to his vessel.

On the fourth wave, the sub popped free, bobbing level in the water before surging forward like a rocket. All aboard felt the sensation, a simultaneous joy and relief passing through them. "Hurray!" they cried out in unison, faces showing disbelief and jubilation as they crowded together. They were saved.

"Zimmermann!" the captain cried out. "All stop!"

"All stop!" repeated the chief.

Linder rushed up the ladder, followed closely by his first officer. From the bridge, they saw the two sailors and the second mate, paddling like madmen back toward the sub. "Reverse, one quarter!" The submarine eased backward, closing the gap. "Full stop!" When the dinghy reached the hull, the raft and its occupants were hauled aboard.

"You did it!" cried the jubilant second officer. "We're clear!"

"Deflate this dinghy and get these men below," Linder replied.

"Aye, aye, sir."

"Forward one-third!" the captain called to his engine room.

"Forward one-third!" repeated the chief.

Linder grabbed the binoculars from his lookout and scanned the horizon for 180 degrees. No Coast Guard cutters in sight. It was beginning to look like they just might make it out of here after all.

For Seaman John Cullen, time was a blur as he sat at a table in the lighthouse station facing two Coast Guard intelligence officers. How long had it been since he'd first spotted those shadowy figures lurking on the beach? Two hours? Three? He couldn't quite say. Long enough for these two officers to arrive from Manhattan and call him off the beach for questioning. Lieutenant Sydney Franken examined the German cigarette pack. "You say you found this in the same location where you first encountered these men?" he asked.

"Not exactly, sir. When I found the cigarettes, we were a little further up the beach. Closer to the dunes."

"How much closer?" asked Lieutenant Fred Nirschel.

"Maybe halfway to the dunes, or a bit more."

Nirschel flipped through the damp bills. Two fifties, five twenties, and six tens. "You say the man who gave you this money had a gray streak in his hair?"

"Yes, sir, I'll never forget it."

"How old would you say the man was? Did you get a good enough look to tell?"

"I'd say he was in his 40's, but I can't be sure exactly."

"So, he wasn't an old man, then?"

"No, sir. He had this gray streak, but he wasn't an old man. That's why I won't forget it. That gray streak was peculiar, I'd say." Cullen watched as Franken jotted down notes on a pad. This was the third time the seaman had been through his story, first to Jennett, then Chief Boatswain's Mate Warren Barnes, the station master, and now these two men he'd never met before. He was beginning to wonder how much longer this would take when Barnes bolted back through the door.

"I think you men had better come with me," said the excited station master.

"What is it?" Franken's eyes lit up.

"We found some things on the beach. I've got my men unloading them from the truck."

"What kinds of things?" Nirschel rose to his feet.

"You gotta see for yourself."

Cullen followed the others out the front door, down a short driveway, and into the boathouse. A group of seamen stood beside four small wooden crates and a sandy canvas duffel. Next to the duffel was a pair of dark blue bathing trunks, a rubber raincoat, and two small shovels.

"We found this buried in the dunes," Barnes explained.

"Have you looked inside any of it?" Franken knelt beside the sea bag.

"That duffel is full of wet clothing. I don't know what's in the crates. We pried the top off one, but it's got a sealed container inside. I thought you should be present before we went any further."

"Good. Let's start with the bag." Franken cautiously opened the duffel and peered inside. Reaching in, he sorted through some of the items of clothing before pulling them out one at a time and laying them on the concrete floor. Four matching naval fatigues and one pair of white canvas sneakers. The intelligence officer turned a button on one of the uniforms. "Look at this. German all right."

A light murmur went up as the men leaned in for a better look. Cullen spotted the naval insignia, complete with a Nazi swastika. A sense of vindication overcame him. If anybody had doubted him before, they certainly wouldn't any longer. Nirschel went through the uniforms, reaching a hand into the pockets one by one until he pulled out another cigarette pack and a soggy book of matches. Holding the matchbook up to the light, he read the inscription out loud. "*Allumettes de Surete.* That sounds like French to me. Does anybody here speak French?"

The men passed wide-eyed glances, slowly shaking their heads.

"Let's take a look at these crates," said Franken.

Chief Barnes took the wooden lid off the crate that they'd already pried open. Very carefully, he lifted out a sealed tin container and placed it on the floor. Nirschel and Franken knelt beside it. "You men have a can opener?" Nirschel asked.

"Sure," said Barnes. "Brooks, get the man a can opener."

Seaman Brooks took off toward the station house. While the others waited, Nirschel examined the cigarettes. "*D. Mosel, Hamburg-Munchen*," he read out loud. "Same as the pack from the beach."

Brooks reappeared and handed a can opener to the Chief.

"You want the honors?" Barnes asked the intelligence officers.

"Go ahead," said Franken. "Just be careful. There could be explosives inside."

Barnes raised both eyebrows. "This isn't going to blow up on us, is it?"

"Not unless something goes horribly wrong."

"I appreciate your confidence…" Barnes knelt on one knee and used the can opener to carefully punch a hole along the top edge of the container. A hissing sound burst forth as pressurized air rushed out of the metal box. The startled chief jumped backward, half expecting to be blown to pieces. Slowly the whooshing noise subsided. "What the hell was that?"

"I don't know," said Nirschel. "Could be saltwater got in there, created some sort of chemical reaction."

"What should we do?"

"Seems all right now," said Franken. "Go ahead."

A somewhat more skeptical Barnes got back down on his knee. Methodically, he worked his way around until the lid was cut free and set aside. Barnes peered into the canister and then began to remove several small cardboard boxes, arranging them on the floor.

Cullen and the other men watched closely as Franken opened one of the small boxes. Inside were what appeared to be pen and pencil sets.

"Are those pens?" a seaman asked.

Franken lifted one and examined it closely. Unscrewing the two halves, he inspected the mechanism inside. "Timing devices. Very clever." He opened a larger box. It was filled with what looked like lumps of coal. Turning one over in his hands, it became clear to the intelligence officer that this was no ordinary coal. "Explosives. Some form of TNT, I suspect." He put the coal back into the box before going through some of the others, where he discovered vials of an unknown liquid and mysterious glass tubes. "I think we've seen enough. Let's pack this up as carefully as possible and your men can load it into our car. Nobody is to mention what we found here tonight. This is a very important point." Franken drove his statement home by looking from one seaman to the next. "As long as the Germans think this stuff is buried on the beach, they might come back for it. When they do, we'll nab them."

Chief Barnes turned to his men. "You heard the lieutenant. Montgomery, put those uniforms back in the sea bag. The rest of you take these other crates out to the lieutenant's car." Barnes packed the cardboard boxes back into the metal tin and then placed it all into the open crate before carrying it out of the boathouse himself.

The eastern sky glowed cobalt blue as John Cullen spotted armed soldiers patrolling the beach below. A mobile artillery unit dragged two howitzer cannons across the sand. Where he'd earlier seen the outline of a stranded submarine, there was nothing left but the frothing sea. What began for Cullen as a normal patrol had turned out to be the strangest night in his life. "Do you have any more questions for me, sir?" he asked Franken.

"Not at this time, seaman." With all the crates and the sea bag loaded inside, the lieutenant swung closed the back door to his station wagon. "We have all we need for the present, but you can expect us to be in touch."

"Have a rest, Cullen," said Barnes. "The army wants us off the beach anyway. You might as well get some shuteye."

"Thanks, Skipper." Exhaustion overtook Cullen as soon as he entered the station. Passing on up the stairs, he entered the crew's quarters and stripped off his uniform. The seaman stepped into the shower and turned the knobs, holding one hand in front of the water until the stream flowed warm from the head. Moving underneath it, he lathered his hands with a bar of soap, absentmindedly washing his body as he thought back to the events of that night, running the encounter with the Germans through his mind once more. "I'll see you in East Hampton," the man had said. What could he have meant by that? And where were he and the others now? Just one day before, the war had seemed so far away. Wandering up and down the beach on lonely patrols in the middle of the night, he'd never expected to actually encounter the enemy firsthand. Maybe he'd spot a suspicious vessel to report, if he was lucky. Not actual Germans, on the beach. Just like that, his perspective changed. The enemy was here. They'd threatened to kill him. For Seaman John Cullen, the war with Europe had arrived.

"Hey, George, look at that," Burger whispered. A thin line of smoke rose from a chimney attached to the station house beside them. "Somebody is in there."

Dasch scrambled to his feet. "Good! That's good. It means there's likely to be a train soon." He approached a window and peered inside. Still no signs of life from this vantage point. He looked at his watch. The time was 6 a.m. "Remember, if anybody asks, we're fishermen."

"And where is our fishing gear?" said Heinck.

"We lost it, when our boat overturned."

Dasch returned to his spot on the bench. Thirty more lonely minutes passed before they began to hear noises. Bangs and thumps emanated from within the ticket office. Next, a bolt on the station house door rattled open. The men sat up straight. Dasch peered left, then right. "I'll see about buying some tickets." He rose and walked to the station house door. This time the handle turned. The door swung open. Dasch walked on through. To his left, a large timetable was attached to the wall. Beside that was the ticket window where a sleepy-looking man with gray hair and glasses sat on a stool behind the counter. "Good morning." Dasch attempted a casual air, doing his best to conceal his jangled nerves. He used one hand to hold together his torn slacks as he moved to the timetable and gave it a quick inspection. The first train of the morning was due to arrive in twenty-seven minutes, at 6:57 a.m. Final destination; Jamaica, Queens. Dasch moved to the ticket window.

The stationmaster raised his eyebrows. "What can I do you for?"

"I'd like four tickets, please. To Jamaica."

The man pulled four tickets from a drawer and placed them on the counter between them. "That'll be twenty dollars."

Dasch reached into his pocket and pulled out his tobacco pouch, stuffed with bills. He peeled off a fifty and slid it across. "The fishing's been lousy around here," Dasch offered.

The stationmaster picked up the bill, counted out thirty dollars in change and slid it and the tickets across.

"Thank you," said Dasch.

"You have a good day now," the man said, though any sense of sincerity was lacking. Apparently, it was too early in the morning for that.

Back outside, Dasch handed a ticket to each man. He sat back down to wait, checking his watch once more. Nineteen minutes to go. Nineteen excruciating minutes. "When we arrive in Jamaica, we will split into two groups," Dasch told the men. "Heinck go with Quirin. Burger, you come with me. We will buy clean clothes and then meet again in the city. Do you know the Horn and Hardart Cafeteria?"

"No," Quirin answered. "Where is it?"

"It is on 8th Avenue, between 34th and 35th streets. Can you remember that?"

"I think so."

"Horn and Hardart. Eighth Avenue. We will meet there this afternoon, in the dining room upstairs."

Quirin's tight mouth and ashen pallor gave away his strain. They heard the train before they saw it, approaching from the east. When it pulled into the station, the men bounced to their feet, eager to put as much distance between themselves and Amagansett as possible. "Where do we sit?" Burger whispered.

"Second class. Follow me." As the train ground to a halt with a squeal of the breaks, Dasch led them onto a second-class carriage. A smattering of seats were already occupied by passengers in suits and fedoras, reading newspapers and smoking cigarettes. A woman with a bundle on her lap sat beside a bouncing toddler in a small navy outfit, complete with a round white cap. Nobody gave the newcomers much notice. The group found four empty seats, two in front of the other.

"I never rode on an American train before," Heinck admitted. The terror that stalked him all morning gave way to a tiny glimmer of joy.

Looking up and down the carriage, Dasch spotted a scattering of abandoned newspapers, resting on one seat here, another there. He quickly gathered as many as he could without calling undue attention to himself and passed out sections to each man. "Read these," he whispered with a light nod. The men quickly buried their faces behind the newsprint. Dasch placed a section across his shredded pants. The train lurched forward. Six hours after landing, they were on their way, headed straight to New York City. Aside from the one small hiccup on the beach, it had all gone reasonably well so far. All they had left to do was buy some dry clothes, find a hotel, and then disappear. The rest of Dasch's master plan would come together in due time.

Chapter Forty-Four

Novgorod Oblast, June 13, 1942

Incessant rain turned foxholes into snaking rivers of mud. Wolfgang Wergin's wet wool uniform clung to his skin as he lay on his belly in the muck, awaiting orders to advance. Fellow soldiers stretched out on either side, doing their best to keep their weapons clean. Ahead of them, a bare hillside angled down into a low gully and then back up to a tree line on the opposite side, a little more than 300 meters from their current position. Within sniper range. Just inside those trees was their objective: a battalion of enemy troops, dug in and waiting.

"How many do you think there are?" Otto Schreiber, Wolf's friend from basic training, lay prone in the trench beside him.

"I don't know," Wolf replied. "More than we got, though."

Otto nodded. "That's what I thought, too."

It was a week since they'd tasted their first combat and the boys had a fairly good grasp of the state of affairs. The Soviets had more men. Russian reinforcements seemed to arrive daily. More artillery. More airplanes. The bombardments were nearly unceasing. Rare moments of quiet on the battlefield did little to quell the tension. Both sides knew what was still ahead. Madness, chaos, death and destruction. During Wolfgang's previous assault on an enemy position they were lucky, or so he was told. Artillery took out two enemy machine gun nests. Wolf's battalion sustained relatively few casualties. He'd fired his weapon, as ordered, in the direction of the enemy lines. Whether he'd actually hit anyone was doubtful, but in the fog of war, it was hard to tell.

This time around the situation appeared to be more dire. The terrain between their positions was rougher, sloped and wet, with a small creek running through the middle. It would slow them down. The Russians were also better prepared, it seemed, with four machine gun nests this time and a battery of their artillery backing them up. Even so, this was ground that must be taken. And so, they waited, Wolfgang slowly sinking further into the muck.

"Fix bayonets!" their commanding officer hollered down the line.

"Fix bayonets!" his sergeant repeated. Each man reached up to the muzzle of his gun, removing the bayonet from the side and attaching it to the front, ready to stab a Russian soldier in the gut and watch him die. 'Better them than me,' Wolf tried to tell himself, all the while picturing a Soviet bayonet thrust into his own belly. If he died here in this muddy Russian field, in the middle of nowhere, his mother would never know. Kate Wergin would never find out what happened to her boy, going to her grave without having solved the mystery.

"I wish we'd just get started," said Otto. "The waiting is killing me."

"The waiting is the only thing that *won't* kill you."

Otto gave a nervous laugh. "I just don't like all of this sitting around. I want to get out of this trench already."

"Be careful what you wish for."

Scarcely had Wolfgang finished his sentence when German rockets and artillery opened up on the Russian lines, pounding the tree line with everything they had. Overhead, projectiles flew through the air. Underneath, the ground shuddered and shook with unearthly violence. Peeking over the wet berm in front of him, Wolfgang saw explosions of smoke and flames shredding the opposite forest into toothpicks. Wolf sank back low into the trench and covered his ears. For a full five minutes the bombardment went on, wave after wave of hot molten death raining down from the sky. "Prepare to charge!" a German officer called out.

"Prepare to charge!" repeated a sergeant.

Silence momentarily descended over the hazy field. Only the anguished cries of wounded Russian soldiers drifted across the lines. This was it. When the order came, the German soldiers leaped to their feet and ran. A few steps late, Wolf quickly followed after, plodding through the sodden earth with his weapon clutched in both hands. There was no time to think. If there had been, any intelligent human would have turned and run the other way. But no, that was not an option, and so, Wolf followed orders, one step after another.

He'd sprinted for 100 yards when the Soviet artillery opened up on them, raining down shells that exploded like black flowers of death, cutting his comrades to pieces. Wolfgang felt a hot shard slice his right calf, yet still he ran, past men writhing on the ground and soaked in blood. Another piece of metal grazed his helmet. Fifty yards further and the machine guns began to fire, raking left to right and back across their line. Wolfgang crossed the small creek, leaping over bodies as he went. The enemy lines were 150 meters away, up a treacherous slope. Soldiers from the battalion were nearly to the tree line as Wolf began his final dash, expecting searing machine gun rounds to cut him down at any moment. All he could do was charge forward, boots sticking in the wet glop as he went. Reaching the enemy trenches, he joined the chaos of men firing at one another point blank, thrusting their steel bayonets deep into each others' flesh, struggling to survive for just this moment. Kill every man in an opposing uniform. Wolf momentarily froze, the eye in a raging storm of carnage. A Russian hurtled forward, bayonet at the ready. This was not a man. It was a mere child in an over-sized uniform. Wolf raised his rifle, yet still the boy came, charging through the wet earth, youthful fury flashing across his face. Twelve yards, ten, five... Wolf heard the crack of his gun and saw the boy drop in a twisted clump, the fingers of one hand reaching skyward as blood spread across his tunic. Moving forward, the battle continued in a blur of motion and noise, chaos and confusion, his overloaded mind paralyzed and numb.

It was not until Wolfgang saw enemy troops fleeing through broken, shattered trees that he realized the battle was won. Fresh corpses littered the ground, inside the enemy trench and out. Germans and Russians, draped across the ground and each other. Surviving Russians were executed, one bullet to the head, no wasting ammunition. Off on their flanks, grenades exploded in the machine gun positions. And then, only the sounds of wounded comrades, clinging to life on this lonely hill. Wolf knelt low to examine the stinging pain in his calf. A tear ripped in his trousers. Blood running down his leg and into his boot. He'd survived. But what of Otto? Where was he?

"Otto Schrieber?" Wolf asked a passing soldier. "Has anyone seen Otto Schreiber?"

"Nein," came the answer. "Who's Otto Schreiber?"

Wolfgang found his friend on the far side of the creek, spread on his back with eyes wide open, his uniform shredded by the metal shards of an exploding artillery shell, a large gash across his left temple. Otto's expression was frozen in bewilderment. How could this have happened to *him* he seemed to ask in perpetuity? Wolfgang stood over the corpse, his mind flashing back to the Russian youth, charging forward, forward, forward. In Wolf's mind, it was Otto's face on the Russian boy. Otto who dropped to Wolf's feet, dead in the mud. It was Otto who Wolfgang had killed. He knelt on one knee and used his fingers to draw down Otto's eyelids, trying in vain to bring a sense of peace and dignity to this broken vessel of a human being. At least Otto's mother would know what became of him. Her son had died in battle, a hero of the Reich. Just as the mother of the young Russian might learn about her own son, in time. Wolfgang flashed to the image of Kate, standing in their kitchen with a white apron over her blue dress. *Her* son went off for a two-week trip to Mexico and simply vanished into thin air. Wolf did his best to feel nothing at all.

Chapter Forty-Five

New York City, June 13, 1942

The train pulled into Jamaica, Queens. End of the line. Four men stood and walked off with the rest of the passengers, clutching small bags as they quietly moved up the platform and out to the street. After pausing briefly, they passed a few words between themselves before heading two to the left, two to the right.

One man did his best to hold a wrinkled newspaper in front of his right leg as he and his partner continued several blocks up the street. Coming to a large clothing store, the pair peered through the front window before walking inside. Wet, dirty, and with pants torn to shreds, George Dasch was overcome by a sense of shame. Perhaps it was his imagination, but mothers seemed to clutch children just a little tighter to their sides when they saw him. Afternoon shoppers gave him an extra-wide berth as he went past. In the men's section, he and Burger found a young clerk behind a sales counter.

"Can I help you gentlemen?" A hint of disdain dripped from the man's voice.

"We are looking for new suits," Dasch answered. "Something casual, perhaps in a tweed."

The clerk's expression brightened somewhat. "Certainly."

"And a new shirt and underwear while we're at it."

"Of course, of course. Right this way…"

Burger and Dasch followed the clerk to a rack of suits where he began to pull one and then another, holding them out for inspection. "How about something like this?"

"Yes, I think this one might work." Dasch took a suit in hand. "You have a tailor on the premises, I presume?"

"We do. Your suit will be ready first thing tomorrow morning, no charge."

"Can you alter it while I wait?"

"Certainly, for a small extra fee."

"Fine. Perhaps you could be so kind as to point me toward a dressing room?"

"Absolutely, right this way."

One hour later, Burger and Dasch exited the store in clean, dry clothing. It made all the difference. They may still have had their accents to consider, but after nearly two decades living in this country, Dasch's was slight. They could blend in. All they had to do was catch a subway into the city, find a hotel, and meet back up with the others. After a rough start on the beach that morning, things were looking up.

To John Cullen, it almost seemed as though the events of the previous night had all been a dream. Here he was, eating a late breakfast of scrambled eggs and toast with two of his fellow seamen. It could almost have been any other morning, except for the topic of conversation, and the electricity still in the air.

"I hear the FBI showed up this morning."

"I thought the army was taking charge?"

"I guess everyone wants a piece of this one."

"Did they find anything else on the beach last night?"

"Yeah, some bottle of something. Schnapps, I think they said."

"What the hell is schnapps?"

"Liquor. German liquor."

"Figures, those krauts would be tying one on down there on our beach. Just think how happy they'd a been if they gutted poor Cullen here!"

The prospect of being carved open by a knife made Cullen look down at his midsection, as if to make sure he was wholly intact. "I'm not sure that character I talked with had it in him. Those other fellows, though… I didn't get a very good look at them."

"They're Nazis ain't they? This is war. You're one lucky son-of-a-bitch they didn't kill you, I'd say."

"Maybe I should have had a gun. How come all we get to take on our patrols is a stinking flashlight?"

"I bet that changes after this."

"If those Nazis are still hanging around here somewhere, I bet our guys will catch 'em. I mean, those krauts have got to come back for their supplies, right?"

"I hope so." Cullen scooped up the rest of his eggs with a fork, plastered them on his last bit of toast, and finished them off.

A third seaman ducked his head through the door. "Hey, Cullen, the skipper wants to see you!"

"Barnes?"

"In his office."

Cullen stood from the table and carried his dishes to a small tub by the sink. He drank the last dregs of his morning coffee, placed the dishes into the tub, and hurried on out of the galley. In Barnes' office, he found the weary-looking skipper sitting behind his desk. Two men in dark suits stood to one side.

"Seaman Cullen, come on in," said Barnes. "These men are from the FBI. They'd like to ask you some questions, if you don't mind."

"I don't mind." Cullen moved on into the room.

"Have a seat."

The seaman took the chair facing his boss. The FBI men moved closer, one of them pulling a notepad and pencil from his pocket. He was a large man with a square jaw and dark hair combed back with grease. "I'm Special Agent Brightman. This is Special Agent Emerich."

"Good morning."

"We understand you were the man who encountered the suspects on the beach. During your patrol last night, is that correct?"

"Yes, sir, that's right."

"Can you give me your name and rank?"

"Seaman Second Class, John Cullen, United States Coast Guard."

"Why don't you tell us the whole story, from the beginning?" The man leaned against the edge of the desk and took notes as Cullen relayed his encounter once more. When he was finished, the two agents eyed one another, as though passing some secret, unspoken code between them.

"If you don't mind, we'd like you to come with us." Emerich spoke this time. He was rounder, with a hint of baby fat still in his cheeks.

"Where to? You're not taking me to the city are you?" Cullen couldn't imagine what else he had to tell them. It all seemed like a spectacular waste of time when they could be busy tracking these Germans.

"We'd like to question you in a neutral location," said Emerich.

"What's a neutral location?"

"Someplace we can talk in private."

"Not far," Brightman explained. "We'd like to take you over to East Hampton so we can go through your story more carefully, in case we missed any important details."

"Sure." Cullen cast a quick glance to Chief Barnes. After a nod of affirmation from his skipper, the seaman stood from his chair. He followed the FBI men out of the station and down the front steps to a nearby car. Brightman opened a rear door to the sedan and stood aside as Cullen climbed in. After heaving the door shut, the agent took his place in the front passenger seat. Emerich was behind the wheel as he started the car and pulled off up the road.

"I think I already told you everything I know." Cullen saw Emerich's eyes on him in the rearview mirror.

"We just have a few more questions, that's all," Brightman replied. "Standard procedure."

"Anything I can do to help." For reasons that Cullen couldn't quite understand, he was beginning to feel a flitting, abstract sense of guilt. He'd fulfilled his duty. Cullen had nothing to worry about. All the same, he couldn't deny the sense that a dark cloud was hanging over him. The only thing to do was tell them exactly what had transpired, as many times as these agents needed to hear it.

When they reached the highway, the car turned left and picked up speed, barreling down the road for two miles until they pulled into the sleepy village of East Hampton. Emerich continued on in silence until they arrived at a small house on the opposite side of town. He pulled into the driveway and turned off the car. All three men got out and the agents led Cullen up the drive and into the house. They walked through a living room with worn couches and a brick fireplace, continuing into a kitchen where Emerich pulled a chair out from the table. "Have a seat." Cullen did as requested. The agents took two chairs directly opposite. Once again the notebooks came out.

"Let's say we go through your story one more time?" said Brightman.

"The whole thing, start to finish?" It was becoming tiresome.

"Humor us."

Cullen heaved a sigh and then began with the start of his patrol, straining to remember every last detail as he went through his tale.

"This second man, the one with the sea bag," Brightman asked. "Do you think you would recognize him if you saw him again?"

"No, sir, I don't think that I would."

"And the two men by the water?"

"No, sir. I never got much of a look at them. We were some distance away. I only saw their outlines, really."

"But the man who spoke with you?" Emerich asked.

"Yeah, sure. I'd recognize him, from that gray streak I told you about."

The questions continued this way, one after another, with Brightman filling his notepad. When Cullen reached the end, the agents traded another conspiratorial glance. "If you don't mind staying put right here, Special Agent Emerich and I have a few things to discuss in private."

"Sure. I got nowhere else to be."

The two men stood from the table, picked up their notepads, and left the room. Bored and restless, Cullen spotted a clock nearby. He watched the seconds tick past, and then minutes, until after nearly half an hour the agents returned and retook their places at the table.

"Thank you for waiting," said Emerich. "There's one more thing that we can't quite understand. Why is it, do you think, that these men didn't kill you?"

The question sounded to Cullen like some sort of accusation, though he couldn't quite understand where they were going with it. "I don't know. I got lucky, I guess."

"You got lucky."

"I guess." Cullen shrugged.

"German agents landing on the beach in the dead of night, and they didn't kill you?" said Brightman.

"No, sir, obviously they did not." The seaman did not like the way this was going.

"You see," Emerich cut back in. "If this whole thing was for real then those men, assuming they were German spies... They would have killed you."

"But they didn't," said Cullen.

"That's right, they didn't," said Emerich. "Four men, speaking German, with German navy uniforms..."

"Surely, you can understand how this looks from an outsider's perspective," said Brightman. "What we're getting at here is, how do we know you're not a part of the whole thing?"

Cullen's mouth dropped open. He was almost too stunned to speak. "You think I'm with the Germans?!"

"They would have killed you otherwise," Brightman repeated. "It only makes sense."

"But..." Cullen stammered. "If I was with the Germans, then why would I turn them in at all? Why would I say anything about it? You think just because they didn't kill me, that makes me a German spy or something?!"

"Frankly, we don't know what to think," said Emerich. "That's why we're giving you a chance to explain yourself. It just seems awfully suspicious. Wouldn't you agree?"

The seaman shook his head. "If I was a part of it, why did I run straight back and tell the skipper all about it? Why did I hand over the money that man gave me, instead of just keeping my mouth shut?!"

The agents' expressions shifted from a cocky self-satisfaction to a look of mild distaste. "That's what we'd like to understand," said Emerich.

"I don't know why they didn't kill me. You go catch them and then ask them that yourselves. I told you everything I know, exactly the way it happened, twice. You believe what you want."

Brightman closed his notebook. He wasn't pleased by this outburst. "I think we're done here for the present. You can expect to hear from us again as the investigation proceeds."

Was this a threat, Cullen wondered? His body shook as they stood and then led him back out to the car. It would almost have been funny if it wasn't so serious. Just the mere suggestion that Cullen wasn't a loyal American made him feel ill. The skipper knew. Jennett, too. They'd back him up. As the two agents drove him to the station, Cullen sat in the back seat running the question through his mind: "If I was a German spy, why would I have turned those Nazis in?" Up front, the FBI agents were no longer in any apparent hurry. Indeed, they seemed to feel they had it all figured out. That still left the larger question, Cullen realized. Where were the Nazis? Looking out the window, he gazed into fallow fields and remnant patches of green forest, straining to spot any suspicious figures hiding in the brush. They had to be around here somewhere. He just hoped these FBI agents were up to the challenge of tracking them down.

With the batteries aboard U-202 running low, it was time to switch from electric power to diesel. That meant surfacing for the first time since their miraculous escape. Captain Linder would have preferred to stay submerged until nightfall, but under the circumstances he had no choice. Before giving the order, he used the periscope to scan the horizon for three-hundred and sixty degrees. No other vessels in sight. Linder retracted the periscope. "Prepare to surface!"

"Aye sir, prepare to surface!" his first officer replied.

With ballast blown from the tanks and stabilizer fins pointing the bow upwards, the men soon felt the sway of the sea. "Open the hatch!" the captain called out. A crewman climbed into the conning tower and cranked open the wheel, sending a stream of seawater spraying into the control room.

"Engineer, switch to diesel!" Linder called over the intercom.

"Aye, aye, captain, switching to diesel!"

Linder ascended to the bridge, accompanied by two lookouts. This time the captain used binoculars to scan for enemy vessels. Still nothing. It seemed they'd made their getaway. Handing the binoculars to a lookout, Linder climbed back down below where he made his way to the infirmary. A medic stood watch over Zimmermann. "How is doing?" the captain asked.

"Better," the medic replied.

Indeed, the sailor's eyes were open. His face was pale, but otherwise the man seemed much improved. No more moaning agony. "How do you feel, Zimmermann?"

"I think I'm going to live, Captain."

"I have no doubt. I've contacted a supply boat with full medical facilities on board. We will rendezvous in forty-eight hours and transfer you to them."

"Thank you, Captain."

Linder shook his head in disbelief. Just a few hours earlier he'd thought all was lost, this vessel itself moments from destruction, yet somehow deliverance arrived. Zimmermann would live, their mission a success. For U-202, the war continued. "A higher power watches over us." It was all the captain could say.

Chapter Forty-Six

New York City, June 13, 1942

At the watch counter in Macy's department store, George Dasch examined the merchandise inside a glass case. Through all of his years in this country, he'd watched every penny. Dasch had survived in the United States. He never thrived. Now with $90,000 in cash stashed away in a rail station locker, he could afford whatever he wanted. He had to admit, it felt pretty good.

"Can I help you with anything?" A sales clerk stood across the counter.

Dasch pointed to a fancy-looking watch with gold bezel and matching band. "How much is this one?"

"Oh, the Lord Elgin. That's one of my favorites. That would be thirty-nine dollars and ninety-eight cents."

George looked up to the clerk. "Can I try it on?"

"Certainly, sir."

Peter Burger stood nearby as the clerk pulled the watch from the case and placed it on Dasch's wrist.

George admired the gleam of gold. "What do you think?" he asked Burger.

"It's a nice watch."

"I'll take it," Dasch said.

"Wonderful, I can ring you up right over here." The clerk moved to a register.

"Are you going to get one?" George turned back to his partner.

"No, that's all right." Peter didn't approve.

"You might as well. We have to blend in, right? Every man needs a good watch."

"Not today. Maybe another time."

"Suit yourself."

"I *would* like to get a camera. I had a Leica back home but my wife had to sell it. You know how things are." Burger thought back to his time in Gestapo captivity, with his wife outside, barely able to survive. "I think they owe me that much."

"Sure they do, boy, sure they do! We'll get you a Leica! First, I think we could use a few more items of clothing. Maybe another suit, with a new hat and scarf? What do you think about that?"

Burger shrugged. "I suppose."

"Enjoy yourself! And don't forget…" Dasch leaned close, reducing his words to a conspiratorial whisper. "It's the Fuhrer who's paying."

After picking out another set of clothing each, along with hats, Burger and Dasch purchased brown leather suitcases with which to cart off their spoils. The men waited for the tailors to work their magic, then carried their goods out of the store in the cases. Stepping onto the crowded sidewalk, they could have been visitors from just about anywhere, swallowed amongst hordes of spectators headed to a massive military parade on Fifth Avenue. Burger's head craned skyward as a formation of B-17 bombers roared overhead. All he wanted was to disappear into the nearest hotel. Just a few blocks away they came to one that looked promising. *The Governor Clinton.*

"This ought to do," said Dasch.

"Fine," Burger agreed.

The pair headed inside and proceeded through the lobby to the front desk. "We'd like two rooms," Dasch announced. "If you have any available, of course."

"Sure, we have rooms." A front desk clerk nodded his head. "Five dollars per night each. How many nights would you like?"

"We'll pay for four nights."

The clerk opened a registry and slid it across the counter. "Sign here."

Dasch wrote the name John George Day along with a date and signature before handing the pen to Burger, who signed his real name one line below.

"That will be forty dollars."

"Can we have adjoining rooms?" Dasch asked.

The clerk gave a quick look through his ledger. "I have two rooms on the fourteenth floor, directly across the hall from one another."

"That would be fine." Dasch slid two twenty-dollar bills across the counter. The clerk found the keys from amongst a wall of mailboxes directly behind him before tapping twice on a small bell. A uniformed bellhop appeared by their side.

"These gentlemen are in rooms 1414 and 1421." The clerk handed the keys to the bellhop.

"Yes, sir." The bellhop dropped the keys into a pocket and then lifted their bags, one in each hand, and placed them on a nearby cart. "Right this way."

Riding up the elevator, Dasch checked the time on his new watch. It was two-fifteen in the afternoon. Ten hours since they'd first set foot on the beach in Amagansett. Forty-five minutes until they were due to meet the others at the Horn and Hardart Cafeteria. Everything according to plan. The elevator opened on the fourteenth floor and the bellhop showed the men to the first room, unlocking the door and then carrying Dasch's case inside. "Thank you." George followed the bellhop back into the hall and then waited while Burger was likewise situated. When the bellhop emerged once more, Dasch shoved a dollar into his hand.

"Thank you, sir." The man gave a quick bow. "If you should need anything else, please don't hesitate to ask."

Dasch watched the bellhop move down the hall and into the elevator. "Clean yourself up," he said when the doors had closed. "We'll leave in thirty minutes to meet the others."

Burger's expression was blank. He'd have preferred to barricade himself in the room and never come out. He felt vulnerable wandering around in public. The FBI was bound to be searching for them. All the same, Peter wasn't ready to argue the point. "Fine."

"I'll knock when it's time." Dasch retreated into his own room and closed the door. Reaching into a pocket, he took out a fresh packet of cigarettes. On a table near the window, he found an ashtray. Resting in the bottom, a pack of matches, white with gold letters embossed across the front. *Governor Clinton Hotel.* George pulled out a chair and sat. Attempting to open the pack, his fingers trembled. With determination, he managed to extract a single cigarette. Striking a match was no less difficult. On the third try, success. George lifted the quavering flame to his cigarette and inhaled, filling his lungs with a desperately needed breath of smoke. Nicotine flooded his capillaries, flowing directly into his blood and then straight on to his brain. Eyes opened. Pupils dilated. It helped, a little bit. Anything to calm his nerves. He was here. The first part of his mission was a success. But now for the second part. George needed to formulate a strategy. The other group would land in just a few more days on a beach in Florida. Dasch's conscience weighed on him as he thought of the Haupt kid. Herbie was no saboteur. Sure, he was annoying at times, but he was no Nazi. Peter either, for that matter. Turning the whole thing in was a complicated business, though he couldn't wait too long. If the FBI caught up with them before he made contact, his entire plan would be ruined. Instead of a hero, Dasch would be branded as a traitor. He lifted the shuddering cigarette back to his lips and inhaled once more. "Get yourself together, George," he exhaled. Dasch stood and moved to admire the view. Skyscrapers ascended into the heavens all around. Fourteen stories below, New Yorkers moved like ants up and down the sidewalks, yellow taxis clogging the streets in between. Dasch opened the window to soak in the cacophony of automobile engines, honking horns and distant sirens. Despite his deep anxiety, George Dasch felt that he was home again at last. If only he'd never left.

Chapter Forty-Seven

New York City, June 14, 1942

Scrambled eggs, toast with jam and butter, sausages, ham, tomato, sliced fruit, orange juice and coffee. To Peter Burger it seemed extravagant, especially during wartime, but as Dasch kept reminding him, "The Fuhrer is paying." George said the same thing the night before when they'd dined on choice cuts of steak in the hotel restaurant. All through the meal, and on a long walk afterward, Dasch openly conveyed his disdain for the Nazi party. Now that they'd arrived in New York, George had no intention of carrying out their mission. That much was obvious. He put on a good show around the others, but whenever it was just the two of them alone, Dasch let his bile and frustration spill forth.

"I know exactly what you're up to," Burger at last confronted him.

"If you knew that, you would have to kill me."

A light smirk crossed Burger's lips. "I am quite sure that our intentions are similar."

On this first morning, Dasch sipped from his coffee as the two men sat at the table in his room, the spoils of their breakfast spread between them with a room service cart parked nearby. George carefully considered his response. "I have some tests that I need to put you through first, before I can confide my plans." The atmosphere shifted, from one of jovial defiance to a wary tension. Dasch ate the last of his eggs in silence, his hand shaking once again as he brought the fork to his lips. When he was finished, George placed the utensils on his plate. He and Burger sat back in their chairs, each taking the measure of the other. "All finished?" Dasch asked.

"Yes."

"I hope the breakfast was to your satisfaction."

"Yes, fine."

Dasch inhaled deeply. During their conversations thus far, he'd openly tested Burger's loyalties. He'd danced around the truth, yet George still hadn't crossed that line. He hadn't come straight out and said what he must say, without a shadow of a doubt. Once he did, there would be no going back. Burger might very well disagree with him. It was possible that George had misjudged him. Pete was guarded. He kept his true feelings hidden, deep inside. He was also one of the earliest members of the Nazi party. Yet George knew what they'd done to him. It was time to put their cards on the table, to find out exactly where things stood, with no more ambiguity. Dasch stood and then lifted the plates and cups, placing them on the service cart. When it was loaded, he wheeled the cart across the room, through the door and out into the hall. Coming back, Dasch closed the door and used his key to lock it from the inside. His anxiety surged as he tossed the keys into the bathtub and then closed the bathroom door. Burger watched with curiosity as Dasch stalked across the room with nervous energy, his expression pale. After opening the window, he leaned out to take a quick look down. A shiver shot through George from head to toe as he pictured himself sprawled on the sidewalk far below, his head cracked open on the concrete. Dasch took two quick steps backward, his face flushed. "You and I need to come to an understanding." He stood straight and tall, fists clenched tightly by his sides. "If we can't, then either I go out the window or you go out the window. I want the truth, nothing else, regardless of what it is. If we can't agree, we will have to fight it out."

Burger laughed out loud, shaking his head in amusement. "There is no need for either of us to go out the window. We both feel very much the same way."

Slowly, the color returned to Dasch's face. His fists unclenched. His head nodded. Relief. "You and I spoke once, during our training." Dasch was still tentative. "You told me some of your history."

"Yes. I remember."

"I didn't let you finish. I was afraid that it was not the right time."

Burger looked away, turning his gaze out the window toward the New York City skyline.

"I would like to hear the rest."

Placing his hands on his thighs, Peter sat up straight in his chair.

"You can speak freely." Dasch closed the window, hoping to put Burger at ease. "I understand you were in a concentration camp, but I don't know why."

"I spoke the truth. That is why." Burger spat the words in anger.

"Ah, the truth. The truth is dangerous business these days in Germany." Dasch retook his seat. "About what, exactly, did you tell the truth? Please, I'm begging you to tell me your story, no matter how bad it is or how good it is. I want you to tell me the truth and nothing but the truth. If you will do that, I will tell you my story exactly as it is. I will explain to you why I went into this undertaking, but before I do that you must show me that we have faith in each other."

For Peter, it was as though a heavy fog was lifting. All of those secrets hidden away inside ate at his very soul. In Germany, confiding them in anyone but Bettina would have amounted to a swift and certain death sentence. Yet here, in this New York hotel room, the man tasked with leading their mission was offering Burger the opportunity to speak his mind, unmolested and without dire consequence. It was an opportunity that Peter couldn't hope to resist. "I was sent to Poland, to write a report. I was tasked with detailing conditions in the camps there. You can guess what I saw."

"Yes, I can imagine."

Burger shook his head slowly as he thought back. "I believed in the movement once. I thought it was a revolution, for a greater Germany."

"You were with the stormtroopers. Correct?"

"Yes. That is correct," Burger acknowledged. "I was with Hitler in Munich, back in 1923."

"Did you know him?"

"Yes, I knew him. I fought with him. When sixteen of our comrades were shot dead in the street, I was there."

"But you left Germany. You came to America. Why did you do that?"

"After Munich, things went badly. When Hitler was arrested, I knew that I must leave. Our lives were in danger, all of us. And so I came to America. Seven years I was here. I served in the National Guard. Did you know?"

"Yes. I saw that in your file."

"First in Michigan and then Wisconsin."

"If you felt safe here, then why return to Germany…?"

"Why did *you*?"

Dasch shrugged and then took another drag off his cigarette. "It wasn't always so easy for me here. I suppose I didn't realize how good I had it until I'd gone."

"So you understand. After '29 there were no jobs. I couldn't find work. Not steady work. My family in Germany, they sent me a ticket so I went home."

"In 1933, correct?"

"Yes."

"How long was it before you went to work for General Röhm?" Dasch tried to coax the information out carefully. He knew that this story took a difficult turn.

Burger's eyes narrowed. He'd spent the past nine years avoiding this topic at all costs, yet the memories were raw as ever. "I worked for Röhm, yes," Peter conceded. "Shortly after my return, I was assigned as the general's aide-de-camp. I traveled with him everywhere. Later I was made assistant to his personal physician, Doctor Ketterer."

"Tell me about that," Dasch pressed. "The night they came for Röhm, you were there?"

"It was morning." In his mind, Burger relived the terror, his blood pressure surging just as it had that very day.

"What happened that morning? What do you remember?"

Fear shifted to rage and frustration. "We were in a hotel, on the outskirts of Munich. A conference was scheduled that day. All the top officials were to attend, Hitler included. The night before was a celebration. Röhm believed that the Fuhrer would finally give him what he wanted. The general would take full control of the Reichswher." Burger thought back to that one exact moment in time. The moment when everything changed. The knock. Loud and insistent. "I was fast asleep, but there was a commotion in the hall. A pounding on the door. When I opened it, the doctor was standing outside with his wife, surrounded by SS officers armed with submachine guns. 'Get your bag," he said. 'We're leaving. Don't waste any time.' The doctor's haunted expression told me all I needed to know. Death had arrived…" Burger paused, swallowing hard.

"It's all right, take your time."

"Just a few meters down the hallway stood a figure in a gray suit and overcoat. A small man, but with such power. The Fuhrer himself. Our eyes met." Peter tilted his head to one side as he tried to make some sense of it. "I don't know if he remembered me. I saw only emptiness in those eyes. That's when it became clear to me. The general demanded too much. He would not take control of the army. Instead… I thought of him, sleeping peacefully just down the hall. It was too late to save him, but perhaps I could still save myself. I gathered my things as quickly as I could."

"Why do you think you were spared?"

"It was the doctor. I owe my life to that man." Peter looked to his hands, resting on the table. "He could have left me behind. He didn't have to knock on my door. He didn't have to save me, but the doctor insisted."

"And you were the only survivors?"

Peter nodded, overcome by a swirling mix of guilt, anger and despair. He pictured the faces of friends and colleagues as they were stood up against a wall in the early morning mist. What had they thought in those last moments, as they struggled to understand? By the time they were gunned down, Peter Burger was in the back of a staff car, driving into the city in tense silence. "The general, he was shot a few days after. And then the real killing began. Three thousand SA men, rounded up…"

"Did you think they'd come back for you?"

"Of course." Elbows on the table, Burger rested his face in his hands. Once upon a time, he'd found a sense of belonging amongst the National Socialists. He'd believed in their stated cause. Hitler and the Nazis would lift the German people to the place of prominence that they deserved. A place of strength and dignity. Sitting here in New York, Peter understood that it wasn't he who would betray the Nazis. No, it was the Nazis who had betrayed him.

By the time their taxi pulled up to the meeting point at Grant's Tomb, Dasch and Burger were late. They'd already missed an earlier rendezvous scheduled for the Swiss Chalet restaurant, but once

Dasch had Burger talking, he didn't want to interrupt. Instead, they'd continued for hours, sharing their deep-seated enmity for the Hitler regime. They'd begun to formulate a plan for turning in their sabotage operation to the FBI. First, however, they needed to maintain the confidence of the other men for a little while longer. They couldn't tip their hand too soon. And so, Dasch paid for the taxi and the pair walked toward the monument, spotting the others side-by-side on a bench. Pretending not to notice, Dasch and Burger continued casually past, heading off down 117th Street. Quirin and Heinck waited a beat and then stood to follow, slowly gaining until they caught up at the intersection of Broadway.

"We were supposed to meet at the Swiss Chalet!" Quirin hissed as they crossed the street together. "Or did you forget?!"

"I apologize," said Dasch. "I was obliged to meet with a certain person who may be of assistance to us."

"Who is this person?" Heinck pressed.

"I am not at liberty to discuss their identity. I can only say that everything is progressing according to plan. Did you find a suitable hotel?" On the far side of the intersection, the men continued together up the sidewalk.

"Yes," Quirin answered. "The Chesterfield, as you suggested."

Dasch suspected that this was a lie. He'd already called the Chesterfield, asking for the agreed-upon aliases. Nobody by either of those names was checked in. These men did not trust him. "You should try to find an apartment," he suggested.

Quirin and Heinck looked to each other without speaking.

"My next task is to ensure that the papers provided to us by German intelligence are sufficient," Dasch continued. "I will be leaving the city for a few days in order to meet with some people in Washington. Peter and I will remain in touch."

"We should return to Long Island as soon as possible to retrieve the supplies!" Quirin protested.

"No!" Heinck countered his partner. "I told you, it is too dangerous!"

"But how will we fulfill our mission?!"

"We can't retrieve the boxes. What if they are watching?!"

"Alas, boys, I think Henry is right," Dasch agreed. "But all is not lost. Remember your training. We will manufacture our own explosives. We can still succeed if we set our minds to it."

Heinck shook his head and mumbled to himself. "Forget it. This job is over…"

Burger kept his mouth shut, afraid that anything he said might reveal his true intentions.

"I must contact the FBI immediately," Dasch explained as soon as he and Burger left the others. "If we are arrested before I speak with them it will be very difficult to explain ourselves."

"Agreed. Shall we call from our hotel?"

"I don't want to waste another minute. Let's find a payphone."

"There's a hotel," Burger gestured as they approached the corner of Madison Avenue and 52nd Street. "They should have a phone."

"Let's check." The men ducked into the lobby. A bank of phone booths lined a far wall. "You wait here while I make the call." Dasch entered a booth and closed the door tightly behind him. Picking up a phone book, he scrolled through the government listings until he found a number for the Federal Bureau of Investigation, New York office. He lifted the receiver, dropped a few coins into the slot, and dialed. Beads of sweat formed on his brow as he leaned against a wall, struggling not to collapse from the anxiety. In his earpiece, he heard the phone ringing on the other end of the line. On the third ring, a voice answered.

"FBI, how can I help you?"

Dasch was already stumped. What was he to say? He hadn't thought that far ahead. "I wonder, are you able to take a statement?" he asked.

"I'll transfer you, please hold."

As he waited, Dasch focused on his breathing, in and out as evenly as he could. Another voice came on the line. "Special Agent O'Sullivan."

"Hello," Dasch tried again. "Are you able to take a statement?"

"What sort of statement?"

Dasch's voice dropped a few octaves. He spoke in a near whisper. "I am a German citizen. I arrived in this country yesterday morning…." He took a moment to collect himself. "I have information of the utmost importance to national security."

"I see. Hold on a minute while I transfer you."

Dasch went through the same procedure two more times with different agents. He was nearly ready to give up when the fourth man came on the line. "This is McWhorter, how can I help you?"

"I'm trying to find somebody who will take a statement!" Dasch pleaded.

"What's this all about?"

"I'm a German citizen. I have some important information regarding national security."

"What kind of information?"

"I can't tell you that exactly." Dasch was cagy. "Not on the phone. This is so big, only Washington is the right place to spring it."

"Washington, huh?"

"The person who should hear it first would be John Edgar Hoover himself."

"Mr. Hoover is a busy man."

"I know that he is, sir, but he will want to hear what I have to say."

"What is your name?"

Dasch pictured agents arresting him before he'd had a chance to properly confess. He wanted to do this on his own terms. "My name is Franz Daniel Pastorius. Are you writing this down?"

"Yes, sir. Why don't you spell that for me?"

"Franz. F-R-A-N-Z," Dasch spelled out each name.

"Uh-huh. So how about you come on down to our office and talk to me yourself, Mr. Pastorius? There's no need to wait for Mr. Hoover, we could take your full statement." Dean McWhorter scrawled the name on a blank piece of letterhead and then leaned back in his chair. On this quiet evening, his unfortunate assignment was to man what was referred to as the "Nutter's Desk," tasked with mollifying cranks, crackpots, and crazies, one loony after another.

"No, I'm not ready to come in yet," Dasch declined. "You tell Washington that they will hear from me soon. I want you to pass a message to your Washington office, in order that they will expect me."

"I'd prefer it if you just came in to discuss this in person."

"No, sir, nothing doing!" Dasch was becoming irritated. "I would like you to pass my message along to Mr. Hoover."

"All right, have it your way."

"I want you to write this out."

"Sure."

"I, Franz Daniel Pastorius, shall try to get in contact with your Washington office this coming week, either on Thursday or Friday."

"How will they recognize you?" McWhorter jotted down the message.

"I'm about forty years old and I have a little gray in my temples."

"OK."

"Please repeat to me the time and date that this message was taken."

"June 14, 1942, 7:51 p.m."

"Thank you. Can you also repeat the message, please?"

"I, Franz Daniel Postorius will be in touch with the Washington office to speak to Director Hoover on Thursday or Friday."

"Franz Daniel Pastorius. With an *a*."

"Right."

"Thank you. I will be in touch with them soon." When he hung up the phone, Dasch felt a faint glimmer of relief. It had begun. If they apprehended him now, he could point to this message as proof of intent. He wasn't a saboteur, he was an American hero, fighting against Hilter and those Nazi thugs in the only way he knew how.

In the meantime, Special Agent Dean McWhorter slid the message deep into a file, never again to see the light of day.

"Who was that?" asked a curious colleague.

"Just another crackpot," McWhorter answered.

Chapter Forty-Eight

Ponte Vedra, Florida, June 17, 1942

Under a pale crescent moon, the men paddled their small rubber boat across a gently undulating sea. Herbie and his co-conspirators were dressed only in bathing suits with German naval caps on their heads, complete with Nazi swastika pins. Four crates of explosives rested in the bottom of the dinghy, along with water-tight bags holding their clothes and money. Small waves lapped the beach as they coasted up onto the sand and hopped out. Not another soul was in sight as they silently unloaded their cargo. With the last crate safely ashore, one of the sailors who accompanied them grabbed a small jar from the boat and hurried up past the water line. Bending low, he scooped up some sand before sealing the jar tight with a tin lid.

"A souvenir," he explained to the others. "For my girlfriend."

Kerling helped the sailors push the raft back into deeper water.

"Good luck." The sailors hopped aboard and reached for their paddles.

"Thanks." Kerling watched them take a few strokes back toward the waiting submarine, just 50 meters offshore. From somewhere further up the beach came the sound of girls, giggling and laughing as they plunged into the sea. "Everybody grab a box!" Kerling whispered. It took the men two trips to carry their things up the beach to a low dune. They chose a spot near two palm trees and beside a long fence, easily recognizable for later retrieval, and began to dig.

When their hole was large enough, they lowered in the crates and tossed their naval caps on top. After filling it all back in, they smoothed over the sand and then walked back to the water's edge where they hurled the shovels into the sea. It was time to put some distance between themselves and their illicit cargo. The dawn of a new day showed on the horizon as they walked north, sea bags slung over their shoulders. They had done it. They were in America. Herbie Haupt was overcome with a swelling sense of joy. He was home, or nearly so. All he had left was to catch a train to Chicago and disappear.

The men approached an elderly couple, out for an early morning stroll. Only Herbie managed to greet them. "Hello," he said as they passed.

"Good morning!" the gentleman answered.

"Lovely, isn't it?" added the woman.

"Yes, lovely."

The men kept on, walking past a quiet golf course. "What do we do next?" Thiel asked.

"I don't know," Kerling admitted.

"Maybe we pretend to be tourists for a while," Neubauer suggested.

From far out over the sea, the rising sun bathed the beach in golden light. A few other people were visible, strolling in the distance. "We could swim and relax for a little while," Herbie agreed. "We haven't had a shower since France."

"Fine, we can swim." Kerling stopped walking. The group dropped their bags and then eased into the water until they were chest deep, ducking under to rinse their heads and then popping back up. After three weeks confined aboard a cramped submarine, this was a small slice of paradise.

"That landing wasn't so bad," said Herbie. "I don't think anybody saw us."

"No," Kerling agreed. "So far, so good. Let's hope the other group had such luck."

They spent half an hour frolicking in the water before getting out to lounge on the sand, the heat of the sun warming their pale skin. Passersby paid them little attention. Over time, families with children began to stake out territory across the beach.

"You think that's Jacksonville up there?" Kerling pointed to a stretch of hotels lining the beach to their north.

"It should be," Herbie answered.

"Scheisse!" Neubauer hissed. "Police!"

Heads swiveled in unison to spot a police cruiser slowly approaching along a frontage road. "Relax!" Kerling tried to calm them but was near panic himself. "Remember, we're only tourists!"

As the patrol car drew close, three out of four men forced a smile and raised one hand to wave. Neubauer struggled to suppress a grimace. The officer waved in response and continued on his way. Just another day at the beach.

"Do you think he suspected?" Thiel asked.

"Nah," answered Herbie. "We look like a bunch of guys on vacation, like anybody. We could be from anywhere." He stood and brushed the sand off his bathing suit. "I'm going back in the water. We might as well have a good time."

"That's all you ever think about, isn't it Herbie?" Neubauer sneered. "Having a good time."

"Why not?" Herbie walked back into the sea as Thiel followed behind.

At the Restaurant Executive Club on 49th Street in Manhattan, George Dasch was running on fumes. Surrounded by a group of fellow waiters, cards and money were spread out across their table. A marathon session of pinochle was winding down. For Dasch, it was the end of a thirty-six-hour binge. Anything to keep his mind off his troubles. George was well-known at the club. Many a night he'd played cards here in the past, yet this time he faced a barrage of eager questions. Each time a new man entered the club it was the same. "George! I thought you were in Russia. How was your trip? How is Snookums? How long have you been back?"

"Don't ask, boys, I can't tell you the truth anyway," he replied. How was his wife? Dasch had no idea. Poor Snookie was still locked up in detention at a British camp in Bermuda. If he could only get through this unscathed, they might be reunited. It was a dream that kept him going each day. For the time being, Dasch scooped up his winnings and counted the bills. It came to $250. "Sorry, Fritz," he apologized to one of his victims. "Let me pay your bill. I'll pay every bill in the house!"

A small cheer arose. The manager, Mr. Koyer, added them all up. When he'd paid, George handed $10 to a broke Polish waiter and then $5 to another. So tired was he that rising to his feet was a struggle. It was two days since he'd last slept. Dasch stuffed what remained of his winnings into his pocket and bid farewell to the boys. He stumbled out into the early morning light and caught a taxi to the Governor Clinton Hotel. Upstairs in his room, Dasch lifted the receiver of his bedside telephone and dialed the extension for Pete Burger.

"Hello?" Burger answered on the first ring.

"Hi Pete, it's George."

"Where have you been? I haven't seen you in two days!" Burger's anxiety was clear.

"It's all right, come over to my room." By the time he hung up the phone and walked back to open the door, Burger was already there.

"Where were you? What happened?!" Peter recoiled at the sight of his partner, with wrinkled clothing, unkempt hair, and deep bags under his eyes. The man looked a wreck.

"Relax, everything is fine." Dasch closed the door behind Burger as he entered the room. "I was gambling with some of the old boys. Believe me, I needed it! I feel much better."

"You look terrible."

"I had to forget about all of this for a while…" Dasch waved a dismissive hand in the air.

"How was I to know? You left me to cover for you, making up stories! The others are suspicious!"

"What did you tell them?" Dasch showed some concern of his own.

"I said you were in New Jersey, meeting with somebody who could check our papers."

Dasch's body trembled. It wasn't merely the exhaustion. All of the stress and strain of the past month was catching up to him. Fear, desperation, sadness… George placed a hand on the wall to steady himself.

"Are you OK?" To Burger, this was beginning to look like a nervous breakdown.

"I need to rest, that's all." Dasch sat shivering on the bed.

"When will you go to Washington?"

"I don't know!" Dasch snapped. "I don't know. I need to sleep. Just keep the others occupied a little while longer."

Peter stood where he was. His entire future was in the hands of this man who seemed on the verge of an emotional collapse. But what could he do, go to the FBI himself? No, Burger would give Dasch a chance to pull himself together. When Peter left the room, Dasch crumpled onto the bed, his consciousness fading away.

It was a small boutique in Jacksonville where Herbie stood at the jewelry counter examining a gold watch, more expensive than he could ever have dreamed of owning before. With thousands of dollars of Hitler's money burning a hole in his pocket, he might as well splurge a little bit. He slid the watch on his wrist and latched the band. "What do you think?" he asked the saleswoman.

"That looks very nice. Is it for you?"

"Yeah. A little welcome home present to myself."

"You were away?"

"That's right, I've been traveling."

"Well, I think it looks fantastic."

"I'll take it."

"Excellent. Should we put it back in the box, or would you prefer to wear it out?"

"I'll wear it, thanks."

When Herbie had paid, he lifted the rest of his parcels from the counter. Already that morning he'd purchased a tan leather bag, a new suit, necktie, underwear, shaving kit and a hat. Along with a much-needed haircut, Herbie felt like a new man. Back in his room at the Mayflower Hotel he found Werner Thiel smoking a cigarette, his own purchases strewn across one bed. "You want to get something to eat?" Herbie asked.

"Sure, I could eat."

"How much time do we have?" Herbie placed his boxes on a table.

Thiel checked his watch. "About an hour. A little more."

"Come on, I'm starving."

After a quiet dinner in the hotel restaurant, Haupt and Thiel met the others at a pre-arranged street corner. All four men wore brand new suits, with pressed white shirts and snappy hats. Neubauer's head seemed on a swivel, eyes darting nervously back and forth as he scanned the passing cars for any signs of trouble. Kerling was calm. "Everything good so far?" he asked.

"Sure," said Herbie.

"We need to go over the plan." Kerling licked his lips. "Let's find a quiet place to talk it over."

"There's a bar at our hotel," Herbie suggested. "Nobody's in it. At least there wasn't before."

"Let's go."

The hotel was only a few blocks away. When the men entered the bar, they saw nine empty tables. The tenth was occupied by a young couple. The group settled in at the farthest table possible and scoped out their surroundings. A bartender polished glasses, paying no attention to his new customers.

"Should we order something?" said Theil.

"How about a round of beers?" said Kerling.

"Is there a waitress?"

"I don't think so."

"Let Herbie get them," Neubauer said under his breath, terrified that if he opened his mouth in public, his thick German accent would give them all away.

"Fine, four beers," said Herbie.

Kerling held out some bills. "Here."

"I got it." Herbie walked to the bar and ordered. When the beers were poured and paid for, Thiel helped him carry them to the table.

"Cheers," said Kerling. "To a safe arrival."

"Cheers," the men tapped their glasses and drank.

Kerling took one last look around to make sure that nobody was listening. The bartender was busy wiping down the bar. The couple were lost in their own world. Newlyweds on a honeymoon. All was clear. "Haupt, you're to travel to Cincinnati. Neubauer, you go to Chicago," Kerling said. "Thiel and I will go to New York and connect with the other group."

"I want to go to Chicago!" Herbie protested at once.

"No!" Kerling was adamant. "Lieutenant Kappe was clear about that!"

"I don't care what the lieutenant said, I'm going to Chicago."

"I can't let you do that. Kappe said explicitly that you are not to have any contact with your family."

"Try to stop me," Herbie challenged his group leader, clenching his hands into fists. "I'm going, I don't care what you say."

The two men stared at each other across the table. Herbie was right. There was no way to stop him, short of physical violence. "Go to Chicago then," Kerling relented. "But you are not to contact your family."

Herbie crossed his arms and scowled. "What about my uncle Walter? Kappe said we could use him as a contact if we had to."

Kerling gave a slow nod. "Fine, but Walter better keep his mouth shut. I'll go to Cincinnati with Thiel and then to New York," Eddie adjusted the plan. "Haupt and Neubauer will both go to Chicago. I'll contact Haupt through his uncle."

Herbie's tension eased. "OK."

"We'll wait a few weeks to make sure there's no heat on and then you can drive me back down to dig up the supplies," Kerling added. "You got it?"

Herbie nodded. "I got it."

Kerling was not at all satisfied. He didn't like having his authority challenged by this kid, the very first day of the mission, yet he wasn't about to fight over it. He slid a leather bag across the table to Herbie. "Your uncle can hold this for us."

Herbie opened the bag and peeked inside. At first glance, it appeared to be empty. He reached in with one hand and lifted the false bottom to reveal bundles of cash.

"That's close to $20,000. Be careful with it. Don't forget, it's not your money."

"I understand," Herbie replied. "It won't leave my sight until I get to Chicago."

Kerling knew the younger man was likely to spend some of it. The only question was how much. At least the money would keep the kid occupied, Eddie figured. And he would be less likely to turn them all in for some type of reward. When the meeting was over, the men downed what was left of their beers and headed back to their respective hotel rooms. So far, at least, everything was going as well as could be expected.

Chapter Forty-Nine

Washington, DC, June 18, 1942

The dinner rush at the Olmsted Grill was winding down when Louis Martin saw a single diner being seated at one of his tables. Martin's face lit up. The waiter recognized his old friend immediately. After quickly delivering coffee to another table, he made his way over. "George!" Martin was bright with enthusiasm.

Instead of the friendly greeting that Martin expected in return, Dasch's face dropped. Fidgeting in his seat, he turned his head away. "I'm sorry, you must have me confused with somebody else."

To Martin, it was as though he'd been slapped in the face. "But surely you remember me?" he sputtered. "From the waiters' club in New York? All of those late nights playing pinochle?"

"No," Dasch shook his head. "That wasn't me." He picked up his menu.

Martin stood by in disbelief. He noticed Dasch's fancy clothes and expensive watch. The George Dasch he remembered could barely scrape two nickels together. He'd come up in the world. Apparently, he was too good to associate with waiters anymore. "I apologize, sir." Martin did his best to bury his displeasure. "Have you decided on your order?"

"I'd like a filet mignon, rare, with a small salad and a glass of house cabernet."

"Excellent choice." Martin took the menu. As he walked away, Dasch called after him.

"Oh, waiter!"

Martin turned back. "Yes, sir?"

"I'll start with a whiskey, if you please."

"Certainly, sir."

Martin conversed with Dasch as little as possible throughout the meal. The snub stung deeply, but the waiter swallowed his pride. By the time Dasch finished his steak, he was the last customer in the place. Louis cleared the plate with a deferential air. "I hope your meal was satisfactory, sir. Can I bring you anything else?"

George took a quick look around. But for a few servers resetting their tables on the other side of the restaurant, they were alone. "No. But I have to tell you, boy, you were correct in identifying the fellow you thought I was."

Martin stood stock still. Of course he was correct, though Dasch's admission did help somewhat.

"I wanted to apologize. You see, I've been under some strain lately, but I wonder if you'd like to join me after work for a drink?"

The waiter wasn't at all sure, still skeptical after Dasch's initial response.

"Come on Louis, I'll buy you a whiskey and we can talk about old times."

Martin slowly shrugged. "OK, George. I'll join you for a whiskey."

"Terrific! Dasch was overjoyed. "I'll wait right here while you close your section."

"I'll bring you a coffee."

"Thank you, Louis."

When they'd moved to a small bar around the corner, Dasch chose a discreet table in the back. The whole episode was highly peculiar, as far as Martin was concerned, though he certainly didn't mind a whiskey to unwind after work. Besides, his curiosity was piqued. They ordered a few drinks and began a conversation about old times in New York, the waiters' club, and some of their mutual acquaintances. Nothing particularly out of the ordinary. It was on their second drink that Martin gathered the courage to broach the subject. "So, what have you been up to since I saw you last?" he asked. "You seem to be doing quite well for yourself."

"Yes, thank you." Dasch's face flushed red. "I have some money, that is true."

"Where did it come from, if you don't mind my asking? You have a new job? Something better than waiting tables?"

Dasch waved a hand in the air to flag down the cocktail waitress. "Two more over here!"

"Yes, sir." The waitress acknowledged.

"You certainly don't seem to mind spending money," Martin added.

"That's because it's not my money." Dasch gave a sly smile.

"Whose is it?"

"I'll tell you a secret. I suppose it doesn't matter anymore." Dasch pulled out a packet of cigarettes and offered one to Martin before taking one for himself. He lit them both and took a long drag on his own. "The money is from the German government. You may find this hard to believe, but I am on an intelligence mission."

"For the Germans? You're working for the Germans?!"

Dasch nodded quickly as he fidgeted with his cigarette. "Yes, technically that is true. They sent me here, sure, but I came only to betray them."

Martin finished his whiskey. Dasch was right about one thing. It was hard to believe.

Leaning closer, George lowered his voice. "I infiltrated a Nazi sabotage school, you see, in Germany! But my plan…" Dasch laughed to himself with barely contained glee. "My plan was to betray them all along. If those Nazis knew what I was thinking, they would have shot me on the spot! And my mother and father, too..."

"I see…"

"No, I don't think you fully understand!" Dasch pointed a finger at Martin to emphasize his point. "I wanted to learn as much about those Nazis as I could! The only way to defeat them is to infiltrate them from within. I wanted to do my part."

"So… What will you do next?"

"Oh, I am not in Washington on some holiday. You'll see…"

The waitress placed two more glasses of whiskey on the table. Dasch waited for her to move on before continuing. "You understand why I pretended not to know you," he said to Martin. "What I am up to here, it is very dangerous."

"You think those Nazis still want to kill you?"

"Of course! They would if they knew what I was about to do. Anyway, I am not here alone. There are others who came with me. Eight of us."

"Eight Nazis?!"

"Some of them are, yes. My partner, Pete, he's no Nazi. He's with me, you see." Dasch took another slug of whiskey. "He is waiting in New York. I left a note for him this morning. I told him I would take care of everything. Peter, he's on our side. The Nazis, they treated him terrible. If you only knew…"

"What about your mother and your father? They're still in Germany, yes? Aren't you worried about them?" As soon as Martin uttered the words, a dark cloud of fear crossed his old friend's face.

"I can't concern myself with that. I must do what's right. That's all. Those Nazis in Germany, they won't have to know it was me."

Martin inhaled from his cigarette. The story was fantastic. It seemed too much to be true, yet the money had come from somewhere. "Good luck to you, George."

"Thank you." Dasch was circumspect. The men finished the last of their whiskey and George paid the bill. "I appreciate your company." As they rose to leave, George put a hand on his friend's back and then escorted him outside. "You will be hearing about me in the newspapers."

"You take care of yourself."

"And you, too, my friend!"

Dasch hailed a cab and then climbed in the back. As the car moved up the street, Martin was left behind to consider this very peculiar evening. On the face of things, it seemed that George had completely lost his mind. Most likely, Martin would never really know. He walked on along the sidewalk, swaying slightly from the whiskey. True or not, it was an entertaining yarn.

Chapter Fifty

Washington, DC, June 19, 1942

George Dasch battled a light hangover as he sat at the desk in his hotel room. Flipping through the government pages of the telephone book, uncertainty danced through his head. Not that he had any second thoughts about his intentions, per se. Quite the contrary, he couldn't wait to spill his guts. The question was, to whom exactly should he spill them? Dasch scrolled through the listings, entirely unsure. Finally, he picked up his phone and asked the hotel operator to connect him with the Government Information Service. After all, he did need some information. On the other end, the phone rang twice before a young woman came on the line. "Information Service."

"Good morning. I wanted to know if you can answer a question for me. Can you tell me the difference between the FBI and the Secret Service?"

A moment of silence followed. "I'm not sure the purpose of your question."

"I have a statement to make of military and of political value and I'm not sure who I should speak with."

The woman considered his request a few seconds longer. "I should think you might speak to the Adjutant General's office."

"Is that with the military?"

"Yes, sir, the Adjutant General is with the War Department."

"That sounds fine. Can you connect me?"

"Certainly. Please hold."

To calm his nerves, Dasch reminded himself exactly why he was here. He had to do everything he could to fight the Nazis, for the sake of the Germany that he still loved. The Germany of his childhood. This was the best way knew how. He didn't have time to dwell on the thought for long before another voice answered.

"Colonel Kramer's office," said a young woman.

"I'd like to speak to the colonel, please."

"The colonel is out presently. Can I take a message for him?"

"When do you expect him to return?"

"I can't say for sure. He should be in sometime this morning."

"Please, can you have him call me as soon as possible? It is of the utmost importance to national security."

"Certainly, sir."

"My name is George Dasch. I can be reached at Mayflower, District 3000, extension 351. Please, as soon as possible."

"I will pass along your message as soon as the colonel returns, Mr. Dasch."

"Thank you." When he'd hung up, Dasch sat and waited, seconds ticking by on the bedside clock. His patience quickly waned. Perhaps he should try the FBI as well? He lifted the receiver once again and dialed zero for the hotel operator.

"Operator."

"Hello, I'd like the FBI, Republic 7100," he said.

"Please hold."

Of course, this was the better alternative. After all, Hoover himself would be expecting to hear from him.

"FBI, how can I direct your call?" a receptionist answered.

"I'd like to speak to John Edgar Hoover, please."

"One moment…"

Yet another receptionist came on the line. "Office of the Director."

"I have a statement of military and political importance," Dasch explained. "I'd like to speak to Mr. Hoover."

"Mr. Hoover is unable to take any calls at the moment. Can you tell me what this is in reference to?"

Dasch tried to explain himself. He was transferred. He tried again. And again. It was just the same as in New York. Finally, on the fifth attempt, his patience was worn thin when the call landed on the desk of Duane Traynor, special agent in charge of sabotage cases for the Eastern Seaboard.

"Traynor," the agent answered.

"Hello." Dasch was hesitant by this point. "I have a statement of military importance," he began yet again.

"What kind of a statement?"

"I recently arrived from Germany. I have information that might be useful in fighting the Nazis. My name is George John Dasch. I left a message with your New York office under the name of Franz Daniel Pastorius. Have they been in touch about me?"

"No…" Traynor's suspicion was evident. "Should they have?"

"I gave specific instructions to pass along my message to the Washington office."

"I haven't heard anything from New York, but if you'd like to come in, you can give me your statement in person."

This time, Dasch felt some sense of relief at the suggestion of meeting an agent in person. Maybe it wasn't Hoover, but at least somebody was taking him seriously. "Yes, I can come in."

"How about eleven o'clock this morning? Would that be convenient?"

"Can we make it earlier?"

"Ten-thirty?"

Dasch glanced at his clock. That gave him a little over an hour. "Sure, I can come at ten-thirty but I don't know how to get there. Could you send a car? I'm at the Mayflower Hotel."

"I'll have a car there in forty-five minutes. Would that suit you?"

"Yes, thank you. My room is three-fifty-one." George hung up the phone. The wheels of his plan were finally in motion. This was it. The Americans would be forever grateful to him. George Dasch was going to be an All-American hero, doing his part for the ideals of liberty and democracy.

As he waited for the mysterious Mr. Dasch to arrive, Duane Traynor sat at his desk reading through reports of suspicious activity. It was mostly mundane stuff. With a war on, the general populace was on the lookout for anything out-of-the-ordinary. So far, every lead had come up empty. The only report he'd seen all week of real interest concerned the possible landing of German spies on Long Island. As many as four men, one in his 40s with a streak of gray in his hair. Could this be Mr. Dasch? Or was his name Pastorius? Either way, Traynor doubted there was anything to it. Nazi spies didn't generally turn up at FBI headquarters of their own volition.

More likely, this was just another wild goose chase. At a quarter to eleven, his phone rang. "Traynor," he said.

"Hey, Duane, this is Mickey. They've got a guy down at the desk named Dasch, insists on seeing Hoover. You know something about that?"

"Right. Dasch. I sent a car for him."

"He seems to think that only the director can take his statement. I've been trying to explain the situation."

"Have him sent him up to my office."

"Right."

It didn't take long before Assistant Director Mickey Ladd gave a quick knock on the door.

"Come in!" said Traynor.

"I thought I'd look in on this one myself."

"Sure."

A moment later, the mysterious Mr. Dasch was escorted into the room. The man was tall and thin, with a long face. He wore a clean-pressed gray suit and held a hat in one hand. As they were introduced, Dasch's rapid-fire handshake revealed a pent-up anxiety. Traynor noticed the gray streak in his hair.

"Do you need anything else?" asked Dasch's escort.

"No, thank you," said Ladd.

The escort retreated.

"Mr. Dasch," said Traynor.

"Yes, that's correct. George Dasch."

"I'm Special Agent Duane Traynor. This is Assistant Director Mickey Ladd." The men shook hands.

"It's a pleasure to meet you," said Dasch.

"Please," Traynor motioned toward two chairs in front of his desk.

"So, Mr. Dasch, what sort of information do you have for us?" said Ladd as they settled in.

"You're sure you heard nothing from New York? I telephoned that office on Sunday."

"Nope. Nothing from New York." Traynor gave a look toward Ladd. "You hear anything, Mickey?"

"Not a word."

Dasch fidgeted in his seat. "First, I would like to inform you that this matter must be handled in a confidential manner. There are innocent people in Germany that could come to great harm if the government there became aware of what I am about to say."

"Whatever you tell us today will remain strictly confidential," said Ladd.

Dasch wasn't entirely convinced, but he'd come this far. There was no turning back. "I suppose I will start from the beginning in that case." He shifted slightly to pull a packet of cigarettes from his pocket, fumbling for some matches before Traynor offered a lighter. Dasch's hands still shook as he lit his cigarette, took a long drag, and exhaled from the corner of his mouth. "I'm the leader of the Pastorius mission that landed several days ago on Long Island. We were sent by the Nazis to conduct sabotage operations throughout the east coast. Our efforts are meant to be directed primarily toward crippling light metal plants in the Tennessee Valley. Instead of carrying out this plan, I consider it my duty as a former member of the United States Army to do everything I can to prevent the attack. I have come to report the matter directly to Mr. Hoover."

Traynor and Ladd's expressions did not change. Blank. Disbelieving. Neither agent was ready to buy in. Instead, Traynor did his best to size this man up. Dasch was a nervous character, that much was clear. He could hardly sit still, with eyes darting back and forth as he continued to puff on his cigarette. Traynor slid an ashtray across the desk. If this had been a trial, he thought, Dasch would make a poor witness. And besides, what he was saying was too spectacular to be true. What was his game? Just another attention seeker?

For Dasch's part, the frustration mounted. After everything he'd been through; traveling back to Germany, through Japan, and then overland all the way through Russia. All of the scheming, and the Heil Hitler salutes... Traversing the Atlantic in a submarine and landing on these shores. Finally, he was here. This was supposed to be the glorious climax of his endeavor. George Dasch should be hailed as an American hero! And yet these two agents, tasked with the simple job of taking his statement, couldn't seem to find it within themselves to even believe him. The men stared at each other in silence. Didn't they at least have some questions? Some mild hint of curiosity? Dasch began to sweat. How could he convince them? He thought back. Some small bit of information that only a German agent might be able to share… Dasch sputtered one word. "Sebold." His face lit up. "William G. Sebold… like me… landed here in 1940."

Ladd leaned forward, his demeanor shifting. "What do you know about Sebold?!"

"Everything, Mr. Ladd, everything!" Dasch laughed out loud with a sudden joy. "All right out of the files of the German High Command! Mr. Sebold came to you then, just like I have today!"

"How do we know you didn't just read about that story in the newspapers?" Traynor asked.

"I know details; things about that mission that even you don't know. Sebold, he was recruited by the Gestapo three years ago, in Hamburg." Dasch leaned one elbow on an armrest and smiled broadly. "Oh, if you only knew how angry the Fuhrer was at that one! I will tell you, he is going to be just as furious this time around!"

Traynor straightened up in his seat. His estimation of this mysterious Mr. Dasch was shifting. Maybe this guy wasn't just some crank off the street after all. "Lock that door, man," Traynor said to Ladd. "I think we've got something real here."

Chapter Fifty-One

Chicago, June 19, 1942

As the train approached its final destination, Herbie Haupt began to recognize the city he called home. Through the window he saw the outlines of downtown skyscrapers in the distance. He was nearly there, a yearlong circumnavigation of the globe complete, almost one year to the day since he and two friends set out on their grand adventure. He longed to see his family and friends. Gerda, too… One year earlier he'd fled from the very prospect but now he wanted nothing more than to kiss his one-time fiancé and hold their child in his arms. Winning her back might be tricky, but with a little luck he knew he could pull it off. The thousands of dollars in his bag would certainly help. That could go a long way toward providing stability at the start. His thoughts shifted to Wolf, off fighting in the German army. That news would not go over well with his parents. Herbie took a deep breath, the guilt weighing on him. In another thirty minutes, he'd be back where it had all started, safe and sound. With each passing second, those downtown skyscrapers loomed larger in his view, each clickity-clack of the rail brought him a little bit closer.

As the train pulled into Union Station, Herbie was struck by a dilemma that he hadn't yet considered. How could he show up at his parents' house unannounced? His mother was likely to pass out from the shock. Perhaps it was better to see his Uncle Walter first, and his Aunt Lucy. At least he could drop off the money and visit with them for a while. It would buy him some time. And anyway, Lucy would know how to handle this.

After lugging his suitcase to the taxi stand, Herbie caught a cab to 3643 North Whipple Street. When the car pulled up out front, the place looked just the same as it always had; a red brick, two-story house with bay windows on one side and a small, covered porch on the other. The green grass was well-tended along with a small plot of flowers planted each spring by his aunt. All-in-all, it was the perfect picture of the American Dream. For Herbie, the dream was simply being back here at all. Anticipation surged through him as he climbed from the cab and set foot on the sidewalk. The driver hopped out to unload his suitcase from the trunk before Herbie slid him a few dollars to cover the fare. "Keep the change."

"Thank you. Have a good afternoon, sir."

"You, too, buddy." Herbie hoisted his suitcase and made his way through a small metal gate, across the garden path and up the front steps. Under a lazy, afternoon heat, he dropped his luggage on the porch and stood facing the front door. They'd certainly be surprised to see him; that much was not in doubt. Herbie steeled himself to their reaction before reaching up to ring the bell. He shifted anxiously from one foot to another while he waited. When the door swung open, Herbie stood up straight. Before him was his utterly astonished Aunt Lucy, her face turning a dark shade of scarlet as she brought one hand to her mouth. "Oh, my! Herbie!"

Herbie broke into a broad smile. "Hi, Aunt Lucy."

"Herbie!" she repeated before taking a step forward and wrapping her arms around him. After a hearty embrace, she let go and quickly stepped back to take another look, as if to make sure he was real. "How did you get here?! Where did you come from?! Nobody told me you were back! How come nobody told me?!"

"You're the first to know."

"What do you mean, the first to know? Haven't you seen your mother and father?!"

"It's a long story."

"I am sure it is. Well, don't just stand there, come in! Come in!" Lucille turned to shout into the house. "Walter! Guess who it is! You'll never believe it!"

Herbie's nine-year-old cousin Esther bounded into the foyer. "Herbie!" she shouted. "Hey, dad, it's Herbie!"

"Hi, Esther." Herbie moved into the house and dropped his suitcase onto the floor.

Walter Froeling poked his head through the living room doorway. "What the heck are you doing here?!"

"Hey, Unc. I'm back."

"From where, Japan? We haven't heard from you in so long and you just ring the doorbell, completely out of the blue?!"

"He says we're the first to know!" Lucille marveled.

"I don't know how my mother would take it if I just showed up like this. The shock of it might upset her."

"Walter, you call right this minute and tell Hans and Erna to come over here!"

"And what do I say is the reason?"

"I don't know… tell them I'm sick or something. Just get them over here!"

Walter moved down a hall toward a small hutch with a telephone. Lucille escorted Herbie and Esther into the living room.

"What did you bring me from Japan?" Esther beamed at him.

"A kick in the pants!" Herbie answered.

"Aw, that's no fun…"

"You must be a whole foot taller since I saw you last time."

"Have a seat, Herbie!" said Lucille. "Are you exhausted? Where did you come from today?"

"I was in Florida."

"Florida! What were you doing there?"

Before Herbie had a chance to continue, his five-year-old cousin Gordon skipped into the room.

"Look who it is!" Lucille said to Gordon. "Do you remember your cousin, Herbie?"

Gordon gave a blank stare before plopping himself down on the couch next to his sister.

"You are a sight for sore eyes, Gordon," said Herbie. "You have no idea. It's good to be home."

Walter returned to the room. "Your dad is out on a job but I'll go pick up your mother and bring her right over."

"Fine." Herbie was still left with the question of what to tell her. Or for that matter, what to tell any of them.

"I'll be back before you know it." Walter moved off.

"Where have you been all this time, Herbie?" Lucille asked. "What have you been up to?"

"I'd rather hear about you," Herbie responded. "What news is there? Have I missed much?"

"Oh, just the usual dramas. Nothing so important. Of course, we got involved in this war. And you, over there in Japan! How in the world did you ever leave that place?!"

"Like I said, it's a long story..." Herbie remained coy while they waited for Walter to return. Lucille filled him in on the latest gossip involving mutual friends and neighbors.

"How *is* my mother? Last I saw her she was still in the hospital."

"Oh, she's fine, Herbie. Never better. You'd never know there was ever any problem."

"Good, that's good... I'm glad to hear it."

When at last they heard the car pull into the drive, Lucy hopped to her feet. "Quick, grab your suitcase, we'll hide you in the bedroom!" she shouted. "You kids be quiet! Don't give anything away! We're playing a little game here, understand?" Lucille peered directly at Gordon, who puffed up his cheeks without saying a word. Herbie lifted his suitcase and followed her down the hall to a bedroom just off the kitchen. When she'd closed the bedroom door behind him, Herbie heard Walter and his mother entering the house through the back. "What is the big excitement?!" said Erna Haupt. "You don't look sick to me, Lucille!"

"I'm not," her sister-in-law admitted.

"Well, something must be going on for you to drag me all the way over here!"

"We have some news," said Walter.

"What sort of news?"

"It's Herbie," said Lucille. "He's home."

"What are you talking about?! If my own son was home, don't you think I'd know it?" Erna's frustration simmered. "Tell me the truth, what is this all about?"

"It is the truth," said Walter.

"He's right in there." Lucille motioned toward the bedroom door.

Erna wasted no time, flying to the door and throwing it open. Her cheeks flushed as she saw her son standing before her, a loopy grin on his face. "Herbie..." Erna said his name in awe, as though she were witnessing an apparition. She moved slowly forward and then threw her arms around her son before kissing him on the cheek. "Look at you. My handsome boy."

"Hello, mother."

Erna stepped back, her chest swelling with joy. "I was beginning to think I might never see you again…"

"I'm fine mom. I went all the way around the world. From Mexico City to Japan… I would have sent you another card, but you know how it is with the war and all. Especially once I got to Germany."

"Germany!" Erna hollered the word. She turned to the others. "Did he tell you he was in Germany?"

"He hasn't told us a thing," said Lucille. "Come on out of there and let's sit in the living room. We all need to hear this. Would anybody like some tea?"

"Not for me, thank you," Erna replied.

"Well, come on out of there, anyway."

The entire group relocated to the living room. Herbie sat on the couch, with his mother on one side and cousin Esther on the other. Walter took one chair while Lucille sat in another with young Gordon on her lap.

"You can't have gone to Germany." Despite her disbelief, Erna Haupt's face radiated joy.

"It's true," Herbie pleaded. "I was in Stettin, staying with grandmother and grandfather!"

"Stettin!" Erna marveled. "You really mean it?"

"Of course I mean it!"

"And are they well?"

"Sure. They're doing all right. Things aren't so easy there these days. You should see what it's like in the shops. They barely have anything. You need special vouchers just to buy a little bit of meat, or some sugar. I couldn't find a job. They wouldn't let me."

"So then, how did you get back to Chicago?" Walter pondered the obvious question.

Herbie stiffened. It was time to decide how much would he tell them. He couldn't lie to his own family. "I came back on a submarine," he admitted.

"A submarine!" Lucille shouted.

"That's right," Herbie confirmed with a hint of pride. "We only landed in Florida just the day before yesterday. I took the overnight train all the way home from there."

"Well, I'll be…" said Walter.

"What in God's name were you doing on a submarine?" said Erna.

"It was the only way I could find to get back here."

"As far as I am aware, you can't just book passage on a submarine," said Walter.

"No, it wasn't like that."

"So how was it?"

"A little cramped, to be honest, but I guess I can't complain."

"You know that's not what your uncle meant," said Lucille. "How did you end up on a sub?"

"And how did you get off?" said Walter. "I don't suppose they just pulled up to a dock in Miami?"

Herbie looked from one adult face to another. Where he had previously seen joy, he now saw apprehension. "I'm doing some work for the German government."

"What kind of work?" said his mother.

"Just some work, that's all!" Herbie snapped.

The room filled with an awkward silence as the import of what he was telling them sank in. Erna used her hands to smooth the wrinkles on her dress. "You understand, this is all a bit much, Herbie. The last I heard from you was one postcard from Japan. I thought you were only going to Mexico! That's what you told us. Just a few weeks in Mexico."

"We did go to Mexico. Me and Wolf. Hugo took off before we crossed the border. He went out to California."

"What happened to Wolfgang?" Erna asked.

Herbie furrowed his brow. "He was living in Koenigsberg, with his grandmother. The last I heard from him, though, he was being drafted."

"Into the army?!" said Walter.

"That's right."

"Why couldn't he come home with you?"

"Wolf, well he didn't want to…" The questions made Herbie uneasy. "Not that he didn't want to, exactly. I mean he wanted to come home…"

"Well, then, why didn't he?" said Lucille.

"He didn't think coming back this way was such a good idea." The uneasy silence returned.

"I ought to call home to see if Hans is back," said Erna.

"You know where the phone is," said Walter.

"I won't be a minute." Erna rose from her seat and raised a finger toward her son. "Don't say anything more until I return! I don't want to miss it!"

"All right, mother."

Erna hurried down the hall.

"Have you heard any news about my friend Larry Jordan?" Herbie asked his aunt and uncle.

"I believe that he was drafted. A lot of the boys around here have been," said Walter.

"No kidding. Which service did he end up in, do you know?"

"I think it was the army. I heard they were sending him to the Pacific somewhere, to fight the Japs. You better get yourself on down to register. They probably wonder whatever happened to you."

"Yeah, I'll bet they do…"

"Your father tells me that the FBI has been asking about you."

"Asking what?" Herbie was gripped by panic.

"Just why you haven't registered."

"What did my pop say?"

"He told them you were out of the country and he didn't know anything more than that."

"I see. I'll go down and sort it out." Goose bumps formed on Herbie's skin. He was in Mexico, for the whole entire year. That's what he would tell them. With a bit of luck, they wouldn't question it. "What about Gerda Stuckmann?" he went on. "Has anybody had news from her?"

"I know that your mother has seen Gerda a few times," said Lucille. "You'll have to ask her."

"Did she…? I mean…" Herbie couldn't bring himself to ask the question.

"He isn't home yet," Erna came back into the room. "I'll try again in a while. He should be home any time."

"Herbie was just asking about Gerda," said Lucille.

"Oh." Erna's face flushed red as she took her place on the couch. "Yes, Gerda…"

"How is she, mother?"

"Fine. Gerda is just…fine." Erna looked away.

"But, what about…?"

"I said she was fine!" Erna shot a steely gaze at her son. "Let's talk about Gerda later."

"Tell us some more about your travels!" said Walter. "How long did you stay in Mexico City?"

"Oh, I suppose it was around five weeks. We tried to come back home from there, but, it's a long story."

"We have time," said Lucille. "I know I'd love to hear it."

"How are your uncles?" Erna asked. "Did you get to spend much time with them?"

"Sure, I saw them. All except for Otto. They've got him in a concentration camp."

"A concentration camp!" said Lucille. "What on heaven's earth for?!"

"What did he do?" added Walter.

Herbie shook his head, uneasy being the bearer of bad news. "I don't know. You don't have to do much of anything over there these days."

"What's a concentration camp?" asked young Esther. "Do they have a lake?"

"No," Walter replied. "I'm afraid there's no lake."

"Then why would anybody want to go there?"

"I'm afraid that people don't *want* to go."

"So why do they, then?"

"That's enough, Esther," said Lucille.

"I thought those places were for bad people," said Erna.

"A lot of people are being sent," said Herbie. "I think that Germany has changed from when you lived there."

"But Otto? It must be some sort of mistake."

Herbie struggled to come up with an answer. How to explain the paranoia of the Nazi regime to Germans who had no experience with it? All he knew was that he'd prefer to have nothing to do with any of it. He was home. That was all that mattered.

"Let me try your father again." Erna rose again from the couch and headed for the telephone.

"Do they have horses at the concentration camp?" said Gordon.

"No, Gordon," Lucille answered. "They don't have any horses."

"I think it's time for little boys and girls to get ready for bed," said Walter.

"Aw, dad!" said Esther. "It's not even dark out yet!"

"You heard your father," said Lucille. "Upstairs, both of you! I want you in your pajamas in ten minutes!"

"But mom…!" said Gordon.

"No complaining. Go, go, go! Don't forget to brush your teeth!"

With heads hung low the two youngsters rose and moved toward the stairs.

On the train to Cincinnati, Edward Kerling sat beside his old friend Hermann Neubauer. One decade earlier they'd stood beside each other in New York City Hall as Edward married his Marie. Now the two friends rode together into an uncertain future, fearful that every civilian was a member of the FBI, every man in uniform on the lookout to arrest them. How could they complete their mission even if they'd wanted to? They'd heard about the wartime gasoline rationing. This was an unanticipated complication. The men's morale was sinking by the day.

When the train pulled into Nashville for a scheduled ten-minute stop, Neubauer hopped off and made his way to a newsstand, eager to search for anything in the headlines about Nazi spies on the run. Approaching the stand, however, he spotted two men in dark suits and fedoras leaning against the counter. Were *these* men FBI? Neubauer held one hand to his temple. The headaches were never far away. One of the men turned toward him with a curious gaze. Hermann ducked his head low and hurried back to the train.

"Where's your paper?" Kerling asked.

"I changed my mind." Neubauer sank into his seat, overcome by a deep, lonely yearning to be with his wife. Alma would know what to do. She was an American from birth. If only she were here with him, perhaps they could negotiate a surrender. Further up the carriage, Neubauer spotted two soldiers as they took facing seats. Hermann pulled his hat low over his eyes. A minute later, the train eased forward out of the station. "How are we going to transport the supplies if we can't even buy gasoline?" he whispered.

"I don't know. I haven't figured that part out yet."

"We can't drive all the way to Florida without gasoline. We don't have ration tickets at all! How are we going to get ration tickets?!"

"I told you, I don't know!"

"The whole thing is finished..." Neubauer mumbled. "It's impossible. They're just going to catch us..."

For Eddie Kerling, it was not the first time he'd mulled over their options. "We might make it to Canada, if we tried. Or maybe Mexico."

"What if they seal the borders?!" Neubauer raised his voice before casting a worried glance at the two soldiers. The pair were busy smoking cigarettes and playing cards on a small table between them. "We should go to the FBI," he said more quietly. "We could turn ourselves in."

Kerling nodded in agreement. "We could."

"Why don't we? If we tell them everything, they might go easy on us!"

Eddie was agitated. "If we decide to do this, it must be everyone together. All eight of us. Nobody should betray his comrades."

"What if Dasch beats us to it? Or Herbie? I don't trust that kid."

"Look, we'll all meet on the 4th of July in Cincinnati. Every man in the same place. Maybe we can discuss the idea. Herbie, he would go along, I'm sure. George, too. Maybe Peter."

"What of the others? What if some of them refuse?"

"Everyone agrees or it is off!" Kerling was adamant. "It must be all of us or none of us!"

To Neubauer, the 4th of July seemed like an awfully long way off. He would do his best to survive day by day. When one of the soldiers looked up at him, Hermann quickly turned away, wishing he had a newspaper to bury his face in.

The car drive home from the Froeling's house was a quiet ride. Hans and Erna sat up front, with Herbie's father behind the wheel. Herbie himself sat in the back, eyeing familiar streets as they went. He'd told them everything, all there was to say about sabotage school, submarines, and his orders from the German government. Of course he didn't plan to go through with it, he'd assured them, but that didn't make the silence in the car any less stultifying. His parents were worried. Herbie hadn't known quite what to expect from them. He'd thought they might be proud of him somehow, for what exactly he wasn't quite sure, yet fear, that was a surprise.

"Why didn't you tell us about Gerda?" His mother broke the silence with a voice that gave away her deep disappointment.

Herbie slumped in his seat, overtaken by shame. It was the same as before yet magnified. This time, they already knew. He pictured the conversation in his mind, with Gerda telling his mother the truth. He imagined the deep disappointment, swelling in her chest. "I'm sorry. I wanted to but… I couldn't."

"Is that why you ran away?"

It was a question Herbie was unable to answer. "Have you seen her?"

"Yes. I've seen her."

"Did she…?"

"No, son," Hans piped in. "She lost the baby."

The news struck Herbie like an electric shock running through his core. "How?"

"These things happen," said Erna. "Sometimes all on their own."

As he absorbed the information, Herbie was filled with despair for his lost child, tempered by an undeniable sense of relief. He wasn't ready to be a father. They could try again in the future, if she'd have him. Next time it would be on their own terms. On purpose. "Is she seeing anybody else these days?"

"No, Herbie. I don't think so."

"Maybe you could talk to her for me, mother. To let her know that I'm home?"

"Why would you want me to tell her? Shouldn't you all by yourself?"

"I'm afraid she might be angry with me. Perhaps you could smooth things over."

"I'll try, Herbie, if that's what you want me to do."

"Thank you, mother."

Hans pulled the car into the driveway and eased to a stop. Herbie opened his door and climbed out. Looking over their house, lit by a single street light, he was overcome with a swirl of emotions. After yearning for it so badly, for so long, Herbie Haupt was finally home.

Chapter Fifty-Two

Leningrad Oblast, Soviet Union, June 19, 1942

The Fuhrer demanded that the city be taken by the ninth of August. Rumor had it that the invitations were already printed for a lavish celebration at the Astoria Hotel. For Wolfgang, just a warm meal would be nice. Or a hot shower. Wolf could hardly remember the last time he'd had one of those. Every day, every minute, blended into the next. Interminable boredom interspersed with moments of sheer terror. They'd driven the Russians back at Demarysk, creating a corridor for the entire 16th Army to move north. Then days on end on a cramped wooden bench in the back of a troop transport, bouncing over pockmarked roads while under sporadic attack by Russian planes. Nothing could stop the convoy. Forward they went, closer each day until Wolf's truck pulled into a field at sunset and skidded to a stop. Wolfgang climbed down with the others as a seasoned veteran. He no longer faced the shame of an unsullied uniform. Indeed, Wolf was caked with dried earth. Only his rifle remained clean. As the men stacked their packs beside the truck, Wolf craned his neck to watch a wave of German bombers pass far overhead from the south. After Demarysk, this assignment would be the next best thing to a holiday. That's what they liked to think, anyway. Maintain a perimeter around the city. Don't let anybody in. Don't let anybody out. Starve them, bomb them, and by the 9th of August, welcome the Fuhrer to his victory celebration.

When the bombers passed over the city center, clouds of black specks drifted silently earthward. The first concussions rattled Wolf's eardrums as Leningrad took a pounding. The fury of the Fuhrer. Billowing clouds of black smoke appeared in the distance. A yellow glow lit the sky. On this evening, it was not Wolfgang's turn. Today was someone else's day to die.

Chapter Fifty-Three

New York, NY, June 19, 1942

"We don't like it. Not one bit… I am telling you, George better not be up to something!" Heinrich Heinck's face was beet red as they stood in Peter Burger's hotel room. Heinck used one finger to poke Burger in the chest. "You neither!"

"Relax." Burger tried to calm him while an equally agitated Quirin looked on from a chair by the window. It was a dangerous game, yet Peter saw no other way than to keep playing. "I told you, he had to go to Washington to sort a few things out."

"He'd better return soon." Quirin stood to loom over Burger, as if ready to pounce.

"If not, we are prepared to take over the mission," Heinck added.

"I told you, everything will be fine." Burger needed a way to distract them, to keep their minds off any homicidal thoughts they might be harboring. "How about we all go and find some girls? We can call Frankie, from last night. She'll set us up. What do you guys say?" Heinck and Quirin turned toward each other, silently conferring on the prospect. Burger felt the tension dissipate. He'd said the magic word. *Girls.* He pulled a few assorted slips of paper from a pocket and sorted through them until he found one that read *Frankie,* along with a scribbled telephone number.

"Sure, call her, I don't care," said Heinck.

Peter lifted the receiver and asked the hotel operator to connect him, then waited nervously for the call to go through.

"This is Frankie," a girl answered.

"Hello, this is Peter. Peter Burger. We met at the Swing Club. Do you remember?"

"Oh, yeah, of course. The three German fellows."

Burger cringed at the association. "Yes, yes, that's us."

"What can I do for you, Pete? Looking for some fun?" Frankie's tone was coy.

"We hoped you might arrange something for us, like you said."

"You bet. Here's what you'll want to do. Go on up to West Eighty-Sixth Street, number sixty-two. When you get there, hit the bell for apartment number five. You'll want to speak to Anna. I'll call ahead to make sure she has three girls for you."

Burger lifted a pen from the top of his desk and scrawled the address onto his slip of paper. "…West Eighty-Sixth Street, number sixty-two. Thank you, Frankie."

"Sure. You boys have a good time."

Burger hung up the phone and looked to the others. What anxiety remained was tempered by desire. "It's all arranged. Just give me some time to shower and have a shave." Pete moved into his bathroom and stripped off his clothes before placing them neatly on a countertop. He ran the shower until the water was warm and then stepped under the stream, doing his best to wash away his worries. When he was finished, he turned off the taps, dried himself with a clean towel and then wrapped it around his waist. Stepping to the sink, he adjusted the mirror on the medicine cabinet so that he could view through the open door and into the bedroom while he shaved. This way, if they did have any funny ideas, at least he'd see them coming. He was lathering his face when he spotted Heinck opening the desk drawer and then rifling through the contents. Burger froze as Heinck pulled out a note from Dasch, read it to himself and then passed it to Quirin. When his partner had scanned the message, Heinck placed the note back in the drawer and carefully slid it closed.

Burger resumed shaving, all the while wracking his brain to recall exactly what that note said. *I came to the realization to go to Washington and finish what we have started so far…* Finish what they had started. Surely that was a tip-off. Right? Burger used a small towel to wipe his face and then stepped into the room, expecting the worst. Would they strangle him? Toss him out the window? Or maybe leave his dead body in the tub, to be found by a hotel maid the following morning? Heinck and Quirin showed no response. "I'll just put on some clean clothes and we can go," Burger stated. He moved to the dresser for some fresh underwear and then to the closet where he chose one of his new suits. When he was ready, he lifted his hat from atop the dresser. "Shall we go?"

"Is Frankie going to be one of the girls?" Quirin asked.

"I don't think so."

"That's too bad… She was pretty."

"I'm sure the other girls will be pretty, too."

Quirin seemed moderately satisfied. As the men stepped into the hallway, Burger took a long, deep breath. They hadn't murdered him. Not yet, anyway, though he was beginning to wonder how long he could keep this up. Dasch better *finish what they started*, and soon already.

Chapter Fifty-Four

New York, NY, June 20, 1942

Five special agents quietly commandeered room 1419 in the Governor Clinton Hotel, just beside the room where Peter Burger was allegedly holed up. The information came directly from George Dasch in Washington, though they had no verification that this Burger character was actually in there. One agent watched into the hallway through the peephole. Another listened at the wall. There was no sign of activity from room 1421.

"Let's call him," said Special Agent Clyde Stillman. "You know, wrong number?"

Agent-In-Charge Stan Verbinski picked up the telephone receiver and dialed the extension. Through the wall, they heard the phone ring in the next room. On the third go came an answer.

"Hello?" Burger sounded groggy.

"Is this room fourteen twenty-two?" Verbinski asked.

"No, it's fourteen twenty-one."

"My apologies. I'm sorry to bother you, sir." Verbinski hung up. "He's in there all right."

It was another forty minutes before the agents heard stirrings. A dresser drawer slamming shut. A flushing toilet. A running shower.

"He's up," said Stillman.

"You take Sandusky downstairs," Verbinski ordered. "As soon as the subject leaves his room, Kaufman will follow him down in the elevator. "I want at least two sets of eyes on him at all times!"

"You got it chief." Stillman stood and nodded to Sandusky. The two agents left the room, closing the door stealthily before padding softly down the hall. In the hotel lobby they met two more agents, sitting in high-backed chairs.

"What's the word?" Special Agent Gladstone asked quietly.

"He's up," Stillman informed him. "Keep your eyes open. Kaufman will point out our man."

"You got it."

Stillman and Sandusky moved through the lobby and out the front door. "You take the right," said Stillman.

"Sure."

Stillman continued up half a block before stopping at a newsstand to pick up a paper. He opened it to the second page and surreptitiously peered over the top.

"You gonna pay for that or just read the whole thing right there?" The newsstand's owner chomped on a cigar.

Stillman dug in his pocket and pulled out a nickel before dropping it on the stack. As he waited, the agent ran the description of their subject through his head. Approximately five-feet-five-inches tall. Dark hair, parted on the left. Round face, medium build. Certainly not the Aryan superman of legend. It wasn't Stillman's job to make assumptions, though. His job was to follow this guy and pounce when he was told to pounce. Round up the whole gang, one by one. With any luck, this Burger character would lead them to two more. He wracked his brains for their names. Heineken and Quiring? Something like that. He continued pretending to read the paper while keeping an eye on the hotel entrance beyond. After a few minutes, a man matching Burger's description strolled out with his hat pulled low over his brow. The man turned left and hurried up the street. Just behind him, Kaufman emerged, giving a quick sideways nod before following after. Stillman folded his paper and tucked it under one arm. "Thanks, Mac." He gave a quick nod to the newsstand owner and then set off in pursuit.

The subject didn't seem to notice as five agents followed him along Seventh Avenue, down Thirty-Third Street, and then up Fifth Avenue. When he came to the Rogers Peet clothing store at 485 Fifth Avenue, the subject stopped in the doorway, turning to scan the sidewalk in both directions. On the opposite side of the street, Stillman climbed the steps of the New York Public Library, blending with library patrons who streamed in and out under massive concrete arches. Taking a seat on the top step, Stillman positioned himself just behind one of the towering columns and opened his paper once more. From this spot, he was able to monitor the subject while being almost entirely hidden from view. Burger seemed to be waiting for somebody, peering impatiently at his watch several times. To the right, Stillman saw two of his FBI colleagues on the corner of East 42nd Street. Another agent passed the subject and entered the store. Stillman would wait where he was.

It took less than ten minutes before two unidentified men arrived to greet the subject. Both were a few inches taller. One wore tweed pants and jacket. He had dark hair and a fleshy face. The other wore a light-colored suit. Large nose, ears protruding from the side of his head, gray hair on the sides, dark and wavy on top. These had to be their guys. Stillman watched as the three men entered the store together. He folded his paper and then moved down the steps, following Fifth Avenue up to his colleagues at 42nd Street. "Looks like we hit pay dirt," he said to Kaufman.

"We'll wait to see if they split up," Kaufman replied. "Take them down one at a time. I want you on the gray-haired fellow. Light suit."

"You got it."

"We've got cars on the way."

"Right." Stillman wandered back the way he'd come. As a relatively recent hire to the bureau, this was the kind of duty he'd signed up for. He'd always loved dime novels, where quick-thinking detectives were pitted against dark-minded criminals. Stillman was captivated by news stories of Hoover's G-Men, taking out gangsters such as John Dillinger and Machine Gun Kelly. He yearned to become one of the "good guys." Shortly after his 24th birthday, he got his wish. Stillman was inducted as a special agent in the Federal Bureau of Investigation. While this was indeed a dream come true, the first year of his employment was anything but glamorous. Instead of chasing down gangsters, he was more often stuck behind a desk filing paperwork. On this bright morning in June, all of that had changed. This was all hands on deck. Busting up an honest-to-goodness German spy ring! Stillman was not about to squander the opportunity. He was going to nab himself a Nazi.

Back in position on the library steps, Stillman continued waiting. When the three men finally reemerged from the clothing store, Burger held a parcel under one arm. The subjects spoke to each other briefly before moving up the block. Stillman stood and walked down the library steps. Before he'd reached the sidewalk, the three Germans entered a café just beside the clothing store. The agent took a seat on a bus bench directly across the street. From here, he saw the subjects take a table in the café as a waitress handed each man a menu. This would still be a while, Stillman realized.

Roughly forty minutes later, the three subjects finished their lunch and exited the café. This time, after a few more words, the men parted, with Burger heading back in the direction he had come and the other two continuing up Forty-First Street. Stillman folded his paper and jumped to his feet. Crossing the street, he tailed his quarry to the corner of Lexington Avenue where he just managed to board a bus without losing the two men. After paying the fare, he spotted a bureau car outside the window, following them toward the Upper East Side. At the back of the bus, his two subjects sat, eyes darting nervously to and fro. Stillman took a seat near the door.

Reaching Seventy-Second Street, the two subjects stood and quickly exited the bus. Stillman was just a few steps behind. Had they *made* him? He wasn't sure. The two men stopped at the intersection. Stillman ducked into a corner store, buying a pack of cigarettes as he watched them converse just out the window. When the streetlight changed, the men parted ways. From across the street, Gladstone followed the man in the darker suit up the block. Stillman was on the sidewalk in a flash, sticking with the man in the light-colored suit as he crossed the intersection. The bureau car pulled to the curb and two more agents climbed out, one following after the other subject as he ducked into a delicatessen. The second agent joined Stillman. "Get ready," he hissed. "We take him as soon as he crosses Third Avenue."

Stillman gave a quick nod, his adrenaline pumping. This was it. His first takedown. The first arrest of his FBI career, and it was a Nazi spy! If only he could tell his dad about it. The old man would probably never believe him. At the next streetlight, the agents caught up to their man, following him closely through the intersection. Just on the other side, the bureau car slowed to a stop beside the curb. Step by step the distance closed. When the subject turned his head to one side, Stillman sensed fear, like an animal hunted in the wild. There was no way this German would get away. Stillman's entire country depended on him to make sure of it. As they approached the car, every fiber in his body was primed to take the subject down. The back door swung open. Another agent emerged. Time to pounce. Stillman and the other agent lunged at the German, wrapping their arms around the man and throwing him on the hood of the car, face down. There was no resistance. The agent from the car held his ID aloft. "Are you Richard Quirin?"

The subject was unable to reply, too stunned to speak.

"Federal Bureau of Investigation. You're under arrest." The agent pulled the German's arms behind his back, then produced a pair of handcuffs and slapped them onto Quirin's wrists before they bundled him into the back of the car, one agent on each side. Stillman slid into the front passenger seat.

"One down," said the driver as he pulled into traffic. "Six more to go."

Back in his hotel room, Peter Burger left the door open for the FBI agents who he expected to appear at any time. He was becoming impatient. The task of stringing along his co-conspirators left him emotionally drained. He stood in front of a mirror, admiring himself in his brand-new suit, wondering what Bettina would think. Picturing her back in Germany filled him with despair. At least she had his parents. They would take care of her as best they could. Burger sat down at his desk and picked up a newspaper. He was scanning the headlines when three men in suits burst into the room. One blocked the doorway to prevent his escape. The other two closed in on either side.

"Ernst Peter Burger?" one of the men asked.

"Yes, I am Peter Burger."

"FBI." The man held out his identification. "We have some questions for you."

"Of course, of course," Burger nodded. He felt no fear or trepidation. Turning himself in was the right thing to do. After so many years of struggle, all of the beatings and abuse… After burying his fury within for so very long, these FBI agents represented one thing to Peter Burger; the opportunity to unburden his soul. An enormous sense of relief welled within him.

"Your friend George Dasch told us where to find you."

"Yes, George, yes. I was waiting for you."

"If you don't mind, we'd like to take you down to our office where you can give us a full statement."

"Certainly." Peter stood, the two men on either side hovering close by. The agent in the doorway backed out slowly and as they escorted him out of the room and down the hall, Burger began to consider what his statement might be. Where would he start? Back in 1923. Munich. From there forward, he would tell them everything they wanted to know.

Chapter Fifty-Five

Chicago, IL, June 21, 1942

Herbie Haupt sat at a table in the Froeling kitchen with his young cousins, each of them sipping from a bowl of chicken soup. With the side door open, Herbie detected the faint fumes of paint as his Uncle Walter worked in the driveway, putting a fresh coat on a set of patio chairs. Near the kitchen stove stood Aunt Lucy. "I could make some grilled cheese sandwiches if the soup isn't enough," she said.

"Grilled cheese! Grilled cheese!" Gordon cried out.

"Grilled cheese it is. You, too, Herbie?"

"Sure. I'd like a grilled cheese."

"What about me?!" said Esther.

"Yes, dear, don't worry. We won't forget about *you*."

"I'll tell you, after what I've been through, this is a luxury," said Herbie.

"Chicken soup and sandwiches?" Esther scoffed.

"Are you kidding? Chicken, in Germany? Forget about it. Maybe once a week, if you're lucky."

"So what do they eat over there?" asked Esther.

"Black bread and butter. Pickled vegetables. Potatoes."

"That's it?!"

"Mostly. It's about all you can get."

"That sounds awful. I don't want to go to Germany. We don't have to go to Germany, do we mother?"

"No, dear. Maybe someday, after the war is over."

"When is that gonna be?"

"I sure wish I knew," said Herbie. As the clock struck noon his thoughts turned to Hermann, whose call he expected at any time. Hermann, with the shrapnel implanted in his head, whose accent was so thick you could pick it out from half a block away…

Lucille was in the pantry when the telephone rang. Esther hopped to her feet and skipped across the room in a flash. In the hallway, she picked up the receiver. "Froeling residence! Who's calling?"

"You give that to me!" Lucille emerged from the pantry and placed a loaf of bread on the table as she hurried past. When she reached her daughter, Lucille grabbed the receiver from her hand. "Hello, this is Lucille Froeling. Yes… Yes, my husband is here. Hang on a moment." Lucy put the phone down on the hutch and came back through the kitchen.

"Who is it?" Herbie asked.

"I don't know. He's asking for Walter." Lucille ducked her head out the door. "Honey, telephone for you!"

Walter came into the house, wiping his hands on a paint-splattered rag. "Who is it?"

"He didn't say."

Herbie's uncle went to the phone and picked it up. "Hello, Walter Froeling. That's right… Yes, my nephew Herbie is right here." Walter put down the phone and came back through the kitchen. "It's for you," he said, but Herbie was already moving toward the phone.

"Hello?" Herbie said when it was finally his turn.

"Herbie?" It was the voice of Hermann Neubauer. "I thought maybe I had the wrong number."

"You in Chicago?"

"Yes, I'm here. We need to talk. When can we meet?"

Herbie looked at his watch. "How about one-thirty? You know the Chicago Theater? It's on State Street."

"Yeah, I know it."

"OK. See you there."

When he'd hung up the phone, Herbie felt a slight bit better. At least Hermann wasn't arrested along the way. As he retook his place at the table, however, Herbie considered the delicate question of what he might say to Neubauer. He just wanted this whole thing to go away. Herbie wanted to simply get on with his life. Neubauer, Kerling, and all of the rest of them… they were a very unfortunate complication. Herbie considered ratting out the whole operation to the FBI. If word got back to Germany that he'd done so, that could lead to serious consequences for Wolf, and his Uncle Otto, too.

Herbie would meet with Neubauer, if for no other reason than to buy himself some time.

After exiting his streetcar, Herbie Haupt walked the last few blocks to the theater. Approaching along the sidewalk, he spotted Neubauer in a spiffy new suit and hat, standing with his hands crossed behind his back as he looked over a poster for that day's show.

"Hello, Hermann." Herbie sidled up beside him.

Startled at the sound of his name, Neubauer stiffened. "There you are."

"Any problems getting here?"

"No. No problems." Neubauer eyed the Sunday matinee crowd milling about outside the theater.

"You found a hotel?"

"Yes."

"Which one?"

Neubauer was hesitant to say, though ultimately relented. "The Sherman."

Herbie nodded. "I know it. Just a few blocks from here. You want to see a movie?"

"I thought we should talk."

"We can talk after." Herbie took a few steps away. "Come on, my aunt told me about a picture at McVickers she thought I should see."

Neubauer walked with Herbie in silence, along North State Street and then onto West Madison. Hermann's anxiety was palpable, in the way he grit his teeth and kept his head low, his hat pulled forward. Herbie wanted to calm his partner's nerves, but what could he say? When they arrived at McVickers Theater, the two men stopped to read the poster out front. *The Invaders!* The title was splashed in large font across the top. Below, an illustration depicted armed sailors in blue uniforms. Facing off against them were Leslie Howard and Laurence Olivier, dressed as lumberjacks. Between them, a German submarine was under attack, blasted by a dive bomber from above. *Adventure aflame with gallantry! A picture ablaze with excitement!*

"This is what you want to see?" Neubauer was skeptical.

"My aunt said she thought I'd like it." Herbie wasn't so certain himself. "It's about some Germans who come over here on a submarine. That's what she said."

"Why would she think you'd like that?"

"I don't know."

"You didn't tell her…" Hermann couldn't bring himself to say any more out loud.

"No, no. Don't worry. I told them I was in Mexico this whole time. Come on, let's just see the picture and then we'll go somewhere and talk."

The pair got in line at the ticket booth with families, young lovers, and a few off-duty soldiers in uniform. When they reached the front, a teenage girl in the booth chewed gum with her mouth open. "How many?" she asked.

"Two." Herbie pulled out his wallet.

"Fifty cents."

Herbie slid across a dollar and got two tickets and change in return. "How is it?"

"Not bad. Some Nazis fight it out with Laurence Olivier."

Herbie felt his blood pressure drop, as though everyone around him knew his deep, dark secret. Maybe seeing this film wasn't such a good idea after all.

"Don't worry, those Nazis get theirs in the end," the girl added.

"Yeah, thanks." Herbie handed one ticket to Hermann and the two moved toward the entrance and on inside. When they'd found their seats, both men peered around the theater, surveying the rest of the audience. Hermann's anxiety was infectious. Herbie found himself wondering if they were being watched. If they might be arrested at any moment. Nobody seemed to pay them any notice. He and Hermann were merely two non-descript men, minding their own business. All the same, Herbie felt better when the house lights dimmed. It was easier to hide in the dark.

The show started with a newsreel. *New York at War* showed the massive parade held in Manhattan just a few days earlier. After that, the picture itself began. Herbie shifted uncomfortably in his seat as a montage depicted a German submarine sinking an oil tanker before moving into Hudson Bay. As the story unfolded, six Germans paddled ashore on a small rubber raft before making their way across

Canadian soil. If this crowd only knew who was sitting in their midst, Herbie thought… One by one, the Nazis were gunned down. Herbie knew he was supposed to feel a sense of joy at their demise, yet for him the opposite was true. Couldn't they allow just one to get away? Of course, it was only a movie. Real life didn't have to end that way. Herbie could write his own ending to their story. By the time the final credits rolled, however, he felt that he'd just seen the future writ large before him. There was no escape, the film seemed to say. You cannot get away. Yet as the lights came up, the families and the soldiers, the young lovers seated all around them, merely stood and wandered out, none-the-wiser. "How about we get some dinner?" Herbie said.

Neubauer nodded, afraid to speak in public lest his accent give him away.

"Come on, there's a place I know next door." The two men joined the rest of the audience, making their way into the lobby and then out to the sidewalk where they squinted in the afternoon sun. Walking into the restaurant, they found the place half empty. It was late for lunch, yet early for the dinner crowd.

"Table for two?" A hostess stood before them with menus in hand.

"Yes, please," Herbie replied.

The hostess sat them at a table near the front. "Your waitress will be right with you." She handed them each a menu.

"Thanks." Herbie perused his choices as the hostess walked off. It was the usual fare. Hamburgers, meatloaf, chicken pot pie, various sandwiches… "What did you think of the movie?" he asked Hermann.

"I didn't care for it," Neubauer replied.

"What about the guy who just wanted to quit the whole thing and be a baker, like he was back home?" In the scene Herbie referred to, one of the Germans tried to leave the mission, only to be shot dead by his own men.

Hermann looked up quizzically. "He should have followed his orders."

The men stared across the table, each trying to get a read on the other. "Yeah," Herbie looked back to his menu. "I guess so."

When the waitress arrived, the two men ordered burgers and fries with bottles of Coke. Waiting for the food, they quietly filled each other in on their travels. After a day in Cincinnati with Kerling, Neubauer had continued on his own to Chicago. "We were so scared," Hermann admitted. "Me and Eddie… We couldn't even get into a taxi cab. Everywhere I look, everyone I see, I think they must be FBI. I can't sleep, I can hardly eat. I keep thinking they're going to get me. I don't know how long I can take it."

"You've got to pull yourself together." Looking around the room, Herbie saw a few families and a pair of teenage girls. Two elderly men occupied a booth along the far wall. No FBI agents in here, it seemed. He looked out the window, where crowds moved in both directions along the sidewalk.

"How about you?" Neubauer was suspicious. "What have you been doing the last few days?"

"I was with my family, but don't worry, everything is fine."

"You had better be careful. You never know who they might talk to. Even your family."

"You worry too much."

"Maybe you don't worry enough."

When the food arrived, the men ate in silence. Hermann managed to swallow only a few bites of his burger before pushing the plate away.

"Not hungry?" said Herbie.

"I told you, I can't eat."

Herbie looked back to the two old men in the booth, his paranoia growing. "Maybe we ought to get out of here."

Neubauer nodded in agreement. They stood and moved to the cash register, paid their bill and left.

"Grant Park is only a few blocks. Let's take a walk," said Herbie.

"All right."

"Did you really mean it, about that baker in the movie? It seemed kind of rough to me, what happened to him. It didn't seem like he deserved what he got. I mean, if the guy didn't want to do it…"

The pair entered the park, heading toward the waterfront. Families with small children played on the grass. A young couple cuddled on a bench. A man and his son attempted to launch a kite. "I understand what you're getting at…" said Neubauer. "I'm so nervous all the time, I don't see how we're going to go through with this."

The statement offered Herbie a hint of relief. It was a starting point.

"Eddie and George are coming to Chicago on the sixth of July," Hermann informed him. "They will stay at the Knickerbocker Hotel. We are supposed to meet there, both groups."

"Good. We can talk things over. Until then we just have to sit tight."

This comment did nothing to ease Hermann's concerns. He was trapped with no apparent way out. Neubauer was a soldier, not a spy. It was never his intention to become one.

"Let's meet again Wednesday, just to check in," Herbie suggested.

"What time?"

"One p.m., back at the Chicago Theater."

"Fine."

They walked back to the street, where Herbie caught a taxi to his Uncle Walter's house. He didn't want to be the baker, shot dead by his own men. Would they do that? This was a complicated game. Herbie just wished that he knew the right moves.

Chapter Fifty-Six

New York, NY, June 22, 1942

Business at Engemann's Grocery was steady for a Monday afternoon. Hedy Engemann sat behind one register, while her mother worked the other. With her well-practiced digits, Hedy punched in the prices of each item. One loaf of bread, 10 cents, laundry detergent a quarter, a tin of coffee, 18 cents, two cans of soup, 12 cents... Hedy pressed the total button and began placing the items into a paper bag. "That will be two dollars and fifteen cents, Mrs. Wilson," she said.

On the other side of the counter, Mrs. Wilson opened a small, green leather purse and began sorting through her coins and lifting them out one at a time. "I think I can get rid of some change. These coins get so heavy if you're not careful." She placed the money on the counter and quickly counted it again.

"That's right, Mrs. Wilson." Hedy scooped the coins up and then placed them in the corresponding compartments in her register before pulling a lever to produce a printed receipt. She dropped the receipt into the bag before handing the whole load across the counter.

"Thank you, dear." Mrs. Wilson took her items.

"You have a nice day."

Turning to the next customer in line, Hedy saw a familiar face. It was Helmut Leiner standing before her with a loopy grin. His gray suit hung loosely on his frame. The man had lost weight. His complexion was pale. "Hi, Hedy. How have you been?"

"Helmut!" Hedy didn't hide her surprise. "How are you?"

"I can't complain. I mean, I could, but what's the point, right?"

"You look good."

"That's kind of you to say. And you as well!"

In the line behind Helmut, Hedy saw her next customer standing with a small basket of goods, scowling with suspicion at this apparent interloper.

"Do you mind standing aside, Helmut?" said Hedy. "I can talk to you, but I don't want to hold up the line."

"Oh, yes, of course!" Leiner moved back a step. With a small show of relief, the customer began to place her groceries on the counter.

"So, what brings you to the neighborhood, Helmut?" Hedy punched in the prices, one after another, as she spoke.

"I have some news. Good news. I think you'll want to hear it."

"What news is that?"

Leiner took on an evasive air, shifting his weight from one foot to the other as he peered around the store. "I'd prefer to tell you in private."

"I'm a little bit busy right at the moment, Helmut. Can you come back later? I'm due for a break in half an hour."

"Can you take your break early? I promise, you'll want to hear this. I have a big surprise for you."

Hedy tilted her head to one side, pausing as she eyed Leiner. Turning back to the register, she totaled the order. "That will be one dollar and fifty-four cents," she said. Her customer fished two dollar bills from her purse and put them on the counter. While Hedy made change, she looked to her mother at the next register. "Mother, do you mind if I take my break early? I've got an old friend here that I'd like to catch up with."

"You go ahead. I think I have things covered."

Hedy helped her customer place the items back into her basket before locking her register closed and pocketing the key. "Let's go." She rose from her stool.

"How about we take a walk to the park?" said Helmut.

"That's fine, I could use the air." Hedy took off a red work apron and draped it over her stool. Next, she reached underneath her register and lifted a pack of cigarettes and some matches before stuffing them into a pocket.

Helmut gave a wan smile as he used one hand to straighten some wayward strands of hair plastered across his forehead. "After you." The pair exited the store on a bright summer morning. From Second

Avenue they turned left on East 86th Street and headed toward Central Park.

"I wish you didn't have to be so dramatic, Helmut," said Hedy. "Why can't you just come out with it?"

"There's somebody waiting for us in the park that I think you'll like to see."

"Waiting for us?!"

"That's right."

"Just tell me, who is it?"

"Patience. You'll see."

Hedy pulled the cigarettes from her pocket and offered one to Helmut.

"No thanks," he said. "It's better that I don't. In fact, I've given them up."

"You haven't been well, have you Helmut? What's wrong?" Hedy struck a match and lit her cigarette as they went.

"To be honest, I… well…"

"Go ahead, you can tell me." She inhaled a lungful of smoke.

"It's a little embarrassing, but I somehow managed to come down with a fairly serious case of consumption."

"Oh… I see. Are you sure that you ought to be out here walking around like this? Shouldn't you be home in bed?"

"I would be, but you see this is a somewhat special circumstance."

"It can't be that special! Who on earth could warrant this type of treatment?"

"You shall see, Hedy."

"It couldn't be Marie?"

"No, no. Not Marie."

Hedy was left guessing as they reached Fifth Avenue and crossed into the park. "I certainly appreciate your dedication, Helmut. It is swell to see you again. How long has it been? Nearly a year?"

"Yes, 'round about a year I suspect." When they reached the reservoir, Helmut looked right and then left, searching for their mystery assignation. "Ah, there he is!" Leiner's face lit up. "Right on time."

"There who…" Before she could finish the question, Hedy saw him. Eddie Kerling, walking toward them with a broad grin on his face.

"Look who we have here!" Eddie beamed. "Helmut Leiner and Hedy Engemann!"

"Eddie?!!" Though she saw him with her own two eyes, it felt more like a dream than reality. Yet there he was, as handsome as ever in a white-collared shirt, with his chiseled features and short hair parted just off center. When he held his arms wide, Hedy fell into them. Holding tightly to her love, she inhaled his masculine scent, so comforting and familiar.

"If you two don't mind, I'll be heading off," said Leiner.

"Thank you, Helmut," said Eddie.

"You bet."

Hedy didn't see Helmut go. Nothing could draw her attention away from Eddie. She pulled back only far enough to give him a playful punch on the chest. "What on earth are you doing here?!"

"I'm back, that's all."

"How did you get back? I thought you were in Germany?"

Eddie leaned close and kissed her. "Ask me no questions and I'll tell you no lies."

"But it seems to me that the only way across the Atlantic these days is by submarine!"

A playful smirk crossed Eddie's lips. Releasing her from his embrace, he took one of Hedy's hands in his own. "Come on, let's take a walk."

"How long have you been in New York?" The pair moved off down the path surrounding the reservoir, merely another couple out for a stroll in the park.

"I only just returned. Aside from Helmut, you're the first person I've seen."

"You haven't spoken with Marie?" Hedy couldn't help but feel insecure when it came to Eddie's wife.

"No, no," he answered. "You're the one I wanted to see first."

"Why send Helmut, then? Why didn't you come yourself?"

"I thought you might have a heart attack if I just showed up at the grocery. Besides, what would your parents say?"

"Good point…"

"Don't worry yourself. You're the one I love, Hedy."

"I know that you love Marie. I've come to terms with that."

"I love you both."

Hedy stopped to look him in the eye once again. "Tell me you're here to stay this time."

"I'm not going back to Germany anytime soon, that's for sure. I thought we could take a road trip, you and me. I'll buy a car and we can drive to Cincinnati and then Chicago, and then all the way down to Florida. What would you think of that?"

"What about the grocery?"

"Don't you think your mom and dad can handle that for a while?"

"You need to slow down a little bit," Hedy laughed uneasily as they moved on down the path. "I just can't believe you're back."

"It's true, Hedy. You might as well get used to it."

Hedy pictured the pair of them on a beach in Florida, with fruity cocktails in hand. In the flash of an instant, her outlook on life had shifted. A sense of peace came over her as Hedy's heart swelled with optimism. Over the past year, she'd nearly forgotten what this felt like, to be young and in love. Hedy was bound and determined to never let him get away from her again.

Chapter Fifty-Seven

Chicago, IL, June 22, 1942

"I want you to go down to register for the draft!" Hans Haupt was adamant as he hovered in the doorway. "You get your card and go straighten things out with the FBI!"

"Don't worry, father. I'll take care of it, I promise." Herbie was still in bed after a late night at Kate and Otto Wergin's house, filling in Wolfgang's parents about the news of their son. It hadn't gone over particularly well.

"I don't want you staying in this house until you've done this for me." The strain was evident in his father's pained expression. "At least if you register…"

"Don't you like me anymore, father?"

"Yes, Herbert, I like you, but do me this favor. Please."

Herbie didn't answer right away. What if they were already looking for him? What if he went to the FBI and was arrested on the spot? Then again, if they knew his true circumstances they'd have found him already. "OK, father. I'll go today."

"Thank you, son." The elder Haupt seemed at least somewhat relieved. "It might help if you tried to get your old job back, too."

"Sure, dad. I'll see what they say."

After breakfast, Herbie caught a cab to the local draft board. Registering was easy enough. When he had his card in hand, he took another taxi to the FBI headquarters downtown. This was going to be more complicated. It was the FBI who had been coming by the house in his absence. Walking into the building, he wondered if he'd be allowed to walk back out.

A receptionist at the front desk listened to Herbie's story before calling upstairs. After a short wait, he was escorted up one flight and into a small office where he repeated his tale to an agent.

"So you were in Mexico this whole entire time?" The agent sat at a desk taking down Herbie's statement.

"That's right," Herbie explained. "I was there the whole time."

"Why did you go there?"

"Because…" Herbie hesitated. "My girlfriend was pregnant."

The agent raised an eyebrow. "And you just had to get away?"

"That's right."

"What did you do there in Mexico for an entire year?"

"I was up in the hills most of the time. Looking for gold."

"Looking for gold?" The agent repeated the words with an air of incredulity.

"Yes. Prospecting."

"Uh-huh. And did you find any gold?"

"No, sir. Not much."

"I only have one problem with your story," the agent cast a suspicious gaze. "We spoke with your mother a few months back. It seems that she got a telegram from you, dated August 1941. From Tokyo, Japan. How do you explain that, Mr. Haupt?"

Confronted with this information, Herbie momentarily froze. "I never was in Japan."

"You never were?"

"No, sir."

"Then how do you explain the telegram?"

"That was just a ruse. You know, to keep my girlfriend guessing. I wanted her to think I wouldn't come back, so I had a friend send that for me."

"A friend in Japan?"

"Yes, sir, my friend Joe Schmidt. He went to Japan, not me."

The agent furrowed his brow. "And why did this Joe Schmidt go to Japan?"

"He got a job working at some monastery. I don't know what he was doing, exactly. Farm work, I think."

"I see… You went to an awful lot of trouble just to avoid your girlfriend."

"Yes, sir."

"I hope it was worth it."

Herbie didn't answer this question. Instead, he waited while the agent jotted some notes on his report.

"If we asked you to go to war for the United States, would you go?"

Herbie shifted in his seat. "I'd prefer not to fight against the German people, but if I have to go to war, I'll go."

The agent made another note. "We have everything we need from you at present."

"Thank you, sir." Herbie hopped up, eager to get out of there as quickly as possible. Exiting the building, he turned to make sure he wasn't being followed. It seemed all was clear. That hadn't gone so badly after all. It was much easier if he avoided thinking too much about his predicament. He'd registered for the draft. He'd explained himself to the FBI. At least his father would ease up on him. Herbie could begin to get on with his life. He still had thousands of dollars in cash, some at Uncle Walters and some hidden under a rug at his parents' house. He could get an awfully nice car with that money. Maybe a convertible, and a diamond wedding ring for Gerda. Herbie tried to look on the bright side. Stepping to the curb, he waved one hand to flag down a cab. He'd head straight home to retrieve some cash. His father could take him down to the auto dealership. Things were going to be all right. When a cab pulled over, he slid into the back seat, picturing himself in that brand-new convertible. Yes, everything was going to be just fine…

Chapter Fifty-Eight

Chicago, June 23, 1942

"She wants to see you." Erna Haupt exclaimed. "When I told her that you were back, she was very excited." Erna stood in the kitchen facing Herbie while Hans Haupt sat at the table.

"You didn't mention where I've been, did you?" said Herbie.

"I said that you were in Mexico, just like you asked me to."

"Good, that's good..." It was exactly one year since Herbie fled from his responsibilities. Gerda was bound to hold a grudge. She deserved to be angry with him. At the same time, the complication he'd tried to avoid was no longer an issue. He didn't have fatherhood bearing down on him anymore. Maybe it took being apart to realize how much Gerda meant to him, but after everything he'd been through over this past year, the thought of settling down appealed to Herbie.

"She's working at the Hotel Bismarck. You can call her there."

"Sure." Herbie was anxious. "I'll call her."

"Do you still want to go over to the car lot?" Hans asked.

"Yes, father. Just give me ten minutes, will you?"

"I'm in no hurry."

Herbie made his way upstairs to use the phone in his parents' bedroom, where he could speak in private. After dialing the Hotel Bismarck, he waited while they pulled Gerda from her shift in the dining room.

"Hello?" Gerda sounded out of breath.

"Guess who?" Herbie replied.

"Herbie…" she said his name quietly, with a sense of awe.

"Hi, Gerda."

"I almost didn't believe your mother when she told me you were home."

"I'm back all right."

"Not even a card, for nearly a year?" Her voice rose. "And then you just show up, out of the blue?"

"I'm sorry, Gerda. I would have written to you if I could."

"What, they don't have mail service in Mexico?"

"I was out in the hills, prospecting."

"Prospecting?!" she scoffed.

"For gold."

Gerda took a moment to let this information sink in. "I find it very hard to believe that you couldn't even send a card."

"I want to make it up to you," Herbie pleaded. "Can I see you?"

"I don't know…"

"Please? Just let me explain."

"Look, I need to go. I'm in the middle of a shift."

"Tell me you'll see me. I just need a chance to explain myself."

After a short pause, Gerda acquiesced. "OK. I'll see you."

"Great, you won't regret it, I promise. Why don't you come by my parents' house, today after work?"

"Look, I've got to get back to the dining room."

"I understand. I can't wait to see you."

"I'll be by this evening."

When he'd hung up the phone, Herbie retrieved his envelope of cash from where he'd hidden it under his parents' rug. Making a quick count of the bills, he found that it amounted to $3,120. For a down payment on a car, he figured that $500 should do. He peeled off an additional $120 for spending money and stuffed it into his pocket before sliding the other $2,500 back under the rug. It was as good a place for it as any, he figured.

Back downstairs, Hans waited for him in the living room. "Are you ready?"

"I am."

"Where do you want to go?"

"I thought we might try Morton Motors. I've had my eye on a Pontiac."

"Fine. Let's go see what they've got."

"Good luck." Erna gave the men a weak smile as they moved toward the door.

"Thanks, mother."

Driving to the dealership, Herbie remembered Lieutenant Kappe's explicit instructions. Don't draw attention to yourself. No big, flashy purchases. Yet, now that Herbie was home, the lieutenant couldn't stop him. Still, it was best to cover his tracks. "Father, how about if we put this car in your name? I'll pay for it, but maybe we should put your name on the registration?"

"Why would you want to do that?" Hans looked at his son sideways.

"Because…" Herbie struggled to come up with an answer before finally coming clean. "That way, if I get arrested, you can still keep the car."

Hans turned his eyes back to the road. "Whatever you feel is best."

"I think it might be a good idea."

"I certainly hope it doesn't come to that." His father pulled into the dealership and parked. As soon as the two men exited their vehicle, a middle-aged salesman in a tweed suit approached. "Good afternoon, gentlemen! Something I can help you with?"

"I'm looking for a used car." Herbie's heart swelled with desire.

"You came to the right place. Plenty of models, new and used. What kind of budget are you looking at?"

"Round about a thousand dollars."

"We can work with that, absolutely. Did you have any particular model in mind?"

"How about a convertible?"

The salesman shook his head. "Not for that kind of money. At least not in stock right at the moment, but you never know, we get vehicles coming in every week. I could take down your name and call you if I see anything come through."

Herbie's disappointment was palpable. He wasn't about to wait. He was set on buying a car, today. "What else do you have?"

"If you want a perfect combination of style and value, we've got a beauty of a Torpedo Sport Coupe." The salesman waved his hand. "Come with me and I'll show you."

"OK, I'll take a look." Herbie licked his lips. He and his father followed the salesman across the lot.

"What's your name son?" the salesman asked as they walked past a row of new models.

"Herbie. Herbie Haupt."

"I'm Fred Sloan. Good to meet make your acquaintance."

"Likewise. This is my father, Hans."

"How do you do, sir?"

Hans merely nodded. At the far end of the lot, the men came upon a sleek black Pontiac with red wheels. Herbie was thrilled by the sight of her. She was a beauty all right. Flowing lines, bullet-shaped hood… He was reminded of the Opel he'd admired in Stettin. This was a car he'd only dreamed of owning beforehand. Now it would be his.

"This is a 1941 model year," Sloan informed them. "Talk about speed, she has a flathead, eight-cylinder engine capable of producing a hundred and three horsepower. We're talking about a two-barrel Carter carburetor, hydraulic drum brakes, and a three-speed manual transmission. And if all of that isn't enough, take a look at those lines! The ladies love a Pontiac, am I right?"

"How much?"

"That's what I like. A man who's ready to talk business. This particular automobile is on sale for one thousand and forty-five dollars. Would you be looking to finance the vehicle, or are you ready to pay cash?"

"I can give you four hundred for a down payment."

"That'd be just fine. Why don't I grab the keys and you can take her for a test drive?"

Herbie looked to his father. "Sure, we'll take her for a spin."

"Excellent. I won't be a moment."

While Sloan headed back toward the sales office, Herbie walked around the car, admiring the details. A maelstrom of conflicting emotions swirled through him. Ecstasy on the one hand, and yet… it still wasn't enough to quiet his demons. Herbie had all the money he wanted. Thousands of dollars of his own, plus the bag he'd left with Walter. He could afford a car, new suits, a fancy new watch. A diamond wedding ring… yet no matter how much money he spent, the stress of his predicament lurked in the deep recesses of his mind. Just like Neubauer, Herbie could hardly sleep these days. He looked over his shoulder everywhere he went. As hard as he tried, Herbie could not fully banish the idea that this whole thing might come crashing to an end. It was supposed to be so easy. He'd hitch a ride on the sub, come back to Chicago, and disappear. He'd forget all about the plot against America. Herbie ran one hand against the Torpedo's smooth black roof. He just wanted some control. Buying this car would help. It gave Herbie the sense that he was in charge; that he could still shape his fate. Spending the Fuhrer's money was his own small act of defiance, and besides… he'd always wanted a car like this one. The overwhelming pull was impossible to resist.

"Here we go!" The salesman reappeared with a set of keys in his hand. "Let's say we get her out on the road!"

"Sure." Herbie reached for the keys. There was no denying the irresistible thrill. "You coming, father?"

Hans nodded. "Yes, son, yes, of course."

Herbie opened the driver's side door and slid onto the leather seat, unable to conceal a smile. Before he even put the key into the ignition, he already knew. This car would be his.

With part one of his plan taken care of, Herbie was left with part two. He'd bought the car. It was time to get his girl back. Walking into the kitchen at his parents' house, Herbie found Gerda sitting at the table with his mother, sharing coffee and a smoke. The women fell silent when Herbie appeared. It took him a moment to process the meaning of Gerda's pale, drawn expression. What he saw in her eyes was fear. Previously, Gerda was always the strong, confident type. Even when faced with an unwanted pregnancy, she'd exuded an air of control. This time, however, things were different.

"Hi, Herbie." Gerda placed her cigarette in an ashtray.

"Hi, Gerda."

The ex-lovers stared at one another. After a year of swirling questions, neither knew quite what to say.

"I'll leave you two alone." Erna quickly stubbed out her cigarette and stood. "You've got a lot of catching up to do."

"Thank you, mother." Herbie moved closer to the table. Unlike his fantasies, there was no falling into each other's arms. No cradling his newborn infant. Instead, he felt the desperate need to plead his case. As his mother left the room, Herbie leaned forward and kissed Gerda on her cheek. "It's good to see you."

"I'm sure."

"I thought about you all the time. Every single day."

"But not enough to write." Gerda paused to take another drag on her cigarette and then exhale. "You told me you were going to California, Herbie. For a few weeks, you said. Do you have any idea how that made me feel when I found out you were in Mexico?"

"I'm sorry, Gerda…" Herbie took a seat across the table. "It's complicated."

"What's so complicated? It's been an entire year! What have you even been doing this whole time?!"

Herbie fumbled to light a cigarette of his own. "I know it looks bad, but it's not like you think. You can't know how much I've missed you!"

Gerda lowered her eyes. Never before had she felt so vulnerable. She would proceed with caution. Given a second chance, he very well might hurt her all over again. "So, you've missed me. You weren't even here when I lost the baby. I thought you'd abandoned me for good."

"No," Herbie shook his head. "I would have come back sooner, but…"

"But what?"

"I can't really say."

"You can't say?!"

"Look, I could use something a little stronger than coffee. Let's you and me go get a drink somewhere. What do you think?"

Gerda tapped her ashes and gave a quick nod. "I could use a drink."

Through sheer force of will, Herbie was determined to get his old life back. "Come on, then," he stubbed out his cigarette. "There's some things we need to talk about."

"I'll say."

Escorting Gerda through the living room, Herbie clung to the optimism that a little persuasion might convince her. "I'm going to take Gerda home," he said to his parents. "I'll be back in a while."

"It was lovely to see you, dear," his mother replied from her place on the couch.

"You, too, Erna."

"We might stop for a drink," said Herbie. "I shouldn't be too late."

"Have a nice time." Hans handed over the car keys. Herbie had wanted to come home with his spiffy new ride, but the loan had yet to go through. He wouldn't take possession until the following day. Until then, he'd make do with his father's old Plymouth. Herbie hadn't yet bought her a ring either, though that wouldn't stop him. He would ask for Gerda's hand in marriage this very night. It was a far cry from one year earlier, but things had changed. He had changed. Herbie's perspective on life was entirely different. He just had to convince her. With some luck, Gerda Stuckmann would say yes.

Chapter Fifty-Nine

New York, June 23, 1942

Walking up Second Avenue toward Engemann's Grocery, Marie Kerling felt ambivalent about meeting with Helmut Leiner. He'd been so enthusiastic when they spoke on the telephone that it was hard to say no, though he'd always been Eddie's friend more than hers. She hadn't even spoken with Helmut once since Eddie left more than a year earlier. Besides that, it seemed like an odd meeting place. Sure, Hedy Engemann and Marie were technically friends, but it was complicated. They were friends because they'd shared a man. Friends in dismay because that man was gone, back to a Germany at war. Even without Hedy in the picture, Marie's relationship with Eddie was complicated, too. He was still her husband. True, she'd encouraged him to take a mistress, though it was only after he'd left that she came to regret the decision. Marie still loved Eddie. She felt it most acutely on the rare occasions when she saw Hedy Engemann. Though she tried to put a positive face on their situation, it was never easy. With Eddie off in Berlin, though, Hedy was one of the last connections she had to her husband. Arriving at the grocery, Marie steeled herself to the emotional fallout to come. She opened the door and walked in.

Behind a register, Marie saw a gentleman she knew to be Hedy's father. There was no sign of Hedy herself, or Helmut either. At just after 9 p.m., the store was nearly deserted. "Excuse me," she approached Mr. Engemann. "I'm looking for Hedy. Is she around?"

"In the back."

"Thank you. Can I just…"

"Go ahead. Through the door there. The office is on the right."

Marie nodded and moved down an aisle to a double door along the back wall. Passing through, she entered a storeroom with shelves stacked floor to ceiling with boxes of groceries. From an open doorway to her right she heard the muffled voice of Helmut Leiner. Marie ducked her head around the doorframe to see Leiner sitting on a couch next to Hedy.

"Marie, there you are!" Leiner rose, a broad smile on his face. "We were just talking about you!"

"Hello, Helmut." She moved into the room, leaning forward to give him a light kiss on the cheek. "It's been a while."

"Hello, Marie." Hedy was demure, keeping her seat on the couch.

"Hi, Hedy."

"How have you been?"

"Not too bad."

"Where are you working these days?" Helmut coughed into his hand, deep and rasping as his whole body shook.

"Are you all right?" Marie took one step back.

"Sure, sure," Helmut raised a hand as he struggled to regain his breath.

"He's been a little under the weather," said Hedy.

"It's nothing. I'm fine," Helmut countered. "Tell me, then, are you managing the bills these days?"

"I always do."

"Yes, you do. I've always admired that about you." The conversation tailed off as Helmut looked uneasily to Hedy and then back. "Look, I'm sure you're wondering why I called you down here," he said to Marie.

"I thought there must be a reason. Not that it isn't nice to see you both."

"I have somebody that I'd like you to meet. You could say that he's the perfect blind date." Leiner's face lit up with enthusiasm.

"Oh, Helmut!" Marie protested. "Tell me you're joking! A blind date is the last thing I'm interested in!"

Helmut strove to maintain his optimism. "But this one is special! I'm telling you, Marie, you'll like him. I promise you that!"

"Helmut…" Marie growled.

"Won't you just meet with him, at least? I'll come along. Hedy, too! Right, Hedy?"

Hedy shrugged. "Sure, I'll come."

Marie shook her head, a sense of panic overcoming her. "Honestly, Helmut, I'm not interested. You might as well get that idea clear out of your head."

Leiner's jaw hung open. "But…"

"No, Helmut! No."

"Perhaps if Helmut told us a little bit about this person," Hedy tried to help.

"I'm sorry to have wasted your time, but I'll be going. Take care of yourselves."

"Wait! Hold on a minute!" Helmut cried out. "It's not like I said!"

Facing Leiner, Marie crossed her arms and tilted her head to one side, anger rising in her core. "What is it like, then, Helmut?"

"It's not a blind date. Not a blind date at all. I didn't want to tell you, but…" He took a deep breath. "It's Eddie."

"What do you mean, Eddie? What are you talking about?!"

"He's back. Eddie is back. He wants to see you."

"You're crazy!" Marie dismissed him with a wave of the hand.

"Honest," Leiner persisted. "I mean it. I've seen him myself. I'll take you to him right away."

When Marie looked to Hedy, she was met with an uncertain shake of the head. "Did you know about this?" Marie asked.

"Me? No! I can't hardly believe it! Eddie, in New York?!"

"It's the truth," said Helmut. "If only you'll come with me, Marie, I'll prove it."

As the news sank in, a mix of emotions surged through Marie. She wanted to believe it, but how could she? Eddie…? Here? How was that even possible? She raised one hand to wipe a tear spilling from the corner of one eye. "You better not be playing games with me, Helmut."

"It's no game, I promise. Eddie will explain everything."

Marie turned to Hedy. "Will you come?"

"Oh, I don't know…" Hedy patted the work apron that she wore over a plain blue dress. "I can't let him see me like this."

"Please?" Marie persisted. Somehow having Hedy along would make the whole thing easier.

"I'd have to change first."

"We don't mind, do we Helmut?"

"No, no, we don't mind. Not at all."

"*Where* are we meeting him?" Marie's reluctance faded. It was more than a year since she'd seen or even heard from her husband. No mail between two warring nations. No transport at all, yet if Helmut insisted…

"The Hotel Shelton, in the bar. He's planning to meet us there at 10:30." Helmut looked at his watch. "That gives us just about 30 minutes."

"Well then, Hedy, you'd better get changed, hadn't you?"

"Yes, yes, of course. I won't be ten minutes."

Marie walked to a mirror advertising Dr. Pepper Soda. As Hedy departed the room, Marie opened her purse and removed a lipstick, carefully applying it before using a brush to tame the wild curls in her hair. Despite everything, she *did* still love him. Then again, so did Hedy, yet after waking up every day for a year thinking that she might never see Eddie again, the prospect seemed like a dream. If Helmut was right, that dream would become reality in just twenty more minutes. For Marie, those minutes could hardly tick by fast enough.

Chapter Sixty

Chicago, June 23, 1942

After the unbearable uncertainty that he'd struggled with over the previous year, Herbie Haupt craved stability. He wanted to banish his doubts and fears. He wanted his job back and his new car. He wanted a home of his own to share with the girl who sat across the table from him. The girl he'd grown to long for. If only Gerda would take him back, then Herbie could make the rest of his problems vanish. He was sure of it. Only, having just asked for her hand, Gerda's reaction was less than enthusiastic. She hadn't come right out and said no, though her expression conveyed no joy. Confusion was a better descriptive.

"Why now?" Gerda asked. "After all of this time apart? Why do you want to marry me so bad?"

"Because I'm in love with you, that's why! Is it so hard to believe?"

"I just don't know what to make of it, Herbie. You didn't write to me for a whole year! I haven't heard from you! Not since that one card from St. Louis, and now you come back and tell me that you want to marry me the very first time you see me? I just want to understand it, that's all."

"I'm sorry that I didn't write. I would have if I could…"

Gerda turned away, unwilling to look him in the eye if he was merely going to lie to her.

"I saw my old boss, down at Simpson Optical," he went on. "They got a big new contract. The foreman says I can start back this Thursday."

"That's great, Herbie."

"Why you don't want to marry me…?"

The sadness in his question nearly broke Gerda's heart. "I never said I don't want to."

Herbie pulled out his wallet and flipped it open. Extracting a ten-dollar bill, he slid it across the table. "Take this and you can get your blood test tomorrow."

"Blood test!?"

"Everybody knows you need a blood test to get married. It's for the license."

This time, Gerda looked at him dead on. The pleading expression on his face suggested he was serious. Slowly, she reached for the ten dollars, clutching the bill in her fingers. At least this would buy her some time to think it over. "I'll get the test. But you better get one, too."

"I will, I promise!" His face lit up. "First thing tomorrow."

Gerda tucked the bill into her purse and snapped the clasp shut.

"To us." Herbie raised a glass of whiskey.

Gerda raised her own. She wasn't entirely sure she would marry this man, but then again, she wasn't entirely sure that she wouldn't.

Chapter Sixty-One

New York, June 23, 1942

"Did you see the headline in the *Mirror* this morning?" Eddie Kerling sat in a crowded, smoky bar, drinking beer with Werner Thiel.

"What mirror?" Thiel asked.

"The paper. The *New York Mirror*?"

Thiel shook his head. "Never heard of it."

"It seems that they have heard of us."

Thiel narrowed his eyes. "What are you talking about?"

"They say the FBI is scouring the swamps down in Florida. Rumor has it that some Nazis landed on the beach."

"The FBI?! I thought we got away clean. I mean, nobody saw us, right?"

Kerling slumped on his stool. "I don't know."

Thiel scanned right and then left. "Even if they did, how would anybody know it was us?"

Eddie shook his head. "There's no way we can go back down there. We'd better forget the whole thing. If we try to dig up those crates, we're as good as done for."

Thiel swallowed his beer. "What about Kappe?"

"What about him?" Kerling growled.

"If he finds out…"

"Look, I gotta go." Kerling was agitated. "I need to meet my wife."

"I hope you haven't told her nothin'," Thiel warned.

"I haven't even seen her yet."

"Yeah, well you'd better keep your mouth shut."

Kerling stood to go. "I'll see you back at the hotel." Eddie stubbed out his cigarette and left the bar, turning right on Lexington Ave. and heading toward East 49th Street. Despite his troubles, his heart sang at the thought of seeing Marie. Was it possible to love two women at the same time? The whole idea was untenable in the long term, but Kerling didn't want to worry about that. He and Marie still shared a connection. They cared for each other, no matter what the future held. She was a ray of sunshine in what had become a dreary existence.

Crossing the intersection at 47th Street, just two blocks from the Hotel Shelton, Eddie saw a large black Chevrolet slow beside him. His posture straightened, all senses on alert. Ahead on the sidewalk, two men stood idly smoking cigarettes. Everybody looked like FBI to him these days. He lowered his head and hurried forward. They were just men, standing on the sidewalk. Nothing more.

Yet this time was different. As soon as Kerling stepped up onto the opposite curb they converged on him, the car pulling to a stop with front and rear doors springing open. Two more men jumped out. Too startled to react, Eddie's muscles stiffened as he was thrown onto the hood of the car, face down. His arms were wrenched behind his back, the cold steel of handcuffs tightening around his wrists.

"Edward Kerling?" The man's voice was calm. Matter-of-fact.

Eddie managed to nod. This was it. The culmination of his fears. "Yes." His mind flashed to Marie. So close. He could see the hotel where she and Helmut waited for him, just up ahead.

"Federal Bureau of Investigation," the agent continued. "You're under arrest."

Yanked off the hood of the car, Kerling was shoved into the back seat, an agent clinging to him on either side. As the doors slammed shut, an agent on the sidewalk tapped twice on the roof and the car moved out into traffic. Racing past the Hotel Shelton, Eddie strained to see through the front entrance, hoping for at least a fleeting glimpse of Marie. He was not so lucky. The car turned at the corner. Any semblance of the life he'd once known was finished. Any chance for escape was gone.

Chapter Sixty-Two

Washington, DC, June 23, 1942

The director sat alone in his office, both hands on his desk. Anxiety coursed through his veins. J. Edgar Hoover was not about to be humiliated. Things were in danger of slipping out of control, and he simply wouldn't stand for it. Glory was there for the taking, yet this Dasch character presented a major problem. The narrative had to change. America needed a victory. The bureau itself was the hero in this story, and the press would tell it exactly as he wanted them to. Through the hard work of dedicated agents, the FBI was solely responsible for cracking the case, period. That was all anybody outside this building needed to know. Those Nazi spies never stood a chance. Dasch's role in the affair must never be disclosed. The director picked up his phone and dialed an extension.

"This is Ladd," the assistant director answered.

"Mickey, I want Dasch arrested in New York!" Hoover bellowed. "Not Washington! You understand me? New York!"

Ladd knew better than to contradict his boss. "New York," he repeated.

"That's right, you take him up to the federal courthouse and arrest him there!"

"How will we get him up there if he isn't in custody?"

"I don't care, come up with a story. He wants to help us, doesn't he? Tell him we need his help! Tell him it's all a ruse to put one over on those other Nazis he came with. Just make sure there's no official record that this man was ever in Washington!"

"I understand."

"We have to be very careful, Mickey, or this whole thing could blow up in our faces."

"He's still asking to meet with you, personally."

Hoover recoiled, the veins pounding in his forehead. "I'm not going to meet with that son-of-a-bitch! You and Traynor deal with him."

"What about a travel waiver? He'll need to sign one."

Hoover gave this unfortunate detail some thought. "Just make sure that nobody outside the agency ever lays eyes on it. We were on their trail from the moment those Nazis landed on Long Island, and that's all we have to say about it."

"Yes, sir."

When he hung up the phone, Hoover felt slightly better. If he could, he'd stick Dasch in the deepest, darkest cell he could find, never to see the light of day again. Or even better, straight to the electric chair. As long as the newspapers never got hold of him, maybe the bureau could still contain this thing. When Hoover considered the prospect of a public trial, beads of sweat formed on his brow. He was not about to let some Nazi bastard siphon away the credit that Hoover and his bureau rightfully deserved. The FBI cracked the case, end of the story. If Dasch had any complaints, they would be buried with him.

Chapter Sixty-Three

New York, NY, June 24, 1942

Special Agent Thomas Donegan was an imposing man, both in stature and attitude. To run the New York office, he had to be. Chasing after hardened criminals, he had no patience for games. Sitting on the edge of his desk, Donegan was determined that the man in the chair before him talk, no matter what it took. No lawyers. No sleep. Edward Kerling's eyes drooped shut, head tilting lazily. Donegan rose to his feet and lunged forward, kicking violently at the suspect's chair. "Where are the explosives?!"

Kerling's head snapped straight, eyes popping open. "I don't know…"

Special Agent Joe Fellner unfolded a map of Florida and spread it on the desk between them. "Show us where you came ashore."

Kerling glanced at the map and then slowly shook his head. "I'm afraid you are mistaken. As I said before, I arrived overland, from Mexico."

Donegan's fury boiled over. He was finished talking. After a long night of pointless questioning, the agent could take no more. Grabbing Kerling by the hair, he jerked the suspect's head to one side. Kerling's eyes were wide with terror as Donegan grit his teeth, face red with anger. There was only one way to handle this. Releasing his grasp, the agent made a fist with his right hand and swung, connecting clean on Kerling's jaw. Donegan hit him again, and then a third time, knocking Kerling out of his chair and onto the ground.

"Easy, boss." Fellner moved forward, placing a hand on Donegan's arm.

Hovering over the prisoner, Donegan stood his ground, hoping that Kerling would get up, that he might try to fight back. The agent wanted nothing more than to continue pummeling this Nazi sonofabitch.

"Maybe you ought to take a break," Fellner interjected.

"What for?!"

"Just take it easy."

"You got a problem with this?!" Donegan snapped.

"No, Tom, no problem. I think you could use some air, that's all. It's been a long night."

Kerling curled in a fetal position, the right side of his face pressed against the cold tile floor. If only they'd leave him, just for a while. So tired… so tired… despite the pain, he yearned to close his eyes and let consciousness drain away.

Fellner leaned low and took Kerling by the arm. "Let's get you back up." There would be no sleeping. The agent helped the suspect off the floor and back into the chair. "Go ahead, Tom, take a few minutes."

A glowering Donegan stomped out of the office without a word. When he was gone, Fellner took a closer look at Kerling's bruised face. "You all right?"

Kerling didn't bother to answer. What was the point? He was at their mercy and there was nothing he could do about it. They'd made that plainly clear. Fellner moved to the door and called out into the corridor. "Send the doctor in here, will you?"

Fellner sat beside Kerling and pulled out a box of Lucky Strikes. Extracting a single cigarette, he saw the suspect's longing gaze. The agent pulled out another and handed it across, followed by a lighter. Kerling struck the flint and lit up before handing the lighter back. The pair smoked in silence. After a few minutes, a thin man with a doctor's bag entered the room. He had a narrow mustache and wore a loose brown suit. The doctor took one look at Kerling and visibly recoiled.

"Just make sure he's all right, will you?" said Fellner.

Dr. Otis Dwyer placed his bag on the desk. He was no FBI man. The doctor was home asleep when the call came through. Of course, he was no stranger to house calls, but this one was different. What exactly the FBI wanted with him, he'd had no idea. As he fished around inside his bag, the answer was still not evident. Dr. Dwyer pulled out a small penlight. Leaning close, he flashed it into Kerling's left eye, away, and back again. He did the same thing on the right. "How do you feel?"

"Tired."

"How have you been treated?"

"Fine. At least until they hit me in the face."

The doctor's expression gave away his concern. He turned to Fellner for confirmation.

"That wasn't me," said the agent.

"Who was it?"

"Don't worry, I'll talk to him."

"I think that would be advisable."

Fellner stepped out of the room, leaving patient and doctor alone. Dwyer placed a finger on Kerling's neck, sliding it back and forth until he found a pulse. Keeping an eye on the second hand of his watch, he counted the heartbeats. "You seem to be all right, though I would suggest you get some rest."

"They won't let me sleep. Every time I close my eyes, they wake me up."

"I'm sorry. I'll try to check back in from time to time." Doctor Dwyer placed his penlight back into his bag and then zipped it closed just as Donegan stormed into the office once more, nearly bowling the doctor over.

Charging across to Kerling, Donegan raised a hand in the air. "Did I strike you in the face?!"

"Um… I…" Kerling flinched as he leaned away.

"Did I strike you?!!"

"Well… you brushed me lightly. On the side of the face."

Donegan grasped the suspect by the shirt, yanked him to his feet and dragged him out the door. Down the corridor they went. The beating would resume, Eddie realized. This time in private. Donegan pulled him into a vacant office and shoved him against a wall. Pressing close, his hot breath caressed Kerling's face. "Did I hit you?!" Donegan's voice was thick with menace.

"No, sir. No, you did not."

"That's what I thought. When the doctor asks again, that is exactly what you will tell him. Do you understand me?!"

"Yes, sir."

Donegan held his clenched right fist in the air. "Don't try anything funny."

"No, sir." Kerling shook.

With veins throbbing in his forehead, Donegan hauled the suspect back up the corridor to his own office and then shoved him into the chair once more. "Ask him if he was hit."

Dr. Dwyer licked his lips in dismay. He turned to his patient. "Were you hit in the face at any time?"

"No." Kerling shook his head. "No, I was not."

"Has anybody here physically abused you in any way?"

"No."

"You can go," Donegan said to the doctor. Dwyer picked up his bag and moved out of the room. Donegan leaned close to Kerling once more. "You're going to tell me about those explosives," he snarled. "Not only that, we're going down to Florida and you're going to show us exactly where you buried them. What do you think about that?"

For Eddie Kerling, any last sense of defiance melted away. They had him. There was no sense in holding out. Slowly, almost imperceptibly, he nodded his head.

"Get me a train schedule," Donegan said to Fellner. "We're taking this man to Florida."

"You got it."

Chapter Sixty-Four

Washington, DC, June 24, 1942

George Dasch was beginning to worry. Special Agent Traynor was pleasant enough. They got along fine, but the man Dasch wanted to see was Hoover. George was eager to help battle the Nazis in any way he could. He drew a careful diagram of the submarine base in Lorient. He disclosed the diving speed and maximum depth of a Nazi submarine. He explained, to the best of his ability, the workings of an Enigma coding machine. After wracking his brain, Dasch finally remembered how to reveal the invisible ink on a handkerchief he carried, exposing his local German contacts. George had grand plans. With his background at the Interior Ministry, he offered valuable assistance in directing propaganda efforts against the Nazis. With each passing day, however, it seemed that any appreciation for his efforts waned.

After a full week of questioning, a transcription of Dasch's statement was typed and presented for his signature. It came to a full 254 pages. George sat in Traynor's office, reading it through carefully and making corrections here and there before signing each page. Is this what he'd said? Was that detail correct? He wanted to make sure the record was straight, but the information had come out in what, at times, amounted to a rambling stream of consciousness. "My mind is all upside down," he said.

"It's fine, don't fret so much over the small details," Traynor answered.

In the chair beside Dasch was another agent he'd come to know. Norval Wills never said much. He was a beefy man. The strong, silent type. George understood that Wills' primary responsibility was to keep an eye on him. Somebody was always keeping an eye on him. Even in his hotel room, Wills slept in the next bed. "I know I've said this before, but if the Nazis ever find out what I've done..." Dasch signed the last page and slid the document across the desk. "You have to understand it's my family that I worry about."

"I do understand." Traynor picked up the statement and put it into a desk drawer. "We've been giving that some thought." He paused. "Your family, I mean."

"What sort of thought?"

"We'd like to stage things so that the other men think that we have you in custody as well. You know, march you past their cells in prison garb so they think we nabbed you, too. Just for show, of course."

"I thought you said the rest of the men were in New York?"

"That's right," Traynor nodded. "We'd take you up to New York."

The prospect of facing the other men in prison made Dasch decidedly uneasy. "I'm not sure how that would help safeguard my family," he countered. "If none of the men have any contact with the outside…"

Traynor leaned forward over his desk. "You'd be doing us a big favor. Some of the others are refusing to talk at all, as long as they think you're still at large and doing Hitler's dirty work. If they saw you in custody, they'd know the jig was up. Of course, there is an added benefit for you. The others won't have any reason to believe that you turned on them."

Dasch held his fingertips together. That made sense.

"We could make it look like one of the others turned you in. Say Heinck, or maybe Quirin."

Dasch tilted his head to one side. "What about my wife? Are you going to get Snookie out of that internment camp? Why hasn't there been any news about that?"

"We're working on it, George, but it's better if we go slowly. If your wife were released right away, that would be a clear tip-off to the Nazis that you're involved with us."

"What about Hoover? If I could only speak with the director…" Dasch pleaded yet again. "If I could explain the situation in person…"

Traynor ran his tongue across his upper lip, trying to quiet his frustration. "The director is a busy man."

"So you keep saying."

"He is being kept up to date on all of the details of your case. One thing that you should understand, George, is that while we do appreciate all that you have done for us, it is important that we give the Nazis the impression that the FBI cracked this case unassisted. Not only for your sake, but in order to discourage any further sabotage missions."

"You want to take the credit? Is that what this trip to New York is about?"

"It is in your interest as well as ours."

"If I hadn't walked in that door of my own free will…" Dasch couldn't bring himself to complete the sentence. All he wanted was the respect that was his due. He wanted to speak to Hoover. He wanted a role in organizing propaganda efforts. He wanted to contact his wife. Yet he was starting to get the impression that they had all they needed out of him. Dasch was hit with a creeping apprehension. Despite all he had done for this adopted homeland of his, they might just hang him out to dry.

"Like I said, you've done a great service, George. I mean that. You took a lot of chances."

"I did it because it was the right thing to do. Don't you understand? I had to do it, or my heart would burst!" Dasch shifted uneasily. "If I go to New York and take part in this little charade, can you promise that you'll keep my name and photo out of the papers? I wouldn't want people to get the wrong idea about me."

"You won't be in the papers. We'll make sure of it."

"That's a promise?"

"Yes, sir, that's a promise."

Dasch acquiesced with a nod. "If you think it's important, I will do it."

Traynor offered the slightest of smiles. He took two single-page documents from his top drawer and slid them across the desk along with a pen. "Great. I just need you to sign these for me."

"What are they?"

"Standard travel waivers. Just a matter of form."

Dasch began to read the first document, full of legal jargon that he couldn't quite understand.

"You can sign right there at the bottom," Traynor prodded.

Without reading further, Dasch signed and dated the first document, and then the second.

"Thank you." Traynor retrieved the pages and then gave a slight nod to Wills, who stood from his chair. "Now if you don't mind, George, could you please stand and place your hands on the desk?"

"Is that really necessary?" Dasch's eyes opened wide.

"I'm afraid so," said Traynor. "It's just standard procedure."

"Am I under arrest?"

"No, George, you're not under arrest."

Confusion swirled through Dasch's mind. He didn't like the shift in tone. He didn't like Wills hovering behind him with menace. Yet George was at their mercy. After some hesitation, he did as he was asked.

"Spread your legs," Wills grunted. Dasch widened his stance and then felt the agent's hands moving first across his arms and chest, then along his torso and up and down each leg. Wills reached into Dasch's pockets and pulled out the contents. On the desk, he placed a gold pen and some spare change before removing George's tie clasp. "Please remove your watch," Wills added.

"The watch, too?!"

"We have to do this by the book," Traynor exclaimed. "I'll take the hat as well."

Dasch reluctantly took off his watch and placed it on the desk. Wills lifted the hat from a rack by the door and added it to the pile. As Traynor began typing a receipt for the items, he stopped to look up. "Relax, George, everything is going to be fine."

Dasch slumped back into his chair. Despite this assurance, he couldn't quite banish his doubts.

Chapter Sixty-Five

Jacksonville, FL, June 25, 1942

An unshackled Eddie Kerling was escorted off the overnight train by four G-Men, with an agent holding tightly to each arm. Waiting for them on the platform was Assistant Director Earl Connelley with a contingent of agents from the Miami field office. "Any problems?" Connelley asked.

"None," replied Special Agent Gerald McSwain.

"Good. Let's move out."

So exhausted was Kerling that if it weren't for the agents propping him up, his feet might have failed him. Instead, he was hauled through an underpass and out to the street where he was loaded into the back of a large black sedan.

"OK, Kerling." Connelley turned to look back from the front passenger seat. "Where to?"

"South." Kerling sat in the back with McSwain on one side and Special Agent Sam Cutler on the other. "A couple of miles. Just past the golf course." Overcome by a rush of nausea, Eddie leaned his head toward his knees and grit his teeth.

"You heard the man," Connelley relayed to the driver. The car moved out, heading south down State Road 140 in the direction of Ponte Vedra. After a few miles, they eased onto a frontage road that ran parallel to the beach. "How far?" Connelley asked.

Eddie peered through the window. "Maybe another mile." As they went, he searched for the telltale palm trees that he knew marked the spot. To their right was the golf course, to the left, white sand. Beyond that, whitecaps gently fluttered atop the wide-open sea. Closer at hand, additional clumps of palms protruded from the dunes here and there. Were any of these the right ones? They all looked more or less the same.

"You recognize anything?"

"I don't know. I need to see it from the beach."

"Pull over," Connelley said, and the car stopped along the side of the road. All but the driver piled out. "Let's go."

The men trudged south across the sand, beneath the tropical sun. Scattered families reclined on blankets, their children frolicking in the water nearby. A few pairs of curious eyes turned toward the gathering of grown men in their suits and felt hats. Kerling paused to get his bearings, gazing first north to the crescent strip of hotels that made up Jacksonville Beach. "We need to go further."

"Fine. We'll walk."

As they started off, the car followed slowly along the road. One mile. Two. With Kerling's laces removed to prevent a suicide attempt, his loose leather shoes filled with sand. Each time he saw a prospective group of palms he'd stop, look north, then south. Was this it? No. "There was a barbed wire fence," he said. "Right next to the palm trees. Perpendicular to the road. If you follow the fence to the road, there's some kind of foundation there."

"What, like a building?" said McSwain.

"Yeah. Concrete."

"Let's walk on the road," said Connelley. The men moved west once more until they hit the frontage road. This time as they walked on, the car tailed them closely from behind.

"Look, Kerling, you better be straight with us," said McSwain. "We didn't come all the way down here to play games."

"I'm not playing games. I don't want anybody to get hurt. Some kids come along and dig these crates up… I don't need that on my conscience."

"Are you sure we haven't passed it yet?"

"Pretty sure." It was half a mile further before they came to a small concrete foundation sticking up from the sand. Beside it was a barbed-wire fence heading off toward the sea. "This could be it." They followed the fence back toward the water. It came to an end atop a low set of dunes. A few yards to the left: three small palms in a cluster.

"Recognize anything?" said Connelly.

"I think so."

"You think so?"

"Yes." Kerling pointed. "This is it. Somewhere right around there."

"There are two shovels in the trunk," Connelley said to his agents.

"You heard the man," McSwain directed Cutler.

"Get on the radio," Connelley added. "I want Parsons out here, and tell him to bring the photographer, Dunlop. And Danner, too."

"You got it chief." Cutler scurried back toward the car.

Connelley turned to Kerling. "You might as well take a seat."

Dizzy and faint, Eddie dropped atop the dune, closing his eyes as he rocked slowly backward and forward. This was more than mere exhaustion. Perhaps it was food poisoning… He couldn't quite know, but a four-mile march through the sand, without shoelaces, had nearly done him in.

Cutler returned a few minutes later with two shovels. "Where do we dig?" He handed a spade to McSwain.

Kerling opened his eyes. Holding one hand to shield them from the sun, he pointed with the other. "Over there."

"Any word from Parsons?" said Connelley.

"They're on the way."

"Good."

The two agents hoisted their shovels and began to dig. For Eddie Kerling, the nightmare that he'd so feared had come to pass. He wondered if Dasch was responsible, or maybe Burger. Even the Haupt kid was suspect. Somebody must have ratted them out. As the agents removed one shovelful of sand after another, Kerling collapsed onto the sand, tucking his knees toward his chest. He heard the thud of a shovel striking wood.

"I got something here!" Cutler called out.

The others dropped to their knees, pushing the sand away with bare hands. Connelley stood close by the suspect. If he thought that Kerling might run, he needn't have worried. Eddie was going nowhere. His part in this drama was finished. The only thing left was to find out what they'd do to him. One thing he did know; here on the beach in Florida, this was the last fresh air he was likely to breathe in a very long time.

Chapter Sixty-Six

Chicago, June 25, 1942

"I heard you know a thing or two about the draft." Herbie Haupt stood in the back of Donath's Grocery with his friend Bill Wernecke. At the register up front, Otto Donath leaned against the counter absentmindedly reading a newspaper.

"What about it?" Bill was a large man with a perfectly round head. His blustery attitude was legendary. Herbie knew well enough to tread carefully.

"I went down to register, but, you know…"

"You don't want to fight in no stupid war that you didn't start."

"Something like that. They say you've got the whole thing figured out."

Bill crossed his arms and tilted his head to one side, a man confident in his knowledge. "You can either get a medical deferment or a religious deferment. I suggest you go for both."

"How does it work?"

"I've got a doctor you can see. He's one of us."

"Deutsch?"

Bill nodded in the affirmative.

"When?"

"I'll walk down there with you right now if you want. It's not too far. If it doesn't work out, you can try joining my church. We're pacifists. Fighting is against our religion." Bill smiled slyly. Wernecke was never one to shy away from a good fight. He also didn't hide his Nazi sympathies.

"Let's try the doctor first."

"Come on, then."

Walking past the counter, Herbie gave a wave. "So long, Mr. Donath, we're heading to the doctor's."

"Nothing serious, I hope!" Otto replied.

"No, nothing serious. You don't have to worry about that. Just a checkup."

"OK, you boys take care."

On the examination table, Herbie sat in his underwear. A doctor in a white lab coat pressed the cool, round steel of a stethoscope against his chest. "Breathe deeply. Good. Exhale." Dr. Otten listened carefully before lowering the stethoscope and then lifting Herbie's chart to make a few notations. He put the chart back down and then held two fingers against Herbie's neck, watching thirty seconds tick off his wristwatch as he counted the beats. Again, he made a note.

"How does it look, doc?" Herbie asked.

"Your heart is beating a trifle fast. Have you been subject to any undue stress lately? Maybe some difficulties at work?"

"Oh, not at work. I've been taking some time off."

"Any trouble sleeping? Are you waking up in the middle of the night?"

"Yeah, sure," Herbie admitted. "I guess I've been a little nervous lately. I only just got home, you know. I was away for a whole year, down in Mexico."

"I see. I'm going to suggest a cardiograph, just to take a good look at your ticker, if that sounds all right with you."

"Fine."

"You can have it done over at St. Joseph's Hospital. If they can't get you in, you might try Grant Hospital. Just have them send the results over here to me when they're ready. I'm going to give you some pills that will help you sleep. I'll prescribe some others to help with your digestion."

"All right."

"Overall, I don't see anything that gives me reason for grave concern. Come back after the cardiograph and we'll have a better idea." Dr. Otten filled out a prescription and handed it to Herbie, along with a small bottle of pills.

"Thank you, doctor." Herbie put on his clothes and then walked out.

In the waiting room, Bill Wernecke sat reading a magazine. "How'd it go?"

"Fine, I guess. He wants me to have a cardiograph. I'm not sure he understood why I was here."

"He knows. Believe me, he knows. He gave you a prescription, right?"

"Yeah, sure."

"You take some of those before the cardiograph and there's no way the Army is gonna want you. Trust me."

With all the stress he *was* under, Herbie wondered what a cardiograph might show even without the pills. Together with Bill, he walked the four blocks back to Donath's store. Inside they found Bill's mother, Eva, sitting at a table near the entrance with Mildred Donath and her ten-year-old daughter, Lucy.

"There they are! How did it go?" Eva Wernecke asked.

"Oh, fine. No real problems," said Herbie.

"They want him to get a cardiograph," Bill added.

"You look all right to me!" said Mildred. She was a small woman with a bright smile.

"Otten, he's a good doc," said Bill.

"What are you two boys up to this evening?" Mrs. Wernecke asked.

"We thought we might go to a show."

"I want to go for a drive!" little Lucy called out.

"We hear that Herbie just got a brand new Pontiac!" said Mildred.

"It's not brand new, it's a year old, and it's only a coupe. I don't think it would fit everybody."

"We could take my Hudson!" Mrs. Wernecke offered. "It is a lovely evening for a drive."

Bill and Herbie took a quick look at one another. "What do you think?" Bill asked.

"Yeah, sure. It sounds all right to me."

"We can go through the country, out toward Des Plains," said Mrs. Wernecke.

From his place behind the counter, Otto Donath folded his paper and tossed it aside. "I still want to take a look at this car of yours."

"It's parked right up the block," Bill answered. "She's a real beaut."

"I don't doubt it!"

Herbie managed a smile. His coupe *was* a real beaut all right. Maybe with time, he'd put his anxieties to rest enough to enjoy it. Until then he was going through the motions, living his days as if there were nothing wrong at all, yet constantly struggling against the gnawing uncertainties.

"Why don't you give me a loosky, before you all take off," said Mr. Donath.

"Sure, I'll give you a look," Herbie swelled with pride.

"Mind the store for a few minutes, will you?" Otto said to his wife before following Herbie and Bill out onto the sidewalk.

"Don't keep us girls waiting too long!" Mrs. Wernecke called after.

"Back in a jiff!" said Otto.

Sitting in the front passenger seat with the window rolled down, a balmy breeze caressed Herbie's face. For perhaps the first time since his return to Chicago, he could finally relax. Here he was, among friends on a leisurely drive through the country. He was doing all right for himself so far. Herbie just had to maintain his optimism and everything would work out fine.

"We should call in on Ernie Scharff," said Bill Wernecke from his place behind the wheel of his mother's Hudson.

"Who is Ernie Scharff?" Mildred sat in back along with little Lucy and Eva Wernecke.

"You know the Scharffs," said Eva. "They have the cleaning and dyeing business."

"Oh, yes, that's right. I remember them."

"I haven't seen old Ernie in ages," said Bill. "That all right with you, Herbie?"

"Yeah, that sounds like a swell idea." Herbie closed his eyes and inhaled the fresh country air.

"I hate to mention it, but has anybody else noticed that Hudson behind us?" said Mrs. Wernecke.

Herbie's eyes snapped open. He looked back to see a car nearly identical to the one they were driving, about twenty yards behind. "What about it?"

"I only noticed because it's the same kind of car as mine, but it's been there ever since we left the city. That seems a little bit unusual, doesn't it?"

"The same car?" Herbie asked.

"The same car," Mrs. Wernecke answered. By this time, everyone's attention was directed toward the black sedan. Two men wearing dark hats sat in front.

Herbie's heartbeat picked up once again as he pictured himself being hauled away in front of his friends, here in the middle of the Illinois farmlands. Yet if it was the FBI, why follow him all the way out here? It didn't make sense.

"It's got to be a coincidence," said Bill, though he sounded nervous himself. As a committed Nazi and a draft dodger, he had his own reasons to be.

"Hey Herbie, there's pen and paper in the glove box," said Mrs. Wernecke. "Hand it to me and I'll write down the license plate number."

Herbie opened the glove box and found the pen and paper while Bill stepped on the gas, stretching the distance between the cars. At the next intersection, he turned to the right. The other Hudson turned right, also.

"See what I mean?" Mrs. Wernecke quickly jotted down the number.

"Pull over, Bill, and see what they do," said Mrs. Donath.

"Are you sure that's such a good idea?" said Mrs. Wernecke.

"What, you think they plan to rob us?"

"I don't know *what* they plan to do."

"Let's find out." Bill stepped on the brakes and pulled the car over to the side of the road. "Herbie, get out and pretend to check the tire."

"Sure." Herbie climbed out and made his way to the rear where he knelt beside the tire, all the while keeping an eye on the Hudson. It slowed to a stop some distance behind, the two occupants peering forward. Neither car moved. After pretending to check the tire stem, Herbie stood and returned to his place in the passenger seat.

"I say we get a closer look." Bill pulled a U-turn. Moving alongside the other Hudson, just a few feet apart, they saw the two men up close; cleanly shaven and well-dressed, in loose-fitting suits. The men refused to make eye contact, instead staring straight ahead, their jaws clenched tight. As he pulled away down the road, Bill watched in his mirror to see what the other car would do. This time, it drove off in the opposite direction.

"There they go," said Mrs. Wernecke.

"I guess it was nothing," said Mrs. Donath. "Just a coincidence after all."

"I don't know. That was a very strange coincidence."

"Forget it," said Bill. "They're gone. Let's go see what the Scharffs are up to."

Herbie turned back toward the front window, struggling to make sense of it. This was no coincidence. The FBI was on to him. They hadn't arrested him for the simple reason that Herbie had done nothing wrong. He hadn't blown up any factories, or bombed any Jewish-owned stores. As long as he kept his nose clean, there would be no reason to worry. That's what he tried to tell himself, anyway. He turned toward the others and forced a smile. "It'll sure be good to catch up with old Ernie Scharff."

Chapter Sixty-Seven

New York, June 26, 1942

Upstairs in the New York Federal Courthouse, George Dasch stood with his back to a blank, white wall. He wore a white cotton shirt, buttoned close to the collar, tan slacks, and brown shoes. His hair was carefully combed. Around his neck hung a booking slate. *F.B.I. – N.Y.C. 65-11065-N4506.* His expression showed defeat. Sadness. Disappointment in humanity. This was all just a ruse, they'd told him repeatedly, yet going through the motions of arrest left him with a sickness in the pit of his stomach. A flash popped in his face.

"Turn to your left." A booking officer faced Dasch with camera in hand. Beside the officer stood his FBI escorts from the Washington office, Johnstone and Wills, along with a uniformed guard. Dasch shifted 90 degrees to his left. The flash popped once more. The booking officer stepped forward, removing the slate from Dasch's neck and placing it on a nearby desk. Next, he rewound the film in his camera and removed the canister before jotting Dasch's name and booking number on a form. He held a pen toward the agents. "If one of you gentlemen would be so kind as to give me your John Hancock…"

Wills stepped forward, took the pen and signed the document.

"That'll do it."

"Which way to the cells?"

"Follow me," said the guard.

"Let's go, Dasch." Wills added. They led him from the booking area, through one locked door and then another until they came to a long row of cells. The doors were solid, with a single peephole in the center of each.

"The men are in here?" Dasch whispered.

"They're here all right," Wills replied.

"They can see me?"

"Shhh… Yeah. They'll see you."

"Eyes straight ahead!" The guard kept a hand on Dasch's shoulder as they led him down the corridor, past five closed cells. When they came to the sixth, he took a key from a large key ring and slid it into the lock. Pulling on a handle, he swung open the door. "Inside."

George entered the cell and spun around, facing these men he'd considered his protectors. They were all on the same side, right? Johnstone and Wills stared back from the corridor, expressionless. No words spoken. No farewells. The guard slammed the door shut with an authoritative clang. Dasch heard the key turn in the bolt. A sense of suffocation overcame him as he peered around his confines. One small light bulb hanging from the ceiling. A cot with a thin wool blanket. A sink. A toilet. This was the punishment he'd wrought upon the others. Guilt seeped in to further rattle his mind. He sat on the cot. How long must he wait here? An hour? A day? It was a question he'd never thought to ask. Surely, they'd be back for him before too long. With the others having seen him in custody, the deception was complete. Out in the corridor, he heard a door open and then slam closed. The footfalls of heavy boots approached his cell. Dasch heard metal scrape against concrete. Moving to his door, he leaned close to peer through the peephole. On the other side, a guard sat in a chair directly opposite. George moved backward and dropped once more onto the cot, lightheaded as a thin rivulet of sweat rolled down his right temple.

Chapter Sixty-Eight

Chicago, June 27, 1942

Early on Saturday, Herbie Haupt lay in bed yearning for Gerda's soft touch. Soon he'd be spending his nights with her, waking each morning to caress her smooth skin, the warmth of her body beside him. Whatever apprehensions he'd once felt over the concept of marriage were gone. He didn't want to spend his life alone and unloved. After a year of turmoil, Herbie wanted stability. He craved it, in fact, more than just about anything. He would get his blood test done that very afternoon. The sooner they married, the better. They could take a nice road trip in the Pontiac, maybe up around the lake.

After rising to his feet, Herbie opened his closet door and set about choosing his clothes for the day. Tweed slacks, white collared shirt, and a favorite old sweater; navy blue with cream-colored sleeves. Finally, a pair of black and white leather shoes. When Herbie was dressed, he lifted a small, felt box from the top of his dresser and flipped open the top. A diamond engagement ring sparkled in the morning light. Gerda would be mightily impressed. At least he sure hoped so. Snapping the box closed, he put it into a pocket and hurried downstairs.

In the kitchen, Erna prepared a quick breakfast for her son. Two eggs over easy, buttered toast and black coffee. Sitting across from him with a mug of her own, Erna didn't say much. She'd hardly said a thing to Herbie since the day he'd returned. Her silence pained him deeply. Herbie understood how she felt, but what was he to do?

Erna sipped her coffee. "You're seeing Gerda tonight?"

"Mmm, hmm, that's right."

"I hope you treat her right this time around. No running away if things don't go the way you'd like them to."

"Don't worry, mother. I'm in it for the long haul." Herbie leaned back in his seat, sliding a hand into his right pocket. He pulled out his small box and flipped it open, beaming with pride as his wide-eyed mother examined the ring.

Erna nodded in approval. "She's a nice girl. She'll make a good wife."

"Thanks. I think so, too."

Herbie put the ring back into his pocket. He finished his breakfast and put his dishes in the sink. "Look, I've got to run. I have a few things to take care of."

Despite the swirling uncertainty, in these quiet moments together, Erna Haupt was immensely grateful to have her son back. It could have been much different, like with Kate Wergin, constantly wondering what had become of her Wolfgang. Instead, Erna had her son right here in front of her. She tried to tell herself that everything would be all right, that whatever he was mixed up in would work itself out. "You have a wonderful day," she said.

"You too." Herbie leaned close to kiss his mother on the forehead before moving toward the door. Leaving the house, he skipped down the front steps toward his gleaming black Pontiac and walked around to the driver's side. With a light smile, he unlocked the car and then slid onto the smooth leather seat, pulling the door closed behind with a heavy thud. After turning the key in the ignition, he tapped on the gas pedal and listened to the rumbling engine come to life. Just wait until Gerda heard that… Herbie rolled down his window and then let off the parking brake. He took a quick look in the rearview mirror before pulling away from the curb. The key to his predicament lay in figuring out how to handle Neubauer and the others. Herbie once more mulled over the prospect of turning them in to the FBI, though the guilt weighed on him. Then there was the fear. If the other guys suspected anything, they might just try to kill him. It wasn't out of the question. Kerling, in particular, seemed dangerous. And what of Kappe's threats when it came to Herbie's uncles, and to Wolf? Herbie needed more time. He'd come up with a plan. Eventually.

Traffic was heavy on Webster Avenue, but Herbie waited for a break and then turned right, continuing up the street and underneath the elevated railway. When he looked into the rearview mirror, his blood pressure dropped. A red light flashed on the top of a black sedan. What was this? Another sedan pulled up beside him with two men in dark suits, the passenger leaning out the window and pointing with one hand. "Pull over! Now!" the man shouted. In his other hand, he held a shiny metal badge. Herbie did as he was told. After pulling his car to a stop, the sedan beside him quickly cut across to block his lane. The other stopped directly behind. Two men burst from each car, guns drawn.

"F.B.I.! Put your hands in the air!"

The ensuing moments flew past in one surreal rush. An agent reached through Herbie's window and turned off the ignition, removing the keys before stepping back to open the door. "Exit the vehicle!"

Herbie's eyes focused on the guns, pointed at him from all directions. He put one foot on the asphalt and then another as he kept his hands up, leaning forward slightly to stand.

"Turn around and put your hands on the roof of the car!"

When he'd complied, two of the men holstered their weapons and were on him, kicking his legs apart and then grabbing him by the wrists, pulling his arms behind his back and slapping on a pair of cold, steel handcuffs. Herbie was patted down, the agent reaching into his pocket and pulling out the small felt box. Flipping it open, he took a quick look at the ring. "That's for my girl!" Herbie protested. The agent snapped the box shut and put it into his own pocket before spinning Herbie around. Four men faced him with unconcealed malice, one flashing the same metal badge.

"Special Agent Earl Hirsh, Federal Bureau of Investigation. Herbert Haupt, you are under arrest."

Two of the agents dragged him away from his Pontiac and tossed him into the back of the sedan in front, slamming the door behind him. Herbie sat up straight, flooded by a mixture of shock and bitterness. More than any other emotion, however, he was overcome most with regret. Not at taking part in the mission. No, that wasn't it. The mission was his only shot at getting home. What he regretted, deeply, was not having turned them all in. He never should have waited so long. Peter Burger beat him to it. Herbie was never so sure about anything in his life. He never did trust Burger, not from the very start.

Special Agent Hirsh leaned through the front window. "Make it easy on yourself, Haupt. Tell us where to find Hermann Neubauer."

"I don't know anybody by that name." Herbie stared straight ahead in defiance. It was too late to rat them out now.

"So that's how you want to play it, eh? We'll see about that." Hirsh nodded sideways to the others. "Let's get him out of here." Hirsh handed over Herbie's keys to one of his agents and then slid behind the wheel of the sedan.

As the three cars moved together down Webster Avenue, Herbie tried to remind himself that he hadn't actually done anything. What could they even charge him with? He hadn't blown anything up, or even tried. Yet, still, the words of his good friend Wolf rang through Herbie's head. "The G-men are gonna get you!"

Herbie slumped in his seat, chin resting against his chest. "You were right, Wolf," he muttered softly. "They got me."

Ever since Hermann Neubauer arrived in Chicago, going to the movies was a daily occurrence. The cool dark theaters offered a good place to hide. Losing himself in the drama on screen allowed him to temporarily forget his troubles. He could tamp down his gnawing loneliness and pretend he was somewhere else, far, far away. Hermann sat through single features, and double features, newsreels and cartoons, for hours at a time. Eventually, he had to eat. As he walked out of the theater on this particular Saturday, he checked his watch. The time was 6:30 p.m., with the sun still shining on a warm summer evening. Hermann paused to scan the crowds of pedestrians, on the lookout for anyone suspicious. The man in the phone booth? Or the hot dog vendor? The smell of sizzling sausages drew Neubauer closer. He considered stopping for one, but no, it was better to head back to his room. He'd order room service.

Making his way along the sidewalk, Neubauer's temples throbbed. The headaches never quite went away. This was his life. Hiding out and in pain. He longed to see Kerling. Eddie would know what to do. He'd find a way out. They could meet with the others and go to the FBI all together, just like Eddie said. If only they could last that long. Hermann lived in constant fear of arrest, yet in some strange sense, he almost longed for it. Anything to quell this unbearable angst.

Returning to the Sheridan Plaza Hotel, Neubauer rode the elevator up to his floor and then continued down the corridor toward another terrifying night alone in his room, waiting for that knock on the door he expected at any moment. He was pulling the key from his pocket when four men emerged from the next room and quickly surrounded him. One held a shiny metal badge in Hermann's face. "Special Agent Earl Hirsh, Federal Bureau of Investigation. Hermann Neubauer, place your hands on your head. You are under arrest."

Part IV – The Trial

Chapter Sixty-Nine

Washington, DC, June 27, 1942

Attorney General Francis Biddle was a dapper man. Tall and narrow, with a thin mustache, he was in many ways the opposite of his F.B.I. director in both appearance and demeanor. Where the heavy-set Hoover was brash and outspoken, Biddle was the more philosophical type. In fact, the Attorney General often felt overshadowed by his subordinate, though on this Saturday evening he was eager to inform the president himself of the latest developments. After an anxious few weeks, everything was coming together. Biddle made the call from his Washington office and then waited while he was connected.

"Francis! You have some good news for me, I hope?" Franklin Delano Roosevelt took the call in the study of his Hyde Park estate. The president was on edge, not sure what to expect.

"We got 'em, Mr. President. All eight Nazis are in custody."

"Ha!" Roosevelt tilted his head back and grinned, a great burden suddenly lifted. No longer must he worry that these Germans might blow something, or somebody, up. A grievous shock to American morale was avoided. Roosevelt was left feeling downright giddy. "That is some terrific news. Nicely done, my hats off to you and everyone in the department!"

"We had our top men on the job, Mr. President."

"You can tell those men I'm very proud. Very proud, indeed. The whole country owes them a debt of gratitude. Pass my thanks to John, will you?"

"Of course. The director is just about to hold a press conference."

"Yes, yes, good. So, what will we do with these eight? We must make an example of them."

"Yes, Mr. President. We ought to have a meeting to discuss our strategy as soon as possible."

"Right, right. I want to move on this quickly." The president laughed to himself once more. After a month of difficult news from the battlefields of North Africa, this was a rare ray of sunshine. He would do what he could to make the best use of it.

"We also recovered a stash of U.S. currency that the men brought to finance their schemes. Roughly one-hundred and seventy-five thousand dollars."

"That's not enough, Francis!" Roosevelt chuckled. "Let's make real money out of them. Sell the rights to Barnum and Bailey for a million and a half! They can take them around the country in lion cages at so much a head."

Biddle snickered in return. "Yes, Mr. President."

"Francis, I want copies of the files on all eight men sent up here right away. I'm going to type up a memorandum with my thoughts on the matter."

"Of course, Mr. President."

Roosevelt pulled a clean sheet of paper and a pen from his desk. As a trained lawyer, he wracked his brain for appropriate precedents. "Francis, just wait 'til old Adolph finds out, he'll be mighty red in the face!"

"I sure wish I could see that."

"That makes two of us. Look, I want to make the biggest statement that we can with this thing. The whole world needs to know what happens to foreign enemies who dare challenge the United States of America on her home soil. These men are as guilty as is possible to be, all eight of them. They must pay for their crimes with the ultimate price."

"I'll do my best, Mr. President."

"No, that's not good enough. There's no room for error here. The death penalty in this case is practically obligatory."

"Yes, sir."

Roosevelt leaned back in his chair. "My congratulations again to you and the bureau. We simply must ensure that these charges stick, no matter what it takes. You can expect to be hearing my thoughts on the matter in short order!"

"Thank you, Mr. President, I will look forward to that." Biddle hung up the phone, giddy himself at having shared such good news. Quickly, his thoughts turned toward prosecution. The FBI had done their job. Next, it was the turn of Biddle's Justice Department to finish it off. First, however, it was time to inform the public. Biddle lifted his phone once again and dialed the FBI's New York office, speaking to a receptionist before being transferred to the director.

"Hoover here!"

"John, this is Francis. I've passed the news to the president."

"What did he say?"

"He was very pleased. Very pleased indeed."

"I take it that you gave the bureau the credit it deserves."

"Of course, of course. I let him know all about your hard work and dedication in cracking the case. He'll be sending a memorandum detailing his thoughts going forward."

"Good. We've got the press gathered downstairs. I'll start my briefing."

"Yes, go ahead. And John, nice job on this one, from me, too."

"Thank you."

When he'd hung up the phone, Biddle clasped his hands, elbows on his desk. The legal battle was only just beginning. The pressure would be enormous, and the stakes, but he wouldn't worry about any of that quite yet. No, for this evening at least, Francis Biddle preferred to simply savor the moment. Finally, a victory against those Nazi bastards. This was something the whole nation could celebrate. History in the making, and Francis Biddle was right at the center.

Chapter Seventy

New York, June 27, 1942

Reporters pressed forward, jostling for position. A podium was set up at the front of the FBI conference room. Whatever story was about to break, it was big, the energy inside the room electric. Something was up. The director himself holding a press conference was unusual enough, but in New York, on a Saturday night… *New York Times* reporter Will Lissner waited amongst the crowd, notepad in hand. Beside him stood the columnist, Walter Winchell. At the podium, a soundman adjusted one of several microphones, ready to record every word. The director himself didn't keep them waiting long. Shortly after 8:30 p.m., J. Edgar Hoover strode into the room, his bulky frame in a loose white suit with a dark tie. He was surrounded by a phalanx of special agents, keeping a tight perimeter around their boss. Hoover positioned himself behind the podium and held a hand in the air to call for quiet. "Gentlemen!" he said. "I have a very important statement to make! I want you all to listen carefully. This is a serious business." Hoover put his hands on either side of the lectern, staring down the reporters who faced him. "Due to the hard work and dedication of numerous special agents within this bureau, I'm here to announce the arrest of eight Nazi saboteurs, landed in this country from German submarines on a mission to blow up key war plants and cause panic in our large cities."

A clamor arose, reporters all shouting questions simultaneously, but Hoover raised his hand once more. "Gentlemen, please, I will take questions at the end of my statement. We will also be releasing full biographies of all eight suspects!" When the rumbling died down, Hoover continued. "As I was saying… these men were highly trained by the German High Command at a special sabotage school near Berlin. Two groups of four men each landed from submarines on Long Island and Florida carrying boxes full of high explosives and nearly one hundred and fifty thousand dollars in cash. Almost from the moment the first group landed in Amagansett, Long Island, on the night of June 13th, special agents from the Federal Bureau of Investigation were on their trail."

As he spoke, Hoover was careful to give credit where he saw that credit was due and nowhere else. That meant the intrepid agents of the Federal Bureau of Investigation. No need to dwell on the contributions of the Coast Guard. After all, they were just in the right place at the right time. And what of the War Department? As far as Hoover was concerned, they merely got in the way. George Dasch? To Hoover, there was a special place in hell already set aside for that man, a traitor to all sides.

"One after another, each of these men fell into our net," the director went on. "Six of the men were arrested here in New York, including the leader, George John Dasch. The last two members of the gangs were arrested today in Chicago. All have confessed fully, providing information that will make repetition of such sabotage invasions difficult. I would also like to point out that since these acts occurred during wartime, all eight men face the death penalty."

Once more, questions rang out. "Did you recover all of the explosives?!" Winchell shouted.

"Yes, all of the explosives have been recovered. We will now pass out photographs of the materials in question, along with biographies and mug shots of each suspect. Hoover nodded to an assistant, who began distributing copies to eager, outstretched hands. This was going just fine, Hoover thought. Exactly as he'd planned it. The story that he presented today was the story that would stand, no matter what he had to do to make it so.

Chapter Seventy-One

New York, NY, June 28, 1942

George Dasch wore handcuffs as a guard led him to an office two floors below his cell. Special agents Traynor and Johnstone rose from their seats as he entered the room. A meatier fellow leaned against a desk to one side, arms crossed.

"How are you holding up, George?!" Traynor turned to the guard. "You can take the cuffs off and leave him."

With his shackles removed, Dasch rubbed his wrists to get his circulation going. He was in no mood for pleasantries. "I hope you're coming to take me out of here."

"Don't worry, your arrest was only a matter of expediency."

"Arrest! Nobody ever told me that I would be arrested! You assured me that this was all just a ruse, to fool the other fellows!"

The unknown agent on the desk rose to his feet and leaned toward Dasch with a menacing sneer. "You're under arrest. How's that? We're telling you."

"After all I've done for you, I think I deserve better treatment than this." Dasch did his best to edge away.

The agent grabbed George by the front of the shirt, pulling him close. Hatred burned in the man's eyes.

"All right, all right, take it easy!" Traynor reached out to separate them. "Let's all have a seat."

The man let Dasch go, reluctantly, and took one step backward.

"Please." Traynor motioned one hand toward a chair. Dasch took it, with Traynor sitting back down across from him. The third man leaned back against the desk once more, the left corner of his lip rising upwards in disgust.

"What was that all about?!" Dasch complained.

"Donegan didn't mean anything by it. Did you Tom?"

The man tilted his head to one side, his sneer turning to a smirk. "No. I didn't mean nothing by it."

"This is Special Agent Thomas Donegan. He runs the New York office for us. If you have any problems while you are here, he's the one to talk to."

Dasch glanced at Donegan with a deepening sense of unease.

"Look, George," Traynor went on. "The director knows that you've performed a great service for us. Coming forward the way you did was courageous. You have helped us a great deal, but now we're asking for your help once again. This time you'll have to master another job for us. You must become an actor."

"What are you talking about, an actor? I don't understand. I'm no actor."

Traynor looked briefly to his partners and back before continuing. "If we are going to fool the Nazis completely, we'll have to try you in court along with the others. It's the only fool-proof way to keep your part in the roundup a secret. To help move things along, we'd like you to plead guilty."

Dasch's eyebrows went up. "You want me to plead guilty to something that you *know* I didn't do?"

"I'm afraid it's the only way. If you contest your case in federal court, your whole story will come out. We must make the Nazis believe that our coastline is impregnable. If they find out your role, not only will your family be in immediate danger, but one of the most valuable aspects of the incident will be ruined. The failure of this mission must discourage the German government from sending anybody else."

Dasch mulled over the logic of the request. He didn't like the idea of pleading guilty…

"Think of your family and friends back in Germany," Johnstone interjected. "If Hitler finds out your involvement in this, he'll wipe them out. You yourself have told us as much."

"It is for this reason exactly that you must become an actor," Traynor prodded. "And a damned good one. You will have to stand up in court under all kinds of false charges, accusations, and evil inventions and admit to their veracity."

"But what will become of me…" Dasch pictured himself in a cell for the rest of his life. The mere idea was more than he could bear.

"George, I am speaking in the name of the attorney general, Francis Biddle, and of Director Hoover himself, and I assure you that your pleading guilty before the court does not mean that you were actually guilty. All of us know that you are not. It is primarily an expedient necessity to keep your part in the case away from the Nazis. After the excitement has blown over and not more than six months after the trial, you will be freed with a full presidential pardon and complete exoneration of all the charges on which you will be tried."

A full presidential pardon. Complete exoneration. This was more in line with what Dasch wanted to hear. It wasn't immediate freedom. He still had to go along with their plan. He still had to admit to crimes he did not commit, but these men had a point. George had his family to think about. Six months in prison was a small price to pay for their safety. "All right," Dasch agreed. "I will do as you request. I will plead guilty to whatever charges you might bring, as long as I have your word that the president will pardon me."

Traynor reached a hand forward. "Have faith. I'm asking for your trust. When this whole thing is over with, we can go back to fighting the Nazis together, I promise you."

Dasch grasped the outreached hand and shook on the deal.

"Thank you, George. You're doing a great service."

Donegan called out for the guard and Dasch was handcuffed again and led upstairs. Alone in his cell once more, he sat on his cot. Six months, he told himself. If only he had a radio, or even a newspaper, it would make things a whole lot easier to take. Still, he could do this. He could manage. *A full presidential pardon.* He ran the words through his head once more.

George heard the sound of boots approaching and then a metal chair scraping on the floor just outside his cell. Peering through his peephole, he saw a guard sitting in the metal folding chair. In his hands was a newspaper, the full front page facing Dasch directly. The masthead read *New York Daily News*. Beneath that, one bold headline: CAPTURED NAZI SPY! Taking up the entire rest of the page was a photo of George Dasch. A flood of despair overtook him, followed in quick order by a hot surge of anger. They'd promised! Hoover himself agreed that Dasch's name and photo would not appear in the press. Dasch thought of his brother and sister, still living in the United States. He thought of his friends. The boys down at the waiters' club. His wife in Bermuda. Would she hear this news? What would they all think? If only he could speak with a lawyer. This was the United States of America, after all. George Dasch was not ready to give up hope, though it seemed as though that was about all he had left.

Chapter Seventy-Two

Washington, DC, June 29, 1942

J. Edgar Hoover sat in the attorney general's office facing Francis Biddle. Hoover didn't like answering to anybody, particularly this effete excuse for a man who was technically his boss. To Hoover, the FBI was his own personal fiefdom. Even so, there were times when he couldn't escape the fact that the bureau was a division of the Justice Department. Being summoned to Biddle's office was an ignominy, though in this particular case the two men's interests were distinctly aligned. Hoover just wasn't entirely sure Biddle realized how much. "You've briefed the president?" Hoover asked.

Biddle touched the tips of his fingers together. "Yes, I've kept him informed each step of the way. He was very pleased that you managed to round up the suspects so quickly."

Hoover's face took on a reddish hue. "The credit belongs with my agents. They worked tirelessly to crack the case."

"Of course." Biddle and Hoover were among very few men who knew the truth, yet the attorney general said nothing to disabuse his FBI director. This was their official narrative after all.

Hoover squirmed in his seat. For a man who strived to present a brash persona, he felt uncharacteristically insecure. "Which details in particular have you shared?" He couldn't bring himself to come right out and state the question plainly, but this was enough. Biddle understood.

"I didn't think that it was a good idea to disclose the contributions of Dasch and Burger over the telephone."

Relief washed over Hoover, tempered by the understanding that eventually the president might be told.

"I feel it is best if we keep that information between us for the time being," Biddle continued.

"Yes, yes, I agree."

"I've also given some thought to the manner in which we try these men. It seems to me that a military tribunal would be best. It would keep the press out, for one thing. The entire proceeding would take place behind closed doors. It would also leave open the prospect of the death penalty. The only complication with pursuing this course is that it would mean transferring the prisoners into military custody." Biddle watched Hoover carefully for his reaction. "Of course, we could spare Dasch and Burger execution if they continue to cooperate. Perhaps life terms for those two."

The FBI director tilted his head back. Handing the prisoners over to the army would mean he no longer had direct control. But… the prisoners would be more isolated, with army officers for counsel. No outside lawyers, and no public trial. That would solve the problem of George Dasch potentially blabbing his mouth to the newspapers. Everything could be handled cleanly. "Will the president go along?"

"I believe that he will. The president is eager to make an example of these men. We are all very eager."

"I have no objections."

"Good. As long as the president signs off on the idea, we can start making arrangements immediately."

"Do you think that the judge advocate general is up to the task?"

At this question, it was Biddle's turn to show his unease. "I plan to handle this prosecution myself. We can't take any chances."

J. Edgar Hoover's gnawing anxieties began to wane. There was no reason the public had to know anything about the contributions of George John Dasch. If transferring custody to the army was the only way to go about that, then so be it. Hoover wouldn't argue.

Biddle waited for his FBI director to leave the office before reaching for his phone. He dialed the President's direct line in Hyde Park.

"This is the President!" Roosevelt answered.

"Biddle here, Mr. President."

"Ah, Francis, how are things coming with those Nazis? No complications I hope."

"No, everything is fine. I've been consulting some of my men and I have a few thoughts to run past you."

"Good, good, what have you got?" Roosevelt sat at his desk with the latest briefing from the War Department. The Germans were engaged in a new assault in Russia, this time moving south toward Stalingrad. Hitler had a point to make, apparently. To Roosevelt, the more resources the Nazis expended fighting against the Soviets the better. As he spoke with his attorney general, the president examined a map of the USSR, showing the latest known troop movements.

"We feel that a military tribunal is the best way to handle this."

"Excellent idea. We need to teach these Germans a lesson!" Where occasionally they differed on policy questions, this time the two men shared the same opinion. The Nazi saboteurs should be punished as harshly as possible. It would send a resounding message to Hitler while at the same time giving a badly needed boost to American morale.

"I'm afraid that if we tried these men in civilian court, we might not end up with the result that we desire," Biddle continued. "The fact that the men didn't follow through with their plans complicates things for us."

"They damned well wanted to follow through!"

"But the truth remains that they did not. Under civil law, just because a man buys a gun with the intention of committing murder, that does not make him guilty of attempted murder. He has to fire the gun."

"Those men came here with the express purpose of blowing up our war plants! They landed on our shores wearing German naval uniforms. They were apprehended in civilian clothes. I see no difference between this case and that of Nathan Hale during the Revolution. Nor John Andre for that matter. Both spies tried and hung!"

"Yes, Mr. President, I agree."

"Those men are as guilty as can be!" Roosevelt shouted. "I want one thing clearly understood, Francis. I won't give them up. I won't hand them over to any United States marshal armed with a writ of habeas corpus, understand?"

"I understand perfectly. However, if we do transfer these men to the War Department, I would still like to handle the case."

The president furrowed his brow. "Who over there in the War Department would normally handle a thing like this?"

"That would be Major General Cramer, Mr. President. I have to say, if the defense does file a writ, this will go straight to the Supreme Court. That would be new territory for the major general."

"Never been before the court, eh?"

"No, he has not."

"I see."

"If the defense counsel is worth their salt they'll bring up the precedent of *Ex Parte Milligan*."

"Remind me, Francis. What case was that?"

"Dating to eighteen sixty-six, the court ruled that civilians may not be brought before a military tribunal at any time when civilian courts are open and properly functioning. Only two of the men arrested were German soldiers. It could be argued that the rest are indeed civilians."

"This is not what I want to hear, Francis." The president's irritation was plain. "These men were spies! Not civilians at all!"

"We intend to argue as much, especially given that all of them landed on our shores wearing military uniforms."

"Yes, of course. Surely the justices will view our arguments favorably, if it comes to that. They know what is at stake as much as you or I."

"If they drag us to the Supreme Court and prevail, I can tell you, there will be one hell of a mess."

"You can handle this case, Francis. Tell Cramer I said so. I don't want any surprises."

"No, Mr. President. No surprises."

"I'm counting on you. The entire country is counting on you. It's time we had a victory against these Nazi thugs."

"Yes, Mr. President. You have my word; these men will get what they deserve."

"We simply cannot rest until we have convictions. I want you to move forward on this as quickly as possible!"

"Certainly. It might help smooth things over with the War Department if you could call over there yourself, just to explain our plans. I suspect the major general will not be happy to be pushed aside."

"I'll get Stimson on the phone right away."

"Thank you, Mr. President."

"If you need anything else, you just let me know."

"Of course. I will send a brief to you this afternoon explaining all of my plans."

"Excellent work, Francis. Remember, the entire nation is counting on you."

"I won't let you down, Mr. President." As he hung up the phone, Biddle's mind churned through potential pitfalls with the prosecution. Two of the men, Haupt and Burger, were United States citizens. That could complicate things, though both were naturalized. Perhaps their citizenship could be revoked. Whatever it took to achieve the desired result, this was a case he simply had to win, for the president, the country, and yes, for himself.

Chapter Seventy-Three

New York, June 29, 1942

From his small cell in the federal courthouse, Herbie Haupt second-guessed every decision he'd made since departing for Mexico one year before. It was all a grand adventure, until somewhere along the line, it wasn't anymore. Where had things gone so wrong? Maybe if they hadn't sold Wolfgang's car? Or if they'd saved enough to pay the import duty? Once they arrived in Germany, Herbie had little choice but to do as the authorities requested. The threat to his uncles loomed large. And then, he never thought he'd actually get caught. Somehow, he'd convinced himself of that, despite Wolf's protestations. Herbie was going to simply go home and disappear. It sounded like such a good plan at the time. In hindsight, he should have turned in the others before Burger beat him to it. He should have gone to the FBI at the very start. But now… it was too late. He was locked up like an animal. The prospect of years upon end behind bars was too dismal to even consider, yet that's what he faced. Or worse. Herbie pictured himself before a firing squad, a blindfold covering his eyes. They wouldn't do that. Not to an American. Not to him. Would they?

Chapter Seventy-Four

New York, NY, June 30, 1942

"Why should I plead guilty if the proceedings are to be held in secret?" George Dasch was beside himself. "It makes no sense!" Facing him across a large conference table were Attorney General Francis C. Biddle and Judge Advocate General, Myron C. Cramer. Between these two men was the director of the F.B.I. Finally, after weeks of pleading, Dasch faced J. Edgar Hoover himself. "I mean, if the trial is secret, I don't see why I can't plead honestly. The Nazis will never know anything about it." Dasch turned his attention to the list of charges in his hand. *Breaking into the United States defense zone. Planned sabotage. Spying. Conspiracy.* It was a damning indictment.

"Yes, you're right. It will be a secret." Biddle looked from Dasch to the others and back with a hint of insecurity. "But I ask you to plead guilty even before the tribunal."

Dasch narrowed his eyes in consternation. "Gentlemen, do you feel that I am guilty as these charges say?"

"No, Dasch, we know you're not guilty," Hoover spoke up.

"We'd like you to plead guilty in order to speed up the trial," Biddle tried to explain.

"That makes no sense to me at all…" Dasch shook his head back and forth. "If you know that I'm not guilty, why should I be made to stand trial at all? Surely there must be some other way to deceive the Nazis? If the trial were to be held in open court, I am still willing to go through with my part in the bargain, but not in secret. I don't see the purpose." George took a moment to contemplate the implications. Perhaps if they were still willing to give him a full pardon after six months… "Can you tell me this, does our prior agreement still hold?"

Biddle's face drew a blank. "What agreement is that? Has somebody made an agreement with this man?" He turned to his FBI director for some clarification.

Hoover raised one hand in an effort to cut off this line of questioning. "Oh, yes, yes! It all stands!"

Fixing his eyes on Hoover, Dasch pressed for clarification. "Can you be specific about the government's side of the bargain?"

"I know what you mean, Dasch!" Hoover snapped. "It all stands. That is all I can tell you."

Silence pervaded the room. An impasse. "Please, George," Biddle continued. "I am asking you to plead guilty, for the good of the nation."

"What you are asking of me is to tell a lie in court, under oath." Dasch shook his head in dismay. "I have to say, this is something that I don't believe should ever be done. I am more than a little bit shocked that you would make this request. Only the best of motives could persuade me to make such a plea, yet you have given no sound reason at all. The best argument you can offer is to speed up the trial? I am sorry, gentlemen, but that is not enough. I plan to tell the truth. I would like to speak with a lawyer to prepare my defense. Under the circumstances, this is the only honest and proper course of action that I can take."

Biddle turned to Hoover. This was not going as the two men had hoped. George Dasch was the wild card in this whole affair. The other convictions were a slam-dunk, even Burger's. But Dasch? That was cause for some concern. Trying the whole case in secret was key. A panel of military judges would certainly find him guilty of something. But if it went to the Supreme Court? That was the open question. Those nine justices had the power to throw the trial into civil court, in which case all bets would be off. George Dasch, spouting off to a jury? Tossing the government's narrative on its head? This could destroy careers, all the way to the top. The infallible J. Edgar Hoover would be revealed as a fraud. Even Francis Biddle would be unable to escape the ensuing wrath. And what of the President himself? No, they could not let that happen. If only George Dasch would do them this favor and plead guilty, all their problems would vanish. Yet it was becoming clear that the red-faced Dasch would not go along. They needed a new plan, with little time to waste. Biddle motioned to two agents standing near the door. "You can escort the prisoner back to his cell."

"What about my lawyer?" Dasch pressed.

"We'll see about that," said Hoover.

"I've asked for a lawyer from the day that I arrived in this place. I think that I am entitled to one."

"And you shall have one." Biddle's voice betrayed his resignation, as though he regretted granting the prisoner his rights. For George Dasch, the full reality began to sink in that the Justice Department was not on his side. For the entire week that he'd spent answering questions in Washington, George believed that the FBI had his back. Now he saw that they were not with him at all. In fact, this government, whose stated ideals he'd respected and admired so much, was entirely against him.

Alone in his cell, Peter Burger desperately missed the company of his wife. He missed Bettina's bright smile and her laugh, always with a hint of incredulity. He missed her musky scent on a Sunday morning, round eyes peering from beneath her gleaming dark hair. At least he knew that his parents were looking after her. No more scraping to get by on her own, like the last time he was imprisoned. But no visits either. Here in an American jail, Burger didn't exist under constant fear of beatings as he had at the hands of the Gestapo. More than anything, however, he simply felt abandoned. No visitors, no access to counsel, nobody to talk to at all. Burger clung to his confidence that in betraying the sabotage mission, he'd done the right thing. His conscience was clear. Surely the Americans would understand that in time. They couldn't keep him locked up here forever. Peter knew what it meant for the existence of time to vanish, when life was divided by headcounts and meals. In the Gestapo prison, terror was his constant companion. Here in an American cell, it was boredom. More than anything else, Burger was resigned to his fate, whatever it might be. From a small shelf above his cot, he picked up a thin paperback novel they'd allowed him. He'd already read through it once from start to finish. Peter opened the cover and began again, losing himself in the story of another war fought long ago, the American Revolution. He hadn't read far when he heard voices in the corridor. A small slat on his door slid open. The eyes of a guard peered through. Next, the sound of a key turning in the lock. Peter sat up straight as the door swung open. It wasn't mealtime. He'd only just finished his lunch. Appearing before him in the cell was a barrel-chested man in a slate-gray suit. Burger recognized him immediately from pictures he'd seen in the newspapers.

"Peter Burger," said the man.

"Yes." Burger dropped the novel onto his cot.

"J. Edgar Hoover." The director moved closer. "How are they treating you, son?"

"Fine." Burger scrambled to his feet. An agent joined them in the cell before the guard swung the door closed and bolted it from the outside once again.

"Good," said Hoover. "We want you to be comfortable."

"Yes, sir."

"You go by Pete, is that right? Can I call you Pete?"

"If you'd like." Burger wasn't quite sure how to respond. For the past two weeks, he'd wanted to meet the director, to be given a chance to explain himself to the man at the very top. That chance had arrived, yet what was left to say? Surely Hoover read the reports.

"Why don't we sit down?" Hoover motioned toward the cot. "Do you mind?"

"No."

Hoover sat first, at the foot of the bed. Burger carefully took a seat beside him. The director turned his attention to the third man who stood by the door with a single sheet of paper in hand. "You can read the charges," said Hoover.

The man by the door nodded his head quickly before beginning to read out loud. "Ernst Peter Burger, you are hereby charged with the following offenses, as an enemy of the United States acting for and on behalf of the German Reich, a belligerent enemy nation. Charge number one, violation of the law of war. Charge number two, violation of the 81st article of war, charge number three, violation of the 82nd article of war, charge number four, conspiracy to commit all of the above acts."

The director was not here to release him, Peter realized. In fact, there seemed to be no clear point to this exercise at all. Burger remained silent, all hope draining from his soul.

"I realize you've been quite helpful to us up until this time," Hoover admitted. "I want to let you know, we appreciate that."

"Yes, sir." Burger could barely get the words out.

"You've provided useful information."

"Thank you."

"It is my hope that you will continue to do so."

Burger stared wide-eyed, waiting. There must be something more to this. If Hoover admitted his contribution, that meant Peter's entire prosecution was merely a charade.

"I don't mind saying, we're more than a little bit worried about your friend, George Dasch," Hoover went on. "He's proven to be somewhat, how shall I say… unreliable."

"I don't understand."

"He doesn't want to play ball, you see. He's not on our side anymore."

"Whose side is he on?"

"His own! He's out for himself and nobody else! I thought I should warn you, to give you a heads-up. He can't be trusted."

Burger took a moment to process this information. Hoover seemed to be saying that Dasch might sell him out. Peter found that hard to believe. He and George were in this together all the way. "Is he accusing me?" Burger asked.

"You? No. He's not accusing you."

"What then?"

Hoover sat up straight and put his hands on his thighs. "I want you to know that we're counting on you to testify honestly in this whole mess. That's all."

"Of course I will." Burger still didn't quite understand.

"Your testimony will be an important part of our case."

"But I'm charged as well…"

"Yes, that is true, but you have my word, I'll look out for you on this. You play ball with us, we'll help you out down the line, that I can promise you."

"Will there be anything in writing?"

"No. Nothing in writing. You'll have to trust me, that's all."

Burger had expected better from these Americans. Maybe not the hero's welcome that Dasch envisioned, but at least more appreciation than this. Peter shared all the information he could think of with the federal agents, openly and honestly. He'd traveled back to Long Island to show the FBI exactly where and how they'd come ashore. And what did he get in return? Federal charges thrown in his face. A last-minute request to "play ball" with no assurances that it would do him any good. All the same, Burger was a man of principle. He wasn't cooperating for any sort of personal gain. From the time he was a child, Peter always had a strong sense of justice, of right and wrong. That was why his treatment by the Gestapo was so emotionally painful. What had he done to deserve it but offer his loyalty? His countrymen took that loyalty and beat it out of him, one blow at a time. And so here he was, in a position to exact revenge, not on his country, but on the entire regime that betrayed him. Peter Burger didn't need special assurances from J. Edgar Hoover or anybody else. He would do what he thought was right. "Of course, I'll tell the truth."

"Excellent." Hoover's shoulders eased. "We'll be transferring you to army custody. As of today, the War Department is in charge. The trial is in their hands."

"Will I have an attorney?"

"Yes, an attorney will be provided." Hoover stood from the cot and moved toward the door. "And of course, I'll look out for you the best I can."

"I do appreciate that."

The director wrapped his knuckles on the door before calling out. "You can open up!" Eyes appeared at the slot. "Good luck, Pete," Hoover added.

"Thank you, sir."

Hoover's assistant dropped the charge sheet on the edge of the bed. The door opened and the two men walked out. Alone once more, Burger ran the conversation over in his head. The entire encounter was mystifying. J. Edgar Hoover promised to look out for him, but would he? Burger picked up the charge sheet and read it over. This seemed like an awfully strange way of looking out for him. Peter dropped the paper back onto the cot. Either way, he would testify honestly. His integrity demanded as much. It was all that he had left.

Late in the evening, a swarm of FBI agents pulled the men from their cells and lined them up in a row along the corridor, hands cuffed behind their backs. It was the first time that all eight stood together since France, one month before. The first time that Kerling got a good look at Dasch, the man most likely to have turned them all in. The former leader of the other group looked forlorn, thin and sickly, his body wracked by the emotional strain. And what of Haupt? Was it the kid who dropped the dime? When their eyes met, Kerling turned away.

"Where are we going?" Neubauer spoke.

"Quiet!" came the answer. "Eyes forward!"

The men complied as the door at the end of the corridor was unlocked. "Let's go." Special Agent Wills led the procession through the door to a stairwell and then down, down, down into the underground garage. Awaiting them was a large black prison van, with the words *United States Marshals* printed in block letters on the side. Once they were loaded in, the men sat on two long parallel benches. Agents chained each prisoner to the floor before retreating out the back. A heavy door was closed and locked behind them, leaving the prisoners in near darkness. Small windows above their heads let in only the faintest electric light, but they were alone, all eight of them. They were free to talk amongst themselves, though they had little information to share. Their strict isolation left them with almost no knowledge of their standing. Withholding information was a weapon, and the government wielded it with impunity. No lawyers, no due process. Just one enormous void, with seconds ticking off the clock day after day. At least something was happening, finally. What that turned out to be was anybody's guess. Only Burger and Dasch had some small idea, but opening their mouths was a dangerous prospect.

"Where are they taking us?" Herbie's query was met by silence. The men felt a rumbling through their seats as the engine turned over. The van began to move forward. "Is the trial starting?"

"I think it's nighttime," said Quirin. "They're not going to hold the trial at night. Are they?"

"Maybe they won't have a trial at all," said Heinck. "They'll just send us to prison."

"They've got to have a trial," said Herbie. "It's not Germany."

"A tribunal," Burger offered, unable to stay silent any longer. "That's what I heard."

"Heard when?" Kerling demanded. "From who?"

"One of the agents was talking about it." Burger could hardly admit that Hoover himself had paid him a visit. The others were bound to find out about his betrayal soon enough. Until then, he'd keep that information to himself. "They're taking us to Washington."

"Don't we get a lawyer?" said Neubauer. "I mean, they've got to give us a lawyer. Right?"

"It's their country," said Kerling. "They can do what they want."

"It's my country, too," Herbie replied.

The truck shifted gears and picked up speed as it moved onto the streets of Manhattan, sirens blaring on their police escorts. The men lost themselves, each in his own thoughts. *A tribunal.* Only Dasch had any real understanding of what that meant. Secrecy. Whatever happened next, the outside world would likely never know. Looking from one man to the next in the dim light, Dasch was overcome with guilt at having turned them all in. If things went as he expected, their deaths would forever be on his conscience, assuming he survived himself. The promise of a pardon ran through his mind, but he remembered Biddle's expression. The attorney general knew nothing about it. That encounter left George gripped by foreboding. He'd been as straight as he could with them. It seemed that Hoover was being anything but straight in return.

After a short journey, the van skidded to a stop. The back door swung open and agents quickly reappeared. When the prisoners were unloaded, Dasch recognized Penn Station. Security was tight as the prisoners were escorted to the platforms and then loaded onto a special train carriage. This time they were separated into alternate rows, with an FBI agent seated beside each man. No chance to talk any longer.

With the men chained to their seats, the train departed. At least he was out of his cell, Herbie thought. The sensation of air from an open window gently brushed his skin. He'd never known how much a light breeze could mean. As the train moved forward, he closed his eyes and inhaled. Diesel fumes, unwashed men, the smells of the city. After two weeks of sensory deprivation, at least it was something.

Chapter Seventy-Five

Washington, DC, July 5, 1942

For a man in his mid-50s, Colonel Carl Ristine's thick shock of hair was strikingly gray. The man was tall and thin, his officer's uniform hanging loosely from his bones. When he spoke, it was slowly and with deliberation. To date, the colonel's career with the Judge Advocate General's office had been relatively quiet and predictable, representing servicemen who ran afoul of the law after drinking too much on a Friday night. He was known by his superiors as dependable if not flamboyant. Just the kind of man they needed, apparently, for the case of a Nazi spy, caught behind enemy lines with a cache of explosives. Ristine would negotiate the best deal he could, and if possible, save the man's life. If you asked him privately, however, things didn't look promising. Waiting in a small reception room at the District of Columbia Jail, Colonel Ristine used his pencil to absentmindedly draw small concentric circles in a notepad. The door swung open. Two guards entered, one on each side of a man he assumed to be his client. George John Dasch. The suspect was roughly the same height as Ristine, with his own thin streak of gray. The lawyer stood as a guard removed the prisoner's handcuffs.

"If you have any problems, give us a holler," the guard said to Ristine.

"I don't think there will be any problems." The colonel flashed a light smile. Truth be told, the prospect of being locked in this small room with a Nazi spy did make him somewhat anxious. The two guards left the room. Ristine offered Dasch a hand. "Colonel Carl Ristine. I'll be representing you."

"George Dasch." He took the measure of the man before him. At least he finally had counsel. It was a start.

"Please. Sit."

The two men took chairs on opposite sides of a small desk. "How much have they told you?" Dasch asked straight away.

"Not much, I'm afraid."

"I see. And how do you plan to handle my defense?"

"Well... I should say as the facts of the case allow." Ristine drawled.

"And what are those facts as you see them?" Dasch couldn't help but sound testy.

"Now, now, you've been arrested by the FBI, haven't you? You came here on a Nazi submarine, and boxes of explosives that you buried on the beach have been found."

Dasch allowed the realization to settle in. His own counsel was led to believe that he was guilty. "That's all they've told you...?"

"Oh, I know a fair deal. I know, for instance, that a coastguardsman spotted you on the beach the night you landed."

"A fair deal indeed! This is what the illustrious FBI is willing to share?!" Dasch spat the words in disgust as the veins in his forehead began to throb.

Ristine's eyes were wide as he sat up straight in his chair. He wasn't used to being challenged by his client, though the source of his information was even less impressive than Dasch suggested. "I read about it in the newspapers," he admitted.

"That's it?!" Dasch couldn't help but laugh. "The newspapers! You haven't seen my statement? They haven't told you anything at all?!"

"What statement?" Ristine's shoulders dropped.

"My FBI statement!" Any vestige of amusement quickly shifted back to anger. Whatever lingering hopes he had concerning the intentions of the Justice Department were gone. Dasch understood. If the attorney general failed to prove him guilty, the whole department would be caught in a massive lie. And here was the lawyer they'd sent to defend him; a man already convinced of his guilt merely from reading newspaper accounts; fairy tales planted in the press by J. Edgar Hoover himself! "If you don't mind, I'd like to give you my account of the situation."

"Yes, of course!" Ristine leaned over the desk and picked up his pencil. He quickly turned to a blank page in his notebook. "By all means, tell me your side of the story."

Dasch almost didn't know where to start. "What would you say if I told you that the FBI never would have arrested any of us if it weren't for me? The FBI didn't track me down! I turned myself in! I'm the one who told them where to find the others. Me and my friend Pete Burger. The FBI didn't bother to share that with you?!"

"No, Mr. Dasch, nobody mentioned that."

"Read my statement and you'll see! It's all in there! I only came to this country to help fight the Nazis. That was my plan all along, to do what I could to help the American war effort, and look how they're treating me!"

Confusion swept across Ristine's expression. "Boy, if that's true, then what in the hell am I even doing here? Why were you even locked up?"

Of course, Dasch knew the answer to this question all too well. The prestige of the FBI was at stake. The reputation of Hoover himself. Looking over his incredulous lawyer, George had a sinking feeling. The prosecution seemed to be doing all they could to stack the deck against him. Together, he and this colonel would have to do the best they could.

Across the river in his Pentagon office, Colonel Kenneth Royall was perplexed. Tasked with defending the other seven suspects, he couldn't quite make out how to proceed. Royall was faced with conflicting loyalties. As a sworn officer in the armed services of the United States, he was bound to follow the orders of his commander-in-chief. Franklin Delano Roosevelt himself explicitly forbade these suspects from access to any civilian court. Yet to Royall's understanding, this order itself was potentially illegal under the U.S. Constitution. Royall was bound by oath to obey the President, yes, but he was also bound to defend his clients by all legitimate means known to law. Should he disobey the President and seek justice in civil court? Or should he disobey law and duty by failing to mount a vigorous defense? Royall rubbed his chin. The answer seemed clear, even if it meant putting his career in jeopardy. If that's what it took to maintain his integrity, then so be it, Royall quickly decided. Across his desk sat Colonel Cassius Dowell, his co-counsel, a bulldog of a man in a tight-fitting uniform. Royall cleared his throat before he spoke. "The way I see it, we've got to do all we can to ensure that these men get a fair trial."

"Of course," Dowell agreed. "That's our job, if I'm not mistaken."

"Even if that means disobeying a direct order from our commander-in-chief?"

Dowell slightly shifted in his seat. "How do you plan to proceed?"

"I haven't figured that out yet." Royall lifted the President's order and read it over one more time. "But I don't want to drag you into this dilemma. I'm willing to take full responsibility."

"I'm with you all the way, Ken, whatever you decide to do."

Royall shook his head. "I'm not career army like you. When this war is over, I'll go right back into private practice. Hell, to be kicked out of the army for defending a client, no matter who that client was… that would be about the best advertisement I could get."

Dowell smirked. "I'm still with you. Our job is to mount a defense to the best of our abilities. I'll be damned if anybody tries to get in the way, even the President. I intend to do my job."

Royall felt a wave of gratitude. "I'll write a letter to the President, politely explaining that his order is unconstitutional. I don't expect you to sign on to it."

"Of course I'll sign it! Don't worry yourself on that score. You just write the best damned letter you can."

Chapter Seventy-Six

Washington, DC, July 8, 1942

Herbie Haupt wore civilian clothing, the same outfit he was arrested in; gray slacks, navy sweater with cream-colored sleeves, white shirt, and a dark tie. Two guards led him down a long corridor to a large steel door. Keys emerged, locks were turned, the door swung open and Haupt was gently pushed from behind. Emerging into the prison courtyard, Herbie was faced by a gauntlet of soldiers armed with machine guns. Beyond them were six motorcycle policemen, a staff car, and two black prison vans. Behind the vans was an open army transport brimming with even more soldiers. More machine guns. Was he really worth such effort?

"Let's go," a guard demanded. "Move it."

Herbie followed the order, past the army transport and on through the yard until they approached the nearest van. A soldier opened the door and made way for Herbie to pass, up a small set of stairs and into the back. Once inside, it took a moment for his eyes to adjust, but he was able to distinguish the muted outlines of three others. Kerling, Neubauer, and Thiel, all chained to their benches. The guards manhandled Herbie into place beside them and then chained the prisoner to his seat. Once the guards retreated, the door to the van clanged shut. Heavy bolts slid into place. The four men chained in darkness heard shouting and commotion in the yard outside. Engines started, sirens blared and the van began to move. Herbie pictured the procession heading out through the prison gates and onto the street. He felt a bump as they passed down a driveway and then… "Boom! Smash! Crash!" The deafening noises echoed through the traveling tomb.

"What is that?!" Thiel called out.

"They're throwing things," said Kerling. "Bottles and rocks!"

"Who is throwing things?"

Bouncing down the road, the answer to this question became clear. Shouts and catcalls rose up from the unseen crowds along the route. "There they go! Nazi spies! Rats! String 'em up! Kill the rats!"

"But what did we do?" Herbie asked of nobody in particular.

The conference room in the Department of Justice building was not intended for use as a military court, but under the circumstances, it would have to do. Major General Frank McCoy sat behind a table with six other members of the tribunal, waiting for news that the prisoners had arrived. At a facing table sat Biddle in a white linen suit. Beside him was J. Edgar Hoover, along with a small team of prosecuting attorneys. The defense counsel, Royall, Dowell, and Ristine, sat at another table to the right. The time was 10 a.m. when a door in the back of the room swung open. A uniformed aide entered, passing a nod to McCoy at the front of the room, who banged a gavel and then cleared his throat. "The commission will come to order! The commission is now open for the trial of such persons as may be brought before it."

Brigadier General Albert Cox, acting as Provost Marshal, stood from his seat. "Bring in the prisoners!" he called out. Each man in the room watched solemnly as a procession entered. Prisoners in civilian clothing were escorted by uniformed guards. Even those who had never before laid eyes on the men recognized each one from their mug shots. First was Burger, then Dasch, followed by Haupt, and on down the line to Thiel at the end. The prisoners were seated in chairs along the left-hand wall, with an armed escort between each one. Haupt eyed the crowd of military men that faced him, disbelieving, as if it were all a terrible dream that he might somehow wake up from. Dasch fidgeted in his chair, unable to sit still, crossing and uncrossing his arms and legs, leaning forward and then leaning back. Of the eight men, Burger seemed most resigned to the situation. He'd been there before, enduring similar trials in Germany just a few years past. He alone fully understood what it meant to be powerless before forces far greater than himself. There was nothing left to do but play his role in this farce and accept his fate.

Before the proceedings could commence, Colonel Royall rose to make a statement. It was a hail Mary pass and the defense lawyer knew it, yet he had to try. "In deference to the Commission, it is our opinion that the order of the President of the United States creating this court is invalid and unconstitutional. We question the jurisdiction of any court except a civil court over the persons of these defendants. We think that the order itself violates several specific enactments as reflected in the Articles of War."

As the head of the tribunal, General McCoy was in equal parts annoyed and confused by this proclamation. He turned to the attorney general. "Are there any remarks on the part of the prosecution?"

Biddle stood to answer, appearing slightly flummoxed himself. "This is not a trial of offenses of law of the civil courts but is a trial of the offense of the law of war, which is not cognizable to the civil courts. It is the trial, as alleged in the charges, of certain enemies who crossed our borders, crossed our boundaries, which had then been described by the military and naval authorities, and who crossed in disguise in enemy vessels and landed here. They are exactly and precisely in the same position as armed forces invading this country. I cannot think it conceivable that any commission would listen to an argument that armed forces entering this country should not be met by the resistance of the Army itself under the Commander-in-Chief or that they have any civil rights that you can listen to in this proceeding."

McCoy furrowed his brow. "The statements of the opposing sides are entered into the record. I will instruct the proceedings of this commission to go ahead."

Royall looked to his co-counsel, Colonel Dowell. The outcome was not unexpected. The defense had stated their opposition. In time, it would assist them in mounting a formal challenge to the Supreme Court. Until then they would argue their case before the tribunal.

"If the commission please, I shall now read the charges and specifications," said Biddle. He lifted a sheet of paper from his desk and began. "In that, during the month of June, nineteen forty-two, the prisoners, being enemies of the United States and acting for and on behalf of the German Reich, a belligerent enemy nation, secretly and covertly passed, in civilian dress, contrary to the law of war, through the military and naval lines and defenses of the United States, along the Atlantic Coast, and went behind such lines and defenses in civilian dress within zones of military operations and elsewhere, for the purpose of committing acts of sabotage, espionage and other hostile acts, and in particular, to destroy certain war industries, war utilities and war materials within the United States."

Herbie Haupt watched the impassive faces of the seven judges. These men held his future in their hands. Innocent or guilty? Life or death? Prison or the electric chair? Surely when they heard his side of the story they would understand. Herbie was no monster. He was no Nazi, hell-bent on destruction. He was an all-American kid, caught up in this scheme by circumstance. If only they would allow him to explain himself… All that he could do was speak the truth. But would that be enough?

With the charges read in their entirety, Colonel P. Granville Munson stood from his place at the prosecutors' table. "I will now ask the accused to plead to the charges and specifications, taking them in the order in which they are named in the charge sheet." Munson adjusted a pair of glasses hanging from the tip of his nose. "Will Ernest Peter Burger rise?"

Burger stood and took one step forward.

"How do you plead to specification one of charge one?"

"Not guilty." Burger's voice rang through the court, clear and true. This was a man who believed wholeheartedly in his innocence.

"Specification two of charge one?"

"Not guilty."

Munson worked his way through all charges, then on to Dasch, and Haupt, and the all of the rest. With the pleas recorded, the prosecution wasted no time in calling their first witness to the stand; Coastguardsman John Cullen. The door to the courtroom opened and Cullen, wearing crisp dress whites, was escorted into the room. All eyes were on the seaman as he settled into a seat on the witness platform. He took a quick look around. When he spotted George Dasch, Cullen momentarily froze. He noted to himself the tall, lanky frame and the gray streak running through the man's hair. Colonel Munson approached the stand, quickly drawing the seaman's attention. "Mr. Cullen. Hold up your right hand. This is not the oath as the witness, but this is an oath of secrecy that you will now take."

Cullen raised one hand.

"Do you solemnly swear that you will not divulge the proceedings taken in this trial to anyone outside the courtroom until released from your obligation by proper authority?" said Munson.

"I do."

"You understand that is an oath of secrecy, for which you can be punished if it is broken. Now, I will give you the oath as a witness. Do you swear that the evidence you shall give in the case now on hearing shall be the truth, the whole truth, and nothing but the truth, so help you God?

"Yes, I do."

"What is your name, rank, organization, and station?"

"John C. Cullen, United States Coast Guard. My rating is coxswain."

"Where are you stationed?"

"I am stationed at Amagansett, Long Island."

"Where were you stationed on June thirteenth, nineteen forty-two?"

"Amagansett lifeboat station."

"Do you remember what occurred on that night?"

"Yes, sir."

"When did you go on duty?"

"Ten after twelve a.m., sir."

"What kind of night was it?"

"Foggy night."

"Describe that a little more, please."

"Well, it was very dark and very foggy."

"How far could you see?"

"Not more than fifteen feet; twenty feet at the most."

"When the events that you are going to testify to occurred, how far were you from the Coast Guard station at Amagansett?"

"Not quite a half a mile, sir."

"Not quite half a mile. What was the first thing that you saw that night after you went on duty at twelve-ten a.m.?"

"I saw a dark object out in the water. It was about twenty feet away."

"I think you had better address your remarks to the commission, so they can hear them, and keep your voice up. What kind of object? Will you describe the object?"

"It was just a dark object when I first approached it. Then I walked up a little further and I flashed my light upon it but quickly put it out again. It did no good. Then I approached a little closer yet, and I noticed there were three men standing there."

"Standing where?"

"Out in the water, sir."

"How deep in the water?"

"Oh, about a little over ankle deep. Not quite at their knees."

"What occurred then?"

"I asked these men who they were. I hollered out. One of the men walked toward me."

"Do you recognize the man in court who walked towards you?"

"I think so, sir." Cullen shifted uneasily.

"Will you stand up and identify him, if you see him in court? Stand up, please."

Cullen stood. He took another glance toward Dasch.

"Now, do you see the man?"

"Yes, sir."

"Which is he?"

"Right here, sir." Cullen nodded his head.

"Go and point to the man that you have in mind. It won't hurt you," Munson urged. "Just go and point at him. Point at him. Which is he?"

"Yes, sir, right here." Cullen stepped down from the platform and took a few steps toward Dasch before raising a hand.

"Will you stand up, please?" said Munson.

Slumped in his chair with one hand on his chin, Dasch straightened himself and then stood. For the first time since that foggy night, the two men faced each other, just a few feet apart yet this time under the full glare of a military tribunal.

"Is that the man that you remember seeing?" Munson asked.

"Would he mind saying a few words?"

"Do you want to identify him by his voice? Is that what you mean?"

"Yes, sir."

Attorney General Biddle quickly spoke up. "Do I have the Commission's permission to permit the person whom the witness has identified to speak, so that he may be able to identify him by his voice?"

"If there is no objection on the part of the defense," answered General McCoy.

"No objection." Colonel Ristine nodded to Dasch.

"What is the matter?" Dasch spoke a few words. He was already frustrated by the way this was going. These facts were not in dispute. He and Cullen saw each other on the beach, he'd happily admit! Why did everybody else in the room seem to take it as an indictment of his guilt? The accusation, the pointed finger. Dastardly George Dasch landed on Long Island on a dark and foggy night! The proceedings had only just begun, yet it felt that the outcome was predetermined.

"Yes, sir, that's the man," said Cullen.

"That's the man you saw at that time?" Biddle asked.

"Yes."

"Let the record show that the witness identified the defendant Dasch as the man whom he saw on the beach," said Biddle.

The eyes of the judges seemed to bore into George Dasch, their hatred and anger visceral. Here before them was a Nazi agent, landed on American shores in the dead of night. Dasch directed his gaze downwards to his hands, now folded in his lap.

When the first day of testimony concluded, the prisoners were once again shuttled back to their cells in the DC jail. Distrust swirled through the mind of Herbie Haupt. Who turned them in? Was it Burger? Or Dasch? That question was not yet answered, though it was overshadowed by a much larger concern. Was there any possible way out? It was hard to conceive of these severe-looking generals and colonels believing in his innocence. Herbie struggled to keep hopelessness from overcoming him. Perhaps these men held some kernel of mercy in their hearts. That seemed to be his only chance. From what he'd seen so far, Herbie Haupt did not like his odds.

Chapter Seventy-Seven

Washington, DC, July 20, 1942

For two weeks, the trial continued. Every morning the defendants were loaded into the prison vans and driven to the Justice Department under armed escort. Each evening they returned to their cells in the DC jail. In between, the accused were merely spectators. The contents from their buried crates were presented in court and examined. Witnesses for the prosecution were called, one after another; officers in the Coast Guard intelligence service, present on that fateful night on Long Island; special agents of the F.B.I., Donegan, Traynor, Johnstone, Wills. Full statements by the defendants, taken upon arrest, were entered into the record. It was only when Pete Burger's statement was read out loud that the full truth became clear to all involved. Herbie was right all along in his suspicions. Burger did betray them. Dasch, too. "I consider Haupt very dangerous," Burger conveyed to his F.B.I. handlers. "He was formerly a wrestler and a boxer and he is extraordinarily strong. I consider Haupt to be very cunning but not intelligent. He is extremely interested in money. Haupt is also a very free spender and can undoubtedly be found among the cafes and nightclubs in whatever city he may be located. Haupt, while we were in Paris en route to Lorient, caused considerable trouble at a hotel where we stayed when he refused to pay a French prostitute for her services."

As this last portion of the statement was read out, Herbie felt a wave of humiliation. He peered down the row to Burger, but Pete kept his eyes fixed straight ahead. When the prosecutors came to Dasch's statement, at least George was more considerate. "I would like to state that he is a romantic type of boy," he'd said of Herbie. That didn't change the cold hard facts as George readily admitted them. No wonder he'd never paid attention during their classes at Quenz Lake. It was George's plan to betray them from the very beginning. Herbie's idea of going home to reclaim his old life was doomed from the start.

After eleven days of testimony and evidence, Attorney General Biddle stood before the commission. "The prosecution rests its case," he stated.

For Colonel Kenneth Royall, the following morning would begin his chance to present evidence. Saving his clients' lives was a steep hill to climb. A mountain, more like it. Despite the secrecy, or perhaps because of it, the entire nation was united against his defendants. The press, the public, the President of the United States, all calling for their execution. The pressure on these seven officers who made up the commission was intense. Royall understood that his only chance rested with a Supreme Court that happened to be in the midst of their annual summer break. If the commission had its way, his clients would be dead before the court came back into session. Royall had already spent the past two weeks attempting to track down individual justices to plead his arguments over the phone. Just a few days earlier he'd managed a meeting with the only justice remaining in the capitol, the Honorable Hugo Black. Standing in Black's study, Royall asked for a hearing.

"You mean the case of these German spies?" the justice was immediately suspicious.

"We don't call them spies, but I suppose that's the case you're talking about."

"I don't want to have anything to do with that matter." Black shook his head as his whole body shivered in revulsion.

Royall reeled. Here was one of the most liberal justices on the court, well-known as a defender of civil liberties, denying the defendants the chance to even be heard. "Mr. Justice, you shock me, that's all I can say to you."

Back in his office, Royall settled into his chair, struggling to fend off a growing sense of despair. If he couldn't have this case transferred to civilian court, his clients were doomed. The swirling of America's bloodlust would not be denied until all eight Germans were dead. But how to argue to the court when the court wouldn't listen, when the justices didn't even seem to *care*? Their minds were made up, just like everybody else's. Never in his professional life had Royall felt so despondent. He leaned forward, intent on formulating a different strategy. On the corner of his desk, a pile of newspapers was neatly stacked. The colonel lifted a copy of the *Washington Post.* Staring back at him from the front page was a photo of J. Edgar Hoover. Royall skimmed through the accompanying article until he came to a quote from the director himself. "Through the diligent efforts of agents within the FBI, these Nazi scoundrels were rounded up and arrested before they could perpetrate their diabolical scheme." With the entire trial held behind closed doors, Hoover was free to present whatever narrative he chose. Royall flipped to the second page, scanning for additional reactions. A small, single-column article near the bottom caught his eye. Not an article at all really, a mere mention. *Justice Roberts to Attend Funeral*, read the headline. Beneath that was one short paragraph. *Supreme Court Justice Owen Roberts returned to the capitol from his farm in Chester Springs, Pennsylvania, to attend the funeral of his former colleague, the Honorable Judge Stanley Crowder, Chief Justice of the United States Court of Appeals for the District of Columbia Circuit. Judge Crowder died of unknown causes Friday morning. Services will be held in the National Cathedral, Wisconsin Avenue, Monday at 2 p.m.*

Royall sat bolt upright. This was his chance! Quick as a flash, his despondency gave way to a faint glimmer of hope. Royall looked at his watch. It was 2:45 on Monday afternoon. He had to speak to Roberts. His clients' lives depended on it, though he couldn't very well go to a funeral and accost the judge in the middle of the National Cathedral. Anyway, the service would probably be over by the time he got there. Where would the judge go afterward? Royall pondered the question, wondering what he himself might do in a similar situation. Would the judge go straight home? Perhaps. But then, he might stop by his office while he was back in town, to pick up his mail, maybe catch up on some paperwork… Yes, he might. It was worth a try. Royall pressed a button on his intercom. "Delores, I need a car right away."

"Yes, sir," his secretary replied.

Royall briefly considered what materials he should take along. In the end, it didn't much matter. He knew what he had to say. The colonel picked up his briefcase and hurried out the door.

In Roberts' waiting room, Colonel Royall sat with his left leg resting across his opposite knee. At a small desk nearby, a secretary pecked away, clickity-clack, clickity-clack on a typewriter. The colonel gazed around the room, a little bit surprised by how sparse it was. For the highest court in the land, he'd expected more somehow. A portrait of their boss, Franklin Delano Roosevelt, hung on one wall. Beside it was an American flag. A potted fern took up one corner. The secretary stopped typing to peer at Royall over the rims of her glasses. "I can't guarantee that the judge will be coming in this afternoon," she said. "I honestly don't know."

"I understand," Royall replied. "I'll take my chances." He glanced at his watch. It was 3:35. If the judge didn't show up in the next half hour, he probably wasn't coming. To make use of his time, Royall opened his briefcase and took out a pad of paper, flipping through his notes. He'd start with Herbie Haupt on the stand. That would burst the narrative of Nazi evil-doers that the attorney general had so carefully crafted over the past two weeks. How could the judges look at this all-American kid and not see the humanity in him? Royall scrolled through his list of questions, crossing a few out and adding more in the margins. He'd lost track of the time when the office door swung open. Justice Roberts hurried into the room wearing a black suit with black tie. When the judge saw Royall, he stopped in his tracks, recoiling at the sight of this interloper.

"Your honor!" Royall rose to his feet. "I was hoping to see you!"

"What is this?" Roberts was annoyed.

"Colonel Kenneth Royall, from the Judge Advocate General's office. I wonder if I might have a moment of your time?"

Roberts shrank further backward. "Now that all depends. I'm a very busy man. Most people make an appointment when they want to see me, or didn't you know?"

"I understand, but this couldn't wait. Please, your honor. If you don't mind?"

Roberts turned to his secretary, as though seeking some way out. He was met with a blank stare. "All right," the judge conceded. "But you'd better make this quick."

"I'll try your honor." Royall followed the judge into his office, where Roberts closed the door behind them. They sat on opposite sides of a desk stacked with briefs and casebooks.

"Royall…" the judge tilted his head to one side as he put it together. "This is about those Nazis, isn't it?"

"It is, your honor."

"You understand, of course, that the court is in recess? I don't believe there is anything much I can do for you. If you want to follow the usual channels…"

"But your honor," Royall cut him off with an air of desperation. "If we do that, I'm afraid it will be too late. By the time we work our way through the lower courts, my clients may well have already been executed. Time is of the essence here."

Roberts leaned back in his chair. He didn't have the time or patience for this. "On what grounds should this court hear your case? You realize that you're asking for a special session? You want to call back all nine justices from their recess to hear a case that has no prior ruling? To jump the line in front of every other case before this court?!"

"Yes, your honor. I believe the very integrity of the constitution is at stake!" Royall didn't want to overplay his hand, yet his contention was valid. All the same, perhaps it was best to jump right to his argument. "I assume you are aware of *Ex parte Milligan*?"

"Of course."

"This precedent has never been overruled, your honor. In 1864, Milligan was sentenced to hanging by a military commission for aiding the southern insurrection. This court ruled by a 5-4 majority that denying a writ of habeas corpus was unconstitutional, in peacetime or in wartime."

"I don't need a history lesson, colonel."

"Yes, your honor, I understand, but the precedent here is clear. As long as civil courts are operating normally, all defendants are entitled to a civil trial. Your honor, the courts are presently operating normally."

"But didn't your clients arrive in this country wearing the uniforms of a foreign government? One from which we are currently at war? Are they not combatants, caught behind enemy lines? Why do they deserve special rights and privileges?"

"I would argue that this is not a special right or privilege. Milligan was also arrested behind enemy lines, your honor. I don't need to remind you of the legal and moral tradition behind a writ of habeas corpus. This protection is enshrined in the constitution itself." Royall fumbled through his briefcase to find a typewritten page. "And I quote from the ruling itself, 'The Constitution of the United States is a law for rulers and people, equally in war and in peace, and covers with the shield of its protection all classes of men, at all times, and under all circumstances.' Your honor, I can't imagine a more clear-cut statement than that. War or not, as long as the civil courts are operating in this country, my clients deserve equal protection under the law. This court has a duty, an obligation, to hear this case before it is too late."

Roberts took on the expression of a man who'd eaten something that didn't agree with him. "It does seem to merit further review, I will admit."

"As I've already stated, my clients have no time to waste. I request that you file a temporary writ asserting jurisdiction."

Roberts lifted his hands before him. "I knew I should have stayed on my farm this week…"

"Does that mean you will consent, your honor?"

"Not before I discuss the matter with the rest of the justices." Roberts leaned an elbow onto his desk. "Why don't we arrange to discuss this matter further at the end of the week? Would that be sufficient? I don't believe your clients will be executed before then."

"Yes, your honor, the end of the week would be sufficient."

"You and the attorney general can come up to the farm and we'll have a right, good pow-wow."

"Thank you, your honor."

"I'll warn you, it might take some convincing to get all eight of my colleagues to agree to a special session. It is highly unusual."

"I understand," Royall replied. "But I believe my argument is persuasive."

"We shall see," Roberts exclaimed. "My secretary will be in touch to help make arrangements. Good day, Colonel."

"Good day to you, your honor." Not wanting to press his luck, Royall quickly rose to his feet and left the room. It wasn't a *yes*, but it was about as close as he could have hoped. For the first time since he'd begun his lobbying effort, it wasn't a *no* either. All hope was not lost. Colonel Royall would take what he could get.

Chapter Seventy-Eight

Washington, DC, July 21-22, 1942

Herbie Haupt's ears rang with a high-pitched whine. As he made his way to the witness stand, it was as if time stood still. The past didn't exist, nor the future. Only right here, right now, in this cramped and crowded room. He sat and faced the eyes of the court.

"Hold up your right hand," Colonel Munson directed. "Do you swear that the evidence you give now shall be the truth, the whole truth, and nothing but the truth, so help you God?"

"I do."

"What is your full name?"

"Herbert Joannes Wilhelm Godhelp Haupt."

"You are one of the accused in this case?"

"Yes."

Munson turned toward the defense table. "Your witness."

Colonel Royall stood. "Mr. Haupt, how old are you?" he began.

"Twenty-two."

"Where were you born?"

"Stettin, Germany."

"At what age did you and your parents come to this country?"

"I came to this country with my mother at the age of five."

"Where did you live from the time you were five years old until the summer of nineteen forty-one?"

"Chicago, Illinois."

"When in nineteen forty-one did you leave Chicago?"

"June sixteenth."

"Where did you go?"

"To Mexico."

"What were the circumstances which led up to your leaving Chicago?"

Herbie took a deep breath before launching into the tale. How many times he had conveyed this story, yet none of them as important as this one. "I was associating with a girl named Gerda Stuckmann and my folks objected to my going with her, and her folks objected to her going with me because I was younger, and she became pregnant and I didn't know what to do, so I talked to two friends of mine and left for Mexico."

Colonel Royall walked Herbie through his journey, from Mexico to Japan to France and finally on to Germany with his best friend Wolfgang. Herbie explained his first fateful meetings with Lieutenant Walter Kappe and the chance he was offered, to return to America. "I told Kappe I had a friend who came across with me, and he says he knew, and he said that Wolfgang…"

"That is Wergin?" Royall interjected.

"Wergin… will be held in Germany in case I had any intentions to turn this thing in, or in any other way double-cross this whole thing."

"Did you see Wergin after that?"

"No, I didn't. Not after that."

"Then you went to this school. Did you know the purpose for which you were going at that time?"

"Not until I got to the school, no, sir."

"What did you learn then?"

"That the purpose of the school was to teach us how to sabotage."

"Did you attend the school?"

"Yes, I did."

"Why?"

"To get back to the United States."

"Did you at that time intend to carry out any of the plans that were taught you in school?"

"I intended to carry out none of the plans ever." Herbie was adamant.

"Why were you going to the school, then?"

"Because it was the only possible way to get back to my folks."

"Did you know of any other way to get back to your parents?"

"None whatsoever."

"How long were you at the school?"

"Approximately three weeks."

"Were any instructions of any kind given to you with reference to harming or hurting any person on this mission?"

"We should not harm or should not hurt anybody."

"Were any instructions given you about getting any military or other information and transmitting it to Germany?"

"No, sir."

"Were any instructions given you with reference to spying of any kind?"

"No, sir."

"Were you given specific orders before you landed in America as to what course you should or should not follow in America?"

"Yes, I was told not to go home to my parents, because that is the first place where they would catch me; not to see any of my old friends; not to see my girlfriend. That is about all."

"Where and when were those instructions given to you?"

"They were given to me in Germany by Walter Kappe and on the U-boat by Kerling."

"That is, the defendant Edward Kerling?"

"Yes, sir."

"What was told you about the name you should use in America?"

"Walter Kappe gave me a registration card with the name of Lawrence Jordan on it, and told me I should use that name in the United States."

"Did you use the name Lawrence Jordan in the United States?"

"No, sir."

"What name did you use in the United States?"

"I used my own name."

"Herbert, at the time you embarked in the U boat and at the time you landed from the U boat in this country, did you intend to commit any acts of sabotage?"

"I never intended to commit any acts of sabotage."

"What did you intend to do?"

"I intended to go home to my folks and about the sixth of July go up to the F.B.I."

"Why did you say the sixth of July?"

"Because I didn't know where any of the other fellows were, and I found out from Hermann Neubauer that they were coming to Chicago, the Knickerbocker Hotel, on the 6th."

"Did you tell anybody in the group what you planned to do?"

"No, I did not."

"Why?"

"Well, it would sort of endanger us."

"When you got to the United States, where did you go?"

"I went to Chicago."

"With whom?"

"Alone."

"Now, did you see Gerda Stuckmann upon your return to Chicago?"

"I saw her two days after I came to Chicago."

"What, if anything, transpired between you and Gerda with reference to a possible marriage?"

"We talked over the point of her having had a child and the child having died, and we decided to get married."

"In accordance with that decision, what did you do to arrange for the necessary blood tests?"

"Gave Miss Stuckmann ten dollars and told her to go get her blood test, which she did."

"I believe you purchased an automobile after you got to Chicago."

"I did."

"What money did you use for that purpose?"

"The money that I brought along from Germany."

"Now, why did you buy the automobile?"

"First to have an automobile and then to take a honeymoon with Gerda."

"Had there been originally a plan proposed before you landed for you to buy an automobile and use it in connection with the sabotage operations?"

"No, not to buy an automobile, sir."

"Now, when you were in Chicago, were you followed at any time by any persons?"

"I was followed by the F.B.I. twice."

"When were those occasions?"

"The first time I was followed was about three days before I was apprehended by the F.B.I., and the second time I was followed was the evening before I was apprehended by the F.B.I."

"After you learned that you were being followed did you make any effort to escape from Chicago or leave your home?"

"I did not."

"Now, with reference to your apprehension in Chicago, what did you tell the F.B.I. about who you thought must have turned you in?"

"I told the F.B.I. that Peter Burger had beat me to it. I told them that I knew all the time that Peter Burger would turn us in, because he had been in a concentration camp and had told me about the horrors he suffered and the horrors he had seen other people suffer in the concentration camp in Germany."

"Did you ever hear the defendant Burger in Germany or France make any remark with reference to the Gestapo?"

"Many times."

"What did he say?"

"He said they are the people that he hates more than anything else on earth, that his wife lost a child because of the treatments of her by them." Herbie tried not to think about what anybody else in the room might have thought of his answers. Only Royall mattered. Herbie laid his trust in his counsel. Whatever Royall asked, Haupt did his best to respond honestly. When the defense was finished, however, it was the attorney general's turn to cross-examine. As Biddle stepped to the edge of the witness stand, Haupt's anxiety spiked. This man's job was to convict him.

"Haupt, when did you leave Chicago to go to Mexico?" Biddle asked.

"I left Chicago in June, nineteen forty-one. The sixteenth of June."

"I just do not understand why you left. I wonder if you would tell us again why you left?"

How many times would he have to go through this? Hadn't they all just heard it? Yet Herbie started once more. "The real reason why I left Chicago was because I was going around with a girl named Gerda Stuckmann, who was a girl my folks objected to, and Gerda Stuckmann's folks objected to my going with her because I was so much younger than she was."

"She was going to have a baby?"

"Objection!" Colonel Royall called out. "May it please the Commission, the witness is being interrupted in his answers. The attorney general asked him why, and I think he should be permitted to complete his testimony without being interrupted."

"All right," Biddle conceded. "Finish your answer. I did not mean to interrupt you. I am sorry."

Flustered, Herbie took a moment before restarting. "The girl came and told me she was pregnant and that I would have to marry her. At that time my mother was in the hospital and I didn't know what to do. I couldn't tell my folks, so I decided to go away."

"Do I understand that you left her because you might have had to marry her?"

"Because of what my folks would think – of the shame it would bring upon my family and the trouble it would bring."

"What would bring trouble upon your family? Your marrying her?"

"It would bring shame."

"What would bring shame?"

"My having a child out of wedlock."

"Oh, you were afraid you would have to marry her if you stayed, and that would cause shame; was that the reason?" said Biddle.

"Because of her condition and the way she had been talked about at the time."

"Then, you left so that you would not have to marry, because it would cause shame if you did; is that right?"

"That is right."

"You saw her before you left, did you not?"

"I did. Three days before I left."

"How long were you with her?"

"About two hours."

"You talked to her for two hours, and you told her why you were leaving her?"

"I did not."

"Did you tell her you were leaving?"

"I did. I told her I wanted to see Mexico."

"What did she say about that?"

"She wanted to come along."

"Didn't she object to your leaving her?"

"Yes, she did. She wanted to come along and so I told her I would probably send for her if I made good down there."

"Did you tell her you expected to come back pretty soon?"

"I did not."

"You did not discuss whether you were coming back?"

"No. She figured I would be back in three or four weeks."

"She did not ask you when you would be back?"

"No, because she thought I was sending for her. I was going to send for her if I would get work in Mexico City."

"You told her you would send for her?"

"She made me promise."

"You had promised to send for her?"

"If I made good in Mexico."

"At what time was the baby born?"

"I don't know when the baby was born."

"When was it expected at that time? Do you know that? How long had she been in this condition?"

"Four months."

"Did I understand you to say that you had eighty dollars when you reached Mexico City?"

"About."

"You personally had that, or the crowd had that?"

"No, I personally had that."

"How long did you live in Mexico on the eighty dollars?"

"Three weeks."

"Was it then substantially gone?"

"My money was gone, yes, sir."

"You had been to the American consulate in Mexico City?"

"I was going to the American consulate and then I changed my mind on the way."

"I asked you if you went to the American consulate," Biddle reprimanded Herbie.

"I did not."

"And what was the reason you did not telegraph your family for any money to get back?"

"I didn't telegraph my family for any money because my mother had just undergone a very serious operation, my car was not paid for, the doctor had to be paid, and my father was occasionally sick; in fact, I was going to send them money if I was working, not try to get money out of them."

"Why did you not go to the American consul?"

"I met a man in Mexico City with a wife and two children…"

"What was his name?"

"That I can't tell you. He asked for a handout. He had gone to the American consulate. He was from Texas and he said the American consulate had said to him that they have no funds whatsoever there to send people back to the United States and he asked me for, I guess, five dollars or something so he could get to the border at Laredo. I couldn't give it to him at the time. I gave him money so he could feed his wife. He had his wife and children sitting near—"

"You have answered the question," Biddle cut him off mid-sentence.

"Wait a minute," Royall interjected.

"He has answered the question," the attorney general repeated.

"I do not know whether or not he has," said Royall. "I think the witness is the best judge of whether or not he has answered the question. He did not sound as though he had finished his answer. May it please the commission, the question which he was interrupted twice in answering was, what was his reason for not going to the American consulate? When a witness is asked, 'Why?' he is entitled to tell you why if it takes an hour to do it. This witness may have finished his answer; I cannot tell. I know that he was interrupted in the middle of a sentence. I should like him to be permitted to give his reasons why he did not go to the American consulate, if he has not finished doing so."

"He will be permitted to continue his answer to the question," said General McCoy.

"Did you finish your answer?" Biddle was exasperated.

"There were only two words there," said Herbie. "His wife and children sitting on a bench by a statue in Mexico."

"I take it, then, that you had, before you talked to this man, planned to go to the American consulate?"

"I had thought of it."

"For what purpose?"

"For getting back to the United States."

"So, at that time you did think of getting back to the United States?"

"I did, but I thought it over again."

"Because this handout had told you they didn't have any more money?"

"He told me that they didn't have any money at all."

"That was the reason why you didn't go to them at all? Because the handout had told you that?" The attorney general put his incredulity on full display.

"Because of that reason and the reason I had."

"You went from Mexico where?"

"I went from Mexico to Japan." Herbie was shaken. He continued to recount his story as Biddle hammered away at him. Who paid for his ticket to Japan? The German consulate. How did he obtain a German passport? The consulate issued it for him. So, he had gone to the German consulate? No, he met a consular official at the Lopez Restaurant. The ticket and passport were brought to him at the Nippon Steamship office.

"What did you state your nationality was?" Biddle was perplexed.

"American."

"I do not quite understand the relationship of the German consul to the passport. Why should he have issued it?"

"Well, I told why he issued that passport."

"Well, I do not yet understand. You were an American in Mexico City, going to Japan. Where did the German consul come into it?"

"He is the man who arranged the work for me in Japan."

"He may have arranged the work, but did he sign the passport or issue it at the German consulate?"

"Yes, he did."

"I still do not understand," Biddle persisted. "I may be very stupid. You were in Mexico City, going to Japan. What has the German consul got to do with your passport?"

"May it please the commission," Royall interrupted. "I think that is a question of law or argument. The witness said that he did not know except that he signed the passport. The attorney general is either arguing with the witness or is asking a question of law, either of which is incompetent."

"Does Colonel Royall object?" said Biddle.

"Yes."

"I should like a ruling on it."

General McCoy turned to the court reporter. "Please re-read the question."

The reporter looked to the record. "Question. I still do not understand. I may be very stupid. You were in Mexico City, going to Japan. What has the German consul got to do with your passport?"

"I think that question can be asked," said McCoy.

"Would you answer?" Biddle said to Herbie.

"I have answered it, sir." Herbie was beginning to sound testy.

"Please answer it again."

"The German consul gave me a passport and gave me a ticket to go to Japan. That's all I know."

"Wasn't the reason that the German consul issued it that you told the German consul that you were a German citizen?"

"No, because in order to tell him that, I would have to show him some papers that I am a German citizen, and I could not."

"You did not say to the German consul or anybody else that you are a German citizen?"

"That I am a German citizen? No, I never did."

"You never said that to anybody in Mexico City?"

"Nowhere."

The questions continued for hours as Biddle tried to break down Herbie's veracity, to catch him in any inconsistency, back and forth through the smallest of details. Whenever Herbie spoke, the attorney general interrupted, drawing repeated objections from the defense. Haupt did the best he could to stick to the truth.

"What was your own plan if you got caught?" Biddle asked, late in the afternoon.

"My plan? I never figured on getting caught."

"But if by any ill chance you should happen to be caught, did you ever think about that?"

"I never thought of that."

"You never thought of it at all?"

"Because I never planned to go through the sabotage, so I had never really planned on getting caught."

"That is because you were going to turn this in?"

"Yes."

"Had you planned to turn it in promptly, or were you going to wait a while, while you were thinking about all this on the submarine?"

"The plan did not come to me in Germany. In Germany, I knew that I would never go through with the sabotage. It was just a means of my getting back to my family. I think I started to think about it after I landed. I said if I didn't go through with it, and some of these fellows do, then I will get into trouble just as well as anybody else. So I figured the only thing for me to do was to turn it in; that is all I can do."

"But you never thought about that in Germany?"

"In Germany all I thought of was getting back to my family."

"You never thought about possibly getting into trouble if a bridge was blown up?"

"I never thought about blowing up a bridge. I never had an idea of blowing up a bridge at all."

"Or if somebody else blew up a bridge?"

"I knew the instructions in Germany to both groups were that they were not to blow anything up for at least three months, to get themselves well established."

Herbie continued on, with answers about his mother, his father, and his uncles, all through the rest of the afternoon before picking up again the following day. Had he taken any oath to the German army? How much was he to be paid? Had he signed any contract? Biddle punched and jabbed. Finally, after the attorney general had exhausted all queries, General McCoy had a few questions of his own.

"What do you believe would have happened to you if you told Lieutenant Kappe that you would not come to America to do sabotage?" McCoy asked.

"In the position that I was, not being a German citizen and having trouble with German officials… Well, I can't definitely state what would happen to me. I would have probably went to a concentration camp. That is about all they could have done to me."

"Did they never state what they would do to you under such conditions?"

"No, but Kappe had stated that they would pick up my friend who was an American citizen, who was 19 years of age, Wolfgang Wergin, if I did not cooperate."

"Did he not say anything about what he would do to your family?"

"No. That is taken for granted after you have been in Germany for a few months."

"Why did he specialize so on your friend?"

"Because I had traveled with my friend from the United States, and he knew his folks were also over in the United States."

"He seemed well informed on all the conditions, with regard to both your families, did he?"

"When you re-enter Germany from France or from any point, they give you a questionnaire: How much money do you have, where you came from, and everything. As I understand it, Walter Kappe had all those records."

"Do you remember the questions you answered on that questionnaire?"

"I remember most of the questions." Herbie licked his lips as he thought back. "What was your name, age, description, and how much money you have... How many relatives you have and where they are located in Germany... What you want to do in Germany, and if you were a member of the Party, and if you were not, your citizenship; and that is about all."

"What did you say in answering about your citizenship?

"American."

McCoy nodded. He turned his attention to the rest of his panel, who sat with grave expressions. "There seem to be no further questions on the part of the commission."

"That is all," Biddle concurred.

"That is all," said Colonel Royall.

Herbie passed a hopeful look to his attorney. Had he done all right? Royall nodded encouragement and Haupt rose from the witness stand. Two guards escorted him back to his seat along the wall, his heart beating so fast he felt as though it might explode in his chest. He'd explained himself as best he could. Herbie's fate was in the hands of these seven judges. Glancing from one grave face to another, he realized that it all came down to one question. Was he just another Nazi to them, or was he an American kid from the streets of Chicago? Herbie tried to calm himself. All he could do now was hope for the best.

Chapter Seventy-Nine

Washington, DC, July 22-27, 1942

One after another, over the next four days, the accused took the stand to answer questions, first from Colonel Royall and next from the attorney general. Details emerged, painting a clearer picture of the men involved and their individual circumstances. After Herbie, Hermann Neubauer sat ramrod straight in the witness chair as he explained to Royall why he left the United States two years before.

"I went to a different employment agency to try to get a job and was sent to different places, and I could not get a job on account of being a German," said Neubauer. "Most chefs were Frenchmen, and so I couldn't get a job."

"When did you arrive in Germany?"

"On August third, nineteen-forty."

"Where did you go at that time?"

"Right home to my family in Hamburg, to my folks in Hamburg."

"Were you drafted in the German army?"

Neubauer paused while the panel of seven American generals awaited his reply. The answer would not go over well. "Yes. I was drafted in the German army. I had to report on November fourteenth, nineteen-forty."

"What were your duties in the German army? Did you get into the fighting forces that were on either of the fronts?"

"Yes, sir."

"Where did your regiment go, and were you engaged in any action or did you receive any wounds?"

"Yes, sir. In May we left Brandenburg for the occupied former Poland, to Prszemysl, on the river San, and when the war started between Germany and Russia we crossed the river in rubber boats and advanced into Russia, into occupied Polish territory in Russia, about twenty miles or twenty-five miles. On Tuesday afternoon we were supposed to go over the top, as they say, around five-thirty, and we were laying in a small village, and the Russians bombarded this village and there I was wounded."

"What wounds did you receive?"

"I have shell splinters in my right cheek and in my leg. I still have one large shell splinter, as large as a lima bean, in my cheek near the jaw bone, and two small fragments above the right eye."

"As a result of the injury to your head did you have any form of paralysis of speech?"

"For two days I was not able to speak at all, and then gradually I was able to speak, and I started like a child would start speaking or talking."

"Were you removed to a hospital?"

"Yes. I was taken first to Krakow in an airplane and then by train to Stuttgart, Germany, where I stayed for six months in the army hospital."

"What was your condition while you were in the hospital?"

"I still have headaches. Not so much anymore. I had pain in my cheek. They wanted to operate on my head, but it was too dangerous, because the splinters are too near the brain."

"What was the condition of your nervous system? How were your nerves?"

"I was sent twice, not exactly to a sanitarium; it was an old castle. I was sent there for my nerves, on account of my nerves."

"How did it affect you? How was your nervous condition? Describe it as best you can."

"I get excited about every little thing very easily, and any noise makes me nervous."

"How long has that condition continued?"

"I would say I am still in this condition. Not as bad anymore as I was in the beginning, but I am still in that condition."

"When you got out of the hospital what date was it?"

"I don't know exactly the date. In the middle of November, nineteen forty-one."

"Where did you go then?"

"I was transferred to an army medical center."

"How long did you stay there?"

"Until I was ordered to report."

"Did you receive a written order to report?"

"Yes, sir. I received a letter at the end of February asking me if I would go on a special assignment to a country where I had been before. It was signed by Lieutenant Kappe."

Royall asked Neubauer about the school for sabotage, their orders, how he felt about them…

"When I found out that I was going as an agent over to the United States, I surely didn't like it. In the first place, my wife was born here in the States, and the family of my wife is here in the States; and another thing if you have been a soldier or are a soldier, you don't think much of an agent or a saboteur and I surely didn't like it."

"What could you do about it?"

"I couldn't do nothing about it."

"While on the boat or on the submarine, did you communicate with anyone back in Germany as to how you felt or give them any instructions?"

"Yes, I did. I wrote a letter to my wife in Hamburg, Germany. We had a big argument the night before I had to report back to the school after the furlough the first part of May. She had been disappointed since she come to Germany and I told that I been wrong in the beginning; I should have stayed in the United States with her. The police had asked her why she didn't go to work and why she didn't have a baby, and about her folks and her family in the United States, and she felt bad about it; she felt like she was watched and being treated just like a criminal. She complained about all those things to me. Well, so, on the submarine before landing I wrote her that she should try to get on one of the Swedish boats taking American citizens and diplomats from Europe to the United States, as they were exchanging citizens and diplomats between the United States and Germany, and she was a born American and as an American citizen would have a chance to go back to the States, and she should try to get on one of those boats."

"Did you show that letter to anyone?"

"Yes, I did. At first, I didn't know what to do about it. I showed it to Edward Kerling. I was kind of suspicious what he might say about it, as he was – well, not exactly my boss, but he was the leader of the group, anyway. If he would have protested about it or would have told me I was doing wrong, I just would have told him I was going to tear up the letter. But when he read this, he just gave me a look, and – well, I was kind of glad that he didn't bawl me out on account of that. I realized that he didn't blame me for it. He thought it was all right."

"You considered him your commanding officer at that time, did you?"

"Yes, he was the leader of the group."

"You were taking orders from him?"

"Yes, sir."

"Hermann, after you landed in the United States from the submarine, what was your feeling?"

"Well, I was sure glad when we had those boxes buried on the beach, that we had them off our hands, so we could get away from the beach. I was nervous all along."

After Neubauer's testimony came Thiel, then Kerling, Heinck, and Quirin. Royall did his best to humanize them, to let them tell their stories. Life in the United States, then a return to Germany followed by recruitment into the sabotage mission. Did they plan to complete their mission? No, replied each man. They were too nervous, or they didn't think they could get away with it, and besides, wartime gasoline rationing made retrieving their explosives impossible. They planned to go to the FBI, or flee to Canada, or to Mexico. To the seven-judge panel, it all sounded like paltry excuses. Only when George Dasch took the witness stand on June 25th did the narrative shift.

"How old are you, Mr. Dasch?" Colonel Ristine began to question his client for the first time.

"Thirty-nine years old, sir."

"I believe you were born in Germany?"

"Yes, sir. I was born February seventh, nineteen hundred and three, in Speyer—in Germany."

"Could you tell the Commission what time you came to the United States the first time?"

"I entered the United States on board an American steamer after being seventeen days a stowaway, in the harbor of Philadelphia on or about the eleventh day of October, nineteen twenty-two."

"Did you thereafter convert that illegal entry into a legal entry?"

"Yes, indeed."

"Do you know what the date of that was?"

"On or about October nineteenth, nineteen twenty-three." For the next several hours Dasch relayed his history, waving his arms in the air and rocking back and forth in his chair as he wound through tangents that the attorney general objected to as irrelevant. Dasch would not be deterred. This was his day in court and he was determined to be heard. Even his own attorney struggled, however, to limit his ramblings. It was not until the saboteurs reached New York City that Dasch's story differed from the rest.

"After you got to New York, did you get in contact with the FBI agents there?" Ristine asked.

"That Sunday morning, while we were talking…"

"Answer my question," Ristine interrupted his own witness. "Did you get in contact with the FBI?"

"Yes, sir, that is correct."

"That was Sunday evening."

"Sunday evening."

"Would you just tell the Commission that conversation you had with the FBI on that occasion?"

"I had taken the telephone number in the morning in the hotel; as a matter of fact, I looked it up from the book…"

"Just tell us the conversation." Ristine's frustration was on full display.

"I told them that I am a German citizen, that arrived in this county yesterday morning and that I had a statement to make, and that I wished for him to instruct his Washington office that I will be in Washington either Thursday or Friday this coming week, because I was mentally not—I was mentally not at ease; I was all tied in knots. So, he questioned me: 'Why don't you come…'"

"Limit your statement to what you said to him and what he said to you."

"Yes," Dasch struggled to maintain composure. "Furthermore, then I…we had a little talk. I said to him. 'Now, mark that down, please. I, Franz Daniel Pastorious, shall try to get in contact either Thursday or Friday with Mr. Hoover in Washington, and kindly refer that to Washington.'" In the courtroom, Dasch watched J. Edgar Hoover himself for a reaction, but the director gave none. "I have told him that I am thirty-nine years of age and that I have a gray streak through my hair," Dasch went on.

"They wanted you to come to the office?"

"That is correct."

"You would not do this?"

"I said, to my way of reasoning, the only person who should know that is Mr. Hoover."

"That was Sunday night?"

"That is right, sir."

"Did you come to Washington on Thursday morning?"

"On Thursday evening."

"Did you get in touch with anybody on Friday morning?"

"Yes, sir. I called up, first, Colonel Kramer. He wasn't in. I instructed his secretary to call me back from his office. After that I got in touch with the FBI and told them that I would like to see them, and I spoke to Mr. Traynor, and he requested me to be down at the office at eleven o'clock. I said, 'Would you be so kind as to send a man over, because I don't know Washington well?' and he agreed to that."

"They did send a man to accompany you over to the FBI?"

"They sent five men, I think."

"Anyhow, you did accompany one of them over to the FBI?"

"Yes, indeed, sir."

"From that time forward, I believe, you discussed the matter with them for some five or six days; is that right?"

"At first when I came to the office…"

"Just answer my question," Ristine struggled to keep his witness on topic.

"Sir?"

"Did you not discuss the matter with them for some five or six days thereafter?"

"Friday, Saturday, Sunday, Monday, Tuesday. Yes, five days."

"Did not Mr. Traynor tell you sometime during that first day, quite a while after you started telling your story, that he thought you were a crackpot?"

"Well, I don't know whether it was at the end of the first day or it was on the next day. He said to me, 'You know, George when you came to my office here, I didn't believe you; I thought you were a crackpot-clown,' something like that... 'I just didn't believe you. Then finally when you opened up, then I knew we had something after all.' That is all."

"Well, you did, insofar as you could, tell the entire story from beginning to end to the agents of the FBI?"

"As I got there, I told them who I was, that I came with a bunch of boys, that some were down South..."

"Do not give detail again. It is all in the statement."

"No, I beg your pardon; that is not in there."

"Well, it is substantially in there."

"No, sir. The first thirty minutes there is nothing mentioned... It starts off..."

"But the whole thing is substantially in there is it not?" Ristine cut in once more.

"Yes," Dasch acknowledged. "As it came out, that is right."

"I do not want to go into the detail again."

"No, I don't wish to either, sir."

"Did you ever at any time have any intention, in your efforts to get out of Germany, to do anything other than fight Naziism and Hilterism?"

"The main reason why I left Germany was to go out and do my share to fight that what is inhuman in Germany."

"I believe it is in the record, but you know that during your entire discourse with the FBI you were in protective custody and not under arrest, is that right?"

"During the time of my stay in Washington, I was in protective custody."

"What time did you first learn that you were under arrest?"

"Officially, I found out when I been the second or the third day in the jail in New York City."

"There was something said about an effort to get you to plead guilty in the District Court or in the Federal Court in New York. I do not care to go into the detail. Did you agree, for the purpose of protecting your father and mother that you would enter a plea of guilty and would therefore receive a Presidential pardon within three to six months?"

At this, the veins in J. Edgar Hoover's forehead began to throb. He clenched both hands into fists.

"I agreed to that on Saturday night, yes, sir," Dasch replied.

"And then after thinking it over did you change your mind?" Ristine asked.

"I didn't think it over. As I was brought back to the cell I happened to look outside, because I was given the promise downstairs 'That's the only possible way for you, George, to keep everything quiet. No one shall know it.' And when I went upstairs, I happened to look out the slit, and there, at 11 or 12 o'clock, sat an agent with a newspaper. My picture was in front. I said to myself, 'What is going on? You have been on the defense continuously. Why don't you look at this for real? They want you to plead guilty to an offense you know you did not commit. You are obstructing justice. I can't do it.' I requested to see an agent or representative of the F.B.I., and I did not…"

"Wait a minute. What are you talking about now?" Ristine was testy.

Dasch's eyes opened wide. Why was his own defense attorney treating him with such disrespect? It made no sense. Unless the whole verdict was a foregone conclusion, courtesy of J. Edgar Hoover himself? "While I have been in jail up there," Dasch tried to answer the question.

"In New York?"

"That's right."

Colonel Ristine turned to the prosecutor. "I think you may examine," he retreated, finished with his questions.

As the prosecuting attorney took his seat, the color returned to Hoover's face. The game was shifting, from defense to offense. He jotted down a few notes and slid them across the table to Biddle. The attorney general read them and then rose to his feet and moved a few steps closer to the witness. "There are just one or two small matters that I would like to clear up. I am not perfectly clear in my own mind about them, Dasch," he began.

"All right, sir."

Biddle wound through some of the dates, clarified a few small issues regarding Dasch's early role with the mission, and then got to the heart of his questions. "Dasch, you were pretty nervous when you got to America, weren't you?"

"Nervous? I was happy, happy-happy and nervous."

"You were happy and nervous?"

"Yes, sir."

"Why didn't you go right away to the F.B.I.?"

"I had three reasons, sir. May I explain all three reasons?" After being cut off so many times by his lawyer, Dasch was uncharacteristically tentative.

"Surely. Do them quickly. All three."

"All right. First of all, I was a mental and a nervous wreck. I was so glad that I was here. And, second of all, I had to be human, and that is it mainly – I had to be human."

"And third?"

"Just one second. Why I had to be human – I have got to explain that to the commission. I know why I came. But I studied every other man to find out a reason why they came here. I knew this boy, Burger. I knew why he came here. But I wasn't quite sure why this little kid Haupt came here, a boy who has remained in Germany only four or five months, who had his mother here and lived here in America. I didn't know why he came here. I could not just run to the police and take this chance away from the kid to prove why he came here. That would have been merely for the sake of my own self-protection. That would have been the rottenest thing in the world. To be a real decent person I had to wait. I had to give every person a chance to say what I had to say. That's the reason."

"You were a nervous wreck, but you were a happy nervous wreck, were you not? If you were a nervous wreck, why did you go to the waiters' club and play cards two nights and a day?"

"That was the best thing I could have done."

"That was good for you?"

"Yes. I didn't think of nothing else but playing cards. When I got out I was dead tired, and I went home and had a good sleep, and the next morning I said, 'Now, let's go to work.'"

"Are you a communist?" The question rang through the hall.

"No, sir."

"Were you ever a communist?"

"No, sir."

"Did you ever tell anyone that you were a communist?"

"Yes, I did," Dasch admitted.

"Who did you tell? Did you tell Pete you were a communist?"

"No, sir."

"You never were a communist?"

"Just one second; I would like to get that straight. You cannot ask a question to a man, 'Are you a communist?' That is impossible."

"I can."

"I beg your pardon. I would like to make that clear, please, what I mean by that. Let us be honest. I have tried to be honest all my life that way. If a person wishes to see the truth, wants to know the truth, he must see the good part and the bad part in everything. That is how you get to the truth. So, if I were asked, 'Are you a communist?' I would say, 'No, I have never been a communist.' As a matter of fact, fighting communism over here was an instrumental reason why I had to leave this country."

"I take it then, that you are not a communist?"

"I would say not."

"So you *are* able to answer that question, aren't you?"

"Yes, sir."

"Are you a loyal German or a loyal American?"

"I am loyal to the people of Germany."

"How about the people of America? Are you loyal to them too?"

"Yes."

"You are loyal to everyone, aren't you?"

"I am loyal to all good, decent, honest, law-abiding citizens, regardless of whether they are in Germany or America or France."

"Were you a slave in Germany?"

"Yes. I was physically a free man. I had a very good job and good money."

"Were you a free man mentally?"

"I dreaded becoming a slave. I didn't want to become a slave like the other poor people, and that is why I had to go…"

"I think that is all." The attorney general's cross-examination was complete.

Last to speak on his own behalf was the defendant Peter Burger. In a clear and concise manner, he laid out his entire story to Colonel Royall, beginning with his years in America and including his work as a tool and die maker, service in the National Guard, and his acquiring United States citizenship.

"Upon your return to Germany in nineteen thirty-three did you rejoin the Nazi Party?" Royall asked.

"I did, sir, in nineteen thirty-three, when I came back."

"What connection, if any, did you have with Röhm? State briefly what your connection was with Röhm and what happened to Röhm."

"I came in the fall of nineteen thirty-three to the High Command of the Storm Troopers, and at that time the chief of staff was Ernest Röhm. I had a position as Aide de Camp and remained on the staff up to June of nineteen thirty-four, when he was killed."

"At that time were large numbers of old Storm Troopers killed?"

"Yes, sir."

"How did you escape?"

"I happened to be assigned to the Chief of the Medical Corps, and he was the only one who had the confidence of Adolf Hitler."

"Who was he?"

"Dr. Ketterer."

"How many of the leaders and their friends were killed at the time of the Röhm purge?"

"Around three thousand."

Describing his incarceration in a Gestapo prison, Burger's antipathy for Hitler and the party was on full display, his motive for betraying the sabotage mission clear. It was under cross-examination by the attorney general that he fully explained the details of his planning.

"Pete, I want to come back to the early morning that you landed in Amagansett. It was quite dark and foggy, was it not?" Biddle asked.

"Yes."

"You had certain objects and put them along the beach?"

"That is right."

"One was a half-empty bottle of schnapps?"

"That's right."

"Where did you put that?"

"I stuck it in the sand, sir."

"Standing up?"

"Standing up."

"Buried in the sand?"

"Not buried, but just stuck in."

"The other was a half-smoked package of cigarettes?"

"Yes."

"You put that in the sand?"

"Lay it on the sand."

"How far from the water?"

"I don't know that. I was very excited, naturally, in a state of mind where I didn't recognize anything. It was foggy. I was thoroughly wet, because three or four big waves hit me, and I just ran out of this boat, having the suitcase, and then taking the cigarette box out of my pocket and putting it, as I remember, flat on the sand. I cannot recall how far it was from the water's edge."

"Let us see. There were cigarettes, a bottle, and the coat. What other objects did you put down?"

"Well, small pieces of clothing. I suppose bathing trunks and a folded vest."

"You did put those down on the beach?"

"No, not on the beach, up on the bank."

"You put those there so that, you thought, whoever was looking for the boxes could follow each one, and they would lead to the boxes, is that right?"

"I left tracks by throwing different items down and left a way marked."

"Clearly marked?"

"Yes."

"Clearly?"

"I suppose. Clear enough."

"Would it not have been a little more simple and a little more certain if you had called up a policeman and told him where the boxes were?"

"On the beach?"

"Anywhere."

"That was done, sir, after we left the boxes."

"Why did you not go up to the Coast Guard and report it?"

"Well, may I explain to you, sir?"

"Surely."

"I did not know that there was a Coast Guard station around or where we were. It was so foggy that we did not, in fact, see from the water's edge the houses or anything."

"Had you decided before to report it at all?"

"I decided that I had to make it impossible to have the explosives used by the members of my group."

"Did you decide while coming over on the submarine that you were going to report it?"

"I decided to make our plan, or our orders, to fail."

"I understand that, but you have not answered the question."

"Well, it is pretty hard for me to answer the question."

"Did you decide on the submarine that you were going to report this to the proper officials?" Biddle pressed him.

"I did."

"When did you decide that?"

"Well, I don't think anyone could answer that question, sir."

"But you let a week go by in all before any report was made, did you not?"

"On the very evening of the day of the landing, George Dasch took the whole business over on his hands, and I was very happy to hear him explain his ideas."

"Did you trust Dasch?"

"I did."

"You have confidence in him?"

"Absolutely."

"For some purpose but not for others?"

"Well, I don't understand your question."

"You had confidence in him for some purposes, but you did not have confidence in him for other purposes?"

"I don't know what you mean by 'other purposes.'"

"I thought a little while ago you said you did not have much confidence in Dasch?"

"I was talking about the feeling of our group as subordinates of the leader."

"Were you not afraid that he would steal some of the money?"

"Not after we had our talk."

"But before you had your talk?"

"We all had the feeling anyone has of a man he doesn't know very well and acts funny and carries a suitcase with eighty-two thousand dollars."

"So, as soon as you had your talk, your confidence was completely restored?"

"After that, it was restored… Yes, that is right."

"You had never suspected Dasch of giving this away before you had your talk with him?"

"No. Of giving it away? No, but I also didn't expect him to carry out the orders which were given to him."

"You never thought Dasch would carry out the orders?"

"I mentioned that before."

"I say, you never thought he would carry them out?" Biddle repeated.

"I am sorry I can't express myself. It's very hard to explain to you. His actions were not the actions of a leader. They were not as a soldier and they were not as a saboteur, or whatever you call it. May I explain a little further?"

"Yes."

"From Berlin to Paris, from Paris to Lorient, and finally on the submarine to the coast of the United States, there was not one order given by our superiors he would not do the opposition -- you know, the contrary -- not the order. There wasn't one place where he did anything that wasn't wrong in the eyes of people -- you know what I mean. Even on the train he lost his papers and made a lot of trouble for anyone connected. So naturally, we didn't feel he was a competent leader for an undertaking like this."

Dasch sat watching impassively, arms crossed as his head nodded gently. After nearly three weeks of witness testimony, statements and exhibits, this trial was coming toward an end. Clearly, he was not guilty, Dasch thought to himself. Any right-minded fellow should be able to see that. But were these seven judges right-minded fellows? This doubt kept him up at night, lying on the sagging cot in his jail cell, a possible death sentence never far from his thoughts. He looked to his attorney, Colonel Ristine, sitting silently at the defense table. Ristine, who'd provided the weakest defense in the history of law. Why hadn't Dasch been assigned someone more like Royall? At least *he'd* fought for his clients. Ristine seemed more in league with the prosecution. Dasch's gloom had grown by the day. There was no escaping it. His life was in the hands of others and the prognosis did not look good.

Herbie Haupt, on the other hand, nurtured a small kernel of optimism in his heart. All he'd wanted was to return to his family. They couldn't execute a man for that. The other defendants were more circumspect. Kerling in particular seemed resigned to his fate, scowling in defiance at the judges, the attorney general, the FBI director. Their only true hope was for Colonel Kenneth C. Royall to somehow pull out a miracle.

Chapter Eighty

Washington, DC, July 29-30, 1942

J. Edgar Hoover was not a happy man. Livid was a word that better described his mood as he rode up Pennsylvania Avenue in the back of a bureau car, assistant Clyde Tolson by his side. "Spineless!" Hoover shouted in frustration. He wore a pressed brown suit with a cream-colored tie. A dark handkerchief protruded from his front pocket. In his lap, Hoover carried a white hat with a dark band. "Incompetent! A man like that, in charge of the justice department?! That's a travesty, is what it is! A fool like Biddle has no place being in charge of a God damned thing!"

"No, sir," Tolson agreed.

"How could he have let this happen?" The car turned onto Constitution Avenue and made its way up the hill past the U.S. Capitol. "How many times did I tell him? We can't let this out of our hands! The President himself was clear, our very security is at stake. You know what Biddle said to me?"

"No, sir, I do not."

"He said he didn't understand the need for such secrecy! Can you believe that? He didn't *understand*!"

"Incredible." Tolson shook his head in wonder.

"You know how many people are going to be in this courtroom? Members of the public! Journalists! Recording every word! Our attorney general actually agreed to this little exercise in democracy. Agreed to it! He'd better hope it doesn't come back and bite us all on the ass. If this court rules in Royall's favor…" Hoover couldn't finish the sentence, the prospect was simply too distressing.

"There's no guarantee that the President will abide by such an outcome," Tolson chipped in. "He could just disregard it and execute those Nazis, despite an unfortunate ruling."

These words calmed Hoover somewhat. "I suspect that's exactly what the President would do. Hell, it's what I'd do! Let's hope it doesn't come to that." The car pulled up in front of the Supreme Court building and came to a stop. As the two passengers climbed out onto the sidewalk a small commotion rang out. They'd been spotted. Spectators and reporters rushed over, with photographers from the major newspapers quickly taking up positions, snapping pictures as the director of the FBI made his way across the marble courtyard and up the stairs.

"Mr. Hoover, what result are you expecting today?" a reporter shouted.

"Where are the Nazi spies?" cried another. "Can we expect to see them today?"

"Any statement director? Come on, give us something!"

Hoover declined, his jaw thrust forward as he hurried past with Tolson by his side. Inside the courthouse, Hoover was escorted into the chamber, already full to bursting. A buzz of excitement filled the gallery as he was seated just behind Biddle, small and fragile-looking in his white suit and black tie. Nearby at the defense table, Royall and Dowell quietly went over their notes.

At exactly twelve noon, the marshal stood from a small desk on the right side of the bench and pounded his gavel three times, the sound echoing through the cavernous hall. Quiet followed as all in attendance rose to their feet. "The Honorable, the Chief Justice and the Associate Justices of the Supreme Court of the United States!" the marshal called out. "Oyez! Oyez! Oyez! All persons having business before the Honorable, the Supreme Court of the United States, are admonished to draw near and give their attention, for the Court is now sitting. God save the United States and this Honorable Court!"

Seven robed justices emerged from separate entrances behind the bench and took their places, dwarfed by the giant marble columns rising floor to ceiling behind them. In the center, Chief Justice Harlan Stone waited for the spectators to retake their seats before he launched into the proceedings.

After opening remarks, it did not take long for Royall to realize that he had at least one adversary on the court. Associate Justice Felix Frankfurter attempted to have the entire case thrown out on procedural grounds. "Why could not the appeal have been perfected before the circuit court of appeals?" he demanded.

"The appeal might have been perfected if we had a little additional element of time," Royall replied. Both men knew what was at stake. If Frankfurter was successful in this gambit, sending the case to a circuit court, Royall's clients would likely be executed before the appeal ever made it back to this chamber. "A man is entitled to an appeal. He is entitled to an appeal that has some prospect of being of practical value."

For Frankfurter, the answer was not at all satisfactory, yet here they were. The court in session, the case being argued. Debating whether to continue or not was pointless, and so the questions continued. Was Haupt a citizen? Did this offer him different status? Had the men signed contracts with the Germans? Worn uniforms? The spectators listened with rapt attention, reporters jotting every word in their notebooks. Royall steered clear of revealing any classified information, focusing his arguments squarely on the issue of jurisdiction.

"All these persons lived in the United States for a considerable period of time," Royall explained. "All of them returned to Germany at varying periods. All of them landed on the American coast from a German submarine. The group brought ashore certain explosives. As we see from the facts, there was no definite plan as to when and where these explosives were to be used. They have not been used. No damage was done and no person injured."

"You say that they landed from a submarine operated by the German government?" said Justice Robert Jackson.

"Right, sir."

"They were brought here by the German government and landed on our shores?"

"That is correct, sir."

"They constituted, I suppose, an invading force?"

"No, sir."

"Why not?" Jackson was skeptical. "If you concede that much, why did they not constitute an invading force that had no rights whatever except, of course, under the laws of war?"

"Certain of the defendants, with varying degrees of corroboration, stated that they were merely using this as a means of escaping from

Germany and reaching America and that they had no intention or purpose of committing violence or acts of sabotage."

"Would your argument be based on believing that or accepting that as fact? "

"The fact is admitted that these men came on German submarines. It is not admitted that they were members of the German military force."

Frankfurter stirred once more, one eyebrow arched in condescension. "Is it your argument that this must be tried before a civil court and not a military tribunal?"

"That would be our contention," Royall replied. "Regardless of whether they are designated an invading force, we think that the order appointing the military commission is fatally defective because it violates express statutes."

"Would it be fair to say from your argument that we must determine here a question of status?" said Justice Stanley Reed.

"Yes sir, I think that is exactly the distinction."

"Do we have to determine the question of guilt or innocence?"

"No sir, I don't think that you do."

All morning long, Royall parried queries, arguing as best he could for his interpretation of the law. As the day stretched into the afternoon, it was the attorney general's turn next. Addressing the seven sitting justices, Francis Biddle held his head high and spoke with conviction. "May it please the court; The United States and the German Reich are now at war. That seems to be the essential fact on which this case turns and to which all of our arguments will be addressed. The other essential fact is that these petitioners are enemies of the United States who have invaded this country. We will show that alien enemies have no rights to sue or enter the courts of the United States under these circumstances. Under the very ancient and accepted common law rule, such enemies have no rights in the courts of the sovereign with which they are enemies."

"I suppose you mean that there is a Law of War which may apply, even though there is no specific provision to authorize this particular prosecution?" said Chief Justice Stone.

"That is precisely what I mean, Mr. Chief Justice. Some of that common law has been codified and expressed in the Hague

Convention, but some of it is common law which certainly existed long before the Convention."

"You are saying that there is power to proceed against and punish in time of war those who are enemies of the United States, according to some rule or other? I suppose you would call it the Law of War?"

"Yes."

"And the President may institute the prosecution without authority from Congress?"

"Yes."

"Specific authority?"

"Yes, and, Mr. Chief Justice, in this case I say he has that specific authority."

Royall watched the expressions of the justices as they considered Biddle's argument. Could they accept that the President had specific authority in this case, even though that authority was never granted by Congress, nor the constitution? Despite the fact that clear precedent denied that authority? If the justices had any doubts, they certainly weren't evident. This was not a good sign, but then Royall's job was not to look for signs. His job was to present his case. By the end of the day, it was all but finished as the attorney general wrapped up his arguments. Royall would be given one more opportunity for rebuttal, to be heard the following day.

When the court reconvened in the morning, Colonel Royall was prepared. This was his last chance to frame things as he saw them, as he believed that precedent demanded. Hypothetical questions from the sitting justices were batted and deflected. Royall quoted extensively from the Milligan case. Yet in the end, the colonel went for an emotional approach. He appealed to each justice's conscience, outlining what was at stake, not just for his clients but for the country as a whole. Royall's voice rang out with the passion of his convictions. "Suggestion was made by the attorney general in his opening remarks that we are fighting a war here. We realize that. We also realize that the constitution is not made for peace alone, and that it is made for war as well as peace. It is not merely for fair weather. The real test of its power and authority, the real test of its strength to protect the minority, arises only when it has to be construed in times of stress. Thank you." Royall retook his seat. Whether his arguments were convincing to these seven justices, the colonel couldn't say. He'd given it his best shot.

"The court stands adjourned until twelve noon tomorrow," said the Chief Justice.

From his seat behind the attorney general, J. Edgar Hoover was eager to leave. After two days of arguments, he'd seen and heard enough. The whole proceeding was a farce as far as he was concerned. These Nazis deserved to die, and their secrets to die with them. He didn't care what the court decided. Roosevelt would be on his side, of that he was reasonably sure. They would get the outcome they desired, no matter what might transpire in this room.

Chapter Eighty-One

Washington DC, July 31, 1942

"The Court has fully considered the questions raised in these cases and has reached its conclusion upon them. It now announces its decision and enters its judgment in each case, in advance of the preparation of a full opinion." The words from Chief Justice Stone rang through the chamber. "The court holds that the military commission was lawfully constituted and that the petitioners are held in lawful custody. The motions for leave to file petitions for habeas corpus are denied."

Colonel Royall felt the energy drain from his body. He'd tried to prepare himself for this outcome, though never before had he been so emotionally invested in a case. And on hearing these words, never so disheartened. How could the court deny such an obvious precedent? What sort of psychological hoops had they forced themselves through to justify such a decision? Royall saw relief cross the attorney general's face, though the colonel himself had no time to dwell on this outcome. He still had a job to do. That very afternoon he would deliver closing arguments to the tribunal. With no hope remaining of an outside intervention, however, his clients' prospects looked very grim indeed.

From his seat along the wall, Herbie Haupt rested a notepad on one knee, a pencil clutched in his right hand. The materials were provided to each defendant for the purpose of taking notes. Herbie couldn't imagine how that might possibly help him, but the writing materials presented an opportunity. He would write a message to his parents. Would they ever get it? Of that he couldn't possibly say, yet still he had to try, motivated by a deep desire to explain himself as best he could, to ease the despair he had wrought. *Dear Mother and Father, please don't judge me too hard. While I was in Germany I worried night and day wondering how you were getting along. I tried to get work in Germany but I could not, and when they told me that they had chosen me to go back to the United States you don't know how happy I was. I counted the days and hours until I could see you again and probably help you. Dear Mother, I never had any bad intentions. I did not know what a grave offense it is to come here the way I did in wartime. They are treating me very well here, as good as can be expected.*

Herbie paused to listen to the proceedings. Though Colonel Royall spoke before the commission, every one of these uniformed officers seemed to have long ago settled on their conclusion. For three weeks, the panel of judges had shown only hostility toward the defense. On this last day, as Royall summed up his arguments, he pled not for exoneration but merely for a merciful sentence.

"We believe that these men have done nothing that warrants the infliction of the death penalty," said Royall. "They did not hurt anybody. They did not blow up anything. They did not affect the conduct of the war, except by the fact that they came over here and enabled us to take preventive measures which will help our conduct of the war. But if it be said that their intentions were bad, according to the prosecution, the law has always drawn a distinction between what a man intends to do and what he does. Those of us who appear in civil courts see every day the charge of assault with intent to kill. Here is a man who shoots another, and if his marksmanship had been good he would have been electrocuted. That is the only difference between his offense and that of the man who is sent to the gas chamber or is electrocuted, because the first man missed aim. He generally gets about 18 months or two years, sometimes three or four years. The law has drawn that distinction for hundreds of years. That is an attempt. As a matter of fact, these men have not gone near that far. To make the cases analogous you would have to say that a man bought a pistol with intent to kill. He would be fined $50 in most jurisdictions."

Royall's voice was gravelly and raw. He appeared gaunt, tired, worn out from his marathon sessions before two different courts, yet he carried on, fighting on behalf of his clients. "The law considers not merely the intent of a man, but the result and the accomplishment, in determining what the sentence will be. In the second place, the law recognizes that it takes a great deal more of a criminal heart to actually perpetrate an offense than it does to prepare for the perpetration of it."

"I do not suppose that any member of this commission or any member of counsel on either side has ever really wished that somebody was dead. But there are people who have done that, and if they had the opportunity, possibly, in the heat of anger, they might do something about killing them. It is terribly wrong to feel that way about anybody. But 99 out of 100 of those people, when confronted with the actual commission of an offense, would never commit it, because it takes much more hardness, much more criminality, much more depravity, to actually do something of that kind than it takes to plan to do it or prepare to do it."

"Let us apply that to this case," Royall went on. "Let us apply those doctrines that are so well established in the English law and in the European law and in every law that I know of, that it is unnecessary to cite authority. What did these men do? Let us take the prosecution's case to the limit. Let us assume that they came over here intending to commit sabotage. Suppose they had reached the point in their hearts where they thought that was the thing to do. They did not do it. Whether you believe what they told you in its entirety or not, the fact is that they did not do it, and that is the consideration that the law takes into account."

"Let us get the proper perspective on this case. These men may have planned something, but they have not done any terrible thing. They prepared to do some things which, if accomplished, might have been terrible. But they have not done it. Let us not let the facts of war absolutely change the character of what they have done. Give it weight, yes, but do not let it destroy our entire perspective of just exactly what has happened. They have done nothing to hurt America, to hurt it in the defense of this war. They may have intended to do it, but they have done nothing that has affected our war effort. As a matter of fact, unwittingly, in the case of those who did intend it, they have probably rendered a real service – unwittingly, I say – to the war effort, by giving us a means of prevention."

Herbie turned his attention back to his notepad. What Royall said was true, and logical, and if this was a jury of his peers it might even hold sway, but the faces of the seven generals were impassive. Their minds were already made up. Consumed by emotion, Herbie struggled to come up with the right words. How to convey his love without merely accentuating his parents' pain? He had to try. *Whatever happens to me, always remember that I love you more than anything in the world. May God protect you, my loved ones, until we see each other again, wherever that may be. Love, your son, Herbie.*

With Royall taking his seat, it was Colonel Ristine's turn to present his final defense of George Dasch. Perhaps inspired by Royall's arguments, Ristine managed to work up the passion so absent from his defense thus far, as though only at this last possible moment had he fully comprehended the stakes.

"I think you have heard enough evidence to know that, except for the action which the defendant Dasch took, this would in all probability be an unsolved problem today." Ristine raised a finger in the air to help make his point. "I do not think the eminent counsel for the prosecution will even dispute the proposition that it was Dasch who came to Washington and who laid this case with the F.B.I., with the solution appended thereto. That is one thing I want you to consider all the way through as I present some of the highlights of this case."

Ristine summarized the facts as he saw them. Dasch never belonged to any German organizations in the United States. To the contrary, he was outwardly hostile to pro-Hitler groups. On the boat back to Europe, five of his fellow Germans beat him up for failure to perform a "Heil Hitler" salute, vowing to report him to the German authorities. Dasch had no intent to aid the Hitler regime, at any point. In fact, it was his plan all along to undermine it. Upon landing on Long Island, Dasch was under direct orders to kill or capture any persons encountered on the beach. Why did he not follow those orders? "Does he lack courage?" Ristine asked. "Is he afraid? I do not think anybody could properly say that about him. All Dasch had to do was to wait with the other two sailors until the Coast Guardsman came up, and the two sailors would take him back to the submarine, and nobody would know that the landing was effectuated, from that source, at least."

Listening to these closing arguments, George Dasch himself tried to remain hopeful. Each and every fact pointed to his innocence. The bottom line was clear. He, George Dasch, had gone of his own free will to turn himself and the others in to the FBI. He had never done anything but cooperate. Obviously, he was not guilty of the charges brought against him. All the same, over the last several weeks he'd begun to understand that larger forces were at play. If it was merely a question of guilt or innocence, then J. Edgar Hoover would have been on Dasch's side. This was a case less about justice than about appearances. It was about a moral victory against the Nazi menace. How ironic that here Dasch was, held up by the prosecution as being one of them. His contribution toward bringing down the Nazi regime was to be punished as their representative. The unrelenting frustration ate at Dasch from the inside. One strong statement in his defense from the FBI director would be enough to clear him, yet on this final day, Hoover was nowhere to be seen. Dasch gave everything to them, willfully, openly, honestly. In return, he was abandoned.

"Gentlemen of the commission," Colonel Ristine drew his argument to a close. "If you had been in his position and you honestly wanted to come back here and fight that thing in Germany, what would you have done, or what could you have done that would have improved on what he did? Our commander-in-chief has, not once but several times, over the radio appealed to the liberty-loving people of the entire world, to do what? To rise up and fight the very thing that we are in this war to fight right now. And here is a man who came across, as he says, to fight it. He certainly carried it out after he got here. What are we going to do in a case like that? Is there one of these charges against Dasch that can stand? Why, I submit, gentlemen of the commission, that every one of these charges must fail. There is but one just and fair finding that you can bring in, and that is; 'We find the defendant Dasch not guilty of every charge and every specification.'"

With that, Colonel Ristine raised a chin in the air. It was up to this panel of generals to agree or disagree, though George Dasch was not keen on his odds. The whole thing had felt like a setup, ever since the day they'd first locked him in a cell. His life was no longer his own. All Dasch could do at this point was wait for final judgment.

Chapter Eighty-Two

Washington DC, August 1, 1942

Judge Advocate General Myron Cramer was an unimposing man, of average height and with little discernible charisma. His wavy gray hair was parted down the middle, shaved close on the sides. He wore round, wire-rimmed spectacles and spoke quietly, without bluster. On this final day of the proceedings, it was the major general who stood before the tribunal to deliver closing arguments for the prosecution. "May it please the president and members of the commission," Cramer began. "After listening to the arguments on behalf of the defense, it seems to me that their idea of the proper specification to be brought before this commission would have been worded somewhat as follows: 'In that, Burger and all the rest of these defendants, with intent to defraud the German government, did unlawfully pretend to said German government that they were saboteurs, and by means thereof did fraudulently obtain from said German government the sum of one hundred and eight-thousand dollars in money, boxes full of explosives, and a free trip across the Atlantic in a submarine.'"

The room erupted in laughter. It was not the reaction Cramer expected. The major general paused to let the disturbance dissipate. When calm was restored, Cramer continued, working his way through a list of the defense arguments. After refuting each one, he came to his ultimate point. "It seems to me that the prosecution has proved all the elements of all the specifications, and that all these defendants should suffer punishment by death. The only question is that which has been brought up by counsel, namely, that one or two of these defendants have in some way assisted the prosecution. That is a question with which I do not think this commission should concern itself. The question before this commission is, are these men guilty or are they not, of the crimes or offenses charged? I respectfully urge the commission to take into consideration the old maxim of courts: that clemency is a matter for the appointing authority and is not a matter for the court. For that reason, we ask for a finding of guilty under each specification and sentence of death." Cramer looked each member of the commission in the eye, one by one, to highlight the severity of his point. When he was satisfied, the major general made his way to the prosecution table and took his seat.

"The prosecution and the defense having nothing further to offer, the commission is closed." General McCoy seemed to take great relief in this statement. It was in the judge's hands now, with the sentence ultimately at the discretion of President Franklin Delano Roosevelt.

One by one the prisoners were escorted from their seats and out of the courtroom. Waiting his turn, George Dasch fumed. Where was Hoover? Why was there no mention of the full presidential pardon he had promised? Where was the gratitude Dasch so obviously deserved? It seemed that the director was too great a coward to even show his face. George's anger was tempered only by fear. The government called for execution. Not only for the others, but for him, too.

After Haupt and his escorts moved down the row, Dasch rose from his chair. All eyes were on him, a doomed man. His feet moved, one in front of the other, but it was as though he were floating, his mind already disconnected from the physical world. This was it, the beginning of the end. He moved through the courtroom and into the hall. Two steps out the door, he was nearly run over by a quickly moving scrum of FBI agents as they barreled past, a swirl of motion coming to a stop as they ran headlong into the prisoner and his two guards. Dasch turned his head, jaw dropping as he came face to face with J. Edgar Hoover himself. The director's eyes grew wide as the two men stood before each other for the briefest of moments. Hoover pushed his way past and quickly moved away.

For George Dasch, this was his one last chance to speak his mind. He couldn't let it get away. "Please, Mr. Hoover, just one question!" George shouted after him. "Mr. Hoover, aren't you ashamed of yourself?!" As soon as he'd spoken the words, Dasch felt a fist against his jaw. The blow sent him sprawling on the floor. When he looked up, a scowling agent hovered over him. The two guards quickly gathered their charge and pulled him back to his feet. The offending FBI man followed after his boss, leaving Dasch with the hot sting of tears running down his cheek. The trial was over. All that remained was the sentence. George Dasch had expected adulation, or at the very least appreciation. Now, he was left hoping that they would find the compassion in their souls to merely spare his life.

Chapter Eighty-Three

Washington DC, August 8, 1942

A small crowd gathered in the rain beside the DC jail under dark, foreboding skies. It was early morning as they huddled beneath umbrellas, eager for any news of the eight Nazi saboteurs. Newspapermen and photojournalists hoped for a scoop. Neighborhood residents were drawn to these towering walls by morbid curiosity. An off-duty soldier approached the solid gate in front.

"Hey, you fellows need any volunteers for a firing squad?" the soldier called out to a guard. "I'm a good shot."

"Nah, I think we got it covered," said the guard. "Thanks anyway."

"All right, just thought I'd see. I wouldn't mind popping one of them Jerry's, you know what I'm saying?"

"I hear you, buddy."

Amidst the cluster of spectators, theories floated through the air about what was happening inside. "My cousin, he works in the kitchen in there," one man confided. "Says the warden requested a two-pound bag of salt last night."

"Salt? What the hell for? It's not snails he's killing."

"Maybe he's making a fifty-pound omelet," another man joked. "You know, last meal."

"You people are imbeciles," the first man replied.

"Salt, did you say?" This question was posed by a reporter in a gray suit and hat, holding a pencil and small notepad. Jack Vincent worked for the International News Service.

"Yeah, that's what I said. Salt!"

"A saltwater solution is used on a prisoner's scalp, to ensure they make a circuit," Vincent explained to the others. "For the electric chair."

"Ohhh!" The faces of the other men lit up.

"See what I'm saying?" the first man retorted.

Clutching his umbrella with one hand, Vincent managed to write down this tidbit of information before putting the pencil and notepad into his pocket. A colleague, Dean Roswell, stood nearby. "I hear when the lights in the prison dim, that's when we'll know."

"Seems they already thought of that." Vincent nodded toward the bulbs that normally illuminated the front gate, now dark. "They shut them off half an hour ago. Just to keep us guessing." An army staff car pulled up to the prison gates and came to a stop.

"Who is it?!" somebody shouted.

Vincent hurried closer to take a look inside, spotting a familiar brigadier general in the back seat. "It's Cox," he said to Roswell. The gate opened to let the car pass and then swung shut once more. "Seems we might not have to wait much longer," Vincent added.

"Get it over with already, is what I say," Roswell replied.

"You got that right," a bystander agreed. "Fry those Nazi scum."

"I just wish they'd let me pull the lever," said another.

Clamping his eyes shut, Herbie Haupt could almost smell his Gerda's sweet aroma. He felt the touch of her soft skin against his own, lounging together in her bed on a Saturday afternoon. He thought back one year earlier, to the moment that set in motion all of the events that led him here. She stood in her kitchen wearing a light cotton dress, the faint hint of anxiety showing as she pulled two coffee mugs from a cabinet above her head. "I'm pregnant," she'd said. Just like that. Afraid to even look him in the eye. The panic that shot through him at that moment was indelible. Just the memory conjured it once more. Those following days and weeks he'd felt trapped, terrified of a future he felt forced to flee. Listening now to the rain pounding the pavements in the prison courtyard, his regret was profound. Yet, how could he ever have expected this? Herbie pictured an alternate reality, married to Gerda, raising a child. Perhaps they might still spare him…

A single pair of boots echoed down the corridor. The guard moved quickly past, lifting Herbie's dirty breakfast tray through a gap below the bars as he went. Since the trial concluded a week earlier, this represented the sum of his human contact. Three meals a day, delivered by a guard who barely spoke a word. The rest of his days were spent in waiting. How much time did he have left? How many days? Hours? Minutes? His sentence might arrive at any moment. He wished they'd just tell him already, to end this unendurable ambiguity. When he heard the gate at the end of the hall clatter open once more, he sat up ramrod straight. This was more commotion than just a few guards. This was a crowd. Hushed voices, shuffling feet. Herbie froze as the entire party appeared before his cell. He saw five guards, a small crowd of uniformed clergymen, and a senior officer he recognized as General Cox. Herbie rose slowly to his feet as one of the guards unlocked his cell door. General Cox entered. A chaplain followed right behind. As the door was locked tight behind them, Cox raised a document before his nose, cleared his throat, and began to read out loud. "Herbert Haupt, as Provost Marshal for the District of Columbia, I am here to inform you that the military tribunal has found you guilty on all crimes as charged and recommended to the President of the United States that you suffer death by the electric chair. The President has agreed to follow this recommendation. Your sentence will be carried out on this day, the eighth of August, nineteen forty-two. Do you have any questions?"

The words reverberated through Herbie's skull. His pulse quickened, eyes dilated, all thought and sensation melting away save for one realization. He was going to die today. Until this very moment, he'd maintained a kernel of hope. Maybe they would understand, in the end. Maybe Roosevelt would spare their lives. With this brief statement, General Cox reached in and yanked that kernel clean out. Herbie Haupt was going to die.

"I said, do you have any questions?" Cox raised his voice.

"How much time do I have?" Herbie spoke the words in a stunned whisper.

The general placed three blank sheets of paper and a pencil on a small table. "It will be a few hours. You can write a last letter to your family. If you'd like, the chaplain will stay to help you make your peace with God."

Herbie slowly lowered himself to his cot, struggling to process the news. General Cox nodded to the guards and then retreated from the cell, leaving the chaplain behind. "But why do I have to die?" Herbie fixed his gaze on the chaplain. "What did I *do*?"

"I am sorry, son, truly I am. Wouldn't you like to write a letter to your mother and father?"

Herbie gazed at the blank pages. What was left to say? All his life he'd yearned to make them proud, to be worthy of their love. He'd been told already that his mother, father, and uncle Walter were all in jail themselves, charged with aiding in his scheme. His own mother, locked up in a cell just like this one. Could she ever forgive him? Could she endure this pain he'd brought upon her?

"Is there something you'd like me to say to them for you?" the chaplain asked.

"Tell them… try not to take it too hard. Tell them…" Herbie's eyes clouded over with tears.

"It's all right, son." The chaplain placed a hand on Herbie's shoulder.

"Can you make sure that Gerda Stuckman gets the ring? The diamond ring? I bought it for her. Tell her that… Tell her that I love her."

The chaplain nodded. "Of course."

In the next cell, Cox made the same proclamation to Heinck before moving along the row to Kerling. Eddie stood at attention as the sentence was read, chin thrust forward in defiance. It was what he'd expected, ever since the tribunal wrapped up a week earlier. In fact, he'd mostly expected it from the very beginning. That didn't make it any easier to face, but he vowed to show no fear. No emotion. He couldn't give them that final victory. He would go to his death like a soldier, proud to the last.

When Cox had gone, Eddie sat at his small desk and began to write. *Marie, my wife – I am with you to the last minute! This will help me to take it as a German! Even the heaven out there is dark. It's raining. Our graves are far from home, but not forgotten. Marie, until we meet in a better world! May God be with you. My love to you, my heart to my country. Heil Hitler! Your Ed, always.*

Kerling put his pencil down. It was only at this last moment that he realized how much he loved her. Marie. His wife. She had endured so much. As Kerling awaited his ultimate fate, it was Marie who filled his heart.

For Hermann Neubauer, there was no such confusion. He'd only ever loved one woman. Alma never wanted to leave the United States. Hermann tore her away from friends and family to drag her off to Germany, a country to which she had no loyalty nor experience. Alma, his Alma, was trapped there now, to suffer through the war as a widow. News of Hermann's death would hit her hard. If only he could ease her sorrow. But what was there to say? Hermann lifted pencil to paper. *Dearest Alma. I never thought that they would take our lives away, but as I write these lines I have control of my nerves again. If it only would not hurt so much, it would not be so hard, but I will try to be brave and take it as a soldier. A priest is with me and he will be with me to the last minute. So my Alma, chin up, because I want you to. Be good and goodbye, until we may meet in a better world, may God bless you! I love you. Your Hermann.*

General Cox found Peter Burger lounging on his cot reading a worn copy of the *Saturday Evening Post.* Burger stood as the general entered with a guard in tow. There was no chaplain. Cox read his statement with an amendment at the end. "The President has commuted your sentence to life imprisonment." Burger let the news set in. He'd escaped death. That was something, anyway. If the previous war provided any indication, perhaps they would commute his sentence when this one was over.

"Do you have any questions?" Cox asked.

"No." Burger sat once again, turning back to his magazine.

In Dasch's cell, Cox read yet another amendment. "The President has commuted your sentence to thirty years of imprisonment at hard labor."

"But no, I need to… you don't understand… My family…!" Dasch's mind spun. He was supposed to be the hero! After all he'd done for them…

"Quiet!" Cox shouted. "Get yourself together!"

Dasch's body shook with a mix of fear and fury. "I can't accept this sentence! No, I simply cannot! I was promised a full pardon by director Hoover himself! After all that I have done for this country, the loss of life and destruction that my actions avoided! No! I demand to be released! I would rather be put to death than made to live through this rank miscarriage of justice!"

"You ought to consider yourself fortunate." Cox looked upon the prisoner with contempt. He turned to leave the cell. As the general and guards moved down the corridor, George Dasch was left to run the sentence through his mind. *Thirty years. Hard labor.* The ideals of American justice that he'd clung to for so long were gone, replaced by the harsh taste of bitterness.

The prison barber was Floyd Patterson, serving a five-year sentence for felony hit and run. Patterson was a slight man just shy of sixty years old, with creases in his face and specks of gray in his hair. Fetched from his cell, he'd been told only what he needed to know. He was to shave the heads of six prisoners, one after the other. He would be paid 25 cents for each and would keep his mouth shut, both during and after. Floyd Patterson was no dummy. He understood what was going on. Everyone in the prison knew what was going on. Secrets like that could not be kept. Not in a place like this. Patterson plugged in his electric clippers and waited for his first customer. It didn't take long before two guards and an army chaplain escorted the man into the room. He was young, in a gray prison uniform, wearing handcuffs and leg chains. Hardly more than a boy, Patterson thought. He stood just shy of six-feet tall. White skin. Dark, wavy hair. Handsome. The guards placed the prisoner in Patterson's barber chair and then stood by to watch.

"Go ahead, Floyd," said a guard.

Patterson lifted his clippers and switched them on. An electronic buzz filled the room. Herbie Haupt saw his reflection in a dull mirror mounted on the wall. Gaunt, defeated, scared… How many times had he stood before a mirror, comb in hand before a night on the town? How many times had he visited a barber for a quick trim? For Herbie, his hair was a part of his identity. It helped define him. Sitting in this chair, whatever denial he'd still struggled with evaporated. It was not only his hair that they were taking. It was his life.

"This won't hurt a bit." Floyd raised the clippers.

Herbie dropped his head, unable to bear witness to his doomed visage. Around him, the room dissolved into a hazy blur. His body convulsed with uncontrollable sobs, chest heaving as he lifted his hands to his face.

"Give him a minute," said the chaplain.

Patterson stepped back, switching off the clippers as warm tears streamed through Herbie's fingers, dripping off the end of his nose. He'd tried so hard to take it like a man. One look in the mirror and that pretense dissolved. His grief could not be denied. Herbie struggled to wipe away his tears.

With a nod from the guards, Patterson switched the clippers back on. Leaning close, he slowly ran the shears over Haupt's head. Herbie straightened in the chair, eyes distant, a sickness in the pit of his stomach as dark clumps of hair spiraled to the floor. Unable to watch, he clenched his eyelids tight.

When Patterson was finished, the two guards lifted Herbie from the chair, each by one arm. "Let's go, on your feet." He was led out of the room and down the corridor as though in a trance, one step at a time, propelling himself to his doom as the chaplain trailed behind. Herbie's legs were weak, nearly buckling, yet still he walked, understanding nothing else but that the pain of ten thousand volts awaited him. As they led him into the execution chamber, Herbie saw it; a sturdy wooden chair, restraints on the handles, electric coil attached to the top.

"The Lord will be thy shepherd," the chaplain tried to reassure him.

From behind darkened glass, twenty witnesses watched in awed silence as the prisoner was placed into the chair, restraints secured tightly around his arms and legs. A rubber mask, with openings for his nose and mouth, was pulled down over his head. For Herbie Haupt, the world went dark, his eyes never again to see the light of day. An executioner dipped a small sponge into a bucket of water before attaching it to the inside of a metal helmet and then fitting the helmet to the top of Herbie's head. A second sponge was attached to his bare leg by means of a metal clamp. The executioner attached a single cable to the clamp, and another to the helmet, giving each a slight tug to ensure a solid connection. "That's it," he said. "Clear the chamber."

Herbie Haupt hyperventilated beneath his rubber mask, desperately sucking in his last lungsful of air as he heard the door to the chamber swing shut. Droplets of water rolled down his freshly shorn head. Thoughts of his mother flashed through Herbie's mind. His father. A quick rush of shame at how he'd let them down was quickly overtaken by terror. The last sensation in his short life would be sheer pain. Herbie clenched his hands in tight fists.

At exactly 12:03 p.m., the executioner flipped his deathly switch and Herbie Haupt's body lifted from the chair, pulling hard against the restraints. Hidden from view, his face contorted in agony. Witnesses recoiled in horror as the electrified prisoner jolted wildly before them, one full minute, then two, finally sinking into the chair, motionless at last. Smoke poured from the prisoner's corpse as the executioner cut the power.

Two guards accompanied a doctor and the executioner back into the chamber. Very carefully, to avoid burning himself on any metal buttons, the doctor checked for a pulse. "This man is dead," he pronounced.

In the observation booth, the witnesses absorbed what they had just seen with varying reactions. "Heaven help me if I ever have to go like that," one muttered under his breath.

"He got what he deserved," said another. "Don't think I'm going to feel sorry for these Nazi scum. This is too good for them, ya ask me."

"I'm just saying… It's a rough way to go."

Herbie Haupt's singed and lifeless body was unstrapped, laid onto a stretcher, and then carted out, one limp arm hanging over the side. It was a matter of only a few minutes before the next prisoner was escorted into the room. The face of Heinrich Heinck shone with fear as he spotted the electric chair, the aroma of charred flesh still hanging in the air. Only the witnesses, hidden behind dark glass, knew what a truly gruesome fate he had in store.

By early afternoon, the rain began to let up. Jack Vincent stood with Dillard Stokes of the *Washington Daily News*, eating ham sandwiches and doing what they could to pass the time. A neighborhood mutt ambled up the sidewalk, stopping at Vincent's feet with a whine.

"Look at that, will you?" said Stokes. "A more pathetic beast was never seen."

"Credit where credit is due," Vincent answered. "Who wouldn't beg for one of my wife's tasty sandwiches?"

"They do hit the spot, I'll give you that."

Vincent tore off a piece of his sandwich and tossed it to the dog. "There, now leave us alone!"

"Oh, no, you're only encouraging him." The dog snapped up the bite of food and came back for more, tail wagging. Stokes was tearing off his own piece of sandwich when the doors to the prison began to slowly swing open. A cordon of twenty soldiers appeared, each carrying a .30 caliber M1 rifle. "At last," said Stokes. "Something is happening."

"Let's go people, give us some room!" a sergeant called out to the gathered crowd. "I want everybody on the other side of the street!" The soldiers lined up arm to arm, rifles held before them. With each step they moved forward, the crowds moved back until the street was clear. Spectators strained to see through the gates and into the prison courtyard beyond, photographers jostling for position. Vincent took out a notepad, ready to jot down his impressions. It only took a few moments before the procession began. One after another, black hearses followed each other onto the street, turning to the left and moving into the dismal mists of a wet and dreary afternoon.

"They're dead!" a spectator called out. "The Nazi spies are dead!"

"It's over!" said another.

"They got theirs!" said a third.

"Six," Vincent mentioned as the last glistening black hearse went past. "Six of them."

"Yeah," Stokes agreed. "I noticed."

Vincent looked back to the prison. Two more inside. They may have escaped execution, but Dasch and Burger would be locked away for a very long time. This story was done.

Part V – The Aftermath

Chapter Eighty-Four

Nancy, France, September 13, 1944

The 553 Volksgrenadier Division was dug in to shallow cover along the banks of the River Moselle. Wolfgang Wergin rose to his knees, using his helmet in an attempt to scrape a deeper trench in the rocky terrain beneath him. The results were not promising. If the Americans were to attack this point in the line it would be hard to hold them back. Not that he wanted to. It was only a few short weeks since Wolf was transferred to his new unit. An eye patch still covered his left eye. Recovering from battle wounds suffered on the Russian front, he'd met another private, Reinhold Schweiger, at an army hospital in Wurzberg. Wolf knew he would be sent back into action as soon as the doctors could clear him. It was Schweiger who suggested transferring to the 553, on the western front. Once the idea was planted Wolf pursued it as hard as he could. As an American himself, he was surprised when the transfer went through, but it was easier for them to send him from Germany to France than transport him all the way back to Russia. In the end, it came down to expediency. And so here he was, facing off against his countrymen. Wolf carried a rifle. He had a box of ammunition. He didn't plan on using either. Instead, he was focused on one thing: how he might surrender without first being shot, by the Americans or the Germans or both…

Wolf switched to his hands as he scooped dirt from his small foxhole. Of course, he also faced the prospect of being shredded by an artillery shell. Or pounded by a mortar. Or blasted by a tank. Wolf knew firsthand the sensation of hot lead tearing into his flesh. He'd long ago lost track of the number of mangled bodies he'd witnessed, heads blown off, rotting on the battlefield. He dug a little deeper. In a hole to his left was Schweiger, manning a grenade launcher. To his right, a soldier named Bachman was splayed behind a small rocky berm. Bachman was small and wiry with a nervous twitch. In civilian life, he was a die-maker. He'd supported Adolph Hitler in the early days. After joining the army, he didn't think much about politics at all. Survival was his only concern. The same went for Wolfgang, though his survival plan had its own unique wrinkle.

"They're coming," said Bachman.

"How do you know?" Wolf flattened his body in the shallow foxhole and peered toward a facing ridge with his one good eye. He saw no signs of movement, heard no mechanized forces; only the dull thuds of artillery coming from a separate part of the battlefield, several miles away.

"The smoke," Bachman pointed.

Wolfgang squinted into the distance and then saw it. The exhaust of an armored column moved toward them from over the hill. "How far do you think?"

Bachman did his best to gauge the distance. "One kilometer. Maybe one and a half."

"How do they expect us to hold off an armored brigade?" Schweiger complained. "Where are our guns?!"

Wolfgang peered behind them, first at the bridge that they were ordered to hold and then down the road on the other side of the river. Three self-propelled artillery guns were poised, waiting. Wolf imagined an entire panzer division appearing to back them up, but then he knew better. The 553, or what remained of it, was on its own. This would be his first combat since Russian shrapnel tore into him three months earlier. It was also a moment of truth. He would survive and be taken prisoner or he would die here on this rocky French soil. He would free himself from servitude to the Wehrmacht, taking his first step toward home, or his corpse would rot here in the sun. At any moment the shelling would commence.

The anticipation was debilitating. Once the fighting began, he wouldn't have time to think about it. During those moments of terror, one operated on instinct alone. He must remain focused on one thing; how to make his way across the line.

The first shells landed behind them, some falling harmlessly into the river or onto the far bank, yet still the shockwaves shook the ground to which Wolf clung. They were exposed here, practically in the open, with only those few self-propelled guns to back them up. When the first of the Americans appeared atop the ridge, the Germans artillery opened up. Wolfgang buried his head in his arms as shells flew over him in both directions. Smoke drifted across the battlefield, obstructing the view.

"We should retreat and blow the bridge!" Bachman shouted. "How can we hold it?!"

"We can't retreat!" countered Schweiger. "Hold the bridge, those are our orders!"

The first American tanks cleared the ridge and began down the slope as U.S. infantry soldiers charged forward, spread across the facing field.

"Open fire!" a German officer called out. The men on either side of Wolfgang began to shoot as the American artillery rounds landed closer, one covering them in a shower of dirt and debris. Along his rifle site, Wolf watched the opposing tanks and infantrymen advance. He fired a few rounds over the soldiers' heads. Despite the raging chaos, the sight of actual Americans was thrilling. At last! But how to join them? He looked to his side. If Wolf made a break for it, Schweiger might just shoot him in the back. The American advance continued. Three hundred yards, then two. German bullets thinned their ranks, but still the Americans came, tank guns ablaze. Behind Wolf, a German artillery piece exploded in an enormous fireball. The American infantry was just one hundred yards away. On the bridge itself, members of Wolf's unit began a harried retreat.

"They're going to blow the bridge!" hollered Bachman.

"Keep firing!" came a reply.

Thirty yards away, a green-clad American soldier led the final assault, closing the distance as he ran toward them into a hail of gunfire, each step a yard closer. He was a mere twenty feet away when a bullet struck, knocking him backward and down, where he collapsed to the earth in a twisted heap. Wolf huddled in his hole, watching from just over the edge. Was the American dead? No. He was moving, squirming in the dirt. Wolf heard a groan. Bachman aimed his weapon. "Nein!" Wolf shouted. Before he had time to reconsider, he was on his feet, closing the distance as the ground shook beneath him. One step, two, three… Tossing his rifle aside, he threw his body over the wounded American, expecting the hot lead of a bullet at any moment. Instead, he felt only the soldier's body, shifting beneath him. "It's OK!" he called out to the man. "I'm American!" Wolf held his helmet on the top of his head with one hand, his face pressed into the man's back as he sensed a swirl of movement all around him. He heard shouts, screams, gunfire, explosions. Wolf kept his head down as the grinding sound of the tanks approached. He feared being crushed by their treads, yet he couldn't look. Slowly, the sounds of battle shifted past and away. Wolf felt a sharp kick to the gut. He rolled to his side. Looking up, he saw the barrel of a rifle pointed at his face.

"Don't fucking move, you kraut son-of-a-bitch!" It was an American soldier about Wolf's age, face smeared with dirt and grime.

"It's OK! I'm American!" Soldiers streamed past as Wolf carefully showed his hands. "I'm American!" he repeated.

"Sure you are. Get the hell off him!"

Wolf slid away from the wounded soldier as a medic stopped and began tending to the man. Peering quickly toward the German lines, Wolfgang saw only bodies, and in the distance, what remained of his unit fleeing across the bridge in retreat.

"He says he's American."

"Bullshit," said the medic.

"How's Collins?"

"I'll live," the wounded man groaned, his left shoulder stained with blood.

The soldier standing over them kicked Wolf in the leg. "You are lucky he's not dead, or I would shoot your ass right here."

"I was trying to save him! Honest! I'm from Chicago!" Wolf tried rising to his knees.

"Easy!" The soldier's eyes were filled with hatred.

Wolf put both hands on his head. On the bridge, Americans flooded across in pursuit. This battle was all but finished.

"On your feet, Chicago, but real slow, you hear?!"

Wolfgang rose, careful not to make any sudden moves. The realization only now fully dawned on him. He'd done it! He'd crossed the line, and survived! Wolfgang Wergin was free. After two bloody and brutal years, his part in this war was over.

Chapter Eighty-Five

Wurzburg, Germany, March 16, 1945

Friday evenings in Wurzburg provided Bettina Burger with the last small sense of normalcy in her otherwise unrecognizable life. Three years living in wartime with Peter's parents was hard on them all. They were kind to let her stay, but the deprivations took their toll. Food shortages, stress, and the constant, shared worry over the fate of Peter... Where was he? What had become of him? Bettina had no way to know. All she did understand was that Germany seemed to be losing this war. With enemy troops approaching from all sides, the end was near. At least Wurzburg had escaped the wonton destruction enveloping much of the country. Dresden, Hamburg, Berlin; all bombed to near oblivion. That's what they'd heard from the sporadic accounts they could gather. Peter was right to send her here, to this small Bavarian city far from any industrial centers, where the few military installations consisted primarily of hospital facilities. She'd managed to find work, in the admissions office of the Luitpold Army Hospital. Processing a flood of incoming wounded gave her an insider's glimpse at the war. The outlook was dire indeed. They came from all fronts, young men with limbs torn off, bullet wounds, shrapnel, head injuries; there seemed to be no end to the mutilated soldiers, sacrificing themselves for their nation. At least Peter was not among them. Peter... Three long years since she'd last seen her husband. Bettina often chastised herself for forgetting; his voice, the contours of his face... The vast uncertainty was the hardest part of all. Rumors circulated of a sabotage plot gone awry. Secret trials. Executions. Bettina carried with her the realization that she may never know what had become of her husband. All she could do was survive as best she could until the end of this terrible war. One day and then another, enduring her pain in silence.

If only for a few short hours each week, Bettina was able to push all cares from her mind and pretend that the world had not collapsed around her. They gathered in a small tavern in the medieval heart of the city to drink wine and forget their troubles. In the dim light of this smoky room, they never talked of the hospital, or the war, or the hardships they all faced. Zara, a nurse, told stories of her life before the conflict, back when she was an eager teenager on a farm not far away. She remembered her first crush, a tall, handsome boy named Marcus. He always seemed so self-assured. Smug even. Zara tried not to wonder what became of him. It was best not to know. Instead, that bright smile would live on in her mind, his youthful vigor never fading.

Elke grew up to the south in Stuttgart. A war widow, she'd moved to Wurzburg to take a job at a grocery, where she let a small room upstairs. Quiet and introspective, she preferred to listen more than talk, gazing around the room at the misfits; old men and the wounded, hiding out here in the dim light from the raging war outside. Over the years, the three women came to rely on each other for comfort and support in these most difficult of times. On this particular night, a nervous energy filled the room. The air raid siren had a way of doing that. A continuous three-minute tone sounded just as Bettina arrived. A warning. Residents were advised to tune their radios to their local station. Enemy planes were detected somewhere over southern Germany. They might be headed to Wurzburg, but then they might be headed anywhere. Frankfurt, Stuttgart, Nuremburg… It was the ascending and descending tone that counted. That meant an imminent attack. It had happened before, five times in the last month alone, resulting in three hundred dead and many more injured. But then, they couldn't dive into a shelter every time a warning sounded. They had to carry on as best they could, and anyway, this was a basement tavern. It provided as safe a shelter as just about anyplace. Bettina approached her friends at their usual table. "Did you hear the siren?"

"Shhh…" Zara lifted a finger to her lips. "No talk of the war here. Remember?"

Bettina took a seat. Sometimes she wished a bomb would come already; that it would land right on top of her and put her out of her misery once and for all. No more fear, no more regret. But then she would think of her husband. Bettina had to survive this war. If she could only manage that, she and Peter might someday be reunited.

Elke lifted a carafe and filled three empty glasses with wine before hoisting one in the air. "What shall we drink to?"

"Life," said Zara.

The women looked at each other with pale expressions. In a world filled with death, such a sentiment seemed a temptation of fate. "Why don't we drink to friendship?" said Bettina.

"Fine," Zara agreed. "To friendship."

They tapped their glasses, looking one another in the eye before taking a drink. Sometimes their prohibition on war talk made conversation hard to come by, but there were always fellow revelers to discuss. One young man in particular caught Elke's eye. He was short and stocky, yet handsome, with a rugged face. He sat drinking beer with another soldier, too old for the private's uniform they each wore, but that's the way things went these days. The army was less particular with who they called to duty. "What do you think of him?" Elke whispered to her friends.

"I think he's a little too old for you," said Zara.

"Not him!" Elke blushed in consternation. Zara only laughed.

"Oh no, don't draw their attention!" Bettina cast her eyes downward.

"Why not?" Zara asked. "If Elke doesn't want the old one, maybe you can have him."

"I'm married." Bettina shot an angry look.

"Relax. Have a sense of humor."

"I'm sorry, but I see no humor when it comes to that."

"All right, all right, I apologize."

Bettina shook her head. "Can we change the subject?"

"What's there to talk about? I can't take any more stories about our childhoods. We can't talk about the war, or work. We can't talk about the other gentlemen here in the tavern. What else is there?!"

"Maybe we should lift the rules this once," said Elke. "There's plenty of news." The women sat in silence as they considered the prospect. Hiding from the war at this small table, in this small tavern, was less tenable with each passing day. Enemy forces were swallowing their entire country, chunk by chunk. It was only a matter of time before they arrived here, in their town. They heard the chatter at their places of work. The only question remaining seemed to be which enemy would get here first. The Russians? Or the Americans?

"What have you heard?" Zara relented.

"Me?" said Elke. "Nothing. I thought you might know something."

Zara lifted her glass and drank some wine. "I may have picked up a few things."

"What things?"

Glancing again at the two soldiers, Zara lowered her voice. "They say the Americans have taken Mainz."

"Mainz!" Bettina gasped. "That's so close!"

"They've crossed the Rhine."

Bettina absorbed this information. Mainz was only 150 kilometers away. She did the math in her head. If the Americans advanced just over 10 kilometers per day they could be here in two weeks. It was the outcome she'd secretly yearned for. Freedom. She was a German, longing for her country to lose this terrible war. It seemed the only way she might ever see her husband again, yet now that the end was so near, terror filled Bettina's heart. A wave of anxiety overcame her. She had to go home, to her in-laws' apartment, and lock herself away until it was all over.

At the bar, a small group of men gathered around a radio, listening to local bulletins. The drone of a radio announcer carried across the room. A mass of enemy bombers was reported to the south over Rastatt. Stuttgart was on high alert. "They couldn't come here," said Elke. "They wouldn't. What would be the point? The only thing we have is hospitals."

"What was the point of Dresden?" Zara countered.

The girls sat quietly, trying to tamp down their fears as they listened to the broadcast. "Maybe we should go," said Bettina. "I feel I should be with Peter's mother and father."

"No!" said Elke. "This is our Friday night! We can't allow them to ruin it!"

"Perhaps Bettina is right," said Zara. "My heart isn't in it tonight."

Elke's shoulders sagged. "At least let us finish our wine!"

Bettina and Zara looked to each other, to ascertain how many minutes they were willing to give. "We'll drink the wine. Then we'll go." Zara lifted her glass and took a gulp. Bettina followed suit.

"Finally, a handsome man comes in, and you two abandon me," said Elke.

"Stay if you'd like," Zara replied.

"I might."

Bettina finished her wine in one long draw. Elke raised the carafe to refill their glasses. At the radio, somebody turned up the volume. *Approximately two hundred enemy bombers now moving northwest, direction Wurzburg. Residents are advised to take immediate shelter.*

Elke froze, carafe in hand. "Did he say Wurzburg?"

Before the others could answer, the blare of the sirens began to echo through the city, ascending and then descending. Two hundred enemy bombers! This was no small raid. Not like before… "Maybe we should find a proper shelter!" Zara eyed the other patrons flooding out the door. A few older men stayed where they were, content to meet their fate with a glass of beer in hand. Bettina leaped to her feet. "I need to get home!"

"No!" said Zara. "You don't have time. It's too late! Come, there's a proper shelter just up the street!"

"But you don't understand! They won't leave the house! Not unless I drag them out! I need to get home!" Bettina joined an exodus, rushing for the door and then out. On the street, men, women, and children ran in all directions as the sirens wailed their ominous warning. Searchlights scanned the skies. Bettina heard the rat-a-tat-tat of anti-aircraft guns as orange tracers soared into the darkness. No planes. None that she could see anyway. But what was that? High above, she spotted what looked to be glowing green flares, descending gently to earth. Bettina turned toward home and started to run, three blocks up to Spiegelstrasse and then right. She could make it. She had to. A dark figure bolted from a doorway on her left, slamming into Bettina and knocking her to the ground. The man stumbled beside her, confused, and then ran off down the sidewalk. Bettina scrambled to her feet. She heard them now. A low buzz high above, steadily growing louder. She was only a few blocks from home when the first bombs began to land on the other side of the city, a wave of destruction closing in on her.

"Come, come!" A woman grabbed Bettina by the arm and pulled her toward an open doorway.

"No, please!"

A man darted out, taking hold of them each by a wrist, and dragging them after him. Bettina felt herself tumbling down a stairway and into a heap of bodies on a crowded basement floor. Seconds later, the earth itself shook with the concussive blast of five hundred pounds of TNT. Screams echoed through the room. One after another after another the blasts came, filling the basement with dust and debris, shaking the walls, ceiling, foundations. Bettina choked on the dirt. Her eardrums bled, and still, she thought of her in-laws, cowering in their apartment upstairs. She was too late...

Bettina crawled further into the dark basement, over cowering masses, and still the bombs came. Clamping both hands over her ears, she curled into a ball. This was the end. The end. She would never survive. Yet somehow, she was still alive. The blasts came in waves. Some close by. Others at a distance. One minute, two, three… Time lost all meaning. She thought of Peter, who would never know what happened to her. So close. They'd come so close. The war was nearly over…

And then the blasts receded. Was that all? No, it couldn't be. Bettina's ears rang with a dull hum. The faint flickering of flames danced off the basement walls, illuminating terrified children, clinging to their mothers. Bettina made her way to the stairs, following the dark shapes of a few others as they crept up to look. Peering through the doorway, Bettina saw only destruction; the ruined shells of what had just moments before been residential apartment blocks. Her neighborhood. Two men stumbled out. The street was covered in bricks and wood, shattered glass and debris. Bettina crawled after. The bloodied body of a woman lay half-buried under the rubble. Metal canisters rained down all around, each landing with a thud before bursting into a white-hot glow. She watched them fall in awe. Fire bombs. But what did it mean? How long did she have before an inferno enveloped them all? Bettina thought of the park, the Hofgarten, not far away. She had to get there.

Fire crept up walls, igniting debris, burning in the streets, in the attics, like hell itself on earth. Buildings collapsed behind her as Bettina stumbled forward, pausing where her in-law's apartment previously stood. Where it was exactly, she couldn't be sure. A woman moved past with a wailing baby in her arms. The sheets of flame all around them voraciously consumed all oxygen as thick smoke swirled through the air. Dropping to her knees, Bettina struggled to breathe. A searing wind scorched her skin. It was too late. Too late. There was no escape. Burning soot filled her lungs. These would be her last moments on earth. Bettina flashed back to her childhood, clinging to her mother's skirt in a crowded shop, a comforting hand on the top of her head. She pictured Peter's parents, buried in the wreckage all around her. She saw her husband himself as the Gestapo hauled him away. Nobody would know, Bettina thought. Nobody would know what became of her. Consciousness drained away. The firestorm devoured everything in its path.

Chapter Eighty-Six

Fort Jay, New York, April 4, 1948

George Dasch was escorted in shackles, chains hanging from his wrists, tied around his waist, attached at his ankles. With an Army guard on each side, they entered a room, small and bare, with just a few wooden benches and a single bulb hanging from the ceiling. "Sit down," said a guard.

"Where are we going?"

"Just sit down."

Dasch did as he was told, lowering himself onto a bench and leaning his back against the wall. He didn't know the time, though guessed that it was very early in the morning. Probably close to dawn. For six years, he'd endured such an existence. No possessions of his own, not even the clothes on his back, no control over any aspect of his life. From a federal penitentiary in Danbury, Connecticut to Atlanta, Georgia, and finally Leavenworth, Kansas. He'd lived and breathed, eaten and slept, all the while waiting for that moment when these chains might finally come off for good. For the past four days, he'd occupied a cell on Governor's Island, just a few miles away from his Snookie, going about her life just across the river in New Jersey. Did she have any idea that he was so close? Of course she didn't. They'd done everything possible to keep the couple apart, why should anything have changed?

From down the hall, Dasch heard the rattling of another prisoner's lanky chains. He looked to see Peter Burger shuffle into the room. Six years since they'd laid eyes on one another... Burger was gaunt, his face thin, his hair turning gray.

"Let's go, keep moving," said a guard. Peter continued until he stood in the center of the room.

"On your feet, Dasch," said another.

The prisoners stood facing one another, just a few feet apart. "Hello, Peter."

"Quiet!" shouted the guard. "No talking!"

After moving down another hallway and through two heavy doors, the pair and their handlers emerged into a cool, damp spring morning. Dasch was correct. Not quite dawn, but close. Chains rattled in motion, boots scuffing asphalt as they made their way down a short path to a pier. They were loaded onto a small boat. Pulling away from the island, they motored across the harbor, the eastern sky glowing a deep blue. To the west, the Manhattan skyline loomed above, lights glittering off still water. The city of his dreams beckoned, yet this was as close as Dasch would get.

Arriving at a Navy pier, a transport ship awaited, smoke billowing from its single stack. *Blanche F. Sigman*, George read the name across the bow. After disembarking their tender, the small party of prisoners and guards was met at the gangway by a lieutenant and two sailors. This was it, then. Deportation. He'd expected it for some time, though why they couldn't come right out and tell him was still perplexing. George paused to take a last look around. He had to hope he'd see these shores again. Dasch would do whatever it took to get back to this country that he still considered home, back to the wife who even at this moment slept just out of reach, completely unawares.

"Got a couple passengers for you," said a guard.

"Deluxe accommodations are all set and waiting," the officer replied.

"Better not be too swank."

"Just what these fine gentlemen deserve."

"Let's go." Another guard pushed Dasch in the back. George took a step onto the gangway, and then another. Burger followed closely behind. Once aboard they were led down, down, down into the bowels of the ship, chains clattering against the iron stairs. A distinct diesel odor permeated the air. The thrum of engines reverberated through the steel beneath their feet. When the stairs went no further, the men continued down a passageway, stepping up and through doorway hatches until they came to a row of cells, side by side. Through metal bars, Dasch saw a cot, a sink, a toilet. A sailor used a heavy key to open the first door. When they'd put Dasch inside, the guards removed his shackles.

"Can you tell me," George gave a hopeful look to the lieutenant, "...where we are going?"

The officer took on a quizzical expression. He turned to the army guards. "You haven't told him?"

"Go ahead," said a guard. "No sense keeping it from him."

The officer looked back to Dasch. "Bremerhaven."

"Will we be released?"

"Our orders are to get you there, that's all." The sailor swung the door shut with a loud *clank* and then turned the key before moving to the adjoining cell, where Peter was locked inside. The lieutenant looked them over, one after the other. "That ought to hold them."

"They're your problem now," said a guard.

"I think we can handle it."

The cortege retreated the way they had come, leaving Dasch and Burger behind. The two men stood in their adjoining cells, unable to see one another, yet able to speak for the first time in six years. The survivors. Dasch worried that Burger might hold it all against him. They'd be heroes, George said all those years before, hailed by a grateful America. He still struggled to understand how it went so horribly wrong. If Pete held him responsible, they'd have plenty of time to hash it out. At least George had somebody to talk to along the way, someone he'd once called a friend. He cleared his throat. "Are you there, Pete?"

"I'm here."

Dasch paused. "You holding up all right?"

Burger cleared his throat. "It's been a long time."

"Yes."

"Have you heard from your wife?"

The mention of Snookie left Dasch hollow. "They let me write to her when I was in Kansas. She came to see me."

"I'm glad."

"They sure want to keep this quiet."

"I try not to think about it too much, or it might drive me mad."

"Have you heard from Bettina?"

Burger fell silent, unable to answer.

"I'm sorry," said Dasch. "Maybe I shouldn't have asked."

Dasch took a step back and sat on his cot. His thoughts turned to what lay ahead. Bremerhaven, but then what? Certainly, they would be set free on arrival. "What do you think it's like there in Germany these days?" he asked.

"I've seen some pictures, in the newspapers…"

"Yes, I've seen those, too, but they've had three years. Three years to rebuild."

"Three years isn't so long after a war like this one."

"No, I suppose not."

"Maybe there are some jobs. Construction jobs."

"Maybe," Dasch answered. "Where will you go?"

"I come from Wurzburg, you remember?"

"Yes, yes, Wurzburg." George recalled a photo spread he'd seen in *Newsweek Magazine*. Photos of Wurzburg, virtually wiped off the map. Dasch couldn't bring himself to ask if Pete had seen them, too. "Your family will be very happy."

"Yes. Very surprised." Burger's voice betrayed his sadness. This didn't sound like a man about to be set free after years of captivity. This was a man resigned to disappointment. As a boy, Peter Burger had such hopes and dreams. In time, he'd learned one lesson above all others. Life was cruel. Yet, all the same, he was still alive. He wondered if the same could be said of his parents, or Bettina. That was the question weighing on him every moment of every day. "George, I have something to ask you," he said. "Do you have any regrets?"

"Regrets?" Dasch perked up.

"If you had the chance to go back, would you do the same thing again?"

"Yes. I would do the same thing."

"We could have gone to Canada. Or maybe Mexico. They might never have caught us."

"I don't regret it for a moment," Dasch answered. "I did what was right. Of course, I've thought about this. We've both had a lot of time to consider it."

"What about the others? Herbie, and Eddie…"

Dasch was hit with a familiar pang of guilt. "I never expected…" He couldn't finish the sentence.

"No. Me neither."

"What happened to those boys was not our fault." Dasch tried to sound convincing, though Burger had no reply. A short time later they felt a soft sway beneath them as the ship pulled away from the dock and moved toward the open sea. They were on their way. After all they had been through, Burger and Dasch were headed back to their homeland. Back to where their stories first began.

Chapter Eighty-Seven

Thirty-thousand feet over the Caribbean Sea, September 4, 1956

The first clear sign of United States territory that Wolfgang Wergin saw out the window was a strand of small islands, like a set of pearls in an azure sea. The Florida Keys. It seemed so easy, soaring over the border at thirty-thousand feet. No customs agents to stop and question him, demanding payment. Wolf flashed back to the last time he'd tried to cross, fifteen years earlier. What if they'd done things differently all those years before? What if he and Herbie simply walked along the border until they found a place to cross? Hopped a fence, ducked through a ditch, run like hell? They would have made it; of that he was sure. They would have gone back to Chicago and lived their lives. They would have been drafted into the U.S. Army. Instead of two years on the Russian front, Wolf would have fought on the other side. Maybe they both would have survived. Maybe not. There was no sense wallowing in regret. No changing the past. Herbie and Wolf made their choices. Wolfgang had to live with his. Herbie was not so lucky.

Turning from the window, Wolf reached into a pocket for his wallet. Opening it up, he slid out an old, worn photograph and carefully unfolded it. There they were on the deck of the *Deutschland*, frozen in time. Wolf on the left, Herbie in the middle, and Schmidt on the right. Whatever happened to Joseph Schmidt? Wolf couldn't hope to guess. But Herbie. Wolf knew exactly what happened to Herbie. The spirit of his friend would live on within him. Wolf remembered Herbie's optimism, his joy. This was a man who'd embraced life and all it had to offer. Perhaps he was in heaven now, smiling down on Wolfgang, returning home at last.

When the plane touched down in Miami, Wolf made his way down the stairs and across the tarmac, escorted into the terminal with the rest of the passengers, his feet on U.S. soil. As they came to the immigration checkpoint, Wolf saw two lines. *United States Citizens*, read one sign. *All Other Nationalities*, read another. It was with deep disappointment that he joined the latter. Wolf considered himself an American. He'd never relinquished his citizenship. Instead, it was stripped from him by a government that considered him an enemy. After he was finally released from the American POW camp at war's end, he expected to simply sail for home and pick his life back up where he'd left off. Unfortunately, the State Department had other ideas. And so, he'd stayed in Germany, married, had two daughters. Eventually, he'd moved the family to Colombia. When his wife left him three years earlier, she took the girls back to Germany. Wolf stayed where he was, but never gave up on coming home… or on seeing his mother and father before it was too late. Finally, more than a decade after the war ended, his visa was approved, and so here he was. Wolfgang moved forward in line, fingering his passport. When it was his turn, he stepped up and placed his documents on the desk.

"What's the purpose of your visit?" asked the immigration officer.

"Visiting family." Wolf's heart beat faster. There was no hopping over a fence this time. He took a deep breath.

"Where is your family?"

"Chicago."

The officer examined Wolf's passport and looked over the visa tucked inside. He stamped the passport and handed it back. "Enjoy your stay."

"Thank you."

And just like that, Wolfgang was back. Perhaps before long, his daughters might join him, eight-year-old Carmelita and six-year-old Arlene. They could start life over, here in America. But first, his parents… He pictured them as he had seen them last. There was a time when he believed they were dead. It was in *Coronet Magazine* that he read the story; they were tried for treason after helping Herbie, along with Mr. and Mrs. Haupt. All four were found guilty, all sentenced to death. For half a year, Wolf mourned the passing of his mother and father, struggling to make sense of it. Only later did he learn that their sentences were overturned on appeal. They were alive after all, still in Chicago, his father managing a bar on the south side.

On into the baggage claim, Wolfgang waited for his luggage and then carried his bags through customs. Next, he re-checked them for his flight to Chicago and made his way to the departure lounge. It was the last leg of a very long journey.

Back in the sky, it was all America beneath him as Wolf passed over the green swamps of Florida and on up to the Midwest farmlands. By the time the plane taxied to a stop on the tarmac, adrenaline surged through Wolf's body, all of his senses on overdrive. Exiting the plane, he felt the moist, warm air of Chicago in late summer. He closed his eyes and inhaled. The familiarity was engrained, deep in his subconscious. He remembered nights just like this one, picturing himself with two friends at a Mexican fiesta so many years before.

Wolf walked on. He'd left as a mere teen. These days he looked more like a middle-aged man. Of course, they'd seen pictures. They knew. As he entered the building and began to scan the crowd, the anticipation was overwhelming, but it didn't take him long to spot them. Otto and Kate Wergin stood side-by-side, his father tall and thin in a charcoal-gray suit and hat. His mother wore a sundress, red with white dots. She held a bouquet of flowers in one hand. When they saw him, their faces lit up, arms waving. Wolfgang hurried across the hall and wrapped his mother in an embrace.

"Wolfgang!" Kate's voice filled with joy as tears escaped from the corners of her eyes. Wolf held her tightly, gently rocking from side to side.

"Welcome home, son," said Otto.

Releasing his mother, Wolf turned to his dad. The two men peered into one another's eyes. What they all had been through, Wolfgang thought. Too much to discuss. Instead, he reached out a hand. His father shook it but then leaned forward to give his son a hearty hug.

Kate held out her flowers. "I thought I'd bring you something."

Wolfgang took the bouquet. "Aw, mom, I have a few things for you, in my bag!"

"They can wait!" Kate smiled. "You are the best gift of all."

"Thank you, mother."

"Should we find your luggage?" said Otto.

"Of course."

The three walked toward the baggage claim, just like any other family reuniting at the airport. Nobody paid them attention, or gave a second look. Nobody knew the epic story that was coming to an end. Nobody, outside of these three people, understood the magnitude of what had just occurred. Wolf's heart swelled with a joy he never knew was possible. At long last, Wolfgang Wergin was home.

Afterword

Like Wolfgang's parents, Hans and Erna Haupt were found guilty of conspiracy charges in 1942 and sentenced to death. Those sentences were ultimately overturned, but the pair were imprisoned until after the war and then deported back to Germany.

After his own deportation, Peter Burger returned to what remained of Wurzburg, 90 percent of which was destroyed during a 17-minute period on that March day in 1945. Burger relocated nearby to live with his sister and brother-in-law, with whom he shared a small room. Destitute, he spent his first winter back without proper clothing, underwear, or even shoes for a time, forced to scrounge for food from garbage cans. Burger continued to write periodic letters to J. Edgar Hoover, with whom he felt an unlikely connection. According to at least one account (Dobbs), Burger's wife Bettina disappeared into the maws of a Soviet concentration camp, though after the firebombing, Wurzburg was occupied by American forces and remained in U.S. control before becoming part of West Germany. Whatever did happen to Bettina, there is no indication that Peter ever found or made contact with her again. Peter Burger himself soon vanished, his remaining days unknown to history.

As for George Dasch, he was joined in Germany by his wife, Marie, aka "Snookie." The couple ran their own small business in Manheim, selling wool goods from a small folding table and later moving into a proper storefront. The pair settled into a rhythm and for four years were happy. That period of stability came crashing down when the German magazine *Der Stern* ran a series of articles on the Pastorius mission and Dasch's part in it. George knew he was in for trouble as soon as the first article appeared, portraying him as a traitor to the German people and responsible for the executions of the six other men. Quickly, he sold the business at a fraction of its value and fled to Switzerland with Marie. Shortly after they'd left

Manheim, gangs of fascist vigilantes began showing up at their former store looking to exact revenge.

Unable to work in Switzerland, the couple returned to Germany six months later, settling in Kaiserslautern, where they invested the last of their savings into starting a restaurant. Before it even opened, their story leaked to the local press and they were forced to flee once again. This time the couple was left penniless. Life continued this way as they skipped from town to town, taking what work they could find until they were discovered each time. Finally, in 1955, they were confronted on the street by a man with a pistol. It was only Marie's admonition that he'd have to kill her, too, that drove the man away. For Snookie, however, this was enough. She returned to live alone in the United States, a broken woman. George Dasch spent the rest of his life in a fruitless effort to obtain the pardon he was originally promised.

Some years after his deportation, George Dasch was walking down a street in Manheim when he ran into Walter Kappe. Both men were shocked to face each other once more, with Kappe terrified that Dasch might turn him in to the American authorities. As it turned out, Kappe had eventually managed to change his name and found a job working for the British army as a personnel officer.

Wolfgang Wergin lived the rest of his days in the United States, regaining his citizenship in 1962. His two daughters came to visit, first in 1958 and then later relocating to the U.S. permanently. For a time, Wolfgang lived in Los Angeles where he was part owner of a scuba diving shop. Later he relocated to Las Vegas where he had a successful career as a photojournalist, despite the permanent loss of sight in one eye that was the result of his war injuries. Working for the *Las Vegas Review-Journal*, he shot images of The Beatles, Muhammad Ali, Frank Sinatra, and many others. After divorcing his first wife, Henriette, in 1953, Wolf later married a former model and playboy bunny, Arline Hunter, in 1990. The couple retired in San Pedro, California, and remained together until his death in 2006 at the age of 83.

What was True? A Note on Sources

In a story as complex as this one, or any story really, the absolute truth is impossible to come by. Sources contradict each other in numerous ways. Sometimes statements taken at different times by the same witness will provide contradictory information. That said, I have endeavored to provide as honest and factual an account as I was able. When incomplete information was available, I was sometimes left to speculate on certain details. I understand that this leaves the reader questioning what was actually true and what was not. I will attempt to answer some of those questions to the best of my ability here.

In the grand scheme of things, this was a true story. The events portrayed here happened. All of the dialogue in the scenes taking place within the courtrooms was taken straight from official transcripts. Areas of discrepancy in the story include the question of whether or not Herbie Haupt knew the ship he and Wolfgang boarded in Manzanillo would stop in Los Angeles on the way to Japan. In interviews long afterward, Wolfgang claimed that he expected to disembark in California. In court, Herbie says he planned to go to Japan. Some have taken that to mean that Herbie was lying to Wolfgang about the ship's destination. I tend to believe that Wolf planned to get off in LA while Herbie didn't, but both were surprised when the ship didn't stop.

Another area of contention involves how Peter Burger was able to survive the purge that came to be known as the Night of the Long Knives. In his well-researched book, *Saboteurs, The Nazi Raid on America*, (2005), Micheal Dobbs writes that Burger survived because he was away on an assignment as aide de camp to Ernst Röhm's personal physician, Dr. Emil Ketterer. It is established in numerous historical sources, however, that Dr. Ketterer was staying at the hotel *with* Röhm and a large contingent of Storm Troopers on that fateful morning. Ketterer was being hauled out of his room and into the hallway when Adolph Hitler and several associates spotted the doctor. After being vouched for by one of Hitler's men, Dr. Ketterer was said to be the only Röhm associate allowed to leave the premises alive. But where was Burger at this time? As aide de camp to the doctor, I posit that he was likely also there in the hotel, and therefore that the historical record may be inaccurate. It is entirely plausible that there were two members of the SA whose lives were spared that day, though Burger does not explicitly state as much and his name never appears on the record as having been present. What is incontrovertible is that roughly three thousand of Röhm's followers were executed in the purge, yet Burger's connection to Dr. Ketterer was what saved him.

Also, I do not know the truth about what became of Bettina Burger. I know that in 1942 she went to live in Wurzburg with Peter's parents. I know that 90 percent of Wurzburg was destroyed during the bombing raid on March 25, 1945. I know that Wurzburg was subsequently occupied by U.S. forces. I also know that Burger was unable to locate his wife upon his return to Germany, and that he was told that she'd been taken captive by Russian forces. Did she leave Wurzburg and relocate to Berlin sometime during the war? And subsequently perish in a Soviet concentration camp? That I do not know. The actual truth about what happened to Bettina died with her.

When it comes to the sections on Wolfgang's war experience, this is the one part of the book that I was forced to largely make up. I know when he was drafted, and that he was sent to Russia. I don't know his unit, or actual combat experience, so I placed him in historical situations that occurred at the time. I am willing to guess that he wasn't sent to Stalingrad, or he would never have made it out. In later interviews, he does describe having been wounded, recovering in a military hospital, and being granted a transfer to a unit on the western front. He also tells of charging into no-man's-land to throw himself on top of a wounded American soldier, just as I recounted here. His obituary, printed in the *Las Vegas Review-Journal*, mentions that he never did regain sight in the eye that was damaged on the Russian front.

In addition to these points, of course, it is impossible to know for sure what went on in the characters' heads. Sometimes I had strong clues. For instance, I do know that the last night Herbie and Wolf spent together at his uncle's house in Stettin, Herbie broke down sobbing. Wolfgang mentions this fact in several interviews years later. Obviously, Herbie was under enormous psychological pressure as he struggled to balance the forces tearing at him. At heart, he was just a happy-go-lucky kid trying to get on with his life, yet on some level, he did understand the gravity of his predicament.

When it came to some of the smaller details in this story, at times I was forced to make decisions involving conflicting pieces of information. For example, in his statement given after the Long Island landing, Coastguardsman John Cullen claimed that after returning to the station and taking up arms, he went back to the beach with five other men. In an interview with a local paper years later, he says it was just three others. So how many should I put in my story? I split the difference, with five in total going down to the beach (including Cullen) and one staying behind to guard the station.

When it came to names of minor characters, like many of the FBI agents, I tried to use the actual names of the people involved if I could find them. Sometimes this was impossible and I was forced to make up a name. Overall, throughout the story I did my best to be as accurate as possible.

Another valuable source was a book about the case written by George Dasch himself in 1959 originally titled, *Eight Spies Against America.* Dasch provides a compelling account of his ordeal, though there are times when his account seems overtaken by hyperbole. For instance, he says that when we first met with Duane Traynor and Mickey Ladd at FBI headquarters, the only way he could get them to believe his story was to dump his briefcase full of cash out onto the desk, sending the bundles of currency cascading to the floor. The FBI statements make no mention of such an incident and claim that they confiscated the money several days later, in Dasch's hotel room. Dasch says that J. Edgar Hoover came to visit him in his cell in the D.C. jail. Records show that Hoover visited Burger, but not Dasch. After the trial, Dasch claims that upon confronting Hoover in the hallway, he was knocked to the floor by an agent. This may have happened, though Dasch's is the only account of it.

The most valuable resource of all in this project was the transcript of the court proceedings themselves. During the military tribunal, all of the major players were questioned on the stand, some numerous times. Also, each defendant's FBI statement was read out loud into the record, including Dasch's voluminous statement that took three full days of the trial to enter. The transcript of the military tribunal was made available online by a project of the University of Minnesota. Citation is as follows:

Title. Transcript of Proceedings before the Military Commission to Try Persons Charged with Offenses against the Law of War and the Articles of War, Washington D.C., July 8 to July 31, 1942
Place. Minneapolis: University of Minnesota, 2004
Editors. Joel Samaha, Sam Root, and Paul Sexton, eds.
Transcribers. Students, University of Minnesota, May Session 2003, "Is There a Wartime Exception to the Bill of Rights?"
Transcript site: http://www.soc.umn.edu/~samaha/nazi_saboteurs/nazi02.htm

A transcript of the Supreme Court case, *Quirin Ex Parte*, is also available online as a PDF file through the United States Library of Congress.

The first I heard of this story was in March 2004, during an episode of *This American Life* on American Public Radio. In producing the story, Ira Glass tracked down and interviewed an aging Wolfgang Wergin, who still sounded chipper and optimistic despite his years. To Wergin, it was a tale of youthful adventure, despite the tragic outcome. As soon as I heard him tell it, the story got into my blood and I knew I had to do something with it eventually. At that time, it was in the news again because the George W. Bush administration was using the Supreme Court decision in the *Quirin Ex Parte* case as a precedent to try prisoners held at Guantanamo Bay, Cuba, in military tribunals instead of civilian courts. I let this story settle inside me, eventually finding another interview with Wergin published in *Chicago Magazine* in 2002, "A Terrorist's Tale," written by Richard Cahan. By the time I tried to contact Wergin myself in the summer of 2006, it was too late. He'd passed away the previous January.

There are a few other books written about this episode in history. *Betrayal: The True Story of J. Edgar Hoover and the Nazi Saboteurs Captured*

During WWII, (2007), by David Alan Johnson, focuses on the dynamic between Hoover and Dasch, relying primarily on the court transcripts and Dasch's own book as sources. Another, *In Time of War, Hitler's Terrorist Attack on America*, (2005) by Pierce O'Donnell, focuses on the legal aspects of the case. While it is interesting to see another take on the story from a lawyer's perspective, O'Donnell's book is littered with inaccuracies, sometimes more than one in a single paragraph. For example, O'Donnell only mentions Wolfgang Wergin once in the book and it is only to say that Herbie Haupt met up with him after returning to Chicago in 1942. O'Donnell seems to have Wolfgang mixed up with the senior Wergin, Wolfgang's father Otto. Similar glaring mistakes are peppered throughout.

One interesting source for information is the press accounts written at the time. Often the newspaper writers had little to go on besides what was fed to them by Hoover's PR machine, but they do give a sense for the prevailing mood in a country at war against the Nazis. Ultimately, the outcome of this case was about sending a message, both of warning to the Germans and of hope to an American public desperate for moral victories. Some who read this book will no doubt feel that I got it all wrong, that portraying these men from a compassionate perspective is a betrayal in itself, to my country and all it stands for. They will say that these men, Herbie Haupt, Kerling, and the rest, got exactly what they deserved. They were Nazis after all. Dasch and Burger, too. My view is that I think Herbie Haupt was a bright-eyed kid who fled his responsibilities for a world of adventure, only to get caught up in something larger than he could fully comprehend. I believe that George Dasch and Peter Burger were men of high morals, despite Burger's SA past. These were men who believed in right and wrong. They had faith in America and her system of justice. Up until the very end, George Dasch wanted nothing more than to receive a presidential pardon so that he might return to the place that he considered his spiritual home. There are valuable lessons in this story, if we are willing to heed them. First and foremost is that things are rarely as clear as we'd like them to be, and despite our desire for easy answers in complex times, humanity dwells amidst the varying shades of gray.

Thank you for reading "Enemies: A War Story"

If you made it this far, then I suspect this tale drew you in as a reader in much the same way it did to me the first time I heard about it. I knew that I had to do something with it, to share this story with as many people as I could. Upon completion, I contacted 370 agents and publishers, yet the book was rejected by each and every one. Luckily, these days self-publishing is a viable option. If you would like to help get the word out, please consider leaving a review on Amazon. Honest opinions by readers like yourself help a great deal. Thanks again, and I hope you enjoyed the book!

- Kenneth Rosenberg